The O. Henry Prize Stories 2017

The O. Henry Prize Stories 2017

Chosen and with an Introduction by
Laura Furman

With Essays by Jurors
David Bradley
Elizabeth McCracken
Brad Watson
on the Stories They Admire Most

Anchor Books
A Division of Penguin Random House LLC
New York

AN ANCHOR BOOKS ORIGINAL, SEPTEMBER 2017

*Copyright © 2017 by Vintage Anchor Publishing, a division
of Penguin Random House LLC*
Introduction copyright © 2017 by Laura Furman

Permissions appear at the end of the book.

Anchor Books Trade Paperback ISBN: 978-0-525-43250-0
eBook ISBN: 978-0-525-43251-7

www.anchorbooks.com

Printed in the United States of America
10 9 8 7 6 5 4 3 2

To Susan Kaderka, in honor of our two-lap talks

The series editor knows that *The O. Henry Prize Stories 2017* reflects the integrity and skill of Diana Secker Tesdell and Anchor's production, digital, and publicity departments, and thanks each and every person involved in making this book.

The editorial assistants for *The O. Henry Prize Stories 2017* were Fatima Kola and Rachel Kondo, whose unique perspectives and love for literature made our work together a pleasure.

The graduate school and Department of English of the University of Texas at Austin gives *The O. Henry Prize Stories* a home and research libraries beyond compare. With the Michener Center, the university provides support for the editorial assistants. The series editor thanks the university, especially professors Elizabeth Cullingford and James Magnuson.

—LF

Publisher's Note

A BRIEF HISTORY OF
THE O. HENRY PRIZE STORIES

Many readers have come to love the short story through the simple characters, easy narrative voice and humor, and compelling plotting in the work of William Sydney Porter (1862–1910), best known as O. Henry. His surprise endings entertain readers, including those back for a second, third, or fourth look. Even now one can say "Gift of the Magi" in a conversation about a love affair or marriage, and almost any literate person will know what is meant. It's hard to think of many other American writers whose work has been so incorporated into our national shorthand.

O. Henry was a newspaperman, skilled at hiding from his editors at deadline. A prolific writer, he wrote to make a living and to make sense of his life. He spent his childhood in Greensboro, North Carolina, his adolescence and young manhood in Texas, and his mature years in New York City. In between Texas and New York, he served out a prison sentence for bank fraud in Columbus, Ohio. Accounts of the origin of his pen name vary: one story dates from his days in Austin, where he was said to call the wandering family cat "Oh! Henry!"; another states that the name was inspired by the captain of the guard at the Ohio State Penitentiary, Orrin Henry.

Porter had devoted friends, and it's not hard to see why. He was charming and had an attractively gallant attitude. He drank too much and neglected his health, which caused his friends concern. He was often short of money; in a letter to a friend asking for a loan of $15 (his banker was out of town, he wrote), Porter added a postscript: "If it isn't convenient, I'll love you just the same." His banker was unavailable most of Porter's life. His sense of humor was always with him.

Reportedly, Porter's last words were from a popular song: "Turn up the light, for I don't want to go home in the dark."

Eight years after O. Henry's death, in April 1918, the Twilight Club (founded in 1883 and later known as the Society of Arts and Letters) held a dinner in his honor at the Hotel McAlpin in New York City. His friends remembered him so enthusiastically that a group of them met at the Biltmore Hotel in December of that year to establish some kind of memorial to him. They decided to award annual prizes in his name for short-story writers, and they formed a committee of award to read the short stories published in a year and to pick the winners. In the words of Blanche Colton Williams (1879–1944), the first of the nine series editors, the memorial was intended to "strengthen the art of the short story and to stimulate younger authors."

Doubleday, Page & Company was chosen to publish the first volume, *O. Henry Memorial Award Prize Stories 1919*. In 1927, the society sold all rights to the annual collection to Doubleday, Doran & Company. Doubleday published *The O. Henry Prize*

Stories, as it came to be known, in hardcover, and from 1984 to 1996 its subsidiary, Anchor Books, published it simultaneously in paperback. Since 1997, *The O. Henry Prize Stories* has been published as an original Anchor Books paperback.

HOW THE STORIES ARE CHOSEN

All stories originally written in the English language and published in an American or Canadian periodical are eligible for consideration. Individual stories may not be nominated; magazines must submit the year's issues in their entirety by June 1. Editors are invited to submit online fiction for consideration. Such submissions must be sent to the series editor in hard copy. (Please see pp. 309–10 for details.)

As of 2003, the series editor chooses the twenty O. Henry Prize Stories, and each year three writers distinguished for their fiction are asked to evaluate the entire collection and to write an appreciation of the story they most admire. These three writers receive the twenty prize stories in manuscript form with no identification of author or publication. They make their choices independent of each other and the series editor.

The goal of *The O. Henry Prize Stories* remains to strengthen the art of the short story.

To Jean Stafford (1915–1979)

When I taught a class on the short story, I used to assign Jean Stafford's "The Philosophy Lesson." If I'd tried to explain my choice rationally, I might have argued that because the story is about college students and being young, it should appeal to undergraduates, but in fact I assigned the story only because I admired it.

Without trying to get her readers to like her young protagonist, Cora Savage, Jean Stafford created someone real and troubled, someone trying to find her place in the world beyond childhood. Stafford gives the reader glances at Cora's childhood: "She loved the snow. When she had first heard of heaven, she had thought it would be a place where snow was forever falling and forever concealing the harshness of the world." But the story is mainly rooted in the present and, excruciatingly, in Cora's body: She stands naked before a life drawing class, holding "a pole upright like a soldier with a spear. It was the most unmerciful attitude she had yet held, for all her weight lay on her right heel, which seemed to seek a grafting with the dais, and the arm that held the pole swelled until she imagined in time that it would be so bellied out that her vaccination scar would appear as an umbilical indentation."

Perhaps Stafford's prose asked too much of my students. They didn't warm to Stafford or to Cora Savage, not even when she bravely stays in place after a boy runs into the studio and blurts out: "Somebody just committed suicide on the Base Line." The class turns chaotic. Cora doesn't move.

The dramatic interruption thickens the plot and adds emotional pressure to Cora's physical discomfort. At this point, Stafford does something unexpected in her prose: she adds parentheses and shifts Cora's memories to first person in a long passage that reveals that Cora, from the window of her boardinghouse, had watched Bernard Allen, the boy who killed himself, and his girlfriend, Maisie Perrine. All the hints given so far add up at once: Cora is poor compared to the other students, and she models for the money, enduring the exposure of her nudity before her peers, proud of her ability to endure and ignore pain. In her suffering, she finds superiority and comfort.

Cora recalls watching Maisie in her gold lamé dress and sable coat, feeling left behind like Cinderella before the ball, imagining that she was witnessing true happiness. Now, she wonders, "And what was the misery that had brought the boy to suicide? Rich, privileged, in love, he and his girl had seemed the very paradigm of joy. Why had he done it? And yet, why not? Why did not she, who was seldom happy, do it herself?"

The bell rings, signaling the end of class. Cora drops her pole and everyone in the class turns to look at her, whose presence they'd all forgotten.

Stafford ends her story about death and its eerie closeness to the young with a return to the snow that's falling outside the studio windows. She writes: "The snow was a benison. It forgave them all."

The snow, a piece of heaven, forgives the students for being young and crass, for not knowing how to react to shocking news about someone their own age. Perhaps it also forgives Cora for being naive enough to worship a golden boy and girl and to fall half in love with the idea of her own easeful death.

"The Philosophy Lesson," a story of an outsider, was a natural one for Stafford. She grew up in California and Colorado with an erratic, moody would-be writer of a father and a depressed, hardworking mother. The family moved time and again, giving Stafford fodder for stories and a lifelong sense of impoverishment and insecurity. She lived on the East Coast as an adult and was married three times, first to the poet Robert Lowell, and then to Oliver Jensen, an editor at *Life*. Stafford stopped writing fiction after the death of her third (and best) husband, the writer A. J. Liebling. As she aged, her alcoholism wore away at her friendships. At her death, Stafford left her property and the post of literary executor to her faithful housekeeper, which makes a kind of sense. After a stroke and other debilitating conditions isolated her, she must have appreciated the care this person gave her, though it would be hard to think of a less qualified literary executor.

Stafford was friends with Howard Moss, a poet and longtime poetry editor of *The New Yorker*. In his book of essays, *Whatever Is Moving*, he recalls Stafford: "She was a special mixture of the outlandish and the decorous. She paid great respect to the civilized, but something ingrained and Western in her mocked it at the same time. Think of Henry James being brought up in Colorado." In another passage, he comments on her writing, which is what survives of Jean Stafford. "She simply couldn't write a bad sentence, excellence was a matter of personal integrity, the style was the woman."

Though we might wish that she'd finished the novels she put aside because she was unable to work on them, and that she'd produced more of her beautifully carved stories, we can call ourselves lucky to have what she did leave us.

—*Laura Furman*
Austin, Texas

Contents

Introduction

In the summer of 1917, the artist Vanessa Bell read "The Mark on the Wall," a short story by her sister Virginia Woolf that appeared in the first publication from the Hogarth Press, recently founded by Woolf and her husband, Leonard. "Why don't you write more short things," Vanessa wrote to Virginia, suggesting that "there is a kind of completeness about a thing like this that is very satisfactory and that you can hardly get in a novel."

Virginia Woolf sought her older sister's artistic approval always. Still, I wonder if the future author of a great novel like *Mrs. Dalloway* really needed to be urged to favor the short story over the novel as better suited to her talents. A novel's charm can lie in discursiveness and its richness in variety, while taking highways and byways can ruin a story. If you think of the novel and the story as containers holding images, characters, relationships, and settings, what makes a stark novel might be an overstuffed story.

So many years after Vanessa Bell's note to her sister, it remains easier to say what a short story isn't than what it is: it isn't an anecdote and it isn't a section of a novel and it isn't an essay.

Short stories sometimes end ambiguously, but they can't end indefinitely and still be a complete story. Short-story endings are sometimes a sore point with readers, who feel they've been thrown off a cliff. What happened? What's going to happen next? If these are the reader's questions at the end, the story might not be right yet. Even when I don't understand the meaning and stretch of an ending, if I don't feel the same finality that I do when someone walks out the door, then something's gone wrong.

Short-story beginnings are even more demanding of writer and reader. The reader must be immediately involved. This doesn't mean that we as readers necessarily understand the beginning. It just means that the writer has succeeded in placing us in the world of the story, and we don't want to leave until it's over because we feel involved, curious, and committed.

The beginning and the ending of a short story are part of the wonderful secret of the form and why it's neither a novel nor a novella nor a footnote nor an anecdote. The short story has a formal completeness—Vanessa Bell chose exactly the right word—but one that doesn't call attention to itself.

The story's present, its ongoing action, and its past—call it background or ghosts—sometimes push against each other. Sometimes the past sneaks in front of the present and tries to block the way forward. But in stories by master writers— Mavis Gallant, Alice Munro, Katherine Anne Porter, William Trevor—there is always a path to follow through the deep forest of the fictional world.

A story that begins by retreating into the past has the cart before the horse. In a good beginning, the reader is right there in the story's world, in the present, and when the past comes lurching from behind, the reader knows the difference between now and then. More and more, short-story writers give little weight to characters' past, to pedigree, to war stories. Yet time is such a powerful force in the short story that even if we don't know the specifics of a character's background, we know something of the burden of the character's past by the way he or she acts and reacts in the present.

In the short story there's always a shadow cast on the present by what has just been said or not said, by what was imagined but not accomplished, or even by a wish. While the plot develops, past and present wrangle, and the characters struggle against that tension. At the end, there's the peace that comes with the release of tension, for good or ill.

The greatest success comes when the writer's skill permits the reader to ride on the narrative current without noticing form or technique. Michelle Huneven's "Too Good to Be True" is such a story. For the parents of Gayle, a junkie in recovery, the past is all about their young daughter's alcoholism and drug addiction. Their housekeeper and friend, Harriet, is herself in recovery and sees Gayle through that lens. Gayle has tried and failed at sobriety before, disappearing into the depraved existence that she describes cheerfully to Harriet on their way to support-group meetings, pointing from the car to a place where she once had sex with a dentist in exchange for pain meds, or where she did worse things—a tour of Gayle's own private Pasadena. She's become a jaunty expert on meetings. "'I like N.A.,' Gayle says, 'because people there get paranoia. They've done enough illegal stuff, and have the arrests to show for it. I mean, their paranoia is *earned*. . . . But A.A.'s more fun.'"

The trio of imperfectly loving adults watch Gayle like hawks, simultaneously wanting to trust her and to preserve themselves from repeated heartbreak. They think they know the future because they've lived through the past. In time, the reader sees that they're blinded to the present, for the ending of "Too Good to Be True" exposes their conspiracy of hope and despair. The future is unknown, Huneven shows us, whatever the past. Juror

David Bradley chose "Too Good to Be True" as his favorite, pp. 285–87.

A similar collusion between hope and despair appears in the very different circumstances of Tahmima Anam's "Garments," set against the grisly garment trade of Dhaka, capital of Bangladesh. The workers in "Garments" are young women who've come to the city to make something of their lives. It's hard for the Western reader to understand that sewing slimming undergarments for women who are overfed to a degree far beyond the workers' experience can be a tenable path to advancement. Pressured to meet their quotas of finished garments, working in unventilated heat, three young women are willing to marry an unknown man because his gender will give them a tiny boost of social power—the ability to rent a living space for themselves.

For those of us whose grandparents or great-grandparents worked in similar conditions in nineteenth- and twentieth-century America, the story has a special resonance, but for any reader, the young women's dreams are moving in their audacity and the high price paid for their fulfillment. The Dalai Lama said in November 2016 that compassion is only felt between equals. In order to respond to the story with compassion, the reader must feel herself the equal of the story's heroines.

Alan Rossi's "The Buddhist" is about a monk, ill with an unnamed and debilitating disease in a monastery in Sri Lanka, who is determined to continue as normal. He must at all times pay strict attention in the Theravada Forest tradition. He was "not shirking his dharma-related responsibilities, was not skipping meditation, was not failing to practice in each and every moment." While he prepares for a Skype tutorial session with an American student, we learn something of his personal pressures. He is Canadian by birth and has been ordered by Ajahn, the leader, to return home, which above all he doesn't want to do. Though he strains to concentrate on the present, he can't resist reliving his past failures and desires. He counts the ways in which he now considers himself unsuited to be back home with his family and old friends. He is no longer who he was: he has his daily practice and his devotion to the Buddhist tradition he's chosen; this—and escape from Canada—is all he wants.

Alan Rossi balances the pain of his story with the inevitable comedy of the monk trying to be only in the present while his mind wanders through past and future. He struggles to perform what he sees as his dharma duties while the reader comes to know his troubled heart. Throughout the story, illness presses on the monk and the narrative until nothing is left but fever and dream.

Amit Majmudar's "Secret Lives of the Detainees" is another story in which the deadly serious—in this case torture and illegal detention—mixes with the comic. "Secret lives" sounds lightly humorous here, but "detainees" doesn't at all.

Majmudar's first detainee is Ansar, who is frustrating his interrogators. Their techniques can't compete with the pain he is suffering from kidney stones. Ansar despises the Western doctors who work with the interrogators:

Ansar had never been treated so kindly by other men in his life. White men, the old ones with silver, the young ones with light-brown hair. Their kindness interfered with his hating of them. He had to remind himself: they are saving you to pass you on. They are fixing you so there is something to break.

The next detainee, Marwan Malik, also experiences constant torture inflicted by his own body, in his case by the restlessness of his hands, which are happy only when they are repairing or making something. It doesn't matter to them what it is: "Tasks were their food." The third detainee is Nadeem Nadeem, who has been imprisoned in error; he must inflict harm on his body before he can be liberated. The comedy pertains both to prisoners and torturers. Each believes the other's lies. Neither side is able to feel compassion for the other's pain, whether inflicted or self-inflicted. "Secret Lives of the Detainees" is Elizabeth McCracken's favorite (pp. 288–89).

In Mary LaChapelle's "Floating Garden," the reader immediately feels suspicion and dread.

After a festival, people are lined up for their rides home. An army truck is labeled TAXI, and, oddly, women are being ushered into the truck ahead of men. It's explained that there's no room in that taxi for men, but why not? The answer can't be heard. The narrator's mother climbs into the truck first, then turns to receive wooden statues of gods: the Water Father who guards the lake where they live, and the Road Guardian. The reader suspects that those in the truck—the narrator with his mother and two lovely girls in festival clothing with their mother—will need all the help they can get. And something else is not what it seems—our narrator. Suspicion and dread lead to the ache of loss.

Then "Floating Garden" takes us by surprise. In its beginning, it is a local story, held in place by its details of costume, setting, and the narrator's home and family. For many writers, the injustice and tragedy of the story's beginning would have been enough, but Mary LaChapelle expands her narrative beyond those moments and creates what the reader wouldn't guess to be possible—scenes of beauty, peace, and time well spent.

In Joseph O'Neill's "The Trusted Traveler," a retired couple have moved from New York City to Nova Scotia, where they plan to stay for a year and then make plans. As they adjust to a new daily life in a beautiful place, they invent titles for the memoirs he's not writing about lives they haven't lived. "In this subjunctive world we are adventurers, spies, honorary consuls, nomads."

One reason they've uprooted themselves is to avoid meaningless, time-eating, and unavoidable social events such as the persistent annual visits from the husband's former student Jack Bail. Or is he a former student? The narrator can't remember—over the years he's taught two thousand students—nor can he figure out how to get Jack Bail to cease and desist from inviting himself over. Nova Scotia is a long way to travel from New York for a dinner, but this isn't discouragement enough. Nothing the host does will dissuade his blockheaded guest.

Along with the genuine comedy of unwanted social interaction, "The Trusted Traveler" is a story of change. There are two passages describing the narrator's view from his house, and a comparison gives the reader a sense of time and place working on the narrator. The first is general: "It's my intention to investigate this vista systematically, since it feels strange to look out the window every day and basically not understand what I'm looking at." The second is specific: "Our beach is a sand and shingle beach. The sand is a common blend of quartz and feldspar." And on it goes, for the narrator is now able to name his world and by doing so perhaps make it his own. With such specificity comes the quiet joy of knowing where you are and why. Best of all, there's always something left to learn: "The Wisconsin glaciation isn't something I'm really on top of."

For Glory, the protagonist of Lesley Nneka Arimah's vivid story of that name, joy is one of many emotions she does not customarily feel. Hers is an uncomfortable existence as she avoids her parents' expectations and contemplates her "caul of misfortune." At her birth, Glory's parents pinned on her "every hope they had yet to realize" and gave her the first name of Glorybetogod. But her grandfather calls her "that girl," and prophesizes her misfortune. As a child, her instincts tell her to stick her finger in a sleeping dog's mouth; that caul of misfortune her grandfather alone sees "would affect every decision she made, causing her to err on the side of wrong, time and time again."

Glory's disastrous instincts are deeply satisfying for the reader. There's something reassuring about watching her take one wrong turn after another. Glory doesn't know why she acts out of spite and resentment; she can't seem to stop herself. She's a self-defeating Cinderella, single at thirty, working at a mortgage call center in Minneapolis that's an outer circle of hell both for its workers and the soon-to-be-homeless callers. Soon, Glory meets Prince Charming. Like Glory, Thomas is Nigerian. He is quite good-looking, the son of two doctors, and on his way up in America as surely as Glory is on her way nowhere good. He is everything she isn't, and he pursues her, much to her surprise. She despises and adores him, and waits throughout their courtship for the expected disaster. It's up to the reader to decide whether or not Glory's fate is to be once more herself. Lesley Nneka Arimah's strong writing keeps us enthralled from Glory's first mistake to the many possibilities of her last.

Courtship of a kind is also the subject of Jai Chakrabarti's "A Small Sacrifice for an Enormous Happiness." Like Glory, Nikhil finds a way to shoot himself in the foot. His lover is Sharma, who beams into the story with his "oiled hair shining in the late-afternoon light," as handsome as a Bollywood star. The match of an older, rich, and indulgent man with a beautiful, poor, and manipulative younger lover is a classic formula for trouble. The disaster in this case is caused by Nikhil's greed and blindness to things as they really are, and to his lover's feelings. "A Small Sacrifice for an Enormous Happiness" is a parable illustrating the limits of money and power. By the end, the reader knows that poor Nikhil never really had his lover at all.

Martha Cooley's "Mercedes Benz" begins with a car accident and turns into a disquisition on the place of accident in the characters' lives, and our own. Cooley sets the reader squarely in a mountainous scene before bringing on the car crash: "Huge clouds bloomed and drifted above them. Twisting below, the wide rocky riverbed of the Taro was intermittently visible, little streams emptying into it: Erbetello, dei Cani, Pizzarotta.

Descending, the streams cut stony runnels that zigzagged erratically downward, as though someone had scored the earth with
a huge sharp stick." Here is nature in its orderliness; water falls
from the Apennines and carves a downward path that's compared to a casual violence. Water through rock also reminds
the reader of time, of which the characters might not have a
sufficiency. Theirs is a second marriage for each, and a happy
one. They're in the husband's native Italy, having used all their
money for the purchase and renovation of a house in an almost
deserted village. The region is emptied of people in their prime
and their children, all of whom live in the cities and return only
for holidays.

The title of the story refers to the wife's newfound interest in
fancy cars. She and her husband drive a hand-me-down Golf,
but she finds herself looking at Mercedes and Porsches with
uncharacteristic interest. This too relates to the accidental: luxury sedans, she thinks, "offered their owners an illusion of safety,
neatly packaged as exclusivity." The same thing, of course, can
be said about marriage. In its beneficent ending, Cooley's story
moves past the car accident toward acceptance of the accidental.

"Protection" by Paola Peroni is also set in Italy, not the
unpeopled countryside this time, but Rome. The narrator
returns from her home in New York to spend a last Christmas
with her grandmother, who might die at any time. Though too
weak to cook the traditional meals, the grandmother is sharp
and accurate when she accuses the narrator of avoiding commit-
ting to her own life and marrying and bearing children. When
the narrator asks her grandmother if she never made mistakes in
her long life, the answer is that she made plenty, "But I did not
run away from them." The narrator *has* run away and half-lies
about it to her beloved grandmother. Exposed to the oncoming death and the loss therefore of her past, home, and family
traditions, the granddaughter faces her own life and memories.

"There is no predicting who can protect us and who can attack us, nor whom we will harm and whom we will save." There is also no knowing if such a thing as protection exists.

In Keith Eisner's "Blue Dot," the reader waits for misfortune to strike. An unfamiliar drug is taken: " 'Do we chew or swallow?' " The drug is called blue dot, but what a blue dot can do is unknown. Despite its undercurrent of foreboding, "Blue Dot" is a sweet story, filled with nostalgia. Its lack of sentimentality allows the reader to savor the experience of the drug trip and gives strength to the recollections of innocence and lost connections.

Innocence is also on display in Kevin Barry's "A Cruelty," an innocence that is an outgrowth of the limited intelligence of the story's protagonist, Donie. The author leads us into Donie's world of deliberate and reassuring sameness through the details of his day as he leaves home and takes a customary round-trip train ride. For Donie, making the same joke about the weather rain or shine, as well as checking the schedule of his train to Sligo, are a kind of job that pays him in security and self-confidence. When the cruelty of the title is enacted on Donie, his routine is changed and his world seems broken. The love expressed in the story's last line gives the reader hope that Donie's world can be rebuilt and his joy in it restored.

Kate Cayley's "The Bride and the Street Party" features Martha, twenty-eight-year-old mother of four children, married to Denton, "a big, jovial man." Denton "was liked.... He liked himself." Martha is less sure of her own worth, especially in comparison to the other mothers on the street. She compares herself especially to Bronwyn, her house to Bronwyn's, and her troublesome wild son Noah to Bronwyn's Max, "a vigorous and noble busybody, like his mother" and Noah's only friend. Martha's discomfort around Bronwyn is mixed with gratitude that Noah has a friend, a bit of shame that her life doesn't measure up to Bronwyn's, and, as it develops, a rare sureness that she knows better than Bronwyn how to handle a conflict with their Portuguese neighbors in their gentrifying neighborhood. The story succeeds so well in sinking the reader deep into Martha's point of view that the ending comes as a surprise. The one thing that seemed sure about Martha is her sturdy motherliness, which is undermined in two short words. All at once, we feel the weight of her family bearing down on Martha.

In "The Reason Is Because" by Manuel Muñoz, teenage mother Nela has dropped out of high school in her junior year to live with her mother. Her baby's father, Lando Quintanilla, is none too bright and takes no responsibility for the baby, yet Nela's mother harps on marriage with him as Nela's only hope: "'His elevator don't go all the way to the top,' her mother said, 'but at least he'll go places.'" Where he'll go we can't imagine, but in their world he has more possibilities than Nela.

Nela's world has become very small. "Nela took to sitting at the top of the stairway leading up to their second-floor apartment. She held the baby and longed for the boring days at the high school. At least there, her daydreaming didn't seem so pointless." Everybody else in their public housing apartment complex has somewhere to go. Nela is stuck.

"The Reason Is Because" is Manuel Muñoz's third O. Henry story. He is a writer of great patience, in no hurry to push his characters either into drama or into reaching false conclusions. He draws the limits of their lives so that the reader understands them viscerally. Muñoz finds the truth of his characters and uses it to write stories in language so plain and straightforward that it becomes beautiful. The core of Nela's character is her intelligence, the way she notices the lives of others and is conscious of her own changing perspective. Drama comes by the end of the story, in an unanticipated rush. What seemed benign is revealed as vicious. Now Nela has even more trouble than she knew, but she also has something important to consider.

Heather Monley's "Paddle to Canada" is about "a family of

risk and adventure," whom we meet while the father is paddling a rented boat like mad in the middle of a lightning storm to get them off the water. Afterward, the father lightheartedly asks his wife and children why they had been required to leave a deposit for the paddleboat. " 'What do they think we're going to do? . . . Paddle to Canada?' " That phrase becomes a family joke, told and retold along with stories of other near disasters. The family seems able to accommodate danger and adventure and keep on going without fear. Then comes the divorce and not only their future but their past changes. The story ends right where it began, on that stormy lake, but everything is exposed in a whole new light.

"The Family Whistle" by Gerard Woodward is set in economically stricken postwar Germany in 1949, and it starts at a high happy point: Florian has had an unusually successful day of shopping around town. Back in her apartment, she lays out her hard-to-come-by prizes on the dining-room table. "She spent a while arranging them, as though she were an artist preparing a still life. The tin of coffee formed the centerpiece. The silk stockings, still folded, shimmered beside it. A packet of eggs. A handful of black cherries. A block of butter. Everything so perfect, beautiful, promising." A knock at the solid oak door interrupts her admiration of the goods, and by the end of the story there's no more beauty, no more promise of anything but punishment for her survival. The war has come home to Florian.

Genevieve Plunkett's "Something for a Young Woman" performs the short-story magic of encompassing a great deal of time. It's also a story in which the characters you'd expect to be major—the protagonist's husband, for example—are minor, while the owner of an antique store where she works as a teenager turns out to be major.

We first see Allison as an irritable adolescent, confiding her sexual trials to her boss. In fact, the author at first seems to be leading us into a story about an affair between the two; Allison breaks up with her boyfriend partly because of "the hook of suspicion" she detects in his gaze. Allison is a naive girl, newly sexual and still innocent. She wants to know everything and also to protect herself from such knowledge. When, after marriage and having a baby, she starts to make choices, it surprises the reader. Very slowly, Allison begins to live her own life, not the one others expect of her, part of the gift from a man she'd forgotten.

The narrator of "Night Garden," Shruti Swamy's second O. Henry story, is afraid: in her backyard, there's a standoff taking place between her dog, Neela, and a cobra. "The cobra had lifted the front of its body at least two feet from the ground. I had never seen one so close, even separated by four strong walls and a pane of glass. I could see her delicate tongue, darting between her black lips. Her eyes were fixed on the dog, and his on hers. Their gaze did not waver." As the fascinating story continues, we too are fixed, watching and waiting to see what snake, dog, and woman will decide to do. There is even more at stake for the narrator than her pet's life: in watching the silent confrontation between her dog and the cobra, she's bearing witness as well to the failure of her marriage and the question of how she will face the rest of her life.

Wil Weitzel's "Lion" begins with a death. The narrator's landlord, a man "as old as old trees," had once been a great teacher, one who'd "reached people, even the most remote, and left a mark on their lives." In his extreme old age, he'd become forgetful and forgotten, someone there and not there, "a herald of brighter times which had faded until he had faded." The narrator, a graduate student, lived with the old man during his last two years and entertained him by telling a story again and again about a lion in southern Africa who is raised as a pet in a rich household, then released into the wild, and the boy who years later goes to search for him. The student would always tell only part of the story, claiming to have forgotten the rest—until the time comes when the end of the story finds its way out. This tale within a tale holds inside it a treasure of emotion and vivid relationship, and the secret of the narrator's feeling for the landlord.

"Buttony" by Fiona McFarlane reminds the reader of how the world of the classroom absorbs young children. ("Buttony" was the favorite of juror Brad Watson. See pp. 289–90.)

The classroom is filled with emotional sparks observed by the formidable teacher, Miss Lewis. She's a figure both distant and all-knowing, and she disciplines and indulges the children as it suits her whims. She's invented a game she calls "Buttony," which she uses to amuse and control the children. Miss Lewis has a favorite, Joseph, who is everyone's favorite for he's "both kind and beautiful, and they loved him." Joseph's beauty gives him an extraordinary power that he wields over the other students and their teacher, who knows a lot less than she believes she does.

The stories in *The O. Henry Prize Stories 2017* give their readers the privilege of involvement in another life. Each story has what Vanessa Bell called "a kind of completeness" that allows the story's readers to feel deeply about people they don't know and places they've never been.

It would feel incomplete to end this introduction without noting that in November 2016 we lost William Trevor, a writer of deep intelligence who gave us for so many years stories and novels in his unobtrusively beautiful prose that his death feels like deprivation of an essential good.

—*Laura Furman*
Austin, Texas

The O. Henry Prize Stories 2017

Michelle Huneven

Too Good to Be True

H ARRIET SAYS SHE WILL take Gayle to A.A. meetings. Lois offers to pay her extra for gas and time, but Harriet says no, being of service is essential to her own sobriety. Plus, she gets a kick out of Gayle.

Gayle climbs into Harriet's Corolla and together they cross town to the noon Keeping It Simple meeting at First Congo. En route, Gayle taps her window, says, "That corner there, you can get any pharmaceutical you want."

"Not today, thanks," says Harriet.

Back in her day, Harriet took a few pills. And snorted a line whenever it was free. At heart, though, she's a garden-variety alkie, sober thirteen years. Her rebuilt life is chugging along, though a little cross-addiction to alcoholic men still kicks in from time to time. (They're now sober alcoholic men—growth!) Putting her addiction next to Gayle's, Harriet feels lightweight, a toast burner. (As in, Oh! I burned the toast! My life is unmanageable. Better join A.A.) Harriet drank too much, got fired off the line at Campanile, a job she'd loved, and that's what woke her up, sent her into the rooms. But Gayle has spent twenty months on the street, and she just turned eighteen.

Every trip they take across town yields another revelation.

"Don't tell Mom," Gayle says, "but I was here in Pasadena for a lot of the time. Yeah. Like behind the Baptist church there? Someone left this old blue Crown Vic and some guy helped me take out the seats. I put in this air-bed thing. A couple girls and I kept it till a homeless took it over."

Of a brick building on Green Street, Gayle says, "I blew a dentist there for pain meds and sometimes pharmacological coke, if he was feeling generous."

Farther down Green Street, where people and tables spill over the sidewalk: "That diner? We'd do the owner for hot meals, and also that pharmacist, but all he ever coughed up was some lousy Darvocet."

Thus, over the weeks, these familiar avenues with their ordinary merchants and office buildings accrue, for Harriet, a shimmering glaze of pain, as if a whole other city lay shriveled and suffering within.

Gayle was gone twenty months, except for thirteen or fourteen hours in the middle when the detective brought her home. A lot of people had told Lois and Dave to check her into Las Abejas immediately, or to hire security, or for God's sake at least nail her door shut, none of which they could bring themselves to do. Which meant that Gayle, who arrived home at noon, departed sometime after midnight with Dave's Bose and all twelve Christofle sterling-silver soupspoons.

This time, though, she came home on her own and already sixty days clean, so she claimed. She checked herself into an outpatient program—or did once Lois and Dave agreed to pay for it. Now she has graduated from the intensive program and has signed up for maintenance, which includes a meeting a day.

One rainy February day at noon, Harriet parks and they

head toward a rec room behind the huge blond stone church. Approaching, they hear laughter.

"That's why A.A.'s best," Gayle says. "Addicts don't laugh like that. You ever been to N.A., Harriet?"

"Nope. Just A.A., A.C.A., Al-Anon. Oh, and O.A."

"I like N.A.," Gayle says, "because people there get paranoia. They've done enough illegal stuff, and have the arrests to show for it. I mean, their paranoia is *earned*. Plus, someone slapping at her eyes in an A.A. meeting is a wacko. In an N.A. meeting, everyone knows she's detoxing Valium. But A.A.'s more fun."

Inside the rec room, the meeting has just started. They find seats near the front.

Harriet squeezes Gayle's shoulder, kisses the side of her head, her rippling yellow hair. She is feeding them hope, drop by drop.

Harriet is the Parrishes' housekeeper—her choice of title. She likes the old-fashioned sound of it. She does not, in fact, clean house. The Parrishes have a cleaning woman for that. Also an ironer, a pool man, a gardening crew, an arborist, pest control (organic), and a handyman. Drew, the youngest child, is too old for a nanny, but he is too young to come home from school to an empty house. Harriet's duties are to shop for and prepare dinner, walk the dog, and be there every weekday afternoon for Drew. He does his homework at the dining-room table while Harriet cooks. She stays until Lois is home and changed and ready to take over.

Harriet and Lois met in Al-Anon back when Gayle vanished the first time, three years ago. They share the same sponsor, Elizabeth T., a tall, thin, fragile-boned black woman whose own son lives on the streets right there in Pasadena. (Elizabeth T. sometimes sees her son filthy and asleep in the park, and, although it goes against everything in her bones, she will not stop to help him out—but that is a different story.) When Bistro Mauriac went out of business and Harriet had to find a new job, Lois proposed this arrangement, with a salary that few chefs at Harriet's level ever achieve.

The Parrishes live on Arroyo Boulevard, a street of architectural treasures. When Harriet first drove over to talk to Lois about the job, she was hoping that the family lived in the museum-piece Craftsman, or in the low-slung Japanese bungalow with the shoji doors, but they lived between the two, in a white Cape Cod with trellised roses and a grinning white picket fence.

Harriet herself lives in a tiny rented house in Altadena whose crabgrass lawn is surrounded by waist-high chain link.

All the houses on Arroyo Boulevard are on the east side of the street. The west side is a sliver of parkland overlooking the arroyo itself, a steep-walled canyon with a stream at the bottom. A narrow path meanders along the arroyo's lip under thick-limbed old oaks and pungent California bay trees. Here Harriet walks Lucky Gus, the family's basset hound, every day before Drew comes home from school, and again when Lois comes home from work. Benches and stone retaining walls provide perches from which to admire the deep, stream-cut chasm, or to gaze, at eye level, into the tops of the sycamores and eucalypti growing lower on the canyon's sides.

Many early westerns were shot down in the arroyo during the first decades of the previous century. Dave Parrish has told Harriet all about this. Dave is a film editor and serious movie buff. Once Harriet expressed an interest, Dave called her into his workroom off the garage, a room filled with film equipment and large computer screens: there he showed her clips of men galloping through the flat space where there's now an archery range and a casting pond. Gunfights were staged where the canyon floor narrowed. Dave kept pausing the footage to point out a familiar rock formation or a young oak tree that is now a brooding giant.

These days, Dave works at a trailer house in Hollywood. No, not a mobile home, but a place that makes movie previews. Harriet asks him about every preview she sees, so she's gotten good at recognizing the ones he made, which are short and alluring and as tightly composed as poems.

Dave used to make movies too, Lois told Harriet, but he is too much the artist, too much of a perfectionist, and he drove his directors and producers out of their minds. He'll still help the occasional student or independent director, and in his spare time he'll take on a worthy project, working at home in his room, with its fancy Avid setup.

Lois is a partner at a downtown firm. She practices contract law. That's where the money comes from. Some of the money. With those two, there was always money.

Drew Parrish is eight, the caboose, or, as Lois says, a happy afterthought. His oldest sister, Ginger, is twenty-four and in her first year of medical school at UCLA. In between them is Gayle. On her fifteenth birthday, she was the captain of her trophy-winning volleyball team; at fifteen and three months, she was a runaway turning tricks on the streets of Hollywood.

Harriet has speculated as to what set Gayle off. Everybody has. What makes a child eat pills indiscriminately from every medicine cabinet, even consuming the dog's tramadol and carprofen? What makes a soft-skinned, wide-eyed adolescent glug a two-buck pint of warm vodka, inhale burning white powder, or slide a needle into the milkiest stretch of her inner arm?

In a meeting, Gayle says, "Living on my own was something I had to do. I had to. I had to see what I was made of."

Another time, to Harriet, she says, "My mom was always very hard to please."

"Not anymore," Harriet says.

Now, many, many things please Lois: Gayle not shooting

dope. Gayle not turning tricks. Gayle sleeping at home in her own bed.

Gayle ran away four times. Each time she came home, she went into rehab, except for the last time, when she disappeared in the wee hours with a bulging knapsack. Each time she took off, there was the nauseated reeling, the forty-eight hours of stunned disbelief, and then the slow, miserable slog through day after day, with Lois doubling down on the shrink appointments and Al-Anon, Dave always in his room, and Harriet, too, hitting more meetings.

The last time, just when they were doing better, which took about a year and only meant that the phone could ring in the Cape Cod without setting off great crashes of terror and hope, Gayle had called. This was around Thanksgiving. She was clean and sober, she said, and had gotten her GED. She wanted to go to junior college. She wanted treatment. She wanted to come home.

Lois said this was the last time. The last time they'd pay for rehab. The last time Gayle could live with them after running away.

The Las Abejas outpatient program cost $11,000 for ten weeks, a bargain compared with inpatient. Gayle was there from eight to eight, morning to night, with family group on Tuesday nights running until ten.

"How many more family groups do we have to do?" Lois asked Harriet. "Dave drives me crazy in there. He acts all bored and restless, and when it's his turn to share, he says, 'I'll do anything and everything I can to help.' Yeah! Anything except actually participate."

Las Abejas had a craft hour, and someone taught the addicts to knit—apparently, knitting during meetings helped them pay attention. At Christmas, Gayle's first at home in three years, she had presents for everyone. She had knitted watch caps for Dave and Drew, scarves for Ginger and her mother, then some big, bright pot holders out of some rolled stretchy fabric for Harriet.

Before the New Year, Gayle said, "I'm taking a chip for ninety days tonight, and I'd love it if everyone could come."

Lois, Harriet, Dave, and Drew went and clapped in the audience. Ginger was in Idaho, skiing with a classmate.

The days passed, most of them rainy. Just dashing to the car without an umbrella, you'd get drenched, as if someone had turned a hose on you. Lois made an announcement at dinner: "People—including me—have got to remember to take umbrellas and stop buying new ones. I counted nine umbrellas in the elephant foot last night."

In January, when her Las Abejas program went into maintenance mode, Gayle enrolled at Pasadena Community College. She signed up for Mandarin and Advanced French, and started going to meetings with Harriet.

This coming summer, Gayle tells them, she'd like to start at the Pasadena Culinary Institute. She wants to work in the hospitality industry, she'll need training in food and languages. She has in mind a job at the InterCon in Beijing, she says, or Bangkok, or Nice. Or all three, and more.

"If that's what you really want to do," says Lois.

"We'll help you out any way we can," says Dave.

Harriet imagines, with some satisfaction, that Lois will someday say, "My daughter, the chef." Although, more likely, it will be, "My daughter, the events manager."

Harriet takes Gayle in hand, teaches her *pâte brisée, pâte sucrée.*

The house is fragrant with baked sugar, cinnamon, the warm spices. Gayle and Harriet have made apple pies for a Las Abejas fund-raiser. Harriet is wiping the counters while Gayle hunches over her calligraphy at the kitchen table. She has a brush, a darkening jar of water, and a small ceramic block on which sits the squat black disk of ink. She writes with quick gestures, pulling back to admire the filling grids.

During a lull in the rain, Gayle takes Drew and Lucky Gus out wall-walking. Their neighborhood is full of rock and clinker-brick walls, most of them fairly low; some have a squared concrete or brickwork crown, others are cobbled with rocks. The kids' stated goal is to walk through the neighborhood exclusively on the walls. Of course, they have to jump down to cross driveways and streets. The longest walls line the arroyo, usually right along the lip, but wide as they are, these are too scary for Drew. Harriet, out picking mint, watches them wall-walk down Arroyo Boulevard, two arm-flapping humans and one ear-flapping basset hound whose toenails clack and slip on the stone.

Lois drives up and gets out of the car, wiping her eyes. "Did you see them?" she asks Harriet, then pushes her forehead against Harriet's shoulder. "I can't believe she's really home."

"The jock salesman at the Porsche dealership was always good for a dime bag. I'd do him in a new Boxster on the 210 at a hundred miles an hour."

Today, Sunday, they are driving to the Armory for the big speaker meeting there. The rain is steady.

Harriet says, "Sounds like a real hard way to make a living."

Gayle drags a finger through the fog of her breath on the window. "It's just a life," she says. "You work at a lousy job to get what you want, then sit around till you have to go to work again."

"More like you do unbearable things to get something that lets you forget what you just did."

"Yeah," says Gayle. "Only it won't stay forgotten."

. . . .

"Hey, Mom." Gayle bursts into the kitchen, her hair curly from the mist. "Guess who I saw today in the bookstore? Honor. She also takes Mandarin. She's coming over, if that's okay. I know you said no old friends."

"You know what I meant," says Lois. "But I thought Honor was away at school."

"Yeah, but her mom's doing a party for her grandma's eightieth and she's home for that."

Honor LeClerc, Lois tells Harriet, was Gayle's best friend at Sequoyah through the eighth grade. A good girl. No problems. Now she's at U. Richmond, a Tri Delt.

The phone rings and Lois talks for a few minutes. Hanging up, she whispers to Harriet, "Jennie LeClerc. Making sure we're not a crack house."

Honor arrives driving her mother's Lexus. Shy, overachieving, a painfully fair redhead, Honor is tall and coltish in skinny jeans. Her orthodontia has yielded perfection. She says, "Nice to meet you, Harriet." Her thick dark coppery hair tumbles down to the floor when she leans over to retie her sneaker, and an inky Tinker Bell shoots out from her T-shirt sleeve.

Lois nudges Harriet, and once the girls go out, says, "I wonder how Jennie LeClerc likes her baby's tat!"

Leaving for the day, Harriet watches as the girls take the low wall along the driveway, single file, arms outstretched, dipping and flapping, hamming it up.

Lois comes home early, at three thirty. "I was thinking I'd take Gayle to Target," she says. "She could use some new T-shirts."

"Not home yet," says Harriet.

Lois glances at the clock.

"Not late yet," Harriet says. "The buses aren't so regular."

At four, Lois calls Gayle's cell phone; it rings until voice mail picks up.

"She just missed her bus," Harriet says. "Or decided to walk."

Lois calls again, and after ten minutes, again.

There is an upholstered bench along the breakfast nook and Lois lies down on this, curls knees to chest. Rain slides along the windowpanes. She puts her hands over her face.

"Don't worry yet," says Harriet.

"I can't help it," says Lois.

Harriet slices cucumbers into a bowl.

Lois calls again, then whimpers, a terrible sound.

Lucky Gus runs into the kitchen, toenails clacking as Gayle comes through the door, water flying off her. "Oh, Gussy, Gus, Gus," she says, stooping. Then, "Hey, Harriet. Oh, Mom! You're home early. Are you sick? It's not a migraine, is it?"

"No," says Lois.

"Guess what? My Mandarin teacher set me up with this Chinese girl who'll tutor me if I proofread her papers. We just had our first session. I learned how to say 'bite my ass' in Mandarin."

"I called you," says Lois.

"You did?" Gayle draws her cell phone from a pocket. "Oh, God, I turned it off in class and forgot to turn it back on." She gazes at the tiny screen. "You did call, didn't you." She sits beside her mother on the bench. "Oh, Mom," she says.

The rain is a steady hum, and a metallic gurgle in the drainpipe.

"What did you do all those months?" says Lois.

"Just stuff," Gayle says, and raises an eyebrow at Harriet. "It wasn't so terrible," she says, and jiggles her mother's hip. "I had a couple jobs. One in a library. I lived in a sober house in Alameda run by this woman Maritta who'd been on the streets too and now helps other girls get off. I got my GED there. But a girl brought some stuff in." Gayle shrugged. "It wasn't so bad this time, Mom."

Lois wipes her eyes. "Why didn't you call?"

"I wanted to wait till I could hold it together. It was kind of a roller coaster for a while."

Lois rises up on one elbow. "I was going to take you to Target for T-shirts," she says.

"We can go," Gayle says. "It's not that late. Besides, Lucky Gus needs a new leash. And I need a new umbrella."

Lois sits up all the way. "The *last* thing we need in this house—"

Gayle laughs, her brown eyes shining. "That got her up," she says to Harriet.

Li Juan, a small young Chinese woman, is soon a regular in the Cape Cod. She oversees the calligraphy, a stern taskmaster. She tells Gayle the Mandarin for: "I belched." "I farted." "You farted." When Gayle repeats these back, Li Juan and Drew shriek with laughter.

Harriet teaches Gayle *pâte à choux,* then puff pastry.

"It really wasn't *all* bad," Gayle says to Harriet as they drive to the big meeting in Hollywood on a Friday night. "It'll be my own wild story. How I lived on the streets when I was a girl. Like in *David Copperfield,* when he's so poor, and walking to his aunt's. The story I'll tell my children. Censored, of course."

"I was going to say," says Harriet.

"But the people I met! Everyone helped each other, they gave us blankets and stuff and kept an eye out. The guys used to intervene with the sicko johns."

Harriet is speechless.

"The best times were, you know, I'd find these beautiful places along the freeway hidden by big trees and bushes, with sometimes a water spigot near, and I'd lie in the sun on a cool day, dozing. Like being an animal. Nobody in the world knew where I was. And it was so *real,* Harriet. Each day figuring how to eat and get high, and meet up with people."

"So why come back?"

"I had, like, this vision one day out there. I saw myself, but years ahead, and I was doing great, like, prosperous? I knew I had to get there. And I wanted to get there."

"Your moment of clarity," says Harriet.

"Exactly. I saw myself out in the world, meeting all kinds of people, international types in like a big, beautiful, clean hotel. I had on this cream-colored silk blouse and a black skirt, very professional, and sleek. High heels. I looked fantastic. And my life was busy and important. You know? And I knew exactly what to do to get there. Languages and cooking school. Maybe hotel school in Europe. I was always good in French."

"And here you are," says Harriet. "Isn't that something."

She had almost said, *Isn't that a miracle.* But she couldn't tempt fate.

"So far, so good," says Gayle. "Though I kind of miss being up against it, when every day's like life-or-death. And you're a little animal rooting for food. Then cooking it for people on a campfire. I mean, we made some great meals from dumpster diving. And Harriet, you wouldn't believe the stories people have." Gayle rolls down her window, tests the air with her hand. "Hey, don't tell Mom all that stuff I just said. She'd freak."

Harriet quotes from the Big Book of Alcoholics Anonymous, the promises. "We will not regret the past," she says, "nor wish to shut the door on it."

"We will not," says Gayle.

"And we will know a *new* freedom, and a *new* happiness," says Harriet.

"And you will teach me brioche."

. . .

Lois and Dave are going out. But Li Juan will be there, and Honor, too, who is home on spring break. The young women say they're happy to watch Drew. Harriet makes cheese pizza, and although she is free to go home, she eats some at the table with Drew and the girls.

Li Juan teaches Gayle and Honor to say, "Lucky Gus has diarrhea. Lucky Gus threw up his food." Drew laughs so hard he inhales his juice.

Li Juan teaches Gayle to say, "Juice came out Drew's nose."

Harriet cleans up the kitchen. Then she drives home. It is late April. And still raining.

She is asleep when the phone rings.

"She's gone," says Lois.

"Who what?" says Harriet.

"Gayle. Gayle's gone."

It is one thirty in the morning, according to the red digital numbers. "When did she leave?"

"We came home at eleven. Drew was asleep. Honor was here alone. Gayle walked Li Juan to the bus stop—two blocks! But she never made it home. Honor called her cell and it rang in her room. She'd taken Lucky Gus too, but he scratched at the door not long after she left, and Honor let him in. His leash was still on."

"Did you call the police?" says Harriet.

"They won't do anything for twenty-four hours. And with her history, they're not inclined to do anything at all. She's eighteen now. Free to go where she pleases."

"Maybe she went home with Li Juan."

"We talked to Li Juan. Gayle put her on the bus."

"Shit," says Harriet. "Shall I come over?"

A long pause.

"I'll come over," Harriet says.

"No, no, that's okay," says Lois. "Dave's out combing the streets."

"Good," says Harriet.

"What do you think happened?" says Lois.

"I think maybe she ran into someone she knew."

"I know," says Lois. "That's what I think. I can't believe she just abandoned Lucky Gus like that. Dave has been knocking on doors in the rain."

"He's doing what he has to."

"Yes," says Lois.

"She'll probably come home in the morning. It might just be a guy."

"I hate this the most," says Lois. "Death seems easier. At least you'd know."

Two policemen are in the house when Harriet arrives at noon the next day. It hasn't been twenty-four hours, but Lois has insisted, perhaps used her connections. They've checked the jails and hospitals. There's nothing more we can do, the police insist, over and over again. She's eighteen.

"She was supposed to meet Li Juan after class," Lois says, "and she didn't show up."

Dave has been knocking on doors. One man saw the three girls walking on the rock wall across the street last night, but early, when it was still light.

Harriet goes into the kitchen. She makes coffee, then sandwiches and soup for dinner, which nobody will eat. The cops refuse everything, even the coffee. Harriet has her own conversation with them, telling them about the pharmacist, the dentist, the car salesman. The cops listen but take no notes.

Thinking she is unobserved, Harriet opens the drawer in the dining room where the silver is kept.

"I already checked," Lois calls from the living room. "Nothing is missing."

Come down and file a missing-persons report if she doesn't

show up, the police say. You can always hire a private detective. Keep us informed.

Ginger, the older daughter, takes off from classes on Friday, but she is so furious at Gayle and impatient with her parents that Lois doesn't object when she leaves after dinner. Dave's brother comes over from the Valley and spends the night. Li Juan and Honor sit with them all day Saturday and tell their stories again and again. Li Juan says, "She say we study next day. She very usual. She very happy. She practice Chinese with me all the way to bus stop."

Honor says, "I couldn't believe how long she was taking. And then, Lucky Gus scratching at the door like that, dragging his leash. I called her cell and heard it ring in her room."

Harriet keeps the sandwiches and coffee and cookies coming.

On the fifth day that Gayle is gone, a Monday, Lois and Dave go back to work. It's time, they say. They've been through this before.

Every iteration, though, is a little different. This time, it's Dave who can barely speak, who has aged years in a few days, his skin like clay, his hair lank, his eyes glittering as if he were ill. Lois is quiet too, but Harriet senses relief. Lois always expected Gayle to leave again, and now that she's gone, Lois's posture has slackened, her eyes are dull.

"No sense waiting on tenterhooks," Lois tells Harriet. "It will probably be months before we hear from her again."

Lois has two big trials coming up. She'll fill the days.

Dave starts coming home at three thirty every afternoon to drive Drew to soccer, to his clarinet lesson, to his reading tutor. Come summer, Dave drives him to tennis camp in the morning, and picks him up at four for swimming lessons. Many of these trips involve ice cream.

Also, somebody is cleaning out the leftovers. Harriet cannot believe how half pans of lasagna or risotto or roast chicken disappear overnight. Both Dave and Drew put on weight. Lois is losing. She asks the ironing lady to take in a pile of summer work skirts.

At the Al-Anon meeting that Harriet and Lois attend together, Lois says the same thing every week. "Dave hates it when I say this," she says, "but I'm done. This time, I'm really done. If she wants to get clean, that's her business. If she wants to use, that's her business. I give up. I'm out of it. Dave thinks I'm cold.

"But I still love her," Lois goes on. "Of course I do. Of all my children, I love her the most. I know. I shouldn't say that. But she's the great unattainable love of my life. I will never stop loving her, not for a single moment so long as I'm alive. Every atom in my body craves her, her skin, her hair, the sound of her voice." Lois is sobbing by this point. "But she will never, ever live in my house again."

Harriet doesn't believe her. Of course Gayle will come home. And Lois will let her stay.

"You know what, Harriet?" Dave has come into the kitchen from his room. He opens the refrigerator, takes out a Tupperware tub of potato salad. "It has to be foul play. I mean, she was getting an A in Mandarin. Most A.B.C. kids can't do that. Something happened. Someone nabbed her. The fucking cops won't lift a finger. And that detective is good for nothing, except sending invoices."

Harriet nods and makes a soft noise, but she doesn't agree. Gayle waxed too poetic about life on the street. Harriet won't tell Dave that the day before Gayle disappeared, it was all that crap about great dumpster-diving dinners. The story she'll tell her kids. Her David Copperfield days.

When Harriet drives past the Porsche dealership, the pharmacy, and the diner on Green Street, a hot fury sets in; she wants to shatter the glass doors, collar the mild-looking white businessmen and drag them before the world. This man had a sixteen-year-old girl suck his dick for a bowlful of chili. This one for a pill. Shame! Shame!

Which one of them had driven by, braked, rolled down a window, spoken into the rain? *Hey there.*

By summer the Parrishes are in marriage counseling again. Lois tells Harriet, "His refusing to talk about Gayle makes me crazy."

Dave says Lois talks and thinks too much about Gayle. "It's not like I'm repressing anything," Dave tells Harriet. "I just don't see the point of getting all worked up over and over again."

"Our counselor talks to Dave like he's three years old," says Lois. "And Dave likes it! He says he appreciates the simplicity and clarity. But I don't think anything is all that simple. And nothing is clear."

After weeks of moving the big red Michelin maps off the dining-room table to set it, Harriet drives the Parrishes—Lois, Dave, and Drew—to LAX in August. Lois's sister has rented a villa in Umbria for three weeks. Ginger will join them later, when she's done with summer quarter. Harriet takes a paid vacation. She doesn't go anywhere, except to swim in a friend's pool. She could swim at the Parrishes' too, but she is glad not to go there for a while. They have hired a petsitter. Harriet could have been that petsitter—she was last year, when they went to New York—but she welcomes a break from the family and the house.

When she pulls up to the Cape Cod on her first day back, she feels sorrow take hold, as if the air were solidifying.

But something between Lois and Dave has eased. They are both in the house, tanned, eager for Harriet to taste the *guanciale* and speck they smuggled through customs. Together, they tell her about the artichokes and tripe they ate in Rome, and they laugh describing an enormous steak they ate at a famous butcher's. This ease has come faster than the last time Gayle left, the time she took the spoons and the Bose. Back then, Lois didn't speak to Dave for three weeks, and Harriet was certain the marriage was over.

Harriet would never say it aloud, but the Parrishes are getting better at bouncing back from Gayle's vanishings; they're quicker to settle their scores, find their balance. Gayle has been gone five months, and already they no longer flinch when the phone rings.

By October, Lois looks less skeletal. Dave is getting fit coaching Drew's track team. Drew studies in his room this year, for he has a computer up there now. Harriet spends more time in the winter garden, planting and weeding lettuces, carrots, beets, and herbs, then harvesting the crops. She feels restless, though. A few days before November, Harriet asks for a raise.

"Of course," Lois says. "We should have thought of that, you're way overdue. How much do you want?"

Harriet asks for five dollars more per day, and the Parrishes give her eight.

In the cooling days of early winter, the smell and dampness of the air remind Harriet of driving across town to meetings with Gayle. She misses her, even as the old fury pounds dully on. She makes tarts and pies, and remembers how Gayle would say, "Slow down, let me see how you add the egg in. . . . Stand back, I need to see you pinch the crust."

Harriet had thought that the raise would mollify her, but other ideas keep coming to mind. A little restaurant space on Green Street is up for lease, and Harriet imagines intercepting the street girls between the pharmacy and diner, giving them free lunches. A friend has just opened a spacious new bakery up in Altadena and needs another baker, possibly a partner. Harriet would take a cut in pay, but that would be true of any job in food.

So she broods and shops at noon, usually pulling up to the Cape Cod around one, in time to take Lucky Gus for his walk. They cross the street and follow the meandering path along the arroyo's lip to the road that takes them to the canyon floor. They continue downstream, cross a bridge, and return on the other side of the water. Harriet has probably walked Lucky Gus along here fifty or sixty times in the past six months.

And yet it is another dog, a mixed-breed terrier named Sinbad, who runs up the canyon walls after a squirrel and does not come back as his owner calls and calls. When he finally obeys, he brings her a gift. At first, she tells the police, she saw only a clump of blackened leaves and white pebbles. But when she made Sinbad sit and drop it, when she finally got a closer look, she saw the bones of a human hand.

Pelvis and right leg fractured, a cervical vertebra crushed. Pinned in a thicket of trees and saplings. Probable cause of death, exposure. Even if she had screamed, she was too far down to be heard. And all that rain and rain.

Not far from the body, a broken umbrella is tangled in a bank of wild cucumber, the spokes bent and rusted, the black cloth rotted.

Even before the remains were lifted onto a stretcher, a dispatcher downtown had typed search terms into the missing-persons database—female, brown sweatshirt, blonde, Arroyo Boulevard—and made a tentative I.D. Later, the coroner checked dental records as a matter of course.

Just where the canyon was so steep, the walls so vertical, a low rock wall ran along its edge. Gayle had walked it dozens of times, arms flapping, and one time—perhaps a gust of wind caught her umbrella—she had slipped, there, across the street and down maybe fifty yards from the Cape Cod.

She'd last been seen up on Orange Grove, at the bus stop, in the direction of town. But she had come home, then crossed the street, to walk on that wall.

Harriet is in the kitchen when the cops come to the house, and she's there in the room when they say what they've found.

She gets up to make coffee. A cop comes into the kitchen to say they are leaving, and not to make any for them. Harriet questions him in a whisper: Why hadn't anyone smelled anything? Why hadn't other dogs found her earlier?

Some dogs had, the cop says. Dogs and maybe coyotes. But flies, maggots, ants, ladybugs, bacteria, crows—he pauses, proud of his list, but also abashed by it—they, uh, make short work of it. And the rain masked a lot. A foot, and that hand, had been carried off. But her jeans and sweatshirt served as a body bag. Her skull—here the cop cups his hands—sat in a nest of hair in the hood.

A memorial service is held in the pretty stone building that can be rented for events on the rim of the arroyo. Gayle's counselor and friends from Las Abejas come, and many of her teachers from Sequoyah. Harriet sits in the second row with Honor and Li Juan, right behind the family. The principal from Sequoyah gives the eulogy. Gayle's counselor says that Gayle's enthusiasm for recovery was an inspiration to them all. Li Juan and Honor go to the podium and announce that they will present all of Gayle's favorite things that she learned to say in Chinese. Li Juan reads the phrase, and Honor provides the translation.

You can see Lucky Gus has worms by lifting his tail.
I just burped up some of that hot dog I had for lunch.
My little brother laughs so hard, juice comes out his nose.

The lights are turned off, the shades drawn, and Dave shows

a ten-minute video of Gayle as a white-blond baby, then a tow-headed toddler crawling backward; ten-year-old Gayle with wet hair in a blue Speedo pumps a tacky gold aquabatics trophy in the air; Gayle, hair a yellow cloud, executes an impressive series of setups and spikes on the volleyball court; Gayle, grinning under a lumpy stocking cap, takes a chip for six months clean and sober.

Genevieve Plunkett

Something for a Young Woman

1

THE SHOP OWNER, BY then, knew all about it: the girl's hatred of elbows and stray pieces of hair; how her boyfriend disliked the taste of her lip gloss; how she referred to far too many body parts as "it." He knew which details she had made up to appear more experienced, even what she had swept over in an attempt to be coy. He listened to her, as bosses do, with hands folded, waiting through her blushes and her flights of qualifiers. The corners of his mouth and eyes remained still.

The girl and the shop owner liked to talk. Once, they had been talking in the storage room, searching a heap of bubble wrap for a lost piece to a tea set, and he had gotten very close to her, blocking the door with his body. She had looked up and met the buttons of his shirt, tugging across his torso, and a flight of nerves had gone up inside her, like someone had smacked a screen door covered in moths. He had joked that someone might walk in and get the wrong impression, as if life could just be so funny.

It had come to this, surely, by the girl's own indiscretion—

not just her candidness, but some kind of postural lingering, something learned, but unconscious. She started to spend more time in front of the full-length mirror on the inside of her closet door, so that she could see all the way to her heels, which she raised off the floor. She saw less and less of her boyfriend, and when they spoke she thought she detected something in his voice, like the hook of suspicion. They broke up two months later, although it had nothing to do with the shop owner.

"If I were to ask you what your preferences are," the boyfriend asked, "what would you tell me?"

The girl told him that he needed to be more specific.

"Your preferences," he said again. It was an odd word for him to be using, she thought, but before she could answer, he continued.

"Well, mine are different. People already know."

When she went to work the next day, the shop owner was there, feeding the woodstove. She told him about the breakup and their strange conversation and he turned his face to the fire, to hide from her, she imagined, whatever satisfaction he could not, for the moment, subdue.

"I was wondering when you were going to find out," he said.

He stayed for the day, when he would have usually left her in charge, and chopped firewood behind the building, hauling armload after armload inside with his sleeves rolled up past his elbows. It was the sight of the sleeves like that—the meat of his forearms darkened by hair—that made her wonder if something had changed between them and if, perhaps, he was waiting for her to do something about it.

There was a large desk where she sat, in the back, by the stove. On one side of it, there was a stack of old magazines, and on the other, a shallow wooden box of loose postcards, mostly photos of old bridges and the fronts of hotels. The middle of the desk was kept clear for the exchange of money, the sliding over of small purchases in a folded paper bag. She didn't know what put it in her head to sit there—some adolescent notion of sexual liberty—but she knew, the instant that he returned and saw her like that, that it was the wrong thing to do.

The shop owner dropped his eyes to the side and waited for her to climb down, then handed her the keys and told her to lock up in thirty minutes. She watched him go and heard the triple clatter of the bell above the door. There would be no more shoppers at this time. People did not like to stop roadside after dark, especially not to lurk through the twilight of scuffed velvet and sad lamp shades. Still, she waited until closing time. She took the money from the cash register and recorded the profit onto a slip of paper. The drawer, now balanced for the next morning, was locked into the register, and the envelope of cash was placed in a small safe beneath the desk.

The next week, the shop owner said that he would be on vacation with his family and, since the girl would be off from school, it was up to her to look after the shop. He assured her, in his instructions, that there would be enough chopped wood for the fire until he returned. She wondered, briefly, how she must have appeared, on top of the desk like that. She knew better than to worry that he would speak of it, but she also knew that it would always exist, as a small loss on her part.

She worked diligently while he was away, even though she was alone and could have easily spent the time reading books or using the phone. She even dusted the stuffed emu that had remained unsold for so long that it had acquired a name, chosen by the girl who worked there before her, who had occasionally been mentioned by the owner with unwavering neutrality.

At the end of the day, she locked herself in to count the register. Because the shop owner was not there to collect it, the money began to pile up in the safe. Then one night, the girl unlocked the safe to find the money gone, replaced by a small brown box. For a moment she feared that they had been robbed overnight, but then she saw that the box had her name written across the top.

Allison.

Inside, under a sheet of crepe paper, was a necklace with an oval black stone. Formal. Something for a young woman.

2

Allison met the man that would become her husband during their last year of college, then followed him to the city. He was always saying that he had friends there. She didn't know why she was surprised when the friends did, in fact, exist, all together in little compartments over the street. Like the college boyfriend, the friends had been biology students, but they spent a lot of time playing guitars plugged into big amplifiers, which they once accused her of moving two inches to the right based on dust patterns. There had been shouting. The college boyfriend had flown to her aid, his ears turning pink with outrage. She had cried and cried from the commotion. The city was making her sick with its fumes, its pockets of hot breath and burnt rubber. She swore that the cupboards smelled like newborn mice.

"I have this thing where I can't be around vomit," the boyfriend had said the first time it happened and put up his hands.

It was the pregnancy that caused them to move back north, to be closer to his family. His parents owned a large property with a barn, but you couldn't call it a farm; the horses were old, likely to trot back from the pasture favoring a hoof, and the chickens were slowly disappearing. There was speculation of a fox, as if such a creature in that area needed speculation.

Their decision to get married seemed not to rely on whether it was the right choice but rather on if his relatives in Canada could make it to the wedding, and if it was better to try to hide the belly or wait until after the baby was born.

"Things usually go back to normal," said the woman who would be her mother-in-law. "Before the third one, at least. And by the fourth, you don't care, just as long as it isn't another boy."

It was a boy. They named the baby after Allison's late grandfather, because it seemed like the right thing to do. He was born in January, in their own undecorated living room, with the rug rolled up, so that it would not be stained. It was how the baby's father had been born, same as his brothers, all four of them. Ideal, maybe, in the old family homestead, with its hearth and its lambskin throws. But this was a one-story ranch, spare of furniture and not fully unpacked. The midwife had needed a pan to collect the placenta and they found one in a cardboard box, next to an unwrapped sushi kit and a ceramic cat with hearts for eyes. *Come on, Mama*, the midwife had said throughout the labor. *Come on*, like someone coaxing a stubborn cow.

By summer, they were married on his parents' property, under a rented arbor. These decisions—the birth, the wedding—as well as others were made with the earnestness of dogs wanting to be good. They painted the nursery yellow, because that was the color of the husband's room when he was a boy. She could not dispute this logic, she knew, without weakening the mortar that had fixed together happiness and bumblebee yellow always in his mind. Even though, the way she saw it, bumblebees were mostly black.

In college, she had played the viola. She had always imagined herself in the symphony, with her straight, narrow back, wearing something thin, dark, and almost glittering. In the city, that may have been possible, but so far north, and now with the child, there were only opportunities in the early and late summer, when there were weddings.

Her husband's cousin played the cello and knew a wealthy couple who had taken up the violin years ago, as an answer to their "echoing empty nest." They formed a quartet and met at the cousin's church, in the basement, playing "Jesu, Joy of Man's Desiring" between spines of stacked folding chairs.

The night before their first performance, she found herself struggling to find something to wear. Something around her middle had changed since the baby, who was now four months old, and there was a veiny tint beneath her eyes. She found the necklace with the black stone in the back of a drawer, still in the box with the crepe paper, and put it on for the first time. The shop owner had never spoken of it, and she had never felt an obligation to wear it for his sake. She had taken it in the way someone might receive a confession: not entirely certain whether power had been granted, or taken away. Still, the weight of the stone flat against her skin brought the small pleasure of knowing that she was once something unknown to the people there, to her son and to her husband.

The boy grew, healthy and cheerful, and often satisfied to play alone. Allison took advantage of this, retreating to her room to work through a bit of complicated fingering. Sometimes, talking to the boy, discussing what color spoon he should use, or whether or not it was a good idea to dip his teddy bear into the bath, left her voice feeling frail, caught in the pitch of adult-to-child deception. Something needed to be purged, and so she would work it through the instrument, following an earthy, resonant phrase, like walking a trusted path.

She worked, too. The husband brought in only so much as a high school science teacher, which had him in fits at the end of the day. Why, he wanted to know, was there always some teenager trying to tell him that whales were not animals?

"They probably just mean to say that they are not fish," she suggested, even though she knew it would make his eyes clench in mock pain; his fight was wearying, the enemy ever more insidious.

It was her husband who got her the tutoring position at the high school's library, which was better than her last job behind the counter at the coffee shop: being looked up and down by the worldly, latte-drinking citizens, scanned by their eyes for general intelligence, sex appeal, usefulness; being asked, in so many ways, what had gone wrong in her life. But even with her pupils, she was always up against a sneer—another dirty attitude, waiting for her to slip up.

Her in-laws took the child during this time, which she was grateful for, even though it depressed her to hear them ask, every day, *Are you a good boy?*, and to hear them say, *Watch your footing, be careful,* until the anxiety was too much for him and he fell. That and they wanted to put him on a horse, which she fought outright, until they wore her down. It was an old horse, they said, a slow horse. Her husband had ridden it when he was a boy. All the boys had.

They saddled the horse on the first warm day in April. The saddle was a western style, large enough that mother and child could both sit without being crowded by the horn. The mother-in-law would ride ahead on her pony and the big horse would follow. There was nothing to worry about.

The husband's family owned acres, stretching into the forest behind the house, but it was no use riding where there weren't any paths, so they followed the neighboring fields. As long as they stayed next to the tree line, where they would not trample the crops, it was fine. Allison felt her shoulders relax. If she closed her eyes, she could feel down through the trunk of the animal beneath her, down to the planting of each giant hoof.

"A tractor," said the boy, as they rounded a line of trees. He was excited to see a piece of machinery, like a familiar face in the wilderness. It was parked at the far tree line, by a woodpile. Allison could make out the form of a man, carrying out a repeated swaying motion with his body. As they approached, it was clear that the man was taking wood from the pile and throwing it into the back of a four-wheeler. Every time a log would crash into the bed, the sound would bounce off the side of the tractor, doubling up in echo.

As they passed, the man threw in another log with a crash, causing the mother-in-law's mare to bounce in annoyance, firing a little blast of warning from under her tail. In response, the big gelding buckled at the knees, then danced from side to side before leaping forward at a full gallop. The reins fell from Allison's hands, the boy shifted to the side, and at the same time she had all the time in the world to think of what to do. There was no hope of stopping, so she kicked off her stirrups, hugged the boy's arms to his body, and let herself roll off the side so that she would hit the ground with her back, her body a cushion for his. It was so very easy to maneuver. She felt like she could laugh.

The ground hit, and, as the air burst from her lungs, she had a clear sense of déjà vu, accompanied by a thought: *This is where it happens. It has always been right here.* It was as if she and the boy had taken the fall over and over again, recycled throughout eternity.

Her breath returned. The child struggled to free himself from her arms so he could watch the big horse thunder back to the barn, kicking up bits of horseshoe-shaped mud along the way. He was unharmed, unconcerned even. No one, for that matter, seemed alarmed. The mother-in-law, in pursuit of the runaway horse, could be heard whooping its name from the next field over. The man at the woodpile, who'd seen the fall, did not slow his swinging arms, nor did he call off his dog when it went to investigate the two figures on the ground. The dog licked the boy with a wet muzzle, pushing its insistent face back into them, no matter how Allison held out her arm.

. . .

They did not call it an accident. There was a lesson to be learned for the boy.

"He'll have to get back on sooner than later," said the father-in-law. "We wouldn't want him to develop a fear."

But that is just what Allison wanted: to come to the edge of a cliff and to back away, preferably on hands and knees; to see a rabid animal and to barricade the doors, call the fire department.

They told her that she was worrying too much. The runaway horse had been found after the incident, standing square in his stall, eyes half-closed. Just a big marshmallow, they said. A teddy bear. We'll just put the boy on his back while the horse grazes in the field. As if that were somehow safer.

They lifted him by the armpits, red-faced and kicking, onto the back of the horse, who chewed, drooling gobs of green saliva.

"There," said the in-laws, with some breathlessness. "Now he can get down."

Allison watched the boy run back into the house, then sat on an overturned feed tub by the pasture fence. She wondered why everything was wrong, why she couldn't just be thankful that everyone was alive, that bombs were not falling from the sky.

3

A year later, she found herself separating from her husband. There had not been an affair, or even an argument; it was just that he had left for a long weekend to attend a job training and she had not wanted him to come back. It was the anticipation of his face, drawn in fatigue and pained by private failures; the dirty swill of his eyes scanning the kitchen, the living room, looking to see what had changed while he was gone, or what still had not been done.

The training was for science teachers, kindergarten through twelfth grade. It was held somewhere in the Adirondacks, at a state park, in a small concrete building filled with beaver pelts, animal scat references, and cicada casings. The teachers slept in cabins and took cold showers in the outbuildings in their flip-flops.

"We learned how to dissect owl pellets today," the husband said over the phone. "You know what they are, right? Tell me what you think they are."

She had been about to throw a basket of laundry into the washing machine but set it down, standing over its armpit smells, the acrid shadow of his pillowcase that she'd washed twice already since he'd left. She sighed.

"It's all the mouse parts that the owl can't swallow."

"Well," he said, the word drawn in, a dumpling at the back of his throat. "The point is that you didn't say owl poop, which is what half the people here said. Half. Can you believe it?"

"No." She gave the basket a nudge and it slid almost the entire way down the basement stairs, hissing, like skis, before it flipped and bounced to the bottom. She knew that the stain on his pillowcase wasn't really a stain, just the place where his head ground into the pillow at night, the one place in the house that would always smell most like him and would always remind her of a thumbprint in cheese.

He was upset to hear that she wanted to leave, but not as upset as she thought he would be. He told her to take the child and move to her hometown, only two hours away by car. He was certain that she would want to come back after some time alone. He would send her money. He would tell his parents that she was going to spend time with a sick family member, so that they would not think poorly of her. Everything would be fine. By the time they were finished discussing it, she was not entirely sure that the separation had not, in fact, been his plan all along.

Her parents' house still had the aluminum swing set in the backyard from when she was a girl, with the same slide, always dappled by the repetition of rain and soil. Their rooms were made up for them, complete with a layer cake of towels laid out on the bed, like a hotel. The boy was adored with quiet gratitude. Her decision was never questioned.

She found work at the elementary school, taking over temporarily for a music teacher who was having a baby. There was a lot of cardboard and glitter and toilet paper tubes, stopped at the ends and filled with beans for shaking. There was no epiphany, no rush of dark pleasure now that she was on her own, just "I'm a little teapot" during the day and dinners at home of macaroni and cheese with little cubes of hot dog.

When she first took out the viola, it sounded dry from the travel. Her mind would drift; her bowing arm would become heavy. There were certain steps to be taken, she knew, for moving on, like chopping her hair, doing something drastic, but not too ugly. Her mother urged her to meet people, to "build a foundation," but she would not; she was comfortable, for the time, living in a blind spot, off the grid of where she had pictured her life heading.

And then one day, in February, a change occurred, marked by a dream. It was one of those dreams where very little happens, but something is injected under the surface, into the commotion of life, drugged by sleep. When she woke, she remained in bed for some time, seeing his face in the rumpled darkness, while falling snow and ice hissed against her window.

In the morning, she was still stirred, but with an added dint of sadness. Her husband had called her the night before, like he did every Sunday, to ask about the boy and to inquire, nervously, about her plans. He told her that he hadn't felt like seeing anyone else, meaning women, and then waited a long time for her to respond. He talked about his students. He wanted to know if she had heard that narwhals were in fact mythical. Did she know that brown cows can only make chocolate milk?

She focused on the slight breakage at the end of his questions, the great effort he put into pronunciation that could only be described as "toothy." She had tried to imagine that this would be the last time that they would ever speak, even though she knew he would call again next week. She had imagined what it would be like to see his traits emerge in the boy as he grew, traits that she may or may not have taken for granted in the past. But there had been only weightless, drifting apathy, like the fatigue from artificial light.

She went outside to clear the snow from her car and then work on the layer of ice on the windshield wipers. You could sometimes forget that there was something to be uncovered once you got to chipping and scraping, as if the point were to just keep working until you hit the ground. Exhausted, she opened the car door and sat, freezing, behind the wheel. She looked at the gray sky, the corroded white of birch trees, through the hole of visibility that she had cleared on her windshield.

In her dream, the shop owner had been sitting behind the desk by the open stove, the same large desk that had been there when she worked for him, years ago. He was writing in some kind of financial log with his sleeves rolled up and his arms glowing in the light from the burning coals. He would not look at her. He would not speak to her.

She turned the key in the ignition and was blasted by cold air. Inside the house, she knew that her mother would be making coffee while the boy ate his cereal in the kitchen, scrutinizing the cardboard box (why he could never put that kind of concentration into a real book, she would never know). If she left now, they might not even notice that she was gone.

By the time the hot air kicked in, she had already taken the exit off the highway and pulled into the gas station across the road from the old antique shop. She would wait for ten minutes, she told herself, and if she did not see the shop owner by then, then she would go home, call in sick to work, and come right back. She would sit there in her car all day if that is what it took.

She prepared herself to wait, but when she raised her eyes, he was already there—just a shadow behind the window of a pickup truck, rolling to a stop in the gravel parking lot in front of the shop. The man emerged, hulking in a gray overcoat, and walked to the shop door, where he kicked loose an icicle on the gutter. Her first impression was, not surprisingly, that he looked older—he had been in his fifties when she worked for him, almost ten years ago—but he still had the same broad carriage, the same security of strength. She could see his beard, now fully gray and trimmed close to his jaw. The rest of his face was hidden beneath the furred brim of his hat. She watched him unlock the door to the shop and disappear behind it, imagined him switching on the overhead lights and then going straight to the woodstove. Something knocked around inside her chest, half-winged and terrible.

She went about the rest of the day distracted, unable to focus on her regular tasks, as though she were still in that frozen car, peering through the narrow hole of cleared ice and snow. At school, she unlocked the storage closet and dragged out the xylophones and frayed squares of carpet for her students. She let the time pass in the clumsy gallop of misplaced mallets and little voices off-key. When the last school bell rang, she drove home, stopping by the neighbor's house on the way to pick up the boy, who had been there since lunch. She must have strapped him in the car seat, she must have put his mittens over his hands, for although she didn't remember doing so, he was there, dressed and asleep, by the time she pulled into the gas station again. The antique shop across the road did not close until six and it was not yet four, so there would be little chance of seeing him. Still, she sat, warming the tips of her fingers in the heating vents, just in case she caught a glimpse of shadow, some small sign that he was inside. That was all that she needed.

Half an hour passed. From where she was parked, she could see the items on display in the window—an iron-ribbed trunk, a stenciled child's sled, a mirror reflecting the purpling clouds overhead—and behind them, a sliver of depth, the only suggestion of the space beyond. So far, nothing had crossed it, even though her eyes had remained fixed, pooling with concentration. When the child woke, he wanted to know where they were. He was hungry and cold. She turned on the radio, she dug through her purse for a candy, but the boy only began to cry. Defeated and annoyed, she drove home, determined to return to the spot in the morning.

But the next morning, she felt differently. With horror, she recalled the events of the day before and found each moment distorted by something that she now felt no connection to. Toward the man, the shop owner, for whom she'd waited so long to see cross behind the window, she felt only disgust. She would never go near the place again.

Weeks passed and the strangeness of the day had not returned. A freak reaction, she told herself, caused by stress, or the long winter. She developed a better practice schedule and, through regular use, her viola regained its familiar give, ripened like a spot of hardwood floor warmed by the sun. When she played, she dipped into something that was always streaming, moving like ants through the veins of a colony. There, she was all feelers, little bits of armor, a million tiny, uncrushable hearts. They poured from her instrument and found their way in swarms through the cracks in the walls, slipping outside beneath the skin of the trees, down into the earth, where the egoless are.

And then, on a day in March, she woke before sunrise and could not fall back to sleep. Her mother's little dog was up, dancing its toenails against the kitchen floor, so she put on her jacket and clipped the leash to its collar. Outside, it was unseasonably warm. Her muscles relaxed and her mind wandered. She wished that she had someone to call other than her husband, whose conversation was still irritatingly stoic.

"We lost another chicken at the farm," he would say. "Maybe you will have an answer for me by spring."

She had tried to speak to her husband about the incident with the horse after it had happened, about how time had slowed and she had maneuvered her body to protect their son. About how she had felt that it had all happened before. *This is where it happens.*

"Adrenaline," had been his response. "An amazing thing."

But that wasn't what she had wanted to talk about. She knew the mechanics of it as much as anyone. What she wanted was for him to ask her about something ridiculous, like her past lives, or if she ever flew in her dreams and, if so, whether she flapped her arms or kicked her feet. She wanted him to ask her about the people in her life who'd hurt her and for him to be surprised at her answer, impressed by the depth of her life before him. It wasn't about revealing her soul—a word that she wasn't sure if people were still using seriously, like *Pluto*—but about giving the tangential a place in their life, casually but also mindfully, just as one might start putting a feeder out for birds in the winter.

She let the dog put its weight into the leash, as if she could get away with following it, across town, to where the houses had shapelier gardens and names on the knockers, to the street where the shop owner lived with his wife. The windows of the house were thick with sleep, with gray-blue deafness.

She took a seat on the curb directly across the street from the slope of his front yard, where the crocuses were already coming up along the lattice under the porch, little wet paintbrushes of purple and yellow. The dog sat on its stump, obediently, and looked with her, working its nose against the wind. There was no bench, no view, no reason to be there. She should not have been there, but she waited as the cars came with their headlights spreading over the road, and as birds dropped down and picked over the new ground. She waited for the light to turn on and when it did, downstairs—a little yellow heart, beginning again—she stood up and walked back.

When she returned to her mother's house, the boy had just risen and was looking for her with a watery, worried stare. He wanted her to pick him up, up, up, as if to break through the atmosphere.

4

She wore the black necklace to the shop owner's funeral that fall. When she read his name in the obituaries, it did not register immediately. Was that really how it was spelled? Was that how it looked on paper? Because it was not how it felt, spun into malleable lint inside her mind. She wanted to know if it was him, or just someone with his name.

She was shocked to see the open casket—as if it were something that he had consented to—and it shook her opinion of him, just a little. She considered reminding her husband, who still called every Sunday night, that she wanted to be cremated, but then wondered if that knowledge would somehow tie her permanently to him, "until death."

She remembered, as a child, dreading the body of her grandfather, her son's namesake—not because of its appearance, but because she feared that she would be expected to say something to it, a prayer that she had not been taught. Her six-year-old cousin, the only other child attending the wake, had huddled by the fireplace, shivering. *I'm cold*, he told the grown-ups, *I'm too cold*, and they shook their heads. *You can always count on that one*, they had said. *Oh yes, you can always count on him.*

Years later, during some unremarkable moment—sitting in school, or riding in the car with her feet on the dashboard—it had suddenly occurred to her that her cousin had been afraid of the body, but did not want to admit it. What a terrible world, she had thought, and still felt, from time to time, that a boy, who was probably scolded for saying things like "cross my heart and hope to die," was expected to see a corpse and act accordingly. Stepping into the funeral home, she vowed silently to save the children, should there be any inside.

There was one, a little girl wearing a purple jumper over a black turtleneck, who swung her legs from a tall armchair while reading a paperback. She did not appear to need saving. Allison stood in a line to the casket. One moment, she was looking at the spider veins at the hemline of the skirt in front of her, and the next, she was over his face. Some nearby vent was pumping cool air, which, although odorless, she wanted desperately to avoid, like the puff of wind from under a train. The face before her looked pained, as if caught in the state of being about to swallow. A poorly executed clay figure; a creased sock at the bottom of the laundry basket. She felt the pressure to move along, so that someone who actually knew him could gaze, move their lips.

And then she was in front of the man's wife, not realizing that she had entered a second line. The wife had an open expression, a face of recognition, perhaps left over from the person who had been in front of her just before. The skin around her eyes was gluey, caked-over red.

"Oh, Allison," she was saying. "Allison, Allison, Allison. Look how you've grown up. Thank you for coming."

The line moved on. Conversation trickled as people willed themselves into circles, trying to place their connection to each other, like stringing beads.

"Do you know how it happened?" It was the girl in the purple jumper, leaning back in the chair, her arms spread wide in ownership.

"No," said Allison. "Do you?"

"My mom said that his heart kicked it, but I don't believe her because my dad looked at her weird when she said it."

"You're not afraid to be here?"

The girl swayed a little, dreamily.

"No. Grandpa looks like the trees when they talk in cartoons. They talk and then their faces just go back to looking like bark. That's what I say." She curled back the front half of her book and forced a sigh.

She walked home with her hands plunged into the pockets of her cardigan, digging into the give of the wool. She waited for a weight to lift, or to descend, some indication that her life was affected by the man's death, but felt only the pain of her shoes where they rubbed, up and down. It was a Friday afternoon, still two more days until her husband would call, leaving openings in his speech, places where she knew she could lay out her decision and have it met tactfully and with absolution. She stopped to look up at the glint of a passing jet, which had been roaring inconspicuously through her head for some time. How lucky I am, she thought, watching the plane blink into the clouds, to still have someone on the other end, waiting for me to make up my mind.

Alan Rossi

The Buddhist

WHILE WAITING FOR THE sickness to pass, the Buddhist was not shirking his dharma-related responsibilities, was not skipping meditation, was not failing to practice in each and every moment, and was now, his laptop resting on his knees, getting ready to have a meeting with a student over Skype. He sat in the air-conditioned meditation hall, which was in the center of a Sri Lankan rainforest, waiting to connect with a student named Elise Grantwell, whom he had been teaching for the past six months.

It was the end of the rainy season. Outside the hall everything was darkly wet and green. The sun was not up yet. It was the time between night and morning where the sky went from a lightened gray to an impossibly clear blue. Out one window of the hall, the Buddhist could see Ajahn meditating with two other monks near the stream in the forest. They sat on bamboo mats. Because they all wore the saffron robes that were both customary and required of all monks in the Theravada Forest Tradition, they stood out against the backdrop of green forest. The monks, seated in variations of meditation posture by the river, were still, and the forest appeared to be moving, swirling around them. The Buddhist knew that the visual illusion was caused by his fever, yet he could not stop looking, fixated and momentarily light-headed, feeling vaguely disembodied, aware of the beauty of the scene and of the fact that he would soon not be in Sri Lanka and might never be there again, if that was Ajahn's wish. Then he inwardly chanted *seeing, seeing*— knowing that his sense perception was ultimately devoid of self. The Buddhist thought of Ajahn's order to return to his home country, Canada, to help open a new temple there, and how he'd have to stay in the basement of his father's house, which had been his old room, now a little putting-green thing. He tried to see his aversion to the notion of returning home for what it was: impermanent thinking of no reality, suffering that originated in ignorance and was caused by selfish craving, the craving in this case, he saw clearly, his own desire not to be where he would have to be, back in his home country. Staying on the Astroturf floor of his father's basement—a man who tried to convey how much he disliked the Buddhist by not talking, choosing only to write him notes on Post-its even while the Buddhist was in his presence—was one of the only things the Buddhist believed he dreaded, even more than dying.

A request to connect through Skype blinked on the Buddhist's screen. He sat for a moment, hands composed in his lap on the saffron robes, and let his thoughts of sickness and returning home settle and calm, becoming clear, like dirt settling in water. He connected through Skype with Elise Grantwell. She was fortyish, lived in Washington, D.C., and was—as she had explained to the Buddhist in an earlier email—having some intense episodes of stress, paranoia, and self-loathing, which often led to panic attacks, all due to her job as a defense attorney. Her face appeared pixelated and slightly fuzzy on the Buddhist's screen. The image strained the Buddhist's fevered and tired eyes, which in turn made for an annoyed mind-state, though he told himself that such an annoyance was merely the discomfort of a certain sense perception, and that discomfort was only the consciousness of a certain physical ailment, namely the pain behind his fevered eyes, and also that it was a discomfort that would pass from his consciousness when the sickness passed from his body, which also meant—the fact that it would pass—that it contained no inherent reality, was not his self, and therefore it was nothing to dislike. It was, like all things, changing.

He tried to focus on Elise Grantwell's face. Elise Grantwell was white, had forty-year-old hair, just slightly thinning dark hair, and her face, almost pretty, seemed pulled down by gravity into a near-perpetual frown of seriousness or worry. She appeared to be wearing a pantsuit of some kind. The Buddhist noted that he felt a slight attraction to her overworried yet almost pretty face, allowing the moment of sexuality to pass and fade.

The Buddhist told Elise Grantwell that he had read her email and was there anything else she wanted to add, any other questions? Elise Grantwell said yes, emphatically, on the Buddhist's screen. She said that since discovering Buddhism, which was at first very calming and stress-relieving, she felt even worse, because it (the meditation, the Buddhist presumed) had made her realize that her job—her life's work, she called it—could be considered something that prolonged or encouraged suffering rather than ending it. On the screen, Elise Grantwell appeared almost puzzle-like for a moment, the screen pixelating her face distressingly. So it's like the thing that was previously relieving my stress, she continued, her face blocky and blurred, the meditation itself and the teachings of dharma, you know, that's making my stress levels worse and causing me to have even more panic attacks. Her face resolved clearly on the Buddhist's screen. My stress is out of control, Elise Grantwell said.

He watched Elise Grantwell, whose eyes were mainly looking down, look very briefly up at the Buddhist then quickly back down again, nervy and submissive as a frightened animal. The Buddhist observed himself in the small boxy corner in the

Skype window: visibly sweating and pale, yet composed. He tried not to scratch any part of the rash that had spread all over his body, and closed his eyes briefly. He inwardly labeled the sensation *itchy, itchy*, seeing that the reality of the sensation was no-self, filled with suffering, and impermanent. The feeling was not him—his body was the jug and his self was no self at all, just the emptiness inside.

Outside, the Sri Lankan morning was coming through the woods, the deep green of the forest revealing itself. The monks had completed seated meditation and the Buddhist could see, farther into the forest, that they were walking on the path, doing walking meditation, looking a little like confused old men.

What if I got someone off who was guilty? Elise Grantwell wanted to know. Wasn't that somehow not Buddhist? Also, she said to the Buddhist, what if instead of making me less stressed and suffering less, I'm actually more stressed and suffering *more*? What if all this Buddhism stuff is bad for me? I'm just in a really bad place, she said, her brow furrowed in anxiety and confusion and her mouth tight. And meditation doesn't seem to be working *at all*, she said.

The Buddhist calmly nodded at his screen, watching Elise Grantwell's response and himself as he calmly nodded. He didn't engage with the fever behind his eyes, nor the intense itchiness of his body, and, watching himself, he noticed he was exaggerating his nod so that if the connection was bad and/ or briefly timed out, Elise Grantwell would still be able to see he was nodding and understanding. Elise Grantwell explained that it was not only that she was suffering more now *privately*; all this meditation seemed to be making her worse off around *other people* as well. All this calmness I'm trying to do is making people around me ask if I'm awake, she said. Like people are saying, *Hey, Elise, you awake over there?*, she said, both laughing and almost crying on his screen. The Buddhist observed himself listening, remaining calm, neutral, accepting. I'm just trying to calmly accept and be in difficult situations, like you've taught me, she explained to the Buddhist. But it's hard to be with angry and obnoxious colleagues in a meeting. It all seems to be making things *worse*, especially around other people, she told the Buddhist. And that's making me feel so alone and isolated, even more alone than before.

The Buddhist took a small breath. He observed himself in the corner of the screen sitting composedly in his saffron robes in lotus posture before his laptop, contemplating Elise Grantwell's situation and her being, acknowledging, with a small amount of pride, that he both felt and appeared earnest and attentive. Outside, the Sri Lankan rainforest was suddenly bright green and hummingly alive, insects making mechanical whirrings, as though someone had flipped a switch. The forest was a stark contrast to both his sickness and Elise Grantwell's sense of personal suffering in a materialistic and consumer-oriented culture, the Buddhist thought. He said to Elise Grantwell that he was deeply aware of how interpersonal relationships could quickly deteriorate once you took the first step on the path. He coughed and paused, momentarily feeling nauseated, a wave-like shuddering moving through his body. He allowed his presence to return to Elise Grantwell. The moment of nausea passed. The Buddhist said that Elise Grantwell's questions about other people and feeling alone were very apt. He was speaking calmly and directly and without hesitation, he thought, like a gentle rain addressing the sullen and dry earth.

For instance, the Buddhist said, these questions are very apt for me personally because I'll soon return to my home country, where I've had many difficult relationships, just as you are experiencing now. The idea of this other country where he had once lived, on the other side of the planet, momentarily passed through the Buddhist's mind, the country like some foreign world, and this idea instantly encompassed the place he was in now so that the Buddhist felt that all of existence, even himself, was foreign, alien, that everything was both alien unto itself and at the same time discovering itself to be completely and wholly unalien. The thought, more an intuitively felt experience of reality, passed so quickly that the Buddhist could easily continue what he was talking about. He explained to Elise Grantwell that his own interpersonal relationships had quickly deteriorated when he had been ordained as a Buddhist monk. While this didn't bother the Buddhist in the least now, it was also rather interesting for the truths it revealed about human behavior and how unaccepting almost all people who lived in a materialistic society were of a person who was no longer going to participate in the delusion of such a society. The immediate effects of such a change for him—of becoming a person who was calm, quiet, not unaffected but disaffected, not distant but detached—the Buddhist explained to Elise Grantwell, was that the people who had known him before intensive meditation and Buddhist study now believed him to be zombified, brainwashed, deadened. Asleep, the Buddhist shared openly with Elise Grantwell, who was nodding vigorously on the screen and saying yes, yes.

When I first came home from Sri Lanka after ordaining, the Buddhist told her, after years of studying Buddhism, when I first returned to see family and friends, many people thought that I was asleep. The same thing people are thinking about you. Elise Grantwell was nodding earnestly, her eyes wide as a child's. Why wasn't I interested in climbing or kayaking anymore; why didn't I care about playing any of the instruments I used to play? I didn't joke the way I used to; I didn't drink, didn't do drugs, or even seem to enjoy eating—everyone was basically saying the same thing. The Buddhist said that it was a strange irony that when one comes to see clearly that the three characteristics permeate all things—that all things have no separate self, all things are suffering and all things are impermanent, and that the only way to approach reality is through calm detachment and insight into this—the people who are actually asleep often accuse those who are really beginning to see of being asleep. Elise Grantwell said that that was just what she was thinking. My mother even went so far as to say I was brainwashed by a cult and wasting my life, the Buddhist told Elise Grantwell. I had to remind my mother that she hadn't approved of any of the activities like rock climbing and music that I'd done before anyway. I remember she said that anything would be better than what I'd chosen. Elise Grantwell nodded in the Skype window. The light darkened in the room, and he saw himself in the square of screen appearing thin and sickly and weak, yet composed. The Buddhist told Elise Grantwell that these were definitely deeply painful things and that he remembered them as being deeply painful and isolating. Yes, Elise Grantwell said. It's a little odd that this way also makes one understand one is alone, the Buddhist said. You're right that that first realization—that one is actually more alone than before, or can see one's aloneness with more clarity—you're right that that's painful. But it's a pain that passes, the Buddhist said.

The abbot came into the meditation hall and asked the Buddhist in Thai how his fever was. The abbot was a very old, very bald, and very short Thai man who had a perpetual scowl on his face. His skin was brown, his face wrinkled. He was missing one of his front teeth and wore large, dark-framed glasses, which obscured his face and, the Buddhist believed, hid much of what he perceived of people. He spoke and responded to everything slowly, as inscrutable as an old dog. The Buddhist said he was feeling worse, but he knew it would pass. The abbot said, That's it! Which was what he said often and was his main dharma lesson, as though the entire world could be reduced to: This, It, Here, Now! The abbot, slightly bowlegged, went out again to look for the cook and said that he would try to round up breakfast. Outside, the high insect whine and buzz of the morning had intensified.

Sorry, the Buddhist said to Elise Grantwell, turning back to his screen. The Buddhist said that while he did remember being shunned, by his mother and, more spitefully, his father, as deeply painful and isolating, he also remembered that he had "stood strong." The Buddhist made air quotes here with a small smile, feeling a little political or like a boxing trainer. He then advised Elise Grantwell to do the same, to "stand strong," again air quoting. Elise Grantwell nodded and opened her mouth to talk. For instance, the Buddhist continued, when my mother claimed that she had lost a son to a cult, I responded by saying to her, I'm sorry I can't satisfy what you want me to be, but I have no one to satisfy except myself and may you one day realize the same. The Buddhist said how he remembered very clearly using the word "may." May you one day realize the same, he said into his screen, playing with the fabric of his robes. It was a ridiculous and condescending way to put it, he said. I was a little attached to the whole Buddhist thing. It made me talk like an idiot. Elise Grantwell laughed in a way that a person laughs when they're trying to show just how comfortable and not insecure they are, the Buddhist observed. He noticed this while at the same time choosing to ignore it, then calmly recalled to Elise Grantwell how his mother had cried a little when he had said this, then how she had slapped him. Such a shock. His mother, he recalled, who was a small, waifish woman who would die of cancer while the Buddhist was teaching in Sri Lanka, had never struck the Buddhist before, even as a child. After striking the Buddhist, his mother's eyes had looked into the Buddhist's eyes, as if searching for the lost former self of her son, the Buddhist recalled. I stood looking at her, calm and accepting, while she cried, the Buddhist told Elise Grantwell. My cheek burning. In the kitchen of the family's house, my father's house. My father was standing in the corner of the kitchen, stroking his beard, a thing he always did in moments of either conflict or reflection. I remember how he gave me a stare of pure anger and hatred.

Such a disgusting stare that I actually lost my composure. I got really angry at him and said, You look like an animal right now.

For a moment, the Buddhist thought he was going to throw up. He put his hand to his mouth; Elise Grantwell asked if he was okay; the feeling passed, and he told Elise Grantwell he had been throwing up all night. Oh my God, she said. You should lie down, you don't need to be talking to me. The Buddhist said he was fine. It was just an unpleasant feeling and would pass. The Buddhist said this, aware that he was using his physical ailment to teach a lesson of impermanence and nonattachment to thoughts, feelings, and physical sensations to Elise Grantwell, as if his body and being were the textbook from which Elise Grantwell was studying. Suddenly, the Buddhist had a terrible desire to scratch his back, and at the same time felt a wave of fever run up his spine and into his head, which made his eyes water. The computer screen blurred in his vision. He closed his eyes hard and took a sip of water, hoping that it wouldn't make him want to vomit. When he opened his eyes, the room spun slightly, moving from left to right, left to right, and the Buddhist closed his eyes again. He waited a moment, following his breath. When he opened his eyes, Ajahn was looking into the hall. Feel okay? he said in English, a subtle yet generous gesture of compassion. The Buddhist nodded. Food soon, Ajahn said. Cook is waking up from drink. Outside, the day was warming and insects were wildly buzzing and the humidity of the forest seemed to be overtaking the cooling of the air-conditioning.

This is all on my mind, said the Buddhist to Elise Grantwell, turning back to his screen, because I'm returning to my home country, to people who had a difficult time accepting me, so all these things that you're going through are also very appropriate for me, said the Buddhist. It's a wonderful lesson for both of us. Elise Grantwell's face distorted into pixelation—the connection seemed like it was about to be lost—but then resolved into clarity. The Buddhist continued by saying that he remembered, shortly after his mother slapped him, that his father had said, privately, away from his mother so as not to upset her more, that he didn't understand how his son, a remarkable person, always a wonderfully caring and selfless individual, could have become so selfish. He said, When did you turn into such a pretentious and condescending shit, not to mention a bum? Look at all this we've given you. We've given you everything, he had said, indicating the house and the material possessions of which his parents were, the Buddhist explained, overly proud.

It was about that time, the Buddhist said, that my father told me to get out of his house, which my father had designed and built and kept up and which I had, he told me, lost the right to live in. Which my mother of course protested. To which my father responded by saying things like, Fine, if you want to let him hurt you repeatedly and without end, fine, go ahead. I'm done. The Buddhist recalled to Elise Grantwell, whose mouth was now agape on his screen, how he had simply walked out of the kitchen to meditate in his bedroom and then packed to leave.

Elise Grantwell said, Wow. The Buddhist saw Elise Grantwell adjust her camera so that it showed more of her upper body and her breasts beneath a tight white oxford shirt. The Buddhist could see her bra through the oxford and noted, with surprise, that her breasts, for a forty-year-old woman, were still very full and pleasant and attractive. The Buddhist observed his sexual feelings with calm detachment, noting that because Elise Grantwell's camera was now more focused on her face and body, which was attractive, that he felt both an attraction toward her and an aversion toward the attraction. He allowed the feelings to pass.

Oh, I forgot the best part, the Buddhist said. On his screen, Elise Grantwell perked up, sitting more upright, which almost caused the Buddhist to say that she looked better when she sat up straight. He observed that in the box of the screen he remained composed and uninterested in Elise Grantwell's appearance. The Buddhist realized that he needed to acknowledge that part of the reason he enjoyed talking to Elise Grantwell was the fact that she was, by conventional social standards, a pretty woman and he liked the attention she gave him. He noted this and tried to understand that his real position here was situated in the universal, helping to usher Elise Grantwell to the shore of nonsuffering. The Buddhist allowed himself to focus on his duty. He then recalled with sarcastic humor to Elise Grantwell that the best part of the whole thing was that before he returned to Sri Lanka to live the rest of his life as a monk, his parents had held a family meeting with the former girlfriend the Buddhist had broken up with to be a Buddhist. An intervention for a Buddhist, he said to Elise Grantwell, who smiled and laughed overly sincerely. It instantly passed through the Buddhist's mind, stopping him completely, like pausing a YouTube video, that Elise Grantwell found the Buddhist attractive—her eyes rarely holding his stare, her general discomfort and insecurity coupled with her need to impress, her frequent movement of body and straightening of her back—all of it suddenly and intuitively seemed to the Buddhist to be her sexual reaction to him, though she may not have acknowledged it consciously. The Buddhist also understood, just as instantly, that even if this were true, all he could do was what he was already doing—it was not related to him, was not his concern, was causing Elise Grantwell suffering, and itself was fleeting and no-self.

The Skype connection went choppy. Elise Grantwell's face morphed into three pixelated blocks of color, green, blue, and black, like a puzzle the Buddhist would have to put back together. Then a moment later the bad connection resolved and there was her face, alien and lost and concerned, staring at him from a different part of the Skype window. There was a counselor present at the family meeting, the Buddhist said. She was this weary and hardened woman of about sixty. With serious wrinkles and a set of dentures that protruded from her greatly sagging face, a former addict who usually intervened in substance abuse, the Buddhist explained. So, my family had hired this counselor woman because my parents and former girlfriend considered me *addicted* to a cult/religion. So, there I was, in my saffron robes, sitting on one side of the family's kitchen table, and then my parents were like really close together, very tense and concerned and clearly not getting any sleep, the Buddhist explained, smirking a little while he explained, and then there was my former girlfriend, who, I remember, was very confused, probably because I was not having sex with her and was wearing somewhat creepy robes and had actually broken up with her. Elise Grantwell responded by laughing exaggeratedly, which the Buddhist was annoyed by, but which he also knew was born out of her attempt to connect, to show the Buddhist she was paying attention. He met her exaggerated laughs with composure and equanimity and acceptance.

His mother, father, and ex-girlfriend sat opposite him on the other side of the table, a very fine, very heavy oak table with marble inlaid flowers at the corners. The wearied gray-haired counselor woman had said: Sean, these people have something to say to you. And I remember the counselor was also looking a little confused, the Buddhist said. Because here I was, very healthy, very in control, and once they all began talking— saying I was lost, saying I was selfish, saying I was hurting all of them, saying I was addicted to a cult, asking what had happened to my passion for life, for playing music and kayaking, for enjoying expensive meals, saying how they had lost a son, had lost a boyfriend, had lost a friend—among all this I maintained an accepting and calm demeanor, and I think this wearied former-addict counselor started to get that maybe my parents, my mother especially, were the ones who actually needed help. Like they were the desperate ones. Anyway, this counselor eventually ended the intervention, the Buddhist said. She said that she was misled and she wasn't needed here, the Buddhist said while Elise Grantwell smiled and said, Oh, wow, wow. It was both a little victory and painful at the time, the Buddhist explained to Elise Grantwell, because I think it distanced me further from my family, or my family distanced themselves further from me. But the point is that I can look back at it with detachment and humor.

So what did you tell them? Elise Grantwell wanted to know. What was said at the intervention that made the counselor know you were right? The Buddhist thought for a moment, vaguely interested in Elise Grantwell's question. He then realized that she wanted an answer, something clear and definitive, that she might repeat to others. It wasn't a question of right and wrong, the Buddhist said. I'm just curious about what you said, Elise Grantwell told him in a very quiet, almost embarrassed way. Well, he said, he had tried to calmly explain to his parents, who were not yet divorced, to his mother who was not yet dead, to his father who was not yet only speaking to him through Post-it notes, that he had no beliefs in particular, he didn't believe in a god, he didn't have any particular kind of faith, that that wasn't what Buddhism was about. As the Buddhist explained this, he watched Elise Grantwell and felt that perhaps she was not sexually attracted to him but that, because of the materialistic and sexually objectifying culture she lived in, she was conditioned, in some basic and unconscious way, to present herself, in any situation, as a sexual object; she looked very pretty, he thought, while also thinking that he didn't like her insecurity, oversincerity, or the fact that she was trying to impress him by asking more and more questions and appearing more and more interested. Though of course, he instantly thought, maybe she genuinely wanted an answer, some simple answer to an equation that would solve her life. Additionally, he told Elise Grantwell, I tried to explain to them that this was about seeing into the reality of life, the nature of the mind and how to end suffering; that it was all very logical and required no mysticism or transcendence or belief in things that didn't exist. That's probably when the counselor decided to leave, the Buddhist said.

The Buddhist felt weak, nauseated, extremely sweaty and at the same time itchy. Again the need to vomit came and passed. The Buddhist used Mahasi Sayadaw's technique, inwardly labeling his sensations *pain, itchiness, nausea*. There were of course protests, the Buddhist said. But you're like a machine now, his mother had said again and again. The Buddhist shrugged a little for Elise Grantwell to see. There's no joy of life in you, his mother had protested. My father told me that I was confused. He repeatedly told me that I was confused and on a fool's errand, that was the phrase he used, fool's errand, as if there could be a bigger fool's errand than continuing to live in a materialistic and oppressive society. A hard and stabbing ache made him close his eyes for a moment. Before he stopped talking to me, before I returned to Sri Lanka, my father liked to talk to me late at night and say very clichéd things, like, What about all the years at school? You have a promising career in front of you. You'd be a great psychiatrist or something like that. You know, I always wanted grandchildren. What about the family name? All those things, the Buddhist said, waving his hands at the world around him. Probably many things you're encountering as well, the Buddhist said to Elise Grantwell, who nodded and said, Oh yes, very much so, yes.

What about your partner? Elise Grantwell asked. The Buddhist withheld a sigh—he was tired, nearly exhausted, and the room had begun spinning again. The light from the computer screen was hard to look at. He dimmed the screen. From the kitchen, pots made clattering sounds and he smelled rice. He felt a terrible need to go to the bathroom and vomit, though such a thought was fearful. He also just didn't want to move at all. She called me the feeling police, the Buddhist said. Elise Grantwell laughed what the Buddhist felt was maybe the first actual laugh she had laughed all day, which he found pleasant, attractive, and he felt the need to make her laugh that way again. He told Elise Grantwell that after he was kicked out of his parents' house, before returning to Sri Lanka to stay at the temple for good, he stayed with his former girlfriend. It was a truly terrible idea, the Buddhist said. I actually found out later that my parents and girlfriend had conspired; they had told her to get me to stay; they even gave her money, on the pretense that they were paying for my "rent." It did not go well, the Buddhist said. She tried to have conversations like we'd once had. She tried to flirt with me. I don't know, the Buddhist said, feeling depleted and nauseated. The Buddhist remembered how she wore sexually revealing clothes, exposing her legs and cleavage. She vacuumed in the nude once, the Buddhist said, which seemed pathetically desperate and sad. The Buddhist noticed that Elise Grantwell looked down more and kind of folded into herself, like the leaves of some plants in Sri Lanka that closed into themselves at night.

He said he told his girlfriend that she couldn't do things like that around monks. His girlfriend had said, I'm not around monks, I'm around you, *Sean*. What did you say to her? Elise Grantwell asked, quietly. The Buddhist shrugged. He had tried to explain to his girlfriend the new way he was following and he had decided to show her how this way could apply to her own life. Whenever she came home upset from work, whenever she was depressed about her life, whenever she was in a dark place, I tried to show her that her feelings contained no reality, they were impermanent, based on the belief of a false self. Elise Grantwell nodded vigorously while also adjusting herself on her cushion and rubbing one of her knees, as if one of her legs was asleep. Elise Grantwell listened and rubbed at the same time. The Buddhist said that he tried to show his former girlfriend, while he stayed in her apartment, that her feelings and thoughts, especially about the current situation between them, were clearly leading to her suffering and that she needed to see into the truth of reality, which was the first line from the Dhammapada, that what the mind is, the world is. She was creating her own suffering, to which his girlfriend had replied, No, Sean, *you're* creating my fucking suffering. The Buddhist recalled that they had sat on her sofa often while he tried to teach her these things, but she just couldn't understand.

What'd she do? Elise Grantwell wanted to know. She told me, often through tears, that she missed Sean, that I wasn't Sean anymore, I was trying to control her and make her a Buddhist or something, when her feelings were real, her thoughts were real, they were the only real things. Elise Grantwell looked down. The Buddhist said that he knew that he had to go back to Sri Lanka right away when his girlfriend interrupted his meditation by kissing his neck, which he tried to calmly move away from, and then reached her hand down his robe, grabbing hold of his penis and telling the Buddhist that this is what she missed too. The Buddhist laughed a slight, embarrassed laugh. Elise Grantwell kept her eyes down. Do you ever miss sex? she asked. The Buddhist, who observed that his face was neutral and calm, was surprised by the question. He said, I miss the idea, sometimes, or maybe the idea of being with another person, of, the Buddhist said, like, um, sharing with them or something. He was unsure of what he was saying. He stopped, composed himself, inwardly thinking *confused, confused*, and said, I don't miss the pleasure of sex because pleasure is fleeting, and therefore I understand it's nothing to miss, though, he admitted, perhaps I miss just closeness, maybe, though that could happen in different ways, the Buddhist said, a little exasperatedly. Elise Grantwell said that that made sense, qualifying the response with, for a monk.

The Buddhist thought for a minute, and then said he was sorry, he would be right back. He hurried to the bathroom, where he vomited. Each retching seemed too fast to keep up with, more intensely uncontrollable than the last. He vomited and vomited again. After the third time it was watery and thin.

He sat, half-lying, on the floor of the bathroom, his hands shaking. He felt cooler, the only good part about it. On the floor, he checked his robes to make sure no vomit had gotten on them. He cleaned partially digested chunks of rice and vegetables off the toilet lid, flushed, and washed his hands and face, feeling shaky and weak and wanting never to vomit again, knowing that such a selfish want was based on ignorance.

The Buddhist returned to his spot before the laptop. Elise Grantwell was saying how sorry she was, she could let him go, and the Buddhist put a hand up, palm out, and said it was all right, such things happened, and they were almost finished anyway. What should she do? Elise Grantwell wanted to know. The Buddhist said the best thing to do was very little. Just keep practicing and living and doing, he said. The Buddhist said that the last time he saw his entire family and girlfriend, nearly five years ago now, before he had gone back to Sri Lanka for what he thought would be the remainder of his life, before his mother had died and his father had stopped speaking to him, he said that they had all had a brunch together. My father sat quietly in his seat, less stoic than confused, he told her. My girlfriend was pale and quiet. My mother was just reserved and sad-looking. I remember how I said that if they could see from my position that they were being pulled around by their emotions, their feelings and their thoughts, if they could see this truth in the same way I could, then they would understand why I was doing what I was doing, and also, more importantly, if they could see this, they wouldn't be suffering as they were right at that moment. I told them they were causing their own suffering, and I felt for all of them. None of them responded. Then my father drove me to the airport. It was a terribly lonely time, the Buddhist said.

It was dengue. The Buddhist had probably contracted it when he was meditating in the forest near the stream, where the mosquito population was dense and the insects were large and aggressive. A doctor came from the village and told the Buddhist and the other monks that the Buddhist could not, by any means, travel, and that what the Buddhist needed was to go to the hospital and get a saline drip right away because he was more than a little dehydrated. The doctor conveyed his irritation at the monks by speaking sternly, abruptly, and slamming things in and out of his bag. The Buddhist could hear and perceive very little when the doctor visited; his fever was dangerously high, causing strange hallucinations (he believed, for instance, that he was back in his father's house, which had somehow been turned into an eighteen-hole golf course, and he kept asking the monks what hole his mother was on), intense and bewildering nightmares concerning a tricycle-cum-lawn-mower, and now diarrhea along with the vomiting. Ajahn said they would begin their walk to the city tomorrow. Tomorrow?, the doctor said. Walk? Ajahn replied that the doctor must know that monks were not allowed to ingest any kind of medicine unless it was absolutely necessary, nor were they allowed any medical help unless it was absolutely called for, and were meant to experience the reality of suffering in order to be free of the fact of suffering. The doctor shoved his things into his case and then left, proclaiming that if the young Canadian Buddhist died Ajahn would live countless lives in Hell, to which Ajahn replied, That's it, my friend!

A rickshaw driver saw the monks as they walked to the hospital. He helped the monks cart the sick Buddhist. It was a day and a half's walk and they stopped and begged along the way and families came out, bowing to the monks and making offerings of rice and fish. The rickshaw man often bowed to the monks, who grew tired of bowing back. The Buddhist could not bow back; his thin body was thinner, paler, his eyes red and deeply sunken into his head, a white crust at the corners of his lips.

At the hospital, two nurses hurried him to a bed and began

a saline drip. The Buddhist dreamed it was snowing. In the dream, the Buddhist sat next to his father while it snowed and his stepmother sat across from them. There was oatmeal with pieces of apple and brown sugar in a bowl before the Buddhist. The bowl was melting the snow. In the dream, the Buddhist was telling his father he was not supposed to eat any food given to him unless it was given with three bows, but the Buddhist's father was no longer sitting next to him. The Buddhist was momentarily walking inside a shopping mall, looking into each store, though he didn't know what for. Then the Buddhist was back in the deep, snowing woods. The Buddhist's father was suddenly there again, eating a bowl of oatmeal, but with his back facing the Buddhist. The Buddhist tried to get around his father to see his face, but as he moved around him he realized his father only had a back, had no face. The Buddhist's faceless father nodded, finished his oatmeal, and took his plate to a sink in the middle of the snowing woods and washed the plate and then just stood there.

The doctor explained to the Buddhist that the Buddhist was probably feeling better. The doctor walked to the edge of the bed and felt the Buddhist's forehead with the back of his hand. He moved away again. The doctor said the Buddhist was feeling better because of the saline drip, but that such a feeling was misleading and the dengue would get worse before it got better. Not only that, the hospital was running low on saline; in fact, the doctor said matter-of-factly, they were out. More would arrive, but not until tomorrow afternoon. Dengue is biphasic, he said. You've just finished the first phase. The second phase will begin any moment now. The Buddhist said okay and explained that he felt better and he was grateful to the doctor. The doctor stood there as though he had something else to add. The Buddhist said, Say it. The doctor said it was not his place to say anything and then said that it was foolish, all of it, and after looking at the Buddhist for a moment, closed the curtain and went out.

He opened his laptop again and saw that Elise Grantwell was contacting him through Skype. Her face resolved on his screen, asking how he was. He told her he felt tired, but was fine. At the same moment, he saw his father was trying to connect with him, but he ignored the call and focused on Elise Grantwell, who was thanking the Buddhist for all his help, telling him he had helped her to understand that there is a difference between being lonely and being alone, and that one is always and forever alone, but loneliness is the extra, the part that's unnecessary, and she saw that now. She continued talking, but he didn't hear her, was instead watching his father's Skype icon blinking on the screen next to Elise Grantwell's face. The Buddhist felt what seemed like a fist lodged near his heart. Then Elise Grantwell was saying, What's wrong? What is it? The Buddhist shook his head. Why are you crying? she said. What is it?

Tahmima Anam
Garments

ONE DAY MALA LOWERS her mask and says to Jesmin, my boyfriend wants to marry you. Jesmin is six shirts behind so she doesn't look up. After the bell Mala explains. For months now she's been telling the girls, ya, any day now me and Dulal are going to the *Kazi*. They don't believe her, they know her boyfriend works in an air-conditioned shop. No way he was going to marry a garments girl. Now she has a scheme and when Jesmin hears it, she thinks, it's not so bad.

Two days later Mala's sweating like it's July. He wants one more. Three wives. We have to find a girl. After the bell they look down the row of sewing machines and try to choose. Mala knows all the unmarried girls, which one needs a room, which one has hungry relatives, which one borrowed money against her wage and can't work enough overtime to pay it off. They squint down the line and consider Fatima, Keya, Komola, but for some reason or other they reject them all. There's a new girl at the end of the row but when Mala takes a break and limps over to the toilet she comes back and says the girl has a milky eye.

There's a new order for panties. Jesmin picks up the sample. She's never seen a panty like it before. It's thick, with double seams on the front, back, and around the buttocks. The leg is just cut off without a stitch. Mala, she says, what's this? Mala says, the foreign ladies use them to hold in their fat and they call them Thanks. Thanks? Yep. Because they look so good, in the mirror they say to the panties, Thanks. Jesmin and Mala pull down their masks and trade a laugh when the morning supervisor, Jamal, isn't looking.

Jesmin decides it won't be so bad to share a husband. She doesn't have dreams of a love marriage, and if they have to divide the sex that's fine with her, and if he wants something, like he wants his rice the way his mother makes it, maybe one of them will know how to do it. Walking home as she does every evening with all the other factory workers, a line two girls thick and a mile long, snaking out of Tongi and all the way to Uttara, she spots a new girl. Sometimes Jesmin looks in front and behind her at that line, all the ribbons flapping and the song of sandals on the pavement, and she feels a swell in her chest. She catches up to the girl. Her name's Ruby. She's dark, but pretty. Small white teeth and filmy eyes. She's new and eager to make friends. I'm coming two, three hours from my village every morning, she complains. I know, Jesmin says. Finding a place to live is why I'm doing this.

The year Jesmin came to Dhaka she said to her father, ask Nasir chacha to give you his daughter's mobile contact. Nasir chacha's daughter, Kulsum, had a job in garments. Her father nodded, said, she will help you. Her mother, drying mustard in front of their hut, put her face in the crook of her arm. Go, go, she said. I don't want to see you again. Jesmin left without looking back, knowing that, once, her mother had another dream for her, that she would marry and be treated like a queen, that all the village would tell her what a good forehead she had. But that was before Amin, before the punishing hut.

Kulsum did help her. Put in a good word when she heard they were looking. She has a place, a room in Korail she shares with her kid and her in-laws. Her husband works in foreign so she lets Jesmin sleep on the floor. She takes half of Jesmin's pay every month. You're lucky, she tells her, I didn't ask for the money up front. But now her husband's coming back and Jesmin has to find somewhere else. She has another relative, a cousin's cousin, but he lives all the way out in Mogbajar and Jesmin doesn't like the way he looks at her. There's a shanty not far from the factory and she heard there were rooms going, but when she went to look, the landlord said, I can't have so many girls in my building. What building? Just a row of tin, paper between the walls, sharing an outside tap. But still he told her he wasn't sure, had to think about it. If you had a husband, he said, that would be a different story.

When Jesmin joined the line, she started as Mala's helper. She tied her knots and clipped the threads from her shirt buttons. The Rana strike was over and Mala's leg was broken and the bosses had their eye on her, always waiting to see if she'd make more trouble. Even now Jamal gives her a look every time she walks by, waiting to see if she takes too long in the toilet. They would have got rid of her a long time ago if her hands weren't so good, always first in the line, seams straight as blades of grass, five, seven pieces ahead of everyone.

To make the Thanks you have to stretch the fabric tight against your left arm while running the stitch. Then you fold it, stretch again, run the stitch back up, till the whole thing is hard and tight. Jesmin trims the leg and takes a piece home. She pulls it up over her leg. Her thigh bulges in front and behind it. She doesn't understand. Maybe the legs of foreign ladies are different.

Jesmin and Mala know a foreign lady, Miss Bridgey. She came to the factory and asked them a few questions and wrote down what they said. How many minutes for lunch? Where is the toilet? If there's a fire, what will you do? In the morning before she came Jamal lined everyone up. There's an inspector coming, he said. You want to make a good impression. Jamal liked to ask a question and supply the answer. Are we proud of the factory? Yes we are! What do we think of Sunny Textiles? We love SunnyTex! That day they opened all the windows and did the fire drill ten times. Then Miss Bridgey showed up and Jesmin could see the laugh behind Jamal's face. He thought it would be a man in a suit, and there was this little yellow-haired girl. Nothing to worry. Aren't we lucky? Yes we are.

When Miss Bridgey comes back Jesmin is going to ask her about the Thanks. But right now they have to explain the whole thing to Ruby. Mala's doing all the talking. We marry him, and that way we can tell people we are married. We give him a place to stay, we give him food, we give him all the things a wife gives. If he wants sex we give him sex. When she mentions the sex Jesmin feels her legs filling up with water. Why don't we get our own husbands? Ruby asks. She's green, she doesn't know.

Ruby looks like she's going to cry. Then she bites her full lip with a line of those perfect little teeth and she says, okay, I'll do it.

When Jesmin was born, her mother took a piece of coal and drew a big black mark behind her ear. Jesmin went to school and learned the letters and the sums before any of the other children. The teacher, Amin, always asked her to sing the national anthem on Victory Day and stand first in the parade. Amin said she should go to secondary. He said, meet me after school. He taught her sums and a, b, c. He put his hand over her hand on the chalk.

Miss Bridgey comes a few days later and she takes Jesmin aside. I'm worried about the factory, she says. Has it always been this bad? Jesmin looks around. She takes in the fans in the ceiling, bars on the windows, rows and rows of girls bent over their machines. It's the same, she says. Always like this. This place good. This place okay. We love SunnyTex! But why, she asks Miss Bridgey, do the ladies in your country wear this? She holds up the Thanks. Miss Bridgey takes it from her hand, turns it around, then she laughs and laughs. Jesmin, you know how expensive these are?

On the wedding day Dulal comes to the factory. He's wearing a red shirt under the gray sleeveless sweater they made last year when the SunnyTex bosses decided to expand into knitwear. Jesmin and Mala and Ruby stand in front of him, and he looks at them with his head tilted to the side. Take a look at my prince! Mala says. He's got a narrow face and small black eyes and hair that sticks to his forehead. Now it's time to get married so they set off on two rickshaws, him and Mala in the front, Jesmin and Ruby following behind. They are all wearing red saris like brides do, except nobody's family has showed up to feed them sweets or paint their feet.

Jesmin watches the back of Mala and Dulal. She knows that Mala's brother died in Rana. That Mala had held up his photo for seven weeks, hoping he would come out from under the cement. That she was at the strike, shouting her brother's name. That her mother kept writing from the village asking for money, so Mala had to turn around and go back to the line. Mala's face was cracked, like a broken eggshell, until she found Dulal. Now she comes to the factory, works like magic, tells her jokes, does her overtime as if it never happened, but Jesmin knows that once you die like that, on the street or in the factory, your life isn't your life anymore.

This morning Jesmin went to the shanty to talk to the landlord. I'm getting married. Can I stay? He looked at her with one side of his face. Married? Show me the groom. I'll bring him next week, she said. He took one more drag and threw his cigarette into the drain and Jesmin thought for sure he was going to say no, but then he turned to her and said, what, I don't get any sweets? Then he slapped her on the back, and she shrank, but it was a friendly slap, as if she was a man, or his daughter. Next she went to Kulsum. I found a husband. Good, she said, you're getting old. Now I don't have to worry about you.

Jesmin sees marriage as a remedy. If you are a girl you have many problems, but all of them can be fixed if you have a husband. In the factory, if Jamal puts you in ironing, which is the easiest job, or if he says, take a few extra minutes for lunch, you can finish after hours and get overtime, you can say, but my husband is waiting, and then you won't have to feel his breath like a spider on your shoulder later that night when the current goes out and you're still in the factory finishing up a sleeve. Everything is better if you're married. Jesmin is giving Ruby all this good advice as their rickshaw passes the Mohakhali flyover but the girl's eyes are somewhere else. Bet she had some other idea about her life. Jesmin puts her arm around Ruby's shoulder and notices she smells very nice, like the biscuit factory she passes on the way to SunnyTex.

Jesmin is the only one who can sign her name on the wedding register. The others dip their thumbs into ink and press them into the big book. The *Kazi* takes their money and gives them a piece of paper that has all their names on it. Jesmin reads it out loud to the others.

After, Dulal wants to stop at a chotpoti stall. Three men, friends of his, are waiting there. They look at the brides, up and down, and then they stick their elbows into Dulal's side and Dulal smiles like he's just opened a drawerful of cash. Who's first? they ask him. The old one, he replies, not bothering to whisper it. Then that one, he says, pointing to Jesmin. Next week Kulsum said she would let Jesmin string a blanket across and take half the bed. Her in-laws will be on the other half and she'll take the kid and sleep on the floor. Best for last, eh? his friend says. Dulal looks at Ruby like he's seeing her for the first time and he says, yeah, she's the cream.

The friends take off and then it's just the brides and groom.

They sit on four stools along the pavement. Jesmin feels the winter air on her neck. Where's your village? Dulal asks, but before she can tell him, she hears Ruby's voice saying, Kuri-gram. Something in the sound of her voice makes Jesmin think maybe Ruby wants to be the favorite wife. She notices now that Ruby has tied a ribbon in her hair. They finish their plates and Mala holds hands with Dulal and they take off in the direction of her place. Jesmin and Ruby are taking the bus to Kulsum's. Ruby's giving Kulsum some of her pay so she can stay there too, just until they find her somewhere else.

Jesmin wants to say something to mark the fact that they are all married now. She can't think of anything so she asks Ruby if it gets cold in her village. Yes, she says, in winter sometimes people die. I'm from the south, Jesmin tells her, it's not so bad but still in winter, it bites. They hug their arms now as the sun sets. I wonder what they're doing, Ruby says. Do you think he's nice? He looks nice.

They're doing what people do, she tells Ruby, at night when no one is looking. They arrive at Kulsum's. She can share your blanket, Kulsum says, throwing a look at Ruby until Ruby takes the money out of her bag. They warm some leftover rice on the stove Kulsum shares with two other families at the back of the building. The gas is low and it takes half an hour to heat the rice, then they crush a few chilies into it. I have three younger sisters, Ruby says, even though Jesmin hasn't asked about her family. Where are they? Home and hungry, she says, and Jesmin gets a picture in her mind of three dark-skinned girls with perfect teeth, shivering together in the northern cold. What about you? Ruby asks. A snake took my brother, Jesmin says, remembering his face, gray and swollen, before they threw it in the ground. *Hai Allah!* Ruby rubs her hand up and down Jesmin's back. His forehead was unlucky, Jesmin says, pretending it wasn't so bad, like this wasn't the reason everything started to go sour, her parents with nothing to look forward to, just a daughter whose head was a curse and the hope that next year's rice would come up without a fight.

It's freezing on the floor. Jesmin is glad for Ruby's back spreading the warm into their blanket. You are kind, Ruby mumbles as she falls asleep, and Jesmin can see her breathing, her shoulders moving up and down. She lies awake for a long time imagining Mala with their husband. The watery feeling returns to her legs. Ruby shifts, moves closer, and her biscuit smell clouds up around them. Jesmin takes a strand of Ruby's hair and puts it into her mouth.

When she gets to SunnyTex the next morning Mala is already at her machine with her head down. Jesmin tries to catch her eye but she won't look up, and when they break for lunch she disappears and Jesmin doesn't see her until it's too late. Finally it's the end of the day and Mala is hurrying along in the going-home line. What d'you want? She squints as if she's looking from far away and when Jesmin asks her what the wedding night was like, she says, it wasn't so bad. That's all? You'll find out for yourself, don't let me go and spoil it, and then her face bends into a smile. She won't say anything else.

After their shift is over Jesmin tells Ruby, let's go to a shop. I don't have any money, Ruby says. Don't worry, we'll just look. They walk to the sandal shop at the end of the street. They stare at the wall of sandals. Ruby takes Jesmin's hand and squeezes her fingers. It's so nice she can almost feel the sandals on her feet.

The week is over and finally it's Jesmin's turn. She scrubs her face till Kulsum scolds her for taking too long at the tap. She wears a red *shalwar kameez*. Ruby wants to do her hair. She makes a braid that begins at the top of Jesmin's head and runs all the way down her back. Her fingers move quickly and Jesmin feels a shiver that starts at her neck and disappears into her *kameez*. Ruby reaches back and takes the clip out of her own hair and puts it into Jesmin's. She feels it tense her hair together.

All day while they're sewing buttons onto check shirts Jesmin can feel the clip pulling at her scalp. Mala, she says, I'm feeling scared. At first Mala looks like she's going to tell her something, but her eyes go back to her sewing machine and she says, all brides are scared. Don't worry, I tested him out for you. Equipment is working tip-top.

After work Dulal is standing outside the SunnyTex gate. He puts his finger under her chin and stares into her face like he's examining a leg of goat. His breathing is ragged and his cheeks are shining. She notices how dirty his shirt is under the sweater and she starts to wonder what sort of a man would want three wives all at once. She shakes her head to knock the thoughts out of it. She has a husband, that's what matters. The road unfolds in front of them as they walk home, his hand molded onto her waist. Kulsum is wearing lipstick and she tells her kid, look, your *khalu* has come to visit, give him foot *salam*, and her kid kneels in front of Dulal and touches his sandal. In the kitchen they pass around the food. Jesmin puts rice on Dulal's plate, and the bigger piece of meat. Kulsum gets a piece too and the rest of them do with gravy. She's given him the *mora* from under the bed so he sits taller than everyone else. The gravy is watery but Jesmin watches Kulsum's kid run his tongue all across his plate. She thinks about Ruby. It's Thursday and she's gone home on the bus to spend the weekend with her sisters. Jesmin fingers the clip, still standing stiff on the side of her head.

Now it's time and they lie down together. The blanket is strung across but Jesmin can see the outline of Kulsum's mother-in-law, her elbow jutting into their side of the bed. Dulal turns his face to the wall and says, scratch my back. He squirms out of his shirt and she runs her fingers up and down his back and soon her nails are clogged with dirt. He takes her hand and pulls it over to the front of his body, and then he takes out his thing. His hand is over her hand, and she thinks of Amin and the chalk and the village, fog in the winter and the new season's molasses and everything smelling clean, the dung drying against the walls of her father's hut. Her arm is getting sore and Dulal's breath is slow and steady, his thing soft as a mouse. She thinks maybe he's fallen asleep but then he turns around and she feels the weight of him pressing down on her. He drags down her *kameez* and tries to push the mouse in. After a few minutes he gives up and turns back around. Scratch my back, he says, irritated, and finally he falls asleep with her hand trapped under his elbow.

The next day is Friday and Dulal says he's going to spend it with his sister, who lives in Uttara. Jesmin was hoping they could go to the market and look at the shops, but he leaves before she can ask. She takes the bus to Mohakhali. Mala's neighbor looks Jesmin up and down and says to her, so your friend is married now. Look at her, like a queen she is. Mala's wearing bright orange lipstick and acting like something good has happened to her. She's talking on her mobile and Jesmin waits for her to finish. Then she asks, is it supposed to be like that?

Mala looks up from the bed. You couldn't do it?

What, what was I supposed to do?

She grabs an arm. Did he put it in?

No.

She curses under her breath. But I told him you would be the one.

The one to what?

The one to cure his, you know, not being able to.

Jesmin struggles to understand. You told me his equipment was tip-top.

Mala shrinks from her. It occurs to Jesmin that she never asked the right question, the one that has been on everyone's mind. Why does a guy working in a shop, who doesn't get his hands dirty all day, want a garments girl, especially a broken one like Mala? Jesmin stares at her until Mala can't hold her eye anymore. Mala looks down at her hands. I paid him, she says.

You paid him?

Then he started asking for more, more money, and I didn't have it, so I told him you and Ruby would fix him. That's the only way he would stay.

She's got her head in her hands and she's crying. She rubs her broken leg, and Jesmin thinks of Rana, and Mala's brother, and her own brother, and she decides there's nothing to be done now but try and fix Dulal's problem, because now that they were married to him, his bad was their bad.

What next?

Try again, try everything. Mala hands her the tube of lipstick. Here, take this.

That night Jesmin asks Kulsum for a few sprays from the bottle of scent she keeps in a box under the bed and Kulsum takes it out reluctantly, eyeing her while she pats some of it onto her neck. Jesmin draws thick lines across her eyelids and smears the lipstick on hard. Dulal cleans his plate and goes outside to gargle into the drain. She stands with him at the edge of the drain and after he rinses and spits he looks up at the night. There's all kinds of noise coming from the compound, kids screaming, dogs, a radio, but up there it looks quiet. Maybe Dulal's looking for a bit of quiet, too. Fog's coming, she says. She asks about his sister. *Alhamdulillah*, he tells her, but doesn't say, I will take you to meet her. I hate winter, he says instead, makes my bones tired.

Winter makes her think of the sesame her mother had planted, years ago when she was a baby. The harvest was for selling, but after the first season the price at the market wasn't worth the water and the effort, so she gave it up. But still the branches came up, twisted and pointy every year, tearing the feet off anyone who dared walk across the field. Only Amin knew how to tread between the bushes, his feet unscarred, the soles of his feet always so soft. Jesmin ran them across her cheeks and it was like his palm was touching her, or the tip of his penis, rather than the underside of his big toe, that's how delicate his feet were. I'm only here to talk, he said, telling her the story of Laila and Majnu. From Amin she learned what it was to be swallowed by a man, like a snake swallowing a rat, whole and without effort. He pressed his feet against her face, showing her the difference between a schoolteacher and a farmer's daughter, and she licked the salt between his toes, and when she asked when they would get married, he laughed as if she had told him the funniest joke in the world. And then his wife went to the *salish*, and the *salish* decided she had tempted Amin, and they said, leave the village. But not before you are punished. And into the punishing hut she went, and when she came out, she looked exactly like she was meant to look, ugly and broken. Like a rat swallowed by a snake. Just like Mala looked after they told her the search was over and she would never see her brother again. Now Jesmin is wondering if something happened to Dulal that made him feel like the rest of them, like a small animal in a big, spiteful world.

Maybe that's why, she offers, speaking softly into the dark. He turns to her. What did you say?

Maybe that's why, you know, it's not—it's not your fault.

He comes close. His breath is eggy. That's when, out of nowhere, one side of her face explodes. When she opens her eyes she's on the ground and everyone is standing over her, Kulsum, her kid, her in-laws, and Dulal. The kid tugs at her *kameez* and she stands up, brushes herself off. No one says anything. Jesmin can taste lipstick and blood where she's bitten herself.

In the morning Jamal takes one look at her and runs her to the back of the line. You look like a bat, he says, you should've stayed home. What if that inspector comes nosing around? Her eye is swollen so she has to change the thread on the machine with her head tilted to one side. Ruby's back from her village and when she sees Jesmin she starts to cry. Don't worry, Jesmin says, it's nothing. She takes a toilet break, borrows a compact from Mala, and looks at herself. One side of her face is swallowing the other. When she comes out Ruby's holding a Choc Bar. She presses it against Jesmin's cheek and they wait for it to melt, then they tear open a corner and take turns pouring the ice cream into their mouths.

They go home. Dulal isn't there. Now look what you did, Kulsum says. They wait until the mosquitoes come in and finally everyone eats. When the kerosene lamp comes on and she's about to bed on the floor with Ruby, Dulal bursts in and demands food. She makes him a plate and watches him belch. The food's cold, he says. After, it's the same, lying there facing his back, holding his small, lifeless thing, except this time Ruby's on the floor next to Kulsum and her kid. Scratch my head, Dulal mutters. He falls asleep, and later, in the night, she hears him cry out, a sharp, bleating sound. She thinks she must have dreamt it because in the moonlight his face is as mean as ever.

On the day of Ruby's turn, she looks so small. When she's cut too much thread off her machine, Jamal scolds her and she spends the rest of the day with her head down. But after lunch she goes into the toilet and when she comes out she's got a new sari on and the ribbon is twisted into her hair like a thread of happy running all around the back of her head. Dulal comes to the gate and when he sees Ruby his face is as bright as money. Ruby says something to Dulal and he laughs. Jesmin watches them leave together, holding hands, her heart breaking against her ribs.

Jesmin covers her ears against the sound of laughter.

In the punishing hut, the *salish* gathered. The oldest one said, take off your dress. When her clothes were on the ground he said, walk. They sat in a circle and threw words like rotten fruit. She's nothing but a piece of trash. Amin said: Her pussy stinks like a dead eel. She is the child of pigs. She's a slut. She's the shit of pigs. Walk, walk. Move your hands. You want to cover it now? Where was your shame when you seduced a married man? Get out now. Get out and don't come back. Afterward, they laughed.

Jesmin covers her ears against the sound of laughter.

It's Friday. She packs her things and says good-bye to Kulsum. The kid wraps his legs around her waist and bites into her shoulder. She hands money to the landlord and he waves her to the room. There's a kerosene lamp in one corner, and a cot pushed up against another. Last year's calendar is tacked to the wall. The roof is leaking and there's a large puddle on the floor. She sees her face in the pool of water. She sees her eyes and the shape of her head and Ruby's clip in her hair. She opens her trunk and finds the pair of Thanks she stole from the factory. She holds it up. It makes the silhouette of a piece of woman. She pulls the door shut and the room darkens. She takes off her sandals, her *shalwar*. She lies on the floor, the damp and the dirt under her back, and drags the Thanks over her legs. When she stands up, she straddles the pool of water and casts her eyes over her reflection. There is a body encased, legs and hips and buttocks. The body is hers but it is far away, unreachable. She looks at herself and hears the sound of laughter, but this time it is not the laughter of the *salish*, but the laughter of the piece of herself that is closed. She knows now that Ruby will fix Dulal, that she will parade with him in the factory, spreading her small-toothed smile among the spools of thread that hang above their heads, and that Dulal will take Ruby to his air-conditioned shop, and her sisters will no longer be hungry, and Jesmin will be here, joined by the laughter of her own legs, no longer the girl of the punishing hut, but a garments girl with a room and a closed-up body that belongs only to herself.

The door opens. Jesmin turns to the smell of biscuits.

Paola Peroni

Protection

For Alexandra Krithades

L AST YEAR, ANTONIO GRECO committed suicide after attempting to kill his wife with a hammer. The doctors refused to speculate on the prognosis of his wife, hospitalized in critical condition. When we heard the news, I said I was only surprised Antonio had waited so long to try to kill Maria.

My grandparents had employed Antonio as a driver and butler when he was a young man. In their house in Rome, Antonio had met Maria, who worked there as the cook. The couple remained a stable presence in our lives through the years, always in attendance to help with Christmas dinners and other celebrations. But my grandmother knew him first.

"I warned him he was making a mistake," my grandmother said whenever discussing his marriage. "That woman is an insufferable litany of complaints. She could drive anybody mad."

Antonio was the most efficient butler she had ever had, and yet after he married, my grandmother willingly let him go and got him a higher-paying job as a driver in the family company. Maybe she felt responsible; after all, he had met Maria while working in her house, and with a family to support he needed a bigger salary.

My family decided not to tell my grandmother of the attempted murder and Antonio's suicide. She had endured enough, they said. I disagreed. She was alive and alert, and for her that meant being in charge. Nobody listened to me. I had been living abroad for many years. I had chosen distance to prevent family's interference; now I was prevented from interfering.

I was living in New York then, but I had returned to Rome to be with my grandmother during her final Christmas, a family festivity I had carefully evaded for the past six years. The chaos that plagued Rome throughout the year became claustrophobic during the holidays. The splendor of its ancient past, alive in its monuments, churches, cobblestoned streets, and fountains, disappeared amidst the frantic activity.

My grandmother lived in a residential neighborhood that was spared some of the turmoil. Her apartment was on the top floor of an eighteenth-century building, austere in its elegance. The high ceilings and the antique furniture were imposing, but the kitchen, with the old stove and sink, devoid of any modern appliances, was an inviting gathering place. The refrigerator was fully stocked at all times, and there was always a freshly baked cake. When I went for a visit, I never failed to stop in the kitchen. A superb cook, my grandmother supervised the preparations of every meal. It was a comfort to know that you could show up at any time and find a snack or a meal as if she had been expecting you.

The day I arrived in Rome, I went directly to my grandmother's apartment. I did not stop in the kitchen as was my habit, but went straight to her room. Her ninety-six-year-old body was ravaged by leukemia, but she had retained her sharp mind.

"I was waiting for you," she said when I entered her bedroom.

I stood at her bedside.

She looked me over and said, "You're too thin."

She said, "When are you planning to get married and have children?"

She had never asked before. "I don't have any plans," I said.

"It's time you start making some," she said. "I don't want you to be alone when you get old."

"A family is no guarantee against loneliness," I said.

She said, "Tell me something I don't know."

Her own father had committed suicide following a financial collapse shortly after she got married. Her husband's death had left her a widow at fifty-four. Her daughters were both divorced. That her family was gathered at her deathbed was evidence of her strength of character in having kept us together.

"What is it you want?" she asked.

"I don't know."

She said, "You built a house in Los Angeles, and as soon as construction was over, you put it on the market and moved to New York. You keep moving, but you're still lost."

On her deathbed she was still a commanding presence, but unlike others, I had never been intimidated by her. From early on, I questioned authority. My defiance was a challenge my grandmother had come to accept, and through our disagreements she had earned my respect.

"I never liked Los Angeles. I only lived there because of my job, but I got tired of it."

"And I am tired of watching people I love make mistakes," she said.

"Didn't you ever make mistakes?" I asked.

"I made plenty," she said. "But I did not run away from them."

In the eighties, Italy was swept by a wave of kidnapping. The prominence of my family made us targets. My uncle had barely escaped an attempt when he left his home earlier than usual, and the kidnappers were not quick enough to snatch him before he got into his car and drove away.

My brother and I were in high school at the time, and my parents were concerned for our safety. My father decided to have Antonio drive us in the company's bulletproof car to the bus stop. We were not allowed out of the car until the bus arrived, and he escorted us onboard. This was a source of great embarrassment to me. I hated being driven in a fancy car to the bus stop and having to wait indoors, apart from the other kids. In winter, we were shielded from the cold and rain, and I watched with envy my schoolmates talking and seeking shelter together. I would have liked to invite them to sit with us, but there was not enough room for everybody, and I could not bring myself to choose among them. My brother made things worse when, because of his slackness, we were late and missed the bus. Antonio was then forced to race after it in an attempt to reach the next stop, as the kids on the bus cheered us on. I remember my desire to disappear from a world where I was forced to be in a sleek car driven by a man in uniform as my schoolmates looked on and my brother, untroubled by a delay of his own making, lounged half-asleep in the backseat.

I doubted Antonio could prevent us from being kidnapped. But I would have also doubted anybody who had told me he was capable of murder and suicide. He was short, flabby, alert, argumentative, and with a sunny disposition. I could imagine him talking the kidnappers out of kidnapping us, if not rescuing us from them. But I was wrong. There is no predicting who can protect us and who can attack us, nor whom we will harm and whom we will save.

An undercurrent of tension marked the days preceding Christmas. The doctor had warned us my grandmother might die any day, but she was determined to spend a last Christmas with her family, and to me that counted more than the doctor's words.

I brought an armchair into her room and sat reading while she drifted in and out of sleep. People came and went, but I did not move. At times when we were alone, I caught her gaze.

She said, "That brain of yours. Does it help you to stay out of trouble?"

"It makes trouble interesting," I said.

"That's what I feared," my grandmother said.

I too feared trouble's appeal. I had just ended an affair with a man in Los Angeles whose sick wife I had befriended and tended to until she died. Dissecting my lack of shame and guilt was a distraction from the heartache of watching my dog die, and the sole reason I had engaged with the couple.

"Is anybody waiting for you back in New York?" she asked.

I looked up from my book. "My job," I lied.

I not only did not have a job, but was not looking for one, simply because I had no idea what to look for.

"You don't give anybody a chance," she said.

I said, "I give plenty of chances."

"Stick with someone; it's the only way to find out if he is worth it," she said.

I said, "Maybe I'm not worth it. Maybe I am the problem."

She said, "Is that what you're so scared to find out?"

"I'm scared of what I am capable of."

She said, "I'm glad to hear it. We should all be scared of what we are capable of."

"I don't know what's wrong with me," I said.

She said, "Nothing is wrong with you, and you're not so different as you like to think. Pass me the oxygen mask. You've used up my breath."

When the nurse came to attend to her, I stayed. I liked the nurse, and so did my grandmother. She was a big woman, and her sense of humor and ease in performing her duties made them less degrading, or so I hoped. That day, she entered the room while I was collecting my books and removed my grand-mother's dentures. In an effort not to show my unease and make my grandmother uncomfortable, I did not look away. But as I stood there, an incident in my childhood returned. I had been spending a few days at my grandmother's, and in the middle of the night I felt ill. I walked into her room, and with a movement of her hand she stopped me from moving forward. She did not prevent me, however, from catching a glimpse of her reaching for her dentures and putting them into her mouth. A woman of taste, she was careful not to elicit distaste from others. This was part of the reason she never discussed her father's suicide with anybody. Though everyone knew about it, she only spoke of it when I had ventured to ask her a few years before.

"There is no end to what you want to know," she said.

"You don't have to tell me if you don't want to," I said.

"Nobody ever asked, and I never told my story. Maybe it was a mistake," she said, and I sensed relief mixed with reluctance.

"I was very close to my father, but I knew nothing of his troubles. His death came as a shock. He did not leave a note, an explanation, not a word. All he left were debts, including those of my lavish wedding he had organized."

He had been a prominent attorney, and she had grown up in luxury, but he had deserted his family rather than face financial ruin. Disappointment in the father she had loved was repugnant to her.

"Did you have to pay the debts?" I asked.

"Your grandfather's family had to intervene. They were gracious and generous, and could afford to be, but it was no less humiliating," she said. The humiliation was exacerbated by her knowledge that her mother-in-law had not approved of the marriage, believing her a spoiled woman, too frivolous for her son. My grandmother was determined to prove her wrong, and her father's suicide only strengthened her determination.

"I never asked for anything. I never pretended anything. I never complained. It took years, but my mother-in-law finally wrote me a letter apologizing for having misjudged me."

"You have nothing to be ashamed of," I said.

"I am ashamed of my father," she said.

After she died, I found, among the correspondence she had carefully preserved, letters from her husband, her children, her grandchildren, other members of the family, and friends, but nothing from her father. Even in her diaries, there was no mention of him. But omissions reveal more than confessions. The unwavering effort to negate him never dispelled his prominence in her life.

Love is grief: love we have, love we lack, love we give, and love we miss.

I remembered Antonio's son, the reserved boy with whom I had played in my childhood, now a married man with two children of his own, having to cope with his father's suicide while he assisted his mother in her recovery. But the gap between what we can imagine and what we can endure leaves room for surprises, and I hoped this son of Antonio and Maria would amaze everyone, and himself above all.

Maria's return to her senses was harder to envision. She might forsake sanity to survive. She might add the tragic topic to her litany of complaints. She might resort to silence to quench the shame. She might be unable to endure the pain and follow her husband, or find the will for a needed change. But the glare of the past would dim the future she had left to live.

The day before Christmas Eve, I did not tell anyone where I was going. It was a chilly afternoon, and the city was all glitter and traffic. Antonio's funeral was being held in a neighborhood that was a peaceful village during the day but lost all its charm at night, when crowds flooded its streets in the desperate pursuit of amusement. The church was not crowded, and in the front row, Antonio's son stood next to the casket. When the service was over, people gathered around him with downcast eyes, unable to face him. I recognized some of them, and we exchanged silent greetings. He saw me and came forward. He extended his hand, and I held it briefly in both of mine.

"Any news about your mother?" I asked.

"Last night the doctors declared her out of danger," he said. "I didn't know what to wish for."

I let go of his hand but not of his gaze.

I said, "My grandmother's father committed suicide."

"Her father did not try to commit murder before he killed himself," he said.

I said, "Her father had a different reason. He had squandered all his money."

"How is she doing?" he said.

I said, "Determined to make it through Christmas."

"I wish I had the same determination," he said.

I set out to make my way home on foot and crossed the bridge. Glimmers of light over the surface of the water dimmed under an unrolling blanket of darkness. Streaks of pastel colors dripped from the sky as if a painter had been rinsing his brush after a long day's work. The pale variations of pink blurring the fading canvas over the Eternal City struck me at once with that familiar torpor I dreaded. To love Rome, I had to leave it.

My grandmother was asleep when I returned. The nurse was resting in the adjacent room. I sat in my usual chair, but I could not read.

"Where have you been?" she asked with her eyes closed.

"To Antonio's funeral," I said.

She opened her eyes. "Antonio Greco died?"

I said, "Nobody wants you to know, and you should pretend you don't know."

I told her what happened without leaving anything out. She

was attentive, but age and exhaustion dimmed shock and surprise.

"You did the right thing," she said, and I was relieved to see she did not need to be spared the truth.

My grandmother made it through Christmas. She got out of bed and sat on the wheelchair at the head of the table the way she always did. She had not cooked the meal but had ordered it from a catering service. She tried a bit of everything and grimaced: It did not compare to her cooking. While I ate, I got my first taste of what Christmas without my grandmother would be like.

The day before, my aunt had asked me to go buy a present from the family for my grandmother.

I was incredulous. "We are exchanging presents?"

"It's Christmas. We always exchange presents," said my aunt.

"Grandmother is dying. She knows it. It's insulting to pretend it's just another Christmas," I said.

"Keep quiet for once, and do as you're told," said my aunt.

"I don't want any part in this charade. Find somebody else to do it," I said and left.

Despite my remonstrations, after dinner we proceeded to exchange presents, and my grandmother asked me to open hers.

"I am not in the mood to open presents," I said.

She said, "Neither am I."

My younger cousin, an apprehensive woman, stepped forward and opened it for her. It was a pretty negligee. It was put on her when she was dressed to be buried. I don't know who had gone shopping for it, but I am sure it was not bought with this in mind. The living have an uncanny proclivity to ignore death when faced with it.

She glanced at her present and said, "I am tired."

I helped to put her back to bed, and it was then I saw the ordeal she had gone through to sit with us at the dinner table.

When we were alone again, I leaned my forehead on the edge of her bed.

"It's hard to stay put," she said without opening her eyes. "But even trouble gets tedious after a while."

A few days later, I received a call in the night, and rushed to her apartment. The nurse was taking her pulse. My grandmother looked exhausted, and I knew she was ready to go. My aunt called the doctor, and when she arrived, the doctor instructed the nurse to add a palliative sedative to the IV. The nurse obeyed. Yet it was not long before my grandmother revived and asked for a sip of coffee. Then her breathing got heavy again, and the agony that lasted twelve hours began.

She was conscious to the very end, and to the end she squeezed my hand to let me know she knew I was there. I believe she wanted to reassure me, but I did not need reassurance. I needed it to be over.

The pain she had to endure in those hours enraged me. The nurse had removed her dentures, and when I protested, she said at that point they were an impediment to comfort. I waited to be alone in the room, and with my grandmother's collaboration I eased the dentures back into her mouth.

"Thank you," she whispered.

My father and his sisters came in and out at brief intervals. I later learned they had been busy making funeral arrangements. I remained at my grandmother's side with my cousin. She could hear me, and I leaned over and said, "I want to find out what I'm worth."

She winked at me. I would have to find out for myself.

I knew my grandmother's religious beliefs were a comfort to her, and I knew she wished I had them too. To her dismay, I had rejected the Church, but it was my friend, a young Jesuit, who came to give her the extreme unction.

"This is the greatest gift," my grandmother said, taking my hand.

That I was the one to have delivered it was unexpected, and maybe promising to her. As I watched her dying, the only idea of paradise that came to mind was the one I heard a friend describe, as that place where we do not hurt the ones we love.

It was night when my grandmother left us.

Nobody can protect us.

Shruti Swamy
Night Garden

I HEARD THE BARKING AT six thirty or seven. It had been a
long, hot day, and evening was a relief. I was cooking dinner. I knew Neela's voice well: the bright happy barking that he
threw out in greeting, the little yips of pleading for a treat or a
good rubdown, and the rare growl, sitting low and distrustful in
his throat when the milkman came around—he was a friendly
dog. This sound was unlike any of those. It was high and held
in it a mineral note of panic. I went over to the kitchen window
that looked out onto the yard, where we had a garden. There
was a pomegranate tree, an orange tree, and some thick, flower-
ing plants—jasmine and jacaranda—and some I did not know
that my husband had planted years before. But I was the one
who kept them alive. Neela stood dead center, in the red earth.
His tail was taut and his head level with his spine, ears pinned
against his skull, so his body arrowed into a straight line, nearly
gleaming with a quality of attention. He was not a large dog,
black and sweet and foxlike, sometimes shy, with yellow paws
and snout. Facing him was a black snake—a cobra—with the
head raised, the hood fanned out.

I let out a cry. The cobra had lifted the front of its body at least two feet from the ground. I had never seen one so close, even separated by four strong walls and a pane of glass. I could see her delicate tongue, darting between her black lips. Her eyes were fixed on the dog, and his on hers. Their gaze did not waver. Her body, too, was taut with attention, shiny back gleaming in the low evening light. The sky, I saw now, was red, low and red, and the sun a wavering orange circle in the sky.

Of course my first instinct was to rush out with a broom, screaming, and scare the thing off. But something stopped me. I stood for a full minute at the sink, shaking all over. Then I took a deep breath and phoned my sister.

"There's a cobra outside with Neela."

She exhaled. She was my big sister, and had been subject, lately, to too many of my emergencies. "It's okay. Call Dr. Ramanathan. He knows about snakes. Do you have his phone number?"

I did.

"Are you crying?"

"No."

"It's okay, Vijji."

"I can't—" Then I stopped myself.

"Can't what?" My sister has a voice she can soften or harden depending on circumstance. She kept it soft with me now, like talking to a child. I wiped my face, like a child, with the bottom of my shirt.

"I'll call back," I said.

I went again to the window. The animals were still there, exactly where they had been when I last looked. The dog had stopped barking, and the cobra looked like a stream of poured oil. I dialed Dr. Ramanathan's number.

"Doctor, there's a snake out there with my dog. A cobra. In my yard."

"A cobra is it?" I could see him in his office, his white hair and furred ears. He had a doctor's gruffness, casual in the most serious of circumstances, and had seen both my children through countless fevers, stomach upsets, and broken bones. "Has it bitten?"

"No, they haven't touched each other. They're not even moving. Just staring each other down."

"Don't do anything. Just watch them. Stay inside."

"Nothing? He'll die," I said. "I know it, he'll die."

"If you stay inside the house, he won't die. The snake was trying to come inside the house, and he stopped it. Now he is giving all his attention to the snake. If you break that concentration the snake will kill him, and it will also be very dangerous for you."

"Are you sure?"

"No one must come in until the snake has left. Tell your husband to stay out until the snake is gone."

After I hung up with Dr. Ramanathan, I took a chair and set it by the window, so I could sit while I watched the dog and the snake. It was a strange dance, stranger still because of its soundlessness. The snake would advance, the dog would retreat a few steps. The hair was standing up on the back of his neck, like a cat's, and now his tail pointed straight up. I could see fear in his face, with his eyes narrowed and his teeth bared. The snake in comparison looked almost peaceful. I didn't hear her hiss. The white symbol glowed on her back. Their focus was completely one on the other. I wondered if they were communicating in some way I couldn't hear or understand. Then the dog stood his ground and the snake stopped advancing. She seemed to rise up even higher. Something was too perfect about her movements, which were curving and graceful. Half in love with both, I thought, and it chilled me. Evening came down heavily; the massive red sky darkened into purple.

The phone rang. It was my sister.

"Well?"

"They're still there. They've hardly moved."

"Vijji, have you eaten? It's getting late."

I had been in the middle of making a simple dinner for myself and had, of course, forgotten. The rice was sitting half-washed in a bowl next to the sink. I didn't feel hungry, less even than usual—I don't like to eat by myself. Instead, I felt hollow, like a clay pot waiting for water. It was pleasant, almost an ache.

"What time is it?"

"Nine thirty, darling—eat something. Shall I come over?"

"No! Dr. Ramanathan says no one can come in or out."

"You phoned Susheel?"

"What's the point?"

"What if he comes home?"

"He's not coming."

"It's his dog too."

"My dog," I said, too loudly. "He's my dog."

Then back to the window. It had grown dark. I hesitated to turn on the light in the house, in case they would startle. Our eyes sharpened as the light faded. There was a bit of light that came in from the street, from the other houses, though it was filtered through the leaves and branches of the fruit trees and the flowers. In it, I could see the eyes of my dog, bright as live coals. There is a depth that dogs' eyes have, which snakes' eyes lack. Snakes' eyes are flat and uncompromising, and reveal no animating intelligence. Perhaps that's why we never trust them.

Now, very quietly, I could hear the snake hissing. The sound had a rough edge to it. Neela advanced. The snake seemed to snap her jaws. I have seen a dead snake, split open on the side of the road. Its blood was red and the muscle looked like meat, swarmed with flies. People said it was a bad omen for me, a bride, to see it then. Imagine the wedding of the Orissa bride, who married the cobra that lived near the anthill, and was blessed by the village. People make jokes about the wedding night, but everyone's marriage is unknowable from the outside. I saw a picture of her in the newspaper, black hair, startled eyes, and I blessed her too—who wouldn't? This same communion, it must have been, two sets of eyes inextricably locked, for hours. The *kumkum* smeared in her part like blood. The dog was gaining ground. He stood proud and erect, still focused, but doggish now, full of a child's righteousness. His ears pricked up. But then, for no reason I could discern, the weather between them turned, and it was the snake who held them both, immense and swaying, in her infinite power.

Who knows how much time passed. I sat there by the window. The three of us were in a kind of trance. Once, I awoke with my head in my arms; I had fallen asleep right there on the lip of the sink. I blinked once, trying to make sense of the kitchen's dark shapes. It seemed as though I had had a dream of a snake and Neela, engaged in a bloodless, endless battle, and when I looked outside there they were, keeping this long vigil. Their bodies were outlined by moonlight. At this hour, they looked unearthly, gods who had taken the form of animals for cosmic battle. But I could see the fatigue in my dog. You see it with people on their feet for hours, even when they try and hide it, a slump in the shoulders, the loose shoulders of the dead. No different with my dog. He would die, I was sure of it. I pressed this thought against me. The empty house. I would let all the plants die in the yard. I would move.

I find that at night you can look at your life from a great distance, as though you are a child sitting up in a tree, listening to the meaningless chatter of adults. I stood up in the kitchen. It had been years since I stayed up this late. Slowly, infinitely slowly, the creatures were inching back, toward the shed at the side of the house, the dog retreating, the snake advancing. Their movements were like the progression of huge clouds that seem to sit still in the sky, and you mark their advancement only against the landscape. I followed them, moving from one window to another. I became very angry with Neela. What arrogance or stupidity had urged him to take on this task? It's easier to be the hero, to leave and let others suffer the consequences. To run barking into the house was all he needed to do, to show me the snake so I could close up our doors.

I stood. The snake hissed up and made a ducking move forward, toward Neela, who snarled, baring his yellow teeth, doing a delicate move with his paws, shuffling back, weaving like a boxer. He let out three high yelps, pure anger, and snapped his jaws, and the snake rose even higher, flaring out her hood, hissing, I could hear it, loudly, like a spray of water. Then she lowered herself. Undulating back and forth on the ground, she slunk away, leaving her belly's imprint in the dirt.

I went outside. The air was clean and cool, thin, as it hadn't been all day, almost as if it had rained. He was tired. He whimpered when he saw me, pricked up his ears, and pressed his wet snout into my hand when I drew close. He was radiant. With his mouth pressed closed between my hands, his eyes looked all over my face, joyful and humble, the way dogs are, filled with gladness. He swayed on his feet with fatigue, then slumped down to his knees in a dead faint, tongue lolling back. His breathing came slow and easy.

Who had death come for, the dog or me? I lifted the sleeping creature into my arms. He was no heavier than one of my children when they were young, and I took them in my arms to bed. The air was very still outside at this time of night—or morning. Hardly any sounds came from the street, and all the lights were off in the neighboring houses. The air rushed in and out of Neela's body, his lungs and snout. What you have left is what you have. I carried him into the house.

Kevin Barry
A Cruelty

H E CLIMBS THE TWENTY-THREE steps of the metal tra-
verse bridge at 9:25 A.M., and not an instant before. Boyle
station, a gray and blowy summer's day. He counts each step
as he climbs, the ancient rusted girders of the bridge clamped
secure with enormous bolts, and the way the roll of his step is a
fast plimsoll shuffle as he crosses—the stride is determined, the
arms are swinging—and he counts off the twenty-three steps
that descend again to the far-side platform. The clanky bamp of
the last metal step gives way to a softer footfall on the platform's
smooth aged stone, and the surge of the Dublin–Sligo train
comes distantly, but now closer, and now at a great building
roar along the track—the satisfaction of timing it just right—
and the train's hot breeze unsettles his hair. The train eases to a
halt, and his hair fixes; the doors beep three times and airily hiss
open: an expectant gasp. He takes his usual place in carriage A.
There is no question of a ticket being needed but the inspector
sticks his head into the carriage anyway to bid a good morning.

"That's not a bad-looking day at all," Donie says.

It is his joke to say this in all weathers. He said it throughout
the great freeze of Christmas and the year's turn, he said it dur-

ing the floods of November '09. Now a roar comes out of the north, also, and the Sligo–Dublin train pulls in alongside, and its noise deflates, with the passengers boredly staring—it is at Boyle station always that the trains keep company, for a few minutes, and for Donie this is a matter of pride. Boyle is a town happily fated, he believes, a place where things of interest will tend to happen.

The beeps and the hissing, the carriages are sealed, and the Dublin train heads off for Connolly station, but Donie's train does not yet move. The schedule declares his train will leave for Sligo at 9:33 A.M. and he becomes anxious now as he watches the seconds tick by on his Casio watch.

9:33:35

9:33:36

9:33:37

And when the seconds ascend into the fifties, his breath starts to come in hard panicked stabs of anxiety, and he speaks.

"We'd want to be making a move here, lads," he says.

It is a painful twenty-eight seconds into 9:34 A.M. when the train drags up its great power from within, and the doors close again and the departure is made.

Why, Donie demands, when the train has had a full eight minutes to wait on the platform, can it not leave precisely at the appointed time of its schedule?

"There is no call for it," he says.

And it is not as if his watch is out—no fear—for he checks it each morning against the speaking clock. The speaking clock is a state-run service; it surely cannot be wrong. If it was, the whole system would be thrown out.

The train climbs to the high ground outside Boyle. He rides the ascent into the Curlew Mountains, and he whistles past the graveyard. The judder and surge of the engine is its usual excitement and he tries to forget the anxiety of Boyle station, but it recedes slowly as tide. Now the broken-down stone walls of the old rising fields. Now the mournful cows still wet from the dew and night's drizzle. Now the greenish tone of the galvanized tin roof on the lost shack. The spits of rain against the window, and the high looming of the Bricklieves on a mid-distant rise, northwesterly, a smooth-cut limestone plateau.

He was allowed to make the journey first on the morning of his sixteenth birthday. This is now the twentieth year of his riding the Boyle–Sligo leg, all the working days of the week, all the weeks of the year. It is Donie's belief that if he is not on the 9:33 train, the 9:33 will not run, and who is there to say otherwise?

And distantly, now, the iridescence of the lakes, a vapor-ish glow rising beyond the hills, and the father is dead of the knees. The father was a great walker and he walked five miles daily a loop of the Lough Key forest park, among the ferns and the ancient oaks, across the fairy bridge and back again. Then the knees went on the father—the two simultaneously—and he could walk no more.

"Oh, I have a predicament now," he would say from the arm-chair, looking out at Boyle; the slow afternoons.

The weight piled up on the father quickly. He turned into a churn of butter on the armchair. He took a heart attack inside the year.

"My father," Donie tells people, "died of a predicament of the knees."

The high land of the south county. The approach to Bally-mote. He names the fields for the elder, the yellow iris (the flags), the dog rose. Past the hill of Keash—a marker—and it is 9:45 A.M. on the nose, the lost seconds have been regained; the breath runs easily the length of Donie again. High above the treetops the tower of the castle of Ballymote appears, it is worried this morning by rooks, the rooks blown about on the fresh summer breezes; the rooks are at their play up there. Two elderly ladies wait on the Ballymote platform and Donie knows they are for the Sligo hospital—he can see the sickness in them; they are gaunt and drawn from its creeping spread.

He rides the descent to Collooney. He wills it along the track. Collooney is the last stop before Sligo and as always an encumbrance—he is anxious again; he wants this stop done with; the train must hit Sligo town on the clock. If the time is out, he will know it is out, and it will be an aggravation. Collooney brings on three passengers and he cannot help but mutter at them as they move along the aisle.

"Ye'd be as quick to get the bus, lads," he says.

Sea's hint on the air, and the surge of the motorway beside, and it is the gulls that are flung about now on the breeze, and the back gardens of the terrace houses are a peripheral blur—unpainted fences, the coiled green of hoses, breezeblock—and his eyes water they are focused so hard on the seconds of the Casio watch . . .

10:08:53
10:08:54
10:08:55

. . . and he knows it is all to the good now, as the train eases into the station, as its surge diminishes, and dies.

10:09:15—the arrival has been made within the named minute of the schedule, and there is a lightness to Donie's step as he walks out through the station; the stride is jaunty, the arms again swinging.

It is time to head down to the Garavogue River and have a check on the ducks.

Where the river breaches before the bridge, the current is quick and vicious. Often here, in summer, a mallard fledgling is swept away from its brood, and more than once Donie has climbed down the stone steps—one careful plimsoll at a time to gauge each step for slickness—and he has made it with great trepidation across the rocks where the water diverges, and more than one family he has remade, the tiny damp fowl held carefully in his hands. On a morning two years ago, schoolgirls applauded as Donie went about his work. The delicate thrum of life fluttered within his cupped palms.

This morning, all seems to be flowing well enough, but he keeps an eye on things, duck-wise, for the full half hour anyway.

Now the satchel.

Donie has taught himself to ignore the presence of the satchel on his back until quarter to eleven precisely. If he does not, the sandwiches and the biscuits will not survive even the train journey. He sits on a bench farther along the riverside than his usual bench but it is not a major annoyance. Often enough, the usual bench is taken, especially on a summer morning, and he is resigned to the fact. It just means that this will not be a 100 percent day, a day when everything falls into place just as it should. A sadness but a mild one.

From the satchel he takes first the larger of the foil packages and carefully unpicks the ends of the foil and releases the warm smell of the bread. Two sandwiches, halved, of white bread, ham, spread, and nothing else. When it comes to sandwiches, Donie is straight down the line. No messing.

Would ye go 'way with yere coleslaw, he thinks, and cheerfully he lifts the first plain bite to his mouth.

The sandwiches are washed down with the bottle of orange. The orange is followed by the four biscuits wrapped also in foil. For a while, the biscuits would vary—if only for variety's sake, was the mother's reasoning—but the variance threw Donie out. It became an agitation to him that he did not know whether it would be fig rolls or Hobnobs he was getting. He could guess accurately enough by shape but there'd come a morning of round biscuits and who was to tell a Chocolate Goldgrain from a Polo? It was a dead loss, and it is specified now that it is Chocolate Goldgrain he will unwrap.

He has just finished the last of the biscuits when someone sits down beside. Donie needn't look up to know that eyes are on him—the heat of a stare burns like nettle sting across every inch of his flesh.

"How're we?" the man says.

Donie raises his glance now and finds a man wearing a thin, half-grown beard, and he is pale-eyed, and yellowish of the flesh.

"What's it they call you?" the man says.

"Donie."

"Ah yeah. Is it short for Domhnaill?"

"It is."

"The Irish spelling?"

"That's right. D-O-M-H . . ."

"Good . . ."

"N-A-I-L-L."

"*Very* good. Give the boy a biscuit."

"I ate my last biscuit."

"It's an expression, you poor dumb cunt."

Donie knows that he must rise and go but the man reaches across and lays a steel-cold hand on his. Clamps it to the bench.

"Stop that," Donie says.

The man giggles.

"I'd say the best part of Donie dribbled down the father's leg, did it?"

The thin hard bones of the hand, the yellow of the skin . . . there is something the man brings to mind but Donie cannot place it specifically. He knows that there is the sensation of an animal.

"I've to go now," Donie says.

"If you get up I'll kick the ankles out from under you."

"Don't do that!"

Donie's voice quakes and the words are tiny and lost almost to the roar of the river.

"He's sobbing!"

Donie looks at the man's hand locked on his and the yellow

of the spots on the back of the man's hand and it comes to him, the word comes from the coloring: hyena.

"You're like a hyena," he says.

The man whistles a laugh down his nose. Another comes in quick succession. He shakes with thin hilarity. He continues to lock Donie's hand to the bench but now moves his thumb slowly and sensuously along the back of the hand.

"Don't."

"Why?"

"It tiddles."

"And what would a hyena do to you, Donie?"

"Will you leave me go now?"

"What would he do? A hyena?"

"I have to go home to my mother. I have the twelve o'clock train to get."

"Would it have a feed off your corpse, would you say?"

"I get the twelve o'clock to Boyle station. It gets in 12:33 P.M."

"Take tiny little bites, would it?"

The man grinds and bites with his teeth rapidly—he gnashes, and he aims a sharp smile at Donie.

"Will we go for a walk so?" he says.

Donie with all the force he can muster wrenches his hand free and rises from the bench to go. The man is up as quickly, and as he walks beside Donie, he places a hand softly on his lower back, and he whispers superfast the bad words now.

"Do you know what I'll do to you when I see you down here again . . ." is how it begins but the rest is lost to the high-vaulted pitch of Donie's screech. The screech is held as a shield against the words. But the man just gently shushes.

"Easy now, honey-child," he says.

The man stops suddenly, and Donie feels the hand lift from his back, and he feels the dread of the pause, and now there is a piston jerk of force from opened palm to small of back, and the man sticks a leg out to trip Donie as he flails forward, and he is sprawled on the pathway by the riverside and there are people all about, but nobody comes forward to help. Donie knows they think it's just mad fellas fighting.

He is on the ground and the man is for a moment above him, is blocking out the sky, and he leans down close.

"Hyena," he says, and walks away.

All is thrown out for Donie now as he goes through the tight streets of Sligo town. He does not stop today to look at the equipment in the mountaineering shop, and usually that is a fifteen-minute dream for Donie, a dream of crampons and frost-in-the-beard and great snowy peaks. He does not today say hello to the wood-carver. He does not count the paving slabs through the arcade shortcut.

An hour is lost to trembles on the platform. And he is sat on the twelve o'clock train now but he misses its departure utterly as the eyes of the hyena burn into him. He misses Collooney and the climb to Ballymote. He has no joke for the inspector. The high land of the south county; hyena. The lost shack, and he does not today fantasize the happy family that once lived there. Boyle station; hyena.

"What's up with you, Donie?"

A kind man notes the distress and says the words on Elphin Road in the town of Boyle but Donie does not stop to talk to him. He does not go to Supervalu for the bag of six donuts. He goes straight back to the terrace.

The sun has come out. It is a pure white screech of sun. He hurries along the row of houses as familiar as the mouthfeel of his own teeth and he must squint into the sun, into the light, and the feeling does not break and it will not ease—hyena—until the door of the house opens for him, and it does so, and she steps outside, the moment timed to his arrival, her silhouette against the glare of the sun, mother-shaped.

Mary LaChapelle

Floating Garden

I T WAS A TRUCK like the army uses, but instead of the metal frame and tarp, the back was enclosed in a wooden box. Painted on the plywood was the word TAXI.

One of the taxi men, the one who took our money, wore orange trousers with many pouches sewn on them, his lips and teeth purple from chewing betel. When my mother paid him the money, he looked over our heads and told the two men behind us in line to stand aside.

I heard one of them ask, "What do you mean there's not enough room for a man?"

The taximan answered him in a voice too low for me to hear.

My mother, gathering her long wrap to the side, was the first to climb onto the metal step, into the back. Still on her knees, she turned to me. That was the last time I saw her in full light.

I lifted one of the wooden statues to her and then the other. She set them down, then reached to wrap her hand around my forearm, helping me up as I climbed in. She was strong from doing men's work. I was embarrassed as soon as I entered the shelter because I saw another woman my mother's age and two girls with lovely faces, dressed in festival clothing.

Narrow benches lined both sides of the compartment. Even after I sat, I needed to bend my head under the ceiling of the box. No, the space wasn't tall enough for a man. We should have been suspicious of this.

"Is that the Road Guardian?" asked the woman seated across from us, nodding toward the statue.

"Yes, we are bringing him back to our house to assist the Buddha," my mother answered.

"The Buddha will welcome him," the woman said. "And it is good in these times to travel with a guardian."

It was my grandmother's wish that we bring these statues back from the festival in the mountains, one to guard the road and the Water Father for the lake where we lived.

The back gate of the truck was the only opening, and it cast a rectangle of light across our knees and feet. I was most aware of the older girl because she was a young woman, but it was the younger girl who, in the dim light, smiled at me. Her eyes sidled down with a secretive pleasure, and she leaned forward so that the light shone on her yellow blouse.

I saw then, protruding from between the buttons of her blouse, the tiniest round face of an infant monkey. His eyes had the filmy look of a newborn and his head lolled to the side. She put her finger to the opening in his lips and his little cheeks hollowed and tried to fill.

When she squirmed and giggled from the sensation of his suckling, the woman beside her looked down and said, "He is not a doll; you see he's hungry and soon enough he'll mess your blouse."

"No, Auntie, he won't mess me! I diapered him in a banana leaf!"

My mother and I laughed.

The older girl crossed her arms and turned her body away from her sister. Then I remembered my own embarrassment.

My mother had insisted that I dress like a girl when we traveled, so that the army would not steal me as they had stolen my father.

One day he did not come back from the market with the ox-cart. A woman from our village had passed my father walking in a column of the army. He looked into her eyes and then cut his eyes down near her feet so she would see he had dropped a ball of paper. She said he was carrying a machine, half as big as he was, up the mountain path. *They have made me a porter*, his balled note said. *They guard us with guns.*

Unless you had your service papers with you, the army expected you to go with them for two years; after that, they gave different reasons to make it four years or six.

And so I had grown my hair long and I tied my long wrap at the side like a girl. The villagers didn't laugh at me; the sons old enough to carry bamboo began to resemble girls whenever they went onto the road.

But then at the road market when I stood alone in front of the machete sharpener, he peered up at me from his grindstone. I could see in his face how a girl's value was dangerous, too.

At night on my mat I could hear my grandmother and mother talking in their mountain dialect, so I did not understand every word. My grandfather and father were lake people, but they both married women from the surrounding mountain tribes.

Grandmother said in these times, more and more people on the road are from the army, or thieves, or opium traders, and that the houses along the road do not float as ours do. When she said "float," I understood how important the word was to her; coming from the mountains, she knew what it was not to float.

To live on this fortunate lake, to have these floating gardens away from the winds, away from the pestilence that moves through the trees, out in the open sun, never too dry, never too wet . . . it was a prayer she said to us: "We have fish; we have bananas and papayas; we have the bamboo to make our houses, our canoes, our baskets and hats.

"More and beyond that," she would say, "we have . . ." She held her hands out to indicate the blue mountains with their always changing faces, the mist over the violet silk of the lake. Even now I don't know a word in your language for the "more and beyond" that we had.

Our family kept two floating gardens, one for seasonal vegetables and tomatoes, one with small trees for fruit. We sold half of our vegetables and half we left at the monastery and with the least fortunate road people. It was our way, our Karma.

Most days we rowed our vegetables to the lake market. I stood at the bow of my father's canoe and brought my mother, and at times my grandmother, to our stall on the shore.

My second cousin took me with him when he harvested the bamboo. The bamboo forest, on the far shore, was too thick for the army or the trouser-leg people. Once when we were among the green stalks, under the net of their gentle leaves, my cousin said, "If ever you must hide, bring the canoe here and pull it into the forest."

Now two young women, younger than mothers, climbed aboard the truck with the help of a man too young to be their father. One of them asked him, "Why can't we just go back with you on the scooter?" He looked down and said, "This is as far as I go."

The auntie asked the new girls, "You came to the festival without a chaperone?"

"Her cousin gave us a ride," said one of the friends with bitterness, "but now he has decided it's too hard to carry three on a scooter."

And so there were six females, the statues, and me, dressed as a girl.

The money taker closed the back gate of the truck; then we heard the passenger door shut and the engine start. We watched the road stream from under us like a moving river with deep green trees along the sides. We saw clumps of people in festival dress. There was a shaman, his face painted like a woman's, singing and dancing backward in front of a walking group. His voice faded, and the dust behind the truck consumed their figures.

When we no longer saw people on the road, the truck stopped. They lowered the gate and gave us two large bottles of water. My mother brought drinking cups from our bundle.

We ate bananas and pickled fish. My mother reached over and put a pinch of mashed banana to the monkey's lips. He suckled tentatively and then more frantically. I laughed and sat beside the girl with the monkey and fed him more banana mash. He put his tiny hands around my finger and licked and sucked.

The driver lifted and closed the back gate. Perhaps because the sunlight came from behind his head, I have no memory of his face. "We will cover this to keep the dust out!" he shouted, as if we were a long distance from him. And up came a board in his hands, which the betel-lipped man helped guide over the last light.

They pounded with their hammers. We waited for some adjustment, for a window to be slid open.

"It's dark!" the auntie called to the men.

But we only heard both truck doors slam and then the motor igniting.

"Mother?" I could not see her across the darkness.

"Come next to me." Her voice was strange and in the black between us rose up something we both feared.

I reached forward and touched cloth over a knee. I knew it was hers, because she put her hand on my hand. She guided me and I squeezed into the corner between her and the wall.

Her shoulder against mine eased my heart. The Water Father's shoulders were smooth under my hands and in the stifling box of the truck, I felt for his cool wooden feet with the bare bottoms of my feet. I remembered that my mother had chosen this statue from the festival stand because he had the long toes of a fisherman. Toes like my father's and mine. My heart sank then, because my father's long toes had not saved him from the soldiers.

We felt ourselves slanted back as the truck nosed upward. "We are climbing," the auntie said. "We should only be traveling down."

I put my eye to a crack of light and air that ran from top to bottom in the corner where I sat. I could see a sliver of changing greens and browns and whites.

After a while my mother muttered something; she sounded to me as she did sometimes when she talked in her sleep. The little girl began to whimper, and the auntie said, "Shhh shhh. We must appease the Road Guardian," and she began to chant in the same low tones as my mother.

I edged close to the crack to breathe the air and from time to time I put my eye to the opening. A forearm's length from the top of our box, a wide metal band crossed the gap. I felt with my finger how the band expanded beyond the gap, and I found the same metal across the gap near the bottom. Then I saw better in my mind what I hadn't noticed before, how narrow the colored letters for the word "taxi" had been and how oddly spaced. This was because they could only be painted in the spaces between the many metal strips that made a cage around the box.

It was hard to judge the hours. I was the only one who could wedge myself through the narrow opening in the corner and pee onto the moving road. In the dark, the others didn't know I was doing this.

Earlier my mother had cut the neck from an empty water bottle so we could collect our urine in it, put the neck back in place, and pour the urine through the crack. "Oh thank you! Thank you!" the two girls said when it was their turn to receive the bottle. "Careful, careful," the others said, as it went hand-to-hand, and then to me to pour out through the crack.

"Auntie," my mother said, "sit near me for now." I felt a shifting around me, and I heard the auntie sigh on the other side of my mother. "The farther away they take us, the more difficult it will be to return."

In time we had no water left. We could now feel the truck's angle of descent down the other side of the mountain.

The auntie said, "I think we are in the other country."

"What is *another country*?" the girl with the monkey asked.

She must not go to school, I thought, a thought from my orderly life, the kind of thought I would not have again for years.

At the monastery, our teacher had unrolled the map, pointing to a small blue spot. "This is a picture of our lake and around it, the picture of our country. The sea, which is a body of water much bigger than our lake, draws a border on this side of our country. And the mountains, not the close ones around our lake, but the ones we see against the distant sky, mark the boundary of the other side of our country. If you were to draw a picture of us from the moon," he said, "it is this shape. Our country has had different names and even different shapes at different times. A fish is always shaped like a fish, but the shape of countries can change."

I pictured our truck traveling across the pink shape on the map, over the mountains, into a differently shaped and colored land. Sometime after our descent from the mountains, the air became sharp and fishy, a smell I would always recognize afterward as the sea. We heard more and more traffic and hollow booms and scrapes, and then a sound bigger than an elephant's trumpet, which I would come to know as a ship's horn.

Through the crack I saw it was twilight. The older girl came close to me and placed her eye against the gap. I smelled her hair and the faint residue of spilled urine. After the truck stopped, we heard voices and then for a short while, no voices, and then the sound of a plank of wood dropping, the startling clatter of metal chains dropped on the top of our box.

We heard the screeching of machinery and I felt the older girl sway against me and begin to fall. She cried out, "Oh, Auntie!"

I squared myself in the corner. "They are lifting us!" I called out. Then we were set down with a thud. We heard two voices near our box, the sound of the chain dragging over the top of us and landing with a clank nearby.

As time passed, quiet descended. "It is cool now, night air," my mother said. And then to me she whispered, "We must break out."

"How?" I whispered back.

"We will batter the wall with one of the statues."

She told the auntie and the girls to back away, to give us room to run the diagonal length of the box toward the outside corner. I began to lift the Water Father, but she said "No, this one." The two of us hoisted the Road Guardian by his legs. The lake figure was the bigger statue but perhaps because his long feet reminded her of my father's and my feet, she did not want him battered.

After several rammings, the head of the statue broke through, but because of the many crisscrossing metal straps, we couldn't chip an opening large enough to climb out.

Sharply, my mother said to me, "Take your clothes off."

I felt something cool mashed against my naked shoulders and back. "I am rubbing him with banana," she said to everyone, "to help him slip through." It was the first the others had heard that I was a boy, but perhaps because of the danger, they didn't respond to this new strangeness. My mother put her nose and lips close to my ear and whispered, "The women are too wide, and the littlest girl is too young to do what needs to be done. Find a way to break the back gate open but if you cannot find a way, you must run."

Because of the metal bands I couldn't climb out. "I need help, Auntie," my mother said, "and one of you older girls." I felt their hands on me, lifting me like a rolled rug. I stretched my arms and pointed my hands over my head to make my shoulders as narrow as I could. Half of me scraped through, but then I had the problem of my ass and boy parts. "Hold him still," I heard my mother say from inside the box. I felt her hands on my penis and balls as she pressed them firmly and quickly into the recess of my thighs. As they pushed the last of me through the opening, they twisted and scraped my feet through the splintered planks, and my hands found a metal floor below.

I was exhilarated and afraid, but I am always sad when I remember. I had assisted with my own birthing, had helped my mother squeeze me out and away from her. Outside it was just as dark as inside, and impossible to see. I felt and found a chain near the box and attached it to the truck. Then, in order to search for a tool, a metal bar, something to pry the gate open, I kept hold of the chain so that as I ventured away from the box, I would not lose my way back, but the chain was shorter than I needed to keep searching in the dark. I felt a rope on the floor and tied that to the chain and searched along the boxes and the floor, which was covered with many circular bumps.

I heard the startling noise of sliding metal. A blinding square of light opened in the far wall and revealed that we were inside a gigantic warehouse. Stacks of boxes like ours surrounded me, some as high as houses. Someone was driving through the open door. I hid behind a stack. I unfastened the rope from the chain and slid the chain away from me.

I watched a tractor with a large, forked tongue roll in the direction of the box that held my mother and the others. It lowered its tongue and, with shifting rumbles, slid under and lifted the crate, then turned toward the open door. I dodged from stack to stack, following it as far as the entry wall. Then I slid around the corner of the open door into the shocking light and salt air.

A young man riding on a bicycle looked back at me as he pedaled past.

I ran behind some boxes and vehicles on the gravel-covered waterfront and watched the tractor lower the box onto the back of a white truck, not the one that had brought us.

I called in my language to a man who was approaching me, "They are taking them!" I pointed to the box. He looked angry and moved toward me, shouting words I didn't know. But he made me aware of my naked body. I ran away from him and hid behind a gigantic yellow tractor on the dock.

I saw the white truck across an open, paved space with stacks of boards and barrels and ropes. One of the men finished fastening the box and went around to the rear carrying a plastic water jug. He pried the wooden board partially open and handed it through. He stood there for a minute, said something, and reached in. He pulled out the baby monkey by his little arm and in one motion threw the infant into a pile of refuse at the side of the road.

When I looked back, the man had covered the opening and was walking quickly to the front of the truck. I saw the red taillights brighten for a second, heard his door slam, and then they were driving forward.

I ran after the truck, but did not call out, following directly behind it so the men couldn't see me in the side mirrors. I felt the hard bones of my feet beating on the pavement and tried to reach the back step to attach myself somehow, but the distance grew too quickly. After it disappeared into the traffic of the city, I realized that there were people by the side of the road laughing at me. "Help us!" I howled in my language. Only later did I picture my jiggling balls, my skin covered with dried and browning banana pulp, a mad dog that no one wanted near them.

I found the baby monkey in a pile of dead fish and shells and graying kelp. He was still diapered in his banana leaf, his legs curled up. He smelled of putrid fish and clung to my neck as I carried him. "They took them! They took them!"

My legs brought us to the edge of the closest pier. With no thought I dropped into the water and swam. The baby clenched my hair and wrapped his tail around my neck tightly, and the pain of his claws encouraged me. I thought, *Yes, you hang on or you die.*

The water was thicker than lake water, but softer and more familiar than the cruel strangeness of the city. I washed myself clean, and the monkey, too. I pulled off his banana leaf, avoiding the sight of his frightened eyes.

The ships around us were taller than any structure I knew, except the temple in the mountains. A nearly naked white woman with round sunglasses was stretched out on the roof of a smaller boat anchored off a buoy near me. Tied to the railing was a large orange-and-turquoise towel. It lifted and fell in the breeze. I watched her pick up a glass and then climb down into a hole in the boat. When I raised myself up, I saw on the deck a worn brown towel in a heap. I would use it as my long wrap. The rag would draw less attention than the bright towel and it would cost my Karma less.

In the distance, the tall buildings stood like giant guards in the direction that my mother had been taken. I couldn't begin to find her.

On the boardwalk I watched some boys with painted lips, dressed only in shorts. They played and teased each other and when men walked by them, they struck different poses. One boy pulled his shorts down and bent over to show his bottom to a man who stopped for a moment and smiled at him. They exchanged words in their language, and then the man walked away.

The boy looked at me watching him and then, with no expression, he bent down, picked up a stick, and lunged at me. He hit me in the face and on the shoulder and another boy grabbed for the monkey, but I took him under my arm and ran back toward the water.

There were great crates and stacks of big metal barrels waiting to be loaded onto the ships. I saw no food anywhere. But I found a faucet near one of the smaller boat slips. I turned it and out of the hose's end came clean water. The baby monkey drank and I drank.

I came upon a stack of long bamboo poles that were tied upon a framework of shelves, and I slid in between one of the shelves, out of the sun. It felt good to smell the wood I knew so well. I closed my eyes and prayed to the bamboo spirit to bring my mother to me and take us home again. I knew so little of the world that I believed this bamboo would know the bamboo that crowded down to the far shore of our lake.

Under its friendly shade, I watched the pack of boys who had chased me walking along now with two men. I didn't think they could see me, but they pointed in my direction. The boy who had hit me held his hand up to his brow. I believed he was showing the men how tall I was, and again he gestured in my direction.

I crawled along the bottom shelf of the stacked bamboo and lay there in the near dark. I adjusted the baby into the crook of my arm. His breathing soothed me.

Drowsily, I listened to the rumblings and sounds of the port. The monkey's little lips and tongue searched my skin for traces of the banana mash. A motor I had been hearing for some time became a roar and shook the lumber beneath me. I felt a jolt. Raising my head, I saw down the tunnel of bamboo poles that the scenery was changing. We were rising. I clung to the bamboo and felt the whole load shift and my stomach lurch as we were swung. The motor slowed, and we were lowered.

The path is not difficult, my teacher at the monastery used to say, *save for the picking and choosing along the way.* I chose to rest with the bamboo, and next I was crossing the ocean to a new world.

I slept on my shelf during the day and foraged at night like a rat. What picking and choosing is there for a rat? You make a nest near what you need and hidden from what you fear.

The cabin where the men ate was empty for long intervals. I took a knife, green bananas, coconut milk, dried fish, and the bits of cooked rice left in their pots.

To make up for what I took, I shaved strips of bamboo and wove hats, which I would leave for them when the time came.

The monkey didn't want to sleep during the day. Little by little he ventured out and soon he was adopted by the crew and eating better than I was.

Some days, half-asleep, I would feel him climb into my arms. It was as if he wanted to be a baby again, and I would be as still and welcoming as I could, but we couldn't have what we had before. He would agitate and pick through my hair. A sound would divert his attention and he would scurry away, not to return for days.

In my bamboo nest, I occupied my mind at times with the question of how to make a floating garden. How did you weave the lake hyacinths to net the silt from the lake? What soil did you choose? Did you add fish and algae for richness? How is the bamboo staked to hold the island in place?

My grandfather made one with my father and his grandfather made another with his sons. Where was my father? I often returned to the thought of the note he had written and balled up in his hand. Did he hold that scrap of words for hours, for days, waiting to pass it to a trustworthy friend? If I ever found my way back, could my grandmother teach me? But then, imagining my grandmother on the lake, my mind wanted to put my mother in the picture. The dust of her disappearing truck blotted out my image of home and I needed to drag my water bottle to me and wet my parched throat.

When we landed in port, I stayed in my shelf with my store of food. The platform of bamboo was lowered onto a truck and driven into a big building. From my hiding place, I could see women sitting at long tables weaving the bamboo into mats and rows of men fashioning the bamboo into screens and tying the poles together for fences.

Early the next morning, I folded the ends of my brown towel back and through my legs and tucked it into the back waist, the way the fishermen did. I washed at a large sink in the corner of the building. I had long hair still, but was bare-chested, no longer a girl. I sat at the end of the table with its piles of shaved bamboo strips and began copying one of the woven mats. Others joined me at the table and nodded their greetings. A woman who was able to speak to the woman across from her but not to the young woman next to her gave me a paper cup. She held up a coin and a mat, so that I understood each mat was worth a coin.

Like one more particle of dust within the day's sweeping, I became part of the group. The people were my color, but no one near me spoke my language and their faces were shaped differently from the people I knew.

The first time I noticed that my mother kneeled as she paddled the canoe, I had said, "You don't stand on the bow like Father and push the pole with your leg?"

She said the fishermen on our lake keep their hands free for their nets. I have never seen leg rowers anywhere else. People have their differences. "Where I come from," my mother had told me, "we eat more yams and drink more milk than your father's people. We carve out places in the mountain to set our houses. Our water tumbles down the hills so we have water-wheels and grind the rice and other grains."

The coins accumulated in my paper cup. For fifty cents you could rent one of their blankets for one night and climb the ladder to the loft and sleep on one of the mats laid out in rows. (Twice, when white people came, they hurried a number of us up the ladder to hide.) The boss woman opened a small market in the corner of the building at the end of the day. With our quarters we could buy used clothes, rice cakes, canned fish, fruits. I bought a T-shirt and loose shorts. As I rolled up the brown towel, I had the odd thought that the monkey might not know me without it. Had his own luck persisted? Was he still skittering over the sides and ropes and decks of the ship? Did the monkey study, as I did, how he could be of use?

The large building was built of corrugated metal that rattled when the wind blew. There were no windows cut into the metal; instead, light shone from the uppermost gap between the roof and the walls. The gap was covered with chicken wire to prevent birds from flying through, and because of the height, the long bars of light fell to the opposite sides of the room, leaving the middle interior in a gray light.

The boss woman saw that I was good with the weaving, and she wanted me to make a new item, a lamp shade. She showed me a pattern that did not look right to me, so I borrowed the pencil she kept over her ear and drew on the table a solution to the problem of the shade.

Then I asked her to watch as I drew a picture of the workroom with all the tables moved close to the far walls, instead of the center. I didn't know how to draw the sunlight, but I walked over to the wall so she could see the light shining across my chest. They moved our table first. Eventually they moved the others, too.

She gave me photographs of other objects to draw plans for. Sometimes she took me to a garden shop owned by white people, where the customers came to buy the things we made but also had ideas for special things they wanted made.

When we left the building that first time, I saw the land around us—cement everywhere, with palm trees jutting out of the pavement and the buildings made of metal or concrete in pastel colors. The long metal containers that you see stacked on the ships or on the beds of trains and the backs of trucks were everywhere, row upon row of them over the planes of cement leading out to the ocean. White metal towers with cranes could lift whole ships out of the water. I didn't know the name yet, but this was the Port of Oakland.

The boss woman entered an angled road and roared the car forward fast into a broad, rushing river of cars. She looked straight ahead, as if everything around us was not worth notice. After we left the monstrous road, we passed glass windows that held headless bodies wearing clothes, a building with a sausage in a roll on top, a shop with a large ice-cream cone painted on its wall. We turned down a shady street with no shops, and then arrived at the garden shop, which was surrounded by small trees and bushes and sculptures and pretty benches.

The proprietors, a man and woman, always looked uneasy when we came through the door. When I was closer, however, and they looked into my face, they smiled and looked at each other and then again at me.

One night on our sleeping mats, my mother had turned to me and said, "You have a face like the moon on the water." I looked for this in the mirror once, but my mother said, "You cannot see how your face looks to others."

The last time we went to the garden shop, I noticed a woman with hair the color of brown rust, waiting with the owners. Though the boss woman put her hand on my back in the way she did when we were with the white people and tugged playfully at my long hair, the customer seemed to know that I was not the boss woman's son. Her eyes looked not just at me, but also at the space around me. I felt she was peering into my story, and my mind floated out, dangerously, toward the question of my mother's fate.

I lowered my own eyes and gazed at the photographs spread on the counter before us. In one of them, the rust-haired woman wore trousers and a white hat. I could look at her more easily in the picture. She was not as old as my grandmother and not as young as my mother.

As I studied the photos, she turned some of the prints so I could see them better. She might have been pouring tea into my long-forgotten cup; that was how her gesture felt, as if I only realized the depth of my thirst at the moment of my relief.

In the photos I could see that her house surrounded her garden entirely. On one of the large prints she had drawn with a pen the things she wanted built: a pond, a bridge across the pond, and a teahouse at the other end of the bridge. On a separate piece of paper, she had drawn a pattern for the bamboo walls of the teahouse. I drew another detail, a suggestion for trim that was customary for our houses, and I added a little porch.

She drew decorative lanterns hanging from the porch eaves, and I smiled and made the marks around them for light shining. I drew the trunk of a tree with a carved spirit shelf in it to hold the statue of the Garden Nat. She drew a bed of lotus flowers in the pond.

The owners waited with blank patience. The boss woman narrowed her eyes as if we might be making fun at her expense.

The husband motioned for the boss woman to bring her order list and follow into the back office. The woman with the rust hair gave the large photo to the wife and she came back shortly with a blurred twin picture on thin paper and gave it to me. I made the gesture of washing my hands to the wife and I went to the little toilet room, placed the paper under my shirt, and drank some water from the faucet.

From there I walked out through the nursery to the front parking lot. Besides the boss woman's car and the owners' van there was only one other vehicle. The backseats were folded forward to make a platform for the boxes of plants and bags of soil she had purchased. I opened the door and saw that, between the overturned seats and the floor, there was a place for me to hide, and I squeezed in.

That night, when I could see that the lights were out in her house, I left the car and found my way through a gap in her fence. With moonlight, I was able to see quite well in the dark. I found my way to the inner garden. I found a shovel with other tools leaning against the house. I had studied the picture closely and I could see the clearing where the pond needed to be dug.

By early morning I dug less quietly, wanting her to hear me, to be forewarned and then to come and see what I had accomplished. The pit was deep to my shoulders. When she arrived at the edge in her white robe, she made a sound in the back of her throat and then she reached in, wrapped her hand around my muddy forearm, and pulled me up.

I made the gesture to go back to digging, but she motioned me away from the hole, and pushed me down firmly on a nearby bench. She told me through gestures that she didn't need me to shovel the pond myself. It was then that my hope diminished. I sat there without the language to tell her how deeply I longed to dig, to dig and dig in the days to come, to dig with my own strength and determination a new lake.

She brought me indoors and over to her desk. She took out a white cardboard. She drew squares and in the squares she drew a man and woman holding two babies. She pointed to one of the babies and then to herself. She drew a house with three children and then another house with four, and in each picture she showed an older girl who was herself among her sisters and brothers.

As she drew I could see around me two screens, and machines that I would come to understand were for making television stories. There were other sheets of cardboard on the table with much more elaborate pictures on them.

With quick, simple strokes, she drew her older self in different cities, like the one my ship had left behind, and then the picture of her here in the garden.

She took up a blank board and made squares on it, and gave

it to me. I drew my mother and father and my grandmother and the lake and the floating gardens near us and our boat and me older in my boat. I could see she enjoyed this way of speaking without words. I drew my father with the soldiers' guns pointed against him. I drew my mother and grandmother. As I drew the black holes of their mouths I felt as though my own sobs were opening on the paper.

When I finished drawing, she brought a map to the table. I had not expected this many shapes in the world. I pointed to a shape that resembled the one our teacher in the monastery had shown us and to another pink one, but I could see from her face that she did not believe it was my country.

She spoke into a little box and then held it up to my mouth and gestured for me to speak. I hadn't spoken in so long. It felt unnatural, like biting into a stone. So I shook my head.

I wanted to work in the garden, but she took me in her car to an office. The office woman took out a book with many photographs of faces and on each page there were faces that were similar to each other. I looked at pictures of people that the woman had called the Asians, and I found the page with my people. I can only say that the shape of their eyes in their brow was the shape of a butterfly.

I understand now that the rust-haired woman was trying to determine my nationality in order to restore me to my home. Is that why I chose to hide in her car—to be returned to my home? Or was it simply because of the pictures of her garden?

How strange choices are. When did my ancestors choose to make the first floating garden? Did the silt simply gather in the limbs of the water hyacinth and reveal its potential to them?

Her name was Laura Wold and of course I had a name, too, but we avoided using them with each other, perhaps because this diminished the boundaries between us, which were so great from the beginning. She called me "you" and I called her "ba," which we say in my language for "you." To have no names between us was a pleasure, the pleasure I still feel in not belonging to a country. And now that I know your language and that I have learned others, I can tell you how far the words for things take us from what matters. A box is not a taxi. A slave is not a porter.

Because of the regime that ruled my homeland, it was difficult to contact my grandmother and eventually when, through diplomatic channels, Laura reached the government office of my village, she found that my grandmother was no longer alive. The translator who aided my benefactor's search said it was likely that my mother was serving at some labor in the next country. I always imagined my mother at night, when she was alone and no one's servant, pouring herself a cup of tea. It was always the side view of my mother's face, that side I'd seen so many times as a child. Though she was in a different kitchen now, her hand was calm on the kettle's handle.

I carved a figure with the long feet of my father and placed him on the shore of our pond for all the time I lived with Laura. I went to middle school and high school in Berkeley. I was a strange boy, smaller than most of the other boys from India, from Mexico, from Africa and Europe, even smaller than most of the girls until I reached manhood. At nineteen I went on a scholarship to the agricultural college in Southern California.

I have learned through my studies about the floating gardens of Babylon. And how the Aztecs, driven by their enemies onto the marshy shore of Lake Tenochtitlan, learned to build rafts of rushes and reeds, and like us, dredged up the rich soil from the shallow bottom of the lake. The roots of the corn, the bean vines, and the avocado trees reached through the floor of the rafts into the water. How happy the garden was in that Mexican sun. Marco Polo wrote of the gardens he found in China. Had the Chinese in their nomadic days carried their ways over the mountains to our people, or is it that we ourselves were the same as those they now call Chinese?

After I left for college, Laura Wold sold the property and moved deep inland to her family's lake. She sent me pictures of pine trees and birch leaning over its glittering surface. And a picture of the lake guardian I had carved near a little cove filled with water lilies.

She grew a berry patch in honor of her own mother and grandmother and a few flowers, "barely domesticated," were her words. She wrote me about learning to tap the sugar maple trees in their forest, about walking among them to check on the slow gathering of their sap. This is something I have not yet seen.

I like how it now says on my passport that I work for a non-governmental organization. I travel from country to country, some still called by other names on last year's map. I study the composition of soils, the habits of seasons, and my method for cultivation is to use only what is naturally available—goat dung, swamp grass. If you develop the intuition for cultivation, as long you have water, you can always devise a recipe for soil.

Once an elder in a tribe took me into the forest and showed me, hidden under a bed of undergrowth, a deep bog. It was the richest mud I had ever seen: there may well have been wooly mammoths at the bottom of it, and our primate ancestors, and beneath that, fish-birds, and insects with the organs of males and females both. There are adaptive mutations we cannot even imagine.

The old man told me he'd remembered the place in a dream. We brought the whole tribe there and carried home bog mud in baskets on our backs. We plowed up the barren dust in our plot with hoes, and then with our feet we kneaded the mud into the dry dust; we turned the dust into soil, so dark, so primordial, it steamed between our toes.

Joseph O'Neill

The Trusted Traveler

For almost a decade, Chris and I have received an annual
visit from one of my former students, Jack Bail. This year
is different. When, as usual, he emails to invite himself over,
I reply that "our traditional dinner" can "alas" no longer take
place: six months ago, Christine and I moved to Nova Scotia.

Jack Bail writes back:

Nova Scotia? Canada's Ocean Playground? I'm there, Doc.
Just say when and where.

"Oh no," Chris says. "I'm so sorry, love."

It's I who should say sorry to Chris. Not only will she have
to cook for Jack Bail but she will also have to manage Jack Bail,
because, even though I'm supposedly the one who's Jack Bail's
friend, it's Chris who remembers the details of Jack Bail's life
story and the details of what transpired in the course of our
meals with him, and who is able to follow what Jack Bail is saying or feeling. For some reason, almost anything that has to do
with Jack Bail is beyond my grasp. I can't even remember having
taught anybody named Jack Bail.

"And I guess Chris will be coming," Chris says, confusingly. "His wife," Chris says.

Of course—Jack Bail's wife, like my Chris, is a Chris by way of Christine. Which is irritating.

I say, "You never know. Maybe he won't be able to make it."

Chris laughs, as well she might. Jack Bail always turns up. Without fail he marks the end of tax season by eating at our table. It is always a strangely fictional few hours. Only after he has left does our life again feel factual.

Chris's long-standing opinion on the Jack Bail situation is that I should effectively communicate to him that I don't wish to see him. It's not her suggestion that I socially fire him in writing—as she acknowledges, "That's pretty much psychologically impossible"—but that I make use of the well-understood convention of email silence.

I've tried it. Email silence only prompts Jack Bail to switch to pushy text messages, for example:

Hi about this dinner thing. Let me know details as soon as you have them, no rush.

This obdurate memorandum and others like it—

Dinner this month? Next month? All good :)

—weigh on me so heavily that in the end it's just easier to spend an evening with the guy. The truth isn't so much that Jack Bail is a terrible or unbearable fellow but that Jack Bail falls squarely into the category of people whom Chris and I really don't want to see anymore as we hit our mid-sixties and apprehend the finitude and irreversibility of human time as an all-too-vivid personal actuality and not just a literary theme to be discussed in high school classes devoted to *The Count of Monte Cristo* or *The Old Man and the Sea*. And, indeed, a central purpose of relocating to this Canadian coastal hilltop has been to shed our skins as New Yorkers and finally rid ourselves of the burrs and barnacles of association that, it seemed to me especially, had crowded our day-to-day existences, which, even discounting work, apparently amounted to one interaction after another with individuals who demanded that we transfer our time to them, sometimes for no better reason than that our paths had once crossed or, would you believe it, that their very demand for our time constituted such a crossing of paths.

(Illustration: A, whom I've never met, informs me by email that he's thinking of applying for a job at the school where we teach. Could he pick my brain over coffee? Further illustration: B writes to Chris to say that her child once attended the school. Could Chris assist B in relation to an overseas research fellowship in which she, B, is interested? Exercising what is, I believe, a universally accepted right to reasonable personal autonomy, we choose not to answer these approaches; whereupon, we find out, both A and B go around telling people that we're rude, selfish, full of ourselves, etc. In A and B's minds, making unilateral electronic contact means that we, the contactees, are somehow in their debt. The difference between Chris and me is that she doesn't let this stuff get to her, whereas I stupidly waste a lot of time and emotion being bothered by the ridiculous injustice and hostility of it all.)

I won't even begin to describe how many hours and years we devoted to the parental body—the Hydra, as Chris named it. You cannot defeat the Hydra. You can only flee it. None of this is to say that we're refugees; but it can't be denied that we've retired, and that to retire means to draw back, as if from battle.

The good news is that Jack and Chris Bail will not be sleeping over. My Chris took it upon herself to warn Jack Bail and his Chris that there was no room at our inn, so to speak, to which

Jack Bail responded, No worries. We'll take him at his word. The other good news is that Ed and Fran Joyce, new Nova Scotia acquaintants, will join us for the dinner in order to absorb the Bails, although of course the Joyces aren't aware that this is part of their function. We don't know the Joyces at all well, but they strike us as good sports. Also, they hosted a kind of welcome event for us, and so we owe them dinner, arguably: one day soon after we arrived, a basket filled with good things was left at our front door, together with an invitation to join members of "the community" for drinks and nibbles. We accepted the invitation—we hadn't come here to be recluses, after all— and enjoyed the occasion, although we were, and still are, a little wary of and astonished by and ironical about the prospect of joining a retiree crowd. Our plan is to have a year of contemplative idleness, after which we'll have a better idea of what to next get up to. We're far from elderly, after all. Time is not yet a victorious enemy.

Shortly before everyone is due to turn up, Chris and I take to the deck and get a head start on the wine, which is white and cold. "I wonder what Jack will have to say about this place," Chris says. "Yes," I say. "That's something to look forward to." She has reminded me of Jack Bail's chronic amazement at our old apartment in Hudson Heights. Every time he came over, from Brooklyn, he would say something like, Hudson Heights? Who knew this neighborhood even existed? Who lives up here? Oboe players? It's like we're in Bucharest or something. How come nobody knows about this place? Should I buy here?

This kind of thing is all fine, needless to say, and absolutely within my tolerance levels in relation to schoolchildren, although of course Jack Bail, who must be in his late thirties, and if memory serves is balding, is no longer a schoolboy. But this question of his personal qualities is beside the point. The point is that Jack Bail is uncalled-for.

It's a mild, semi-sunny, slightly windy June evening. "Just look at that," I declare for about the millionth time since we moved into our cottage, which offers a panorama of a pond, green seaside hills, a semicircular bay, and a sandbar—or spit, perhaps. To the south, there's a wooded headland that may or may not be a tombolo. It's my intention to investigate this vista systematically, since it feels strange to look out the window every day and basically not understand what I'm looking at. Right now, for example, I'm observing an extraordinary horizontal triplex: in the offing, a distinctly ultramarine strip of ocean water is topped by a dull-blue band of unclassifiable vapor, itself topped by a purely white stratum of cloud. Then comes sky-blue air and, almost on top of our own hill, an enormous hovering gray cloud. This outlandish hydroatmospheric pileup, which is surely not unknown to science, leaves me at a terminological and informational loss that's only intensified when I look at the bay itself, where the migrant and moody skylight, together with the action of the wind and current, I suppose, and maybe differences in the water's depth and salinity, constantly patterns and textures and streaks the surface. It's unpredictable and beautiful. Sometimes the bay, usually blue or gray, is thoroughly brown, other times it features Caribbean swirls of aquamarine or is colorlessly pale, and invariably there are areas where the water is ruffled, and there are smooth or smoother areas of water, and areas that are relatively dark and light, and dull and brilliant, and so forth, ever more complexly. There must be some field of learning that can help me to appreciate these phenomena more fully.

"*The Salty Rose*," Chris says. "For the Lunenburg whaling episode."

"Not bad at all," I say. She's running with her joke about the memoir that I am not writing of the lives that we have not led. In this subjunctive world we are adventurers, spies, honorary consuls, nomads. For example, Chris has proposed *The Hammocks of Chilmark*, about our fictitious summers on Martha's Vineyard, and our nonexistent Corfu years will be the subject of a trilogy: *The Owl in the Jasmine, Who Will Water the Bougainvillea?*, and *A Pamplemousse for the Captain*. Other than a four-year stint in Athens, Ohio, our thirty-one-year-old marriage and thirty-two-year teaching careers and almost all of our vacations have unfolded in and around the schools and streets of New York, New York. Jack Bail claims to have been in my class at Athens High, which is confounding. I have a pretty good recall of those Athens kids.

"Goddamn it."

Chris: "Leg-bug?"

I pick it off my ankle and, because these lentil-size spiderlike little fuckers are tough, I crush and recrush it between the bottom of my glass and my armrest. I call them leg-bugs because these past couple of weeks every time I've set foot outdoors I've caught them crawling up my legs—to what end, I don't know; they're up to no good, you can bet—and because I can't zoologically identify them. They're certainly maddening. Often my shin prickles when there's nothing there.

"Here they are," Chris says.

Our guests have arrived simultaneously, in two cars. Fran and Ed get out of their red pickup and Jack Bail gets out of his rented Hyundai. There's no sign of his Chris.

Dispensing with the steps, Jack Bail strides directly onto the deck. He's extraordinarily tall, maybe six foot six. Has he grown?

"Adirondack chairs," Jack Bail says. "Of course."

As the young visitor who has gone to great lengths, Jack Bail is the object of solicitousness. There's no way around this: once Jack Bail has traveled all the way from New York, he must be received with proportionate hospitality. "Jack first," Fran says, when I try to pour her a glass of wine. "He deserves it, after his voyage."

"The flight was great," Jack Bail tells us. "Newark airport—

not so much." Ed says, "You might want to think about the Trusted Traveler program. Might speed things along." "I am a Trusted Traveler," Jack Bail says. "It did me no good. Not at Newark." "What happens if you're a Trusted Traveler?" Chris says. Ed says, "You don't have to take your shoes off." We all laugh. Jack Bail exclaims, "They gave me a piece of paper saying that I didn't have to take my shoes off! Then they still made me take my shoes off!" We all laugh again. Ed asks Jack Bail, "Which program you with? NEXUS?" "Global Entry," Jack Bail says. Looking at Fran, Ed says, "That's what I'm all about. Global entry." That gets the biggest, or the politest, laugh of all.

Soon we're eating grilled haddock, asparagus, and field greens. "Delicious," Jack Bail is the first to say. "Thank you, Jack," Chris says, with what seems like real gratitude. Jack Bail inspects the ocean, parts of which are ruddy and other parts dark blue. "That's some view, Doc," Jack Bail says. "Well, it's not Hudson Heights," I say. "I thought you lived in Manhattan?" Fran says. I say, "Hudson Heights is in Manhattan." Ed says, " 'Doc,' eh? You're a dark horse." "That's what they called me," I declare, very heartily. I didn't invent the custom of recognizing a teacher's academic title. Ed continues, "How about you, Jack? You a doc too?" Jack laughs. "No way, man. I'm just a C.P.A." "Just?" Fran says, as if scandalized. She tells me, "You must be very proud of this young man," and this is a tiny bit infuriating, because I don't like to receive instruction on how I ought to feel. How proud I am or am not of Jack Bail is for me to decide. "Certainly," I say, Mr. Very Hearty all over again. Fran says, "How was he in the classroom? A rascal, I'll bet." I make a sort of ho-ho-ho, and Jack Bail says to Fran, "Hey, don't blow my cover!" He adds, "Doc was a great teacher." I say, "Well, we've come a long way from Ohio," and Ed says, "We've all come a long way, eh?" and he tells Jack Bail that he's from B.C. but that Fran is a Maritimer and Maritimer women always want to return home eventually and you'd have to be crazy to stand in the way of a Maritimer woman.

Fran says very attentively, "Your wife can't be with us, Jack?"

"No, Chris is not able to come," Jack Bail says.

"Maybe next time," Fran says. Chris somehow catches my eye without looking at me and somehow rolls her eyes without rolling them. Or so I imagine.

"Unfortunately we're currently separated," Jack Bail says.

This gives everyone pause. "I'm sorry to hear that," Ed says. Jack Bail says, "Yep, it's not an ideal situation."

Now Chris gets up and says, "We have assorted berries, and we have—chocolate cake. Jack's favorite."

"Do you have children, Jack?" Fran asks, which is surely a question whose answer she can figure out by herself. "We don't," Jack Bail says. "A couple of years back, we tried. You know, the I.V.F. thing. Didn't work out." I'm refreshing the tableware at this point. Jack Bail says, "As a matter of fact, I just got this letter from the clinic demanding nine hundred dollars for my sperm."

This silences even the Joyces.

Jack Bail continues, "So three years ago, as part of that whole process, we froze sperm. Yeah, so anyway, we go through the whole thing, an ordeal I guess you could call it, and this and that happens, and we forget all about the frozen sperm. Now here's this invoice for nine hundred bucks because they've stored it all this time—they claim. I call them up. I speak to a lady. The lady says they've sent letters every year informing me that they're holding my sample. Letters? I don't remember getting any letters. But first things first, right? Destroy it, I tell her. Get rid of it right away. She tells me that they can't do that—they need a notarized semen-disposition statement."

"Okay, here we go," Chris says. "Jack's cake. And berries for anyone who might be interested."

"Now, I know their game," Jack Bail says. "I know what's going to happen. I'm going to mail them the notarized statement and they're going to say they never got it. And they're going to make me go to a notary all over again and they're going to make me mail them another statement and they're going to drag this thing out. And every extra day they store it, they charge more, pro rata. See? They're literally holding my sperm hostage."

"Corporations," Ed says. "Remember, Fran, that time—"

"Exactly," Jack Bail says. "It's not that the employees are evil-doers. It's the corporate systems. When it comes to getting mail they don't want to get, mail that reduces their profits, their systems are chaotic. When it comes to billing you, their systems are never chaotic. And I mean: retaining my genetic material without my consent? It's insanely wrong. So—do you ever do this?—I tell the lady I'm an attorney and that I've got assistants who'll be all over this shakedown like a pack of wolves."

Ed says, "That would blow up in your face in Canada. We're—"

"In the U.S. it's different. In the U.S., you don't register on their systems unless you threaten a lawsuit. That's how they operate. Human reasonableness is just seen as an opening to make more money. So I say to Chris, Do you recall us ever getting a letter about a frozen sperm sample? She's like, I don't know, all those letters look the same. I'm like, Wait a minute, this is important, I want you to think hard. She's like, I can't do this, I've got to keep my eye on the ball. I'm like, What ball? This is the ball. I mean, think about it. My genes are in the hands of strangers. Never mind the nine hundred bucks. We're talking about my seed. For all I know, I could have children out there in the world right now. Offspring. It's far from impossible, right? Mistakes happen all the time. And foul play. People think that foul play doesn't really exist. They're wrong. Foul play is a very real thing, especially when there's money to be made. Believe me, I know."

Nobody has made a start on the cake or the assorted berries. I say to Jack Bail, "You're right to be concerned. You have to take care of this."

"That's what I did, Doc. Cut a long story short, I caved on the nine hundred bucks and I went to the clinic personally with the documentation. I made sure to get a receipt."

"That was smart," Chris says.

Jack Bail says, "I had no option: I got a letter from a debt-collection agency. I had to cave. What was I going to do, risk my credit over nine hundred bucks? No, I had to cave. And I don't even know if they've actually disposed of the semen. I've got to assume they have. But I'll never know for sure, will I?"

Jack Bail spends the night on our sofa. In the morning, when Chris and I go down, there is a thank-you note.

Then a year passes and with it a tax season, and we are walking on the beach, and I stop and I say to Chris, "You know what? We haven't heard from Jack Bail."

Our beach is a sand and shingle beach. The sand is a common blend of quartz and feldspar. The sand emerges from the ocean, so to speak, and continues inland until quite suddenly shingle replaces it. The shingle, or gravel, consists at first of pebbles, next of a mixture of pebbles and cobbles, and finally almost only of cobbles. This progressive distribution of the beach stones, apparently methodical, is in fact natural: a storm's waves will force rocks small and large landward, but retreating waves have less power and will move only smaller rocks seaward. The result is a graduated stranding of the rocks, which amass in a succession of steep slopes and berms. Our beach walk begins when we scramble down one berm and then a second, and I always take care to hold Chris's hand as we go down. Countless large spiders somehow make a life among the cobbles, and my job is to help Chris to put them out of her mind. Out of my mind, too. There are no leg-bugs out here. Leg-bugs are deer ticks. Every evening from May through November, Chris and I must examine each other for ticks. Sometimes we find one.

From the sand beach, the brown drumlin cliffs are exposed to our contemplation. The drumlins have been here since the Wisconsin glaciation. Their crosscut formation is the result of erosion by the ocean and the wind and the rain, a battering that is ongoing, I can testify after two winters here. As the hills retreat, they leave behind rock fragments that will, in due course, form part of the beach. This sort of fact is difficult for me to really understand; it must be said that much of my newly acquired geologic knowledge is basically vocabularistic. I can't recognize feldspar, for example, or a granitic boulder. The Wisconsin glaciation isn't something I'm really on top of.

Chris and I scan the water, instinctively, I suppose. Sometimes we see a seal's head. It disappears for a while, then surfaces once more. They have large, cheerful, doglike heads, these seals. It would feel good to see our warm-blooded kin out there today: this is one of those strolls when the up-close ocean daunts me more than a little and, as we skirt dainty rushes of water, I sense myself situated at the edge of an infinite and relentless eraser. I'm not sure that there's much to be done about this: awe, dread, wonder, and feelings of asymmetry come with the terrain. There must be something appealing about it, though, or we'd be elsewhere. The question is, where? It's places that are going places. This part of Nova Scotia, the paleogeographers tell us, was once attached to Morocco.

"I hope he's okay," I say to Chris.

"I imagine he is," she says. She says, "You could always call him."

Yes, I could call him. But where would it end? I have taught, I once calculated, almost two thousand children.

No seal today. We keep walking.

Chris says, "*The Last Fez.*"

I say, "About the Constantinople mission? We were sworn to silence about that."

Chris says, "Remember that night we crossed the Bosporus? With that surly boatman?"

"Ali?" I say. "How could I forget?"

Keith Eisner

Blue Dot

Once upon a time, you and I climbed out the front window of the second story where I lived and onto the roof of the porch. We blinked and sniffed the air. Even in the city, we could smell spring rising from the small yards of the neighborhood and from the patch of ground by the bus stop. You looked up and down the street, then opened the top button of your shirt. Slipping two fingers inside your bra, you pulled out a square of aluminum foil. We bent our heads together as you unwrapped it, revealing a pair of tablets, pale blue like a robin's egg.

"Do we chew or swallow?"

"Doesn't matter," you said.

I put one in my mouth and held it there while a car with a lot of chrome passed. There was a tang of aluminum as I swallowed. We held hands and made self-conscious talk, waiting to see when one of us would do something strange or funny. Nothing happened. Sparrows darted from tree to tree. The sun slipped behind a cloud. Somebody in the house put on a record. Bob Dylan. It was always Dylan in that house. The floors and ceilings were made out of layers of his distorted syllables. I hummed along for a while, but "Like a Rolling Stone" didn't seem to have anything to do with me today. So I pointed to Fred Fisher, a city landmark a mile away.

Fred's peak was green during the day, then orange at dusk. At dawn, the custodians switched off the colored floodlights and he'd be green again. When we first got together, we'd go out on the roof in the evenings to watch Freddy change. If we'd been up all night (as we often were), we'd watch him change again. Our urban sunrise and sunset, we said. Now I told you I was looking forward to seeing Fred change a lot more colors today than his usual two.

"Huh . . . colors?"

Okay, it was dumb—one of those small, dumb jokes, barely worth the telling. It was taking forever to explain when a bus suddenly stopped in front of the house. Buses came and went all the time, but this one glowed. We felt its vibrations all the way up to the roof. The doors hissed open and dispensed a small brown man, elegantly dressed in black. Astounding and comical that so ponderous a machine would deliver such a neat little human package with a leather-covered book onto our street. The young man looked about and then began walking away with full, energetic strides. But why did it take so long for his front shoe, hard and shiny, to actually touch the sidewalk?

Then we knew. We gasped and laughed. I was still talking, still swimming from one word to another about Fred. The bus was still gliding up to the curb, idling, then pulling away. The man with the Bible was still taking his first step. Dylan was still asking, *How does it feel?*

"My God," you said.

I couldn't speak. I had assumed it would be like pot or a good drunk—everything becoming close and warm, permeable. It was the opposite. Before and behind us, above, below, and on either side, time was immense. This is no drug, I thought. This is the way things are. I turned to find something I knew. Your mouth was open. You rocked back and forth, staring at the street. I was aware of your skull and the hair flowing from it. *Kids*, you had told me the night before. *People will look like kids.* I had looked forward to that. Now I wasn't so sure. You did look like a child, but not cute and innocent. You were stark and beyond description, like one child seeing another for the first time.

I turned away and watched the small, brown man—from India, I guessed—walk up the street, studying addresses. Several doors down, he turned up the walk of an apartment.

"It may be a little rough for a while," you said.

"Sure, rough," I repeated, though I didn't know what you meant.

"Just go with it." You leaned back against the house and closed your eyes. I wanted you to show me what to do. But you had withdrawn. Stoned, I reminded myself. I would do what you did. I leaned against the house, closed my eyes. I did feel like a stone in the sun. Round and inside myself. Keep your eyes closed. No one will know.

"C'mere," you said.

"I am here."

"No, you know what I mean." You patted the shingle beside you. I slid over and we held hands again, but it wasn't comfortable. My neck didn't feel right. "Love you," you said. I wanted to say it too, but I couldn't. The words would fly away over the rooftops and we'd never get them back. You opened your eyes and looked at me. You said my name. "You need to know something," you said very deliberately. "I am not going to take care of you."

"Wha? What d'you mean—take care of?"

"You know. Take care of. Make you feel okay. I can't do it."

"I never asked you to take care of me. Never asked anybody, did I?"

"No. Yes."

I let go of your hand and crossed my arms.

"Let's go inside," you said.

"What?" It had not occurred to me that we could move. You crawled back in through the window. I stayed. Much better out here. Take *care* of me? When did I ever ask anybody to—? Never. Always. From my mother on down. Well, not anymore. I'll stay out here. Take care of myself.

You stuck your head out. "Come on."

"I don't think so."

"Come on," you said, laughing. "It's okay."

It was always dark inside, and the living room looked more like a bedroom. Posters covered the windows. A paisley print, tacked to the four corners of the ceiling, drooped over the room. There was a low, round table (a utility spool) and a sagging leather armchair. On the far side of the room, Denny lay on a row of cushions. He was at least ten years older than anyone else in the house—maybe even in his forties. He had a long, color-less face and hair down to his waist—hair that always seemed to intrude into whatever I was trying to say or do. He wore a leather car coat, even inside, and was always pretending not to stare at you. Now I froze. A knife quivered in his chest. He turned his head and laughed. It was only a magazine, a rolled-up magazine he was using to tap out the beat.

"Hey," he said in his flat voice.

"Hey, Denny," we said.

"What d'you kids got?"

"Got?" I said.

"Yeah. Windowpane, White Knights . . . ?"

I didn't know what to say. This must be one of his jokes, I thought, one of his tricks to invite himself along. "Oh, man, you are royally fucked up. Totally," he announced in that way he had, as if he owned whatever was going on. Which he sort of did, as he was the only one in the house with a steady income, and the lease was in his name.

"He means what did we take," you said to me. "It's Blue Dot, Denny."

"Blue Dot?" he said, sitting up and shaking back his long hair. "No shit, got any left?"

"No, I just got these two from Louise."

"Louise? She got any more?" He said this casually, but to me his long-legged, leather-coated presence was obscene with envy and loneliness.

"I don't know," you said.

"Louise . . . bitch didn't tell me."

"I don't know," you said softly. "I only got these two."

Denny sank back into the cushions. The fire went out of his eyes. I felt sorry for him until he rose and leaned forward again. "How about a joint?" he said to you. "Killer Jamaican shit."

"Oh, hey, thanks," you said, "but not right now. Maybe later. You be around?"

He glanced at me and nodded. "Sure. I'm here forever." Then he laid his long body, segment by segment, back on the cushions, closed his eyes, and stared at the ceiling. You motioned toward my room and went down the hall. It took me a long time to cross the living room, avoiding his lidded eyeballs. In the hall, I paused to catch my breath. I felt warm and rubbery: intense vibrations passed through my knees, elbows, lips. I heard Denny get up and come down the hall, laughing at me. When I turned around the hall was empty. Pressing my fingertips against each wall, I made my way to the door of my room.

You were lying on my mattress with one knee up and your shirt off. I spread myself out next to you. You had that look on your face, and I couldn't imagine how you could feel that way because I already felt like I was coming out of every pore, only a breath or two away from being empty. You unbuttoned my shirt and stroked my chest. The rushes felt like they would never stop. You moved your hand below my waist. No use. You rolled away. I found that place on your shoulder my hand knew so well. You shrugged it off. I found the place again. You didn't move. I kept my hand on your shoulder and closed my eyes.

The rushes were dying down. They weren't big waves anymore, just pulses. Like someone turning a switch on and off: *brrrr-on, brrrr-off*, a buzz in my head.

You turned. "The door. It's the doorbell."

"No, it can't be. You're hearing things."

"Listen."

I listened. Nobody ever used the doorbell. People just walked in. Salesmen didn't do our neighborhood. The doorbell *was* ringing. "It'll go away," I said.

"No, they know we're here."

"Who knows?"

"The people at the door."

"What people? Denny?"

"No, Denny's in the front room."

"Why doesn't he answer it?"

"He's stoned, remember?"

"Oh, yeah. But—we are too. Aren't we?"

"Go answer it."

The shortest way to the front door was through the living room and down the stairs. But I'd have to pass Denny. So I took the long way down the back stairs and through the first-floor corridor. I was pleased with my firm, even tread. I wasn't so stoned anymore, at least not in the legs. Reaching the door, I stopped and stared. Who could be on the other side, ringing the bell so long and hard—who could care so much?

When I opened the door, it was summer. The sun blazed off the windshields of the parked cars and the green shards of a broken bottle on the curb. The small brown man stood to one side. He smiled. He was thinner, more angular than he had appeared from the roof. Clasping the Bible in both hands, his elbows stuck out from his sides. We looked at each other. Finally he spoke.

"Good day, sir." His voice was bright and musical, his teeth small and pearly. I was engulfed by a wave of Sen-Sen.

"Sorry, I'm not interested." I shut the door and turned to go, but he rapped several times on the wood—a soft, rhythmic sound as if he was sending a message. "Not interested," I called through the door.

"Ho, ho," he laughed. "Not interested? Sir, I can tell you are interested—in everything."

"No man, not really. Not today."

"Yes, really. Today!"

Meanwhile, you and Denny were facing each other on cushions in the living room. "I better go find him," you were saying.

"He'll show up. Always does." He pulled the joint out of his mouth and, still inhaling, floated it to your lips. "This first," he said.

"I gotta go. It's his first trip."

"Ah, little boy's all right. Weren't you just with him in his room?"

"He left."

"Aw, that's too bad. Just up and left you all alone?"

You thought. "That's right, he went to answer the door. I asked him to. Didn't you hear it ringing? Someone was ringing and ringing and ringing."

"I never pay attention to that shit."

"Well, he left and it stopped."

"See? Leave it alone and it'll stop. That's my philosophy."

"I should go. He might be out on the street."

"Whoa, whoa. Hurrying's bad for the digestion. Pass me that bag behind you, will you? No, the leather one by the spool. Nice, huh? Moroccan. Ever touch anything so smooth?" He set it between you and him, zipped it open, and pulled out a bulging baggie. "Smell this," he said, lifting it to your nostrils. "Go ahead, breathe deep."

You inhaled, scooted back, and swayed to your feet. "I'm going, Denny. Go on, roll some more. I'll be right back when I find him. We'll all smoke some together."

"Yeah? Well, I might not be around. I got things to do."

"Wait. Someone's on the stairs. It's him."

"Yippee," said Denny, then "Oh, shit," as the smiling man in the black suit stepped into the room. Denny slapped a magazine over the leather bag, brushed debris from his pant legs, and waved the air with the flat of his hand. "What the f—"

As for me, I was speechless in the doorway. On the way up the stairs, I had hoped I'd know what to do or say when we got to the living room. But I didn't know why I was bringing this stranger into the house any more than you or Denny did. Down on the porch, it had made sense to invite him in—who could resist such unswerving cheer and determination? Now I wished I hadn't. Denny's eyes told the story: *narc, cop, at the least some do-good bastard who will call us in at the nearest pay phone.*

"I, uh, he just wants to talk," I began.

Asshole, mouthed Denny.

No one spoke until you stepped around the spool table, offered your hand, and said, "Come in, sir, please."

"Thank you for your kindness, ma'am." He made a small bow.

"Je-sus," said Denny.

"No, sir." The man giggled. "Only one of his messengers." Springing forward and nimbly making his way around a stack of paperbacks and a candle stuck in a wine bottle, he took Denny's hand and shook it vigorously. "I am honored to meet you, sir," he said, with more energy than I think anyone had addressed Denny in years. Maybe ever.

After that we were all tense and uncomfortable except for the strange man who waited in the middle of the room. I felt wretched. What had possessed me to bring in someone who didn't belong? Denny was right. This guy could smile and nod his head and act like everything was fine, then stop at the drugstore and make his call. Even if he wasn't a narc or a cop, this wasn't his scene. We'd all have to pretend we were someone we weren't.

The stranger closed his eyes and sniffed. "Do I smell marijuana?" Despite my confusion and paranoia, I couldn't help smiling at the way he said it, like a children's song: *merry* WAH *na?*

"No," said Denny, "it's just incense, man."

"Yeah, incense," I said.

"Yes," you said to the man, "it is marijuana. We were just smoking and talking together. Would you like to sit with us for a while?" You gestured to a cushion. "I'm Faith."

"Faith," he repeated. In one motion, he sank cross-legged onto the cushion. He told us his name. It was long and incomprehensible—a wild terrain of *v*'s and *k*'s. "That's all right," he said, laughing, "my American friends call me Val." This was the end of his first year in America, he explained. His entire family—grandparents, uncles, aunts, and cousins, too—had been saved by Pentecostal missionaries in Calcutta. He and his older brother studied engineering at Wayne State and witnessed on the weekends. He smiled at Denny. Nodding toward the leather bag beneath the magazine, he said, "I can give you stronger medicine than that, sir." He tapped the Bible in his lap.

"Bullshit," said Denny. "Look, Val, I like you and all that— sort of—nothing personal, but I know all about your medicine. I'll go one-on-one against the Bible any day. I been there. Here, let me see it."

Val hesitated, pressed the book to his lips, then handed it to Denny who rifled through the pages. "Yeah, here it is. I *know* this book. You don't have to ring my bell to tell me about this book. See, here. This line was written in my heart: *Enoch walked with God; and he was no more, for God took him.* That's who I was—Enoch. That was my verse, my mantra. God in every-thing. Walking with Him everywhere. On the street, in the woods, the bars, round and round my goddamn room."

Closing the book, he dropped it back in Val's lap. "Saint Augustine, Aquinas, Meister fucking Eckhardt, Saint Francis—all those dudes. The Totality of God. Nobody's been deeper than I was." Pulling the leather bag out from under the maga-zine, he rolled a joint, licked it closed, twisted the ends, and lit it. You and I looked at each other. His nostrils flared as he sucked in the smoke and blew it out like a cigarette.

"You know what happened? You want to know what turned me around? The Badlands, that's what. I was in a sweat lodge on sacred Indian ground—the only white guy there. I prayed. I fasted. I mortified the flesh. I took the holy sacraments: pey-ote, mescaline, pure Owsley acid. And I wasn't fucking around, either. I wasn't one of these groovy little hippies you see splash-ing around the shallow end of the pool. I was in *deep*. Seven days and seven nights, man, the fire *and* the flood.

"Finally, the last morning, I'm on a rise watching the sun come up across the plains. Hundreds of shades of red, gold, pur-ple. Every color you can imagine. Pulsing. Alive. Majestic. Then off to one side comes this burning little white shape, no bigger than a dime. It gets bigger and brighter till I can hardly look at it—like magnesium. Nobody had to tell me who that was. And you know what He had to say? In all this power and glory, you know the *only* thing He had to say—"

"Oh, yes," said Val, patting Denny's knee, "*suffer.*"

It was darker now that the sun had moved to the back of the house. Denny passed the joint to Val with a strange, possessive tenderness. Val was in his shirtsleeves, his suit coat draped across his lap. Without bringing it to his lips, he held the joint aloft, studied it, then passed it on to you. You three were close, your knees almost touching. I sat a little ways off and to one side. I wasn't so sure of things—like how long would this last, and for that matter, what was *this*? Until I figured it out, I thought it best to keep quiet.

You were getting Val to talk about himself. He said the Pentecostal meetings, here and in India, were like nothing we'd ever seen, much stronger, he said with a laugh, than "your merry-wah-na." The spirit moved people to sing and shout, dance, too. Some spoke in tongues. Others interpreted. A few had visions.

"You too?" you asked.

He nodded.

"Like what, man?" asked Denny. "Fire, serpents? Flood?"

Val rocked on the cushion and laughed. "No, sir, those I see all the time. In our meetings, I have had two visions only. Both times the same—the Holy Ghost."

"Wow," said Denny.

"Only he is a woman, sir. A beautiful woman from my country. All in white with white slippers and white gloves." Val stared above Denny's head. "It is this time of day. She moves from side to side." Val closed his eyes. After a moment, he began to hum, then to sway.

"Then what?"

"That's all there is, Denny," you said. "There doesn't have to be any more."

Val opened his eyes and smiled. "Oh, no, there is more. I have neglected the crickets, or what you might say, locusts. They cover the walls. They land upon her."

"Oh, yeah," said Denny, "I know this one—the eighth plague Moses lays on Pharaoh's Tribe. Giant locusts with beady eyes. And this woman, the Ghost, she zaps them with the end of her finger, right?"

"Oh, no, sir. They are green and not giant. No bigger than this," he said, taking the joint from Denny and holding it up. "And she does not—what you say—*zap* them. She lets them crawl." Val stared at the marijuana burning between his fingers, then raised it to his lips. Thoughtfully, he inhaled. The tip of the joint glowed and Val's body rose off the cushion. No more than an inch—but definitely off the cushion. Neither Denny nor you seemed to notice. A second later, when the joint flew out of his mouth and he was wracked with coughing, you leapt up and slapped him on the back.

"Water," you said to me, "get him a glass of water!"

Why me? I thought, skulking down the hall. Why not Denny? Why don't you tell *Denny* to get a glass of water?

A foothill of dirty pans and dishes sat in the kitchen sink. I studied the scallops of sunlight on the dirty dishes and wondered why I was there. I heard Val cough and your low, soothing voice and Denny giving advice. Water. I extricated a glass and turned on the hot water faucet. It was cold a long time before it got hot. Then it was very hot. I squirted some Ivory Liquid into the glass. The detergent looked like sperm on the side of the glass. I held it under the faucet. The suds ran over the lip of the glass and down my arm. After a while, there were no more suds, only water.

I remembered there was a pitcher of lemon water in the fridge. I filled up the glass and took it to Val. You and he and Denny were seated on the cushions as before, except that Val's eyes were watery and his face had that slack-jawed, receding look of people smoking dope for the first time. But his eyes brightened as he took the glass from me. "Thank you," he said in a husky whisper. "I've not forgotten you, sir."

I sat down, not quite in the circle, but near enough. I watched him very closely. He did not rise off the pillow again, but seemed to elongate and soften with each turn of the joint. "And you, sir?" he asked me. "Have you a story about the Spirit?"

"Uh, no. No spirits. Not yet."

"I got a story, Val," you said. "But not like yours or Denny's. I never had visions or talked in tongues or fasted or anything like that. I was just a regular churchgoer. That was up in Marion, a couple hundred miles north of here. It's nothing but a crossroads really: a couple of bars, an IGA, a Sunoco, and a beauty shop my aunt owned. My mom disappeared when I was little, so I lived with my aunt and uncle above the shop. My dad slept in a little trailer out back. Most of the time he was in one of the taverns or tending my uncle's cows outside of town.

"Anyway, when the farmers' wives came into the shop, they all told me how pretty I was, how they wished they had my soft skin and fine hair. I liked the attention but I didn't like the way they said it or the way some of them would hold my chin and inspect me like some kind of fruit. I got some revenge by watching them sit in their plastic smocks under the dryers, their eyes turning red and teary from the chemicals in their perms. They looked so sad afterward, opening their big purses to pay for hairdos that looked like somebody else's hair on their heads. I was young then and sort of liked the mean feeling I got from watching them. Then, the next time in church, I liked being sorry and promising never to be mean again and feeling pure and forgiven.

"You know what I mean? Well, never mind, what I want to tell you about is when I was sixteen. There was this woman, Mrs. Trent. She was a huge woman, enormous. Pink and blotchy all over. The floor creaked when she walked over it. She came in every month and whined the whole time. She'd say my aunt rolled her hair too tight. She'd complain that the dryer was too hot or not hot enough. People would pass the window and she'd make little comments about them. She was always looking out for me. She'd catch me staring at her and wither me with those two sharp eyes down inside her face. I tried to stay away when she came in, but I couldn't. I was drawn to her. She was ugly like a man's ugliness—layers and layers I could never get to the bottom of.

"One Saturday, it snowed like it never had before. We could

hardly see the other side of the street. It was just my aunt and me. My dad and uncle were out getting the cows in. People called and canceled their appointments. Then the phones went dead and we were sure nobody would come in."

You paused and stared at the joint in your hand. You'd been holding it for a while. Though there were several tokes still left in it, you dropped it in the Mason jar with the other butts. I thought you'd forgotten what you were going to say or maybe decided not to tell us anymore, but after a moment, you raised your head.

"Late that afternoon, I was kneeling on a chair looking out the window. It was like something alive, the way the snow blew down the street and the howling it made. I had this thought, though I wasn't really religious, that it was God's arm coming down the street. Not a vision really, like you two had, but more an imagining. His arms and His fingers searching everything out, including me. Not in a bad way, but kind of gentle in the middle of all that fury and howling.

"So I'm amazed when I see Mrs. Trent come barreling up the sidewalk as if no snowstorm could stop her. She glares at me through the window. I should have gotten up and opened the door for her like I usually did for customers. But I couldn't move, I was so stunned to see her. Resentful, too. My aunt, who'd been upstairs, comes down when she hears the bell.

" 'Why, Betty,' she says, 'what a nice surprise.'

"It was the worst time ever, with no other people or place to go or errand to run. I tried to read a magazine, but I kept feeling her eyes on me.

" 'This storm ain't nothing,' she says to my aunt, 'nothing at all.'

"My aunt gave her a rinse and did her hair and was starting her nails when the phone gave that little *ding* that tells when the lines are clear again. I picked it up and it was Mrs. Ball down at the IGA who had to talk to my aunt. Some kind of trouble—

maybe with the snow, I never found out. My aunt told me she'd be right back and to keep Mrs. Trent company.

"I sat down on a stool by the manicure table. I don't know why. I could've sat in one of the chairs across the room. In fact, I meant to, but I didn't. I sat near her. We didn't talk. I listened to her breathe. There was so much inside of it—wheezing and sighs and groans.

"'Well, ma'am,' she says after a while, 'how 'bout my nails?'

"'Oh, I'd love to, Mrs. Trent, but I'm afraid I'd just ruin them.' This wasn't a total lie because even though I'd watched my aunt for years, I hadn't really done anyone's nails but my own.

"'No,' she says, 'You'll do just fine. Look how fine you do your own. I want you to do mine. Please?' It was the first time I'd ever heard her use that word.

"I didn't see how I could get out of it, so I gritted my teeth and slid my hand under hers. I expected her touch to be heavy and clammy, like a fat person's, but her hand was soft and light as a little girl's. I did her nails and she talked—not about herself or her family or her farm, but *me*. I was amazed at how much she knew—not just what grade I was in, but the horse I hoped to get, my friends, the boys I liked, my mother. It was awful. I knew what to do with her meanness, but not her niceness. I just kept my head bent and my eyes on her nails, saying, 'Yes, ma'am, no, ma'am.'

"Then when I was doing her second hand, she reached the hand I'd just done up to my face and touched my cheek. I was so afraid I couldn't move. I looked up and tears were running down her fat cheeks. She stroked my face. It was as gentle as anybody's ever touched me.

"'You're so pretty,' she says, 'I won't hurt you. I'll stay right here under this dryer. Just look at me. Look how big I am. Why, there's three of you inside of me.'

"She told me crazy things. 'I've loved you all your life,' she says. Loved me before I was born, would love me after she died, loved me more than her husband or any of her own kids. The only reason she comes to the beauty parlor, she tells me, is to see me, to be near me even if I hated her. She says not to worry, that there's only this moment inside the storm, and then everything will be back the way it was.

"'My nails will even grow back,' she says, joking about the terrible job I was doing. Then she laughed at her own joke until she started crying again. 'Don't you think my nails will grow back, honey? Don't you . . . don't you think you could come around this table and let me hold you? I told you I'd stay right here under the dryer and I will. I won't move an inch. I can't. But won't you come on around that table?'

"She reached her other hand up and stroked both my cheeks. I admit that for a second I leaned into that touch. Then the next thing I know, I'm out the door with no coat and the nail file still in my hand. I ran across the street, just crazy, screaming into the blizzard. Nobody heard me. I could hardly hear myself. I stopped on the other side of the street, panting and shivering. It must have been below zero with the wind chill, but all of a sudden I felt calm and burning as if nothing in the world could hurt me.

"Then I see a dark shape coming down the street. My aunt. I hustled back into the shop. Mrs. Trent was standing by the dryer, jerking the pins out of her hair. 'Well,' she says, 'it's not quite dry yet, but I better be moving on before dark, don't you think?'

"'Yes, ma'am,' I say, keeping near the door. I wasn't going to look at her, but she snuffled a little and I did look and she put her eyes down on the floor. That was strange—to have this woman who always bullied me look away. My aunt came in and fussed over Mrs. Trent's wet hair and kept apologizing for having to leave. Mrs. Trent didn't say a word until my aunt goes upstairs to get change for her twenty. Then she looks at me, and there's the old Mrs. Trent again—fierce and direct. But different. Almost in a whisper, she says, 'I'll never touch you again. Won't even look at you. But I will always love you. Always. Now you know what it's like.'"

Denny fidgeted. "Wow," he said, "bummer. We had a priest like that."

"Shh, Denny," I said.

"So what happened?" he asked, ignoring me. "You tell your aunt?"

You didn't respond. A mist seemed to be slipping into the room. The past, I thought. You looked stoned again, diffused and distant.

"You became ill," said Val, "for seven days and seven nights."

"No," you said, "it was only four days. But never mind, I did get sick. Really sick. In my fever, I kept seeing her, hearing her, hating her. Wishing her dead. I didn't actually see the real Mrs. Trent again for six months. She was walking down the street with a cane and a bandage over one eye. I found out later that she'd had a stroke and a cataract, too, and had lost a lot of weight. I wasn't going to say anything, but in that town you never ignore anyone. 'Hello, Mrs. Trent, how are you?' I asked. But she stared through me with her one good eye and says, 'God so loved the world that He gave His only son. . . .'

"I saw her less and less. She never came to the shop, and didn't come to church anymore. Her skin started to sag on her, and because nobody bought her any new clothes, her old things sagged on her, too. But she was always smiling and quoting scripture. Her voice changed, too. It was higher, like a little kid's, always trying to please.

"As far as I know, she never mentioned that time in the storm to anybody, and until today, I didn't either. She died a week before I graduated. I didn't feel much of anything then. But a couple months later, her grown daughter, who'd been taking care of her father and cleaning up the place, comes into the shop with an envelope with my name on it.

" 'Guess this is for you,' says the daughter. 'She sure didn't leave much to nobody else.' She looked me over with her mom's eyes. She had that sourness in her voice, but not her mother's snap.

" 'Aren't you going to open it?' says my aunt.

"I made some excuse about waiting till things were quieter in the shop. Actually, I was pissed at the daughter. I'd steamed enough envelopes to know this one had been opened and reglued. Probably wanted to see if her mom had left me any money. The truth was I was scared. I didn't want any messages from the dead. I didn't want to think about her ever again. When I did open it in my room that night, I almost laughed, it was such a corny card. There was Tinker Bell, all glittered up, flying over Never Never Land. It was something you'd send to a six-year-old. The printed message said *On Your Special Day!* There was writing inside. It took me a long time to make it out—her handwriting was so thin and shaky. It said,

Place me like a seal over your heart, like a seal on your arm
for love is as strong as death, its jealousy unyielding as the grave.
It burns like blazing fire, like a mighty flame.

"There was more, but I can't remember it."

"Many waters," said Val with his eyes closed, "cannot quench love; rivers cannot wash it away. If one were to give all the wealth of his house for love, it would be utterly scorned."

"Thank you," you said. You looked down at your hands. "Sometimes I think I had something to do with her death. In a weird way, thinking that gave me some comfort. It gave her death meaning, and let me feel something: rotten and guilty at first. So I'd pray for forgiveness and then feel purified on the other side. I think that less and less now. I didn't kill her, she just died."

"Amen," said Denny. "A-fucking-men. Hey, I'm sorry, but so what? I mean, this fat, old broad feels you up in a snowstorm, gets sick and dies. I'm supposed to be impressed?"

When none of us answered, he went on. "Okay, I'm rude and I'm crude, but I tell the truth. Val and me, we've been talking about vision, man, *vision*. Your story is touching and all, but it's just a story, just coincidence."

You clenched your jaw. Val stirred but did not respond. It was my turn now. I didn't know what would come out of my mouth, but I'd win you back.

"Denny—," I said.

"Oh, man, look who's back from la-la land. Don't—don't even start, man. Look, she's your girlfriend and all, but don't get into shit with me you don't understand."

"Yeah? Let me tell you something. I can take any—"

"Sirs!" cried Val. He pointed past me, toward the hall.

"Holy Fuck," said Denny, "what is this shit?"

Mist—or the past or *something*—was filling the room. It was too weird to be real and too wet to be another vision. Steam. Steam was coming down the hall, out of the kitchen. I was the first to the hallway, you, Denny, and Val coming behind. Up the hall near the kitchen was a lake.

"Shit, shit, shit," said Denny.

The kitchen was terrific. The kitchen was better than drugs. The low afternoon sun filled the room, making a golden, misty cave. The refrigerator was a monolith, the stove an altar. Beside it, the dishes in the sink were fantastic bones and artifacts. At the same time, what made it the best thing of the day, the best thing in months, was that it was just a kitchen in Detroit, just a hot water faucet I'd left running in a plugged sink. You and I looked at each other, then laughed harder than we had in weeks.

We held each other and shook with laughter. "I know exactly what this is," I cried, "I know exactly!"

"What the fuck, man?" That was Denny, stuck in the hall behind Val.

"Finally, *I* get a vision."

"Shit!" he said, splashing past us. "Turn the fucking thing off! What are you, crazy?"

"Absolutely."

"Fucking-ay." He wrenched the faucet. "This is not funny, not fucking funny at all. This water, asshole, is going to leak through the floor, ruin the ceiling. You got that?"

We understood, but couldn't stop laughing. Val tried not to smile. I looked at his feet. "C'mon, Val," I said, patting his back, "get down from there. Get in the swim with the rest of us."

"Sir?"

"Fuck, I'm not, I am *not* cleaning this up. You hear me? I'm not lifting a finger."

"I see you hovering about. Come on down."

"No thank you, sir. My soles are extremely thin."

"Talking a fucking thousand dollars here."

"Hey, look." You pointed to a cockroach swimming by a chair leg.

"Great," I said, "flood the place. Drown the bastards."

"Christ!" Denny had sloshed a bowl of water on his shirt. He turned toward us with a wooden spoon in one hand and a saucepan in the other. We were laughing about the cockroach, but he didn't know that. "All right, fuck you guys. Clean up your own mess." He splashed across the kitchen, flung open the utility room door, and grabbed the mop. "Where's the goddamn bucket?"

"Denny." I made myself stop laughing. "Go put on a record."

"Huh?"

"Give me the mop. I'll take care of this, every drop. Why don't you go put on a record. How about Bob Dylan for a change?"

He looked lost for a second. Then his face settled into its familiar lines. "Well," he said, "you got to get *all* the water up."

"Okay."

"I mean even a little water will warp everything."

"I know. I'll get it up. I'm sorry about the mess, man."

We stared at each other for a few moments. Finally, he let go of the mop. "Well, I guess the water hasn't been sitting long enough to ruin anything, long as you get it all up now." He started down the hall, then turned and gave you his hangdog look, "Hey, you want to smoke some more?"

You gave me a look. It was okay. It was okay. "Sure," you said.

Then it was just Val and me in the kitchen. He stood in the doorway, a few inches off the floor. "How do you do that, man?"

"Do what?" he asked.

"Is it an Eastern deal or a Pentecostal thing?"

"Do you have a bucket, sir?"

"Yeah, it's on the back landing. I'll get it." It was okay if he didn't tell me. There really wasn't much to say about it. Besides, the linoleum was completely dry around his shoes. When I came back with the bucket, Val was doing the dishes. I told him thanks, but to go join the others in the living room. I needed to use the sink to change the mop water. This wasn't true. I could have used the bathtub, but I wanted to be alone for a while.

I got up all the water I could with the mop. Then took some old towels and got down on my hands and knees and rubbed the floor dry. I was surprised to see how clean it could get. What I had assumed were permanent stains and cracks were only dirt marks. The linoleum gleamed. Its pattern emerged. I thought about the people who lived here before us, probably before I was born; how happy they must have been the day the new linoleum went in. I washed and dried the dishes and put them away. Since they'd never all been cleaned at the same time, I had to make up places to put them. I was grateful for the work, even wiping down the refrigerator and the stove, cleaning under the burners. It wasn't that I was avoiding you or the others, I was simply relieved to be away from visions for a while.

I expected to find the living room all dark with you three sitting together as before. But the room was brightly lit, brighter than I'd ever seen it. You'd even brought in some lamps from other rooms and had taken the poster off the front window. And it wasn't Dylan on the record player, but *Appalachian Spring* from way back in the album stack. Denny was sitting where we'd found him that morning. Val sat beside him, his Bible in his lap and his tie around his forehead. Out the window and a mile away, Fred was fully orange.

You stood in the center of the room on top of the spool table. You had on that long, white dress: the strange, elegant one you got at the Salvation Army. You had even found your scarab pin—ruby red with green rhinestones, but it could pass for a locust. You weren't quite dancing, but posing to the music. Funny, I'd seen you pose nude before. That's how we met— both of us posing for an art class at the Institute. There'd been nothing sexy about it. We were so serious and self-conscious. Now, in this old-fashioned, long-sleeved dress with the high collar, you were as hot and direct as an electric current.

Things were okay again. I'd ridden the drug into the twilight. Later, in my room, we'd hold each other. We'd be lovers again. We'd laugh and do the spontaneous, trippy things young lovers did. Then we'd part. You knew this too.

You bent low, then stood on tiptoe. You raised your arms toward the ceiling, then lowered one arm out straight and drew the other back past your ear like an archer sighting her arrow. You turned toward Denny. You turned toward Val. You turned toward me.

Wil Weitzel

Lion

·

WHEN THE OLD MAN died, I laid him out in the bathtub because he was small and fit neatly. I took him by the ankles first and then, moving slowly toward his neck, gently scrubbed him down. I lifted him at the back and washed his ribs all the way around until he was like an old moist cigarette. Then I dressed him the way he always dressed, in a corduroy suit—this one was a dun brown—and laid him in his bed and called his wife.

No one had been able to tell me why they lived apart. She was the one, most of them said, who insisted upon it. She needed relief from their intimacy, or she'd never loved him at all, or she was someone who thought only of herself. There were many reasons thrown about by the people who'd known the old man when he was young and teaching at the university or by others who cared for him now in his home as a paid occupation.

They were all men, these people of the house, who had keys and came in and out and bought food and delivered it and even ate some of it, standing in the narrow pantry and gazing at the shelves. Pickled artichokes and Sicilian olive oil and healthy breads from the best, the purest, companies would come to rest in the cupboards. Often I would eat with them, and they would talk of the old man in his presence as though he were only partially there.

He *was* only partially there. He was as old as old trees, their bark haggard or worn, that have survived the succession of the forest and long seasons of shade and then the drought years of bone-dry springs and catastrophes of wind. He had long, tired memories that flowed in and out of events just like the wind. And up until the end, he had great gaps like any dry forest where he knew nothing at all about his life and it was as though it had never happened.

While I was attending my classes at the graduate school, he'd invited me through a colleague—as a favor to his former department and because I was an international student—to live with him. It was an honor to live with such a one. There were rumors of his teaching, of how he'd reached people, even the most remote, and left a mark on their lives. He had survived atrocities, it was said, while still a young man and was not supposed to be alive. To me, though, he appeared only a sad, old lord or a herald of brighter times which had faded until he had faded.

"More soup, I see," he would say over our bowls in the low, dark living room that creaked like a boat with uneven boards at the floor and his books hovering above us as though they were preparing to fall from the walls. "More soup and more soup."

"It's wholesome soup," I'd tell him, encouragingly. "You should have more."

He would only grunt in such moments and reply, "So they say," and then slurp his canned pea soup as if he were suddenly the ocean and it was a great turbulent river he was swallowing from the hills.

. . .

Once, during the last year I lived with the old man—when my program of study was nearly complete and I was preparing to shove off again to points unknown—I told him the story of the lion, a story about a young boy in southern Africa who'd grown up on polished tile floors in a household of tutors and money with a lion cub. They had been forced to release the lion into the bush, when he had become so powerful and strong that even the boy, who loved him, could not in good conscience hold him any longer inside the courtyard.

Years went by and the lion allegedly flourished, at first under the eyes of authorities, until they lost track of him in the wild. They thought he had perhaps migrated to the north where there were green, algal lakes and the herds slept in ancient gallery forests for longer segments of the year. No one knew exactly what had happened to the lion, but the prides had been shrinking for years in the scrublands, and their prey had been gently seeping out of the blackthorn and crossing the burnt pans and fossil riverbeds to drift off into the hills. Finally, before he had married, when for several brief seasons of rain there had been no word, the boy—who was already a grown man and the pride of his family—went out searching northward for the lion, carrying no weapon and against everyone's advice.

"By now," I explained quietly, staring up at the rickety shelves, "he's been gone a long time." I could feel my voice catch. "It's possible now that he will not go back."

I assured the old man that honestly I didn't know the rest of the story. We were sitting together drinking cognac, which I never actually drank but only smelled when I raised my glass to keep him company. He didn't much watch me anyway but only listened through his one good ear with a kind of ferocity when I spoke. It was in the winter, when for weeks it had done nothing but snow until a layer of white had risen above the lower sills of our windows, and I'd been shoveling for the old man so he could walk slowly from the house to the street through a high, narrow corridor that constantly refilled. In those days, I awoke early in the mornings and went back to my shovel.

The old man stared at me directly, as he had never done before, when I told him there was no more to the story. Or that if there was more, then I couldn't tell it. Because I wasn't yet sure how it ended. He glared at me from behind his heavy glasses with both eyes squinting intently, furiously it seemed, and waited a long time. He began to list in his chair as though we were poised together on a restless sea.

"Tell me this story again," he said finally.

"That's all I know," I told him.

"Again."

For months, all the way into May when the snows had melted at last and he drank Kir rather than cognac, and all I did around the house was empty the garbage, I told him the story of the lion. He in turn would tell me of Russia during the war and of the cold and how everyone had been hungry. He would come back to his hunger again and again as though it were the line that held him to the present, the long filament he followed backward into his life.

"What would you eat?" I'd ask. "What would there be for dinner?"

"For dinner—," and he'd pause, hovering over the bowl, and then clean his spoon and place it carefully down on the table.

Sometimes for the rest of the meal, even after I'd heated more red lentil soup and come back to him hunched at the table, he'd say nothing. Then just when I'd think he was asleep in some inward way that was deeper than sleep, and I was sneaking glances to measure the strength of his breathing, or just when it felt like I should turn on his Schubert or repeat a host of questions from which he could choose just one, or that I should dim the lights nearly to nothing and silently step out of the room, he would ask me to tell him again about the lion.

On his last day, it was unseasonably cold, and the men who usually came in and out to make his bed or gather his laundry or arrange the mail or deliver his Belgian chocolates must have been shuffling their schedules or preoccupied with others who were sick or elderly in other parts of town. His wife, as usual, was nowhere about.

When I returned from class, the old man was bent at the table alone in the low dark room that buckled beneath the world as though it had sunk to the very bottom.

I was silent. It was my final semester. I'd been living with the old man for nearly two years. I sat there with him and tried not to move at all.

"I've been remembering all of it," he said suddenly, loudly for one so close, as though he were a broad standing clock that had at last hit the hour. "It's all coming back."

"Tell me," I urged him.

"First, I should think," he said very slowly, the way he said all things, with great spaces of silence stretching in between, "you should speak again about the lion."

I drew out the childhood of the boy in great detail, lingering over the way the sun smote the tiles of the courtyard, the way the lion would turn over onto his back in the afternoons in the shade of the mopane tree, and how if one stepped beyond the walls one needed to watch for the long, curved sickles of acacia thorns. For as long as I could do it honestly, I deferred the ending. Finally I came to the part about the boy, grown up, leaving the great sprawling farmhouse in the south and climbing the first escarpment, gazing back down at the maize fields belonging to his family. I related yet again that with twin weights of sadness and longing in his heart, he turned to wander out toward the lion.

Throughout these moments the old man ticked soundlessly beside me, swaying slightly in his chair, nodding now and again with a calm I would never have believed, as if to encourage me. I admitted then for the first time what I hadn't told a soul, that the boy's father had assured him if he left on such a fool's errand—which he, the father, could explain to no one—if he threw himself at the world without so much as a knife at his belt, and if, of all things, he sought a lion that outsized him four and a half to one, then he was not welcome to return. It would be a final parting. He had no place in their lives.

And I could tell as I went on, stumbling at first and then gaining my courage, the old man had been patiently waiting for my story through the length of our long winter, and that after so many years of searching, and for the second time in my life, I was suddenly alone.

Heather Monley

Paddle to Canada

THE CHILDREN WERE TOO young to know the trick of counting seconds between lightning and thunder, but the parents did this in their heads, without speaking of it to each other. There had been families on shore when they'd set out in the boat, children playing in the grass, but now when the mother looked back, the last families were running toward their cars. The rain was getting harder, filling the boat's hollow places. Lightning flashed again, then again, and the mother and father each noted, without speaking of it, that the time between flash and boom had shortened. They pumped their legs faster, but the paddleboat wasn't built for speed. The mother's feet slipped off the wet pedals, and though the father held tight to the rudder, the boat kept turning to the left. In the back, the boy and girl, wanting to bail, splashed at the water with their hands and laughed. Their father yelled, "Stop that! Hold on to the boat."

A thunderclap boomed and the children put their hands to their ears and screamed. They were getting close to the dock now, but the lightning was coming fast, one flash then another, too fast for the mother and father to count. The children held tight and stared through the rain out the back of the boat. That's when they saw it: lightning strike a tree on the far side of the lake.

But the boat thudded against the dock, and the parents lifted the children and unsnapped their life jackets. There was no sign of the teenage boy who had rented them the boat, so the father tied the rope to a cleat, and they ran back to the car.

They waited for the storm to die down. They were soaked and shivering, and the father turned the heat as high as it would go. On the foggy windows, the children drew pictures: a sun wearing sunglasses, a dog with long, spindly legs.

It was not until the next day that the father remembered he'd left his driver's license as a deposit, and he drove back to retrieve it. The road curving through the park was littered with leaves and branches that had fallen in the storm. At the boathouse, the teenager was gone, replaced by an older man, the manager. The way the father had tied up the paddleboat, the man said, it was a wonder it didn't come loose and drift away. Because the family had neglected to sign out at the boathouse, there was no proof that they had returned the boat when they said they had. He should charge them for the full day, not just the hour they had already paid for. When the father asked him to consider the circumstances—the storm, the lightning, small children—the manager gave him a hard look and said they shouldn't have been out on the lake in that weather. But he opened a desk drawer and handed the father his license.

Because they had survived, it all became something to laugh about: the father pedaling so hard his face was red, the mother unable to keep up, and the boat turning in circles. The mother yelling to slow down, the father yelling to speed up, the kids splashing water in the back, the father yelling that they should stop splashing and hold on, because the last thing they needed was the kids to fall in the lake. Then, at the boathouse the next day, the angry manager—a bald man, their father said, with a patchy moustache—complaining they had left the life jackets in the boat where anyone could have stolen them, as if anyone would want a set of waterlogged life jackets scrawled with the name of the park in permanent ink.

Their father even laughed at the very idea the boat rental required a deposit. "What do they think we're going to do?" he said. "Paddle to Canada?"

For weeks, he had only to say, "Canada," and the children would dissolve into giggles, but they didn't understand. Their father saying "Paddle to Canada" made it possible. They imagined one lake connecting to another, like a paper chain, all the way to a vague northern border.

They were a family of risk and adventure—those were the types of stories they told of themselves. The time Jessie sprained her ankle on a hike and the father carried her three miles back to the trailhead. The day on the road trip when their car ran out of gas in the middle of the desert. The time Michael wandered off on the beach and no one noticed, and when they finally found him, two hours later, he wasn't afraid. He and another boy had been walking around the boardwalk, collecting change off the ground and in pay phones, and had found enough to buy themselves an ice-cream cone, which they traded turns licking.

The paddleboat was the family's favorite story: the time they almost died on the lake. They had pulled through and made it to shore—they were a family of survivors.

They pushed everything to the brink. The parents tickled the children, held them upside down, and teased them until their eyes filled with tears. The mother and father's fights were loud, with screaming and broken dishes, and the brother and sister, too, wailed at each other and inflicted bloody noses and bruised skin. The family told stories of packed suitcases and trips to the emergency room. They laughed, and this they believed was their strength—that they could make light of it all. And so they kept pushing, until they found an edge and toppled over.

After the divorce, the stories took on a different tone. "Your father took too many risks," their mother said, "and he wouldn't listen." Taking the kids on strenuous hikes, refusing to fill up the gas tank. That day in the desert, they had passed a gas station in a small town, but he had claimed there would be another town, another gas station, and they had driven on. On the beach, the mother had gotten back from the restroom and asked where Michael was. The father had shrugged—shrugged! "And if he hadn't been so cheap," she said, "he would have *bought* the kids ice-cream cones, and Michael wouldn't have run off in the first place."

He was always cheap. Complaining about the paddleboat deposit. Why shouldn't the boathouse take his license, when people like their father tried to get more than they paid for? If the storm hadn't come, he would have kept them out past the hour reserved, and then he would have argued and argued against the extra fee.

Their father had insisted on taking the family out on the lake, even though the sky was dark and cloudy, and he wouldn't turn back when it started to drizzle. "We could have been killed," their mother said, "but your father was determined."

The children didn't hear their father's side of things as often as they did their mother's. When he married his second wife, he moved to another state. He made offhand comments—"Your mother *would* say something like that"—but when the children grew into teenagers and sometimes believed they hated their mother, they wanted more. What would he say about the men their mother had dated, about her new husband, the stepfather they despised? What stories would he tell about the years when he and their mother were still married? Sometimes—when their stepfather yelled, when their mother said, "I've had it up to here"—they wanted their father to tell them that the fighting, the divorce, had really all been their mother's fault. They imagined how he would tell the paddleboat story: their mother hysterical, shrieking, and no help on the pedals. And then, when their father didn't call or he canceled a visit the day before, they believed he had been careless, that day in the boat, and had risked all their lives.

The lake was not far from the mother's house. The paddleboat rental had closed years before, but the dock was still there, and on hot days the girl walked to the end and dangled her feet in the water. The boy sat on a bare patch of shore and threw rocks out as far as he could. It seemed impossible now: the family together in a little boat. In itself, the story of the thunderstorm was small, but the family had told and retold it so many times that it loomed large, and it seemed important to know its essential truth. How had it really happened? Their memories had become muddled with what they had been told, and what they wanted to believe.

Jessie remembered, or thought she remembered, her father's hands under her arms, lifting her out of the boat, and the steamy car in the rain, and her and Michael's fingers tracing pictures on the glass. Michael remembered getting back to the house, and his mother in the living room holding him close and breathing in his wet hair. They turned these memories over and examined them, shuffled and rearranged them, as if thinking of them hard enough or in the right combination would lead somewhere, would form a pathway to a world that had been lost in the confusion of their lives. They remembered their small hands splashing water, and their father's voice, stern, and his eyes betraying fear. Their mother, in the front seat of the car, wrapping her arm around their father's, and leaning over to rest her head on his shoulder. And lightning, tonguing down to the upper branches of a tall tree, and the tree, for one brilliant flash, illuminated from within, and then dark, and breaking off into the lake.

Jai Chakrabarti

A Small Sacrifice for an Enormous Happiness

F ROM HIS BALCONY, NIKHIL waited and watched the street as hyacinth braiders tied floral knots, rum sellers hauled bags of ice, and the row of elderly typists, who'd seemed elderly to him since he'd been a boy, struck the last notes of their daily work. Beside him on the balcony, his servant, Kanu, plucked at the hair that grew from his ears.

"Keep a lookout for babu," Nikhil shouted to Kanu. "I'll check on the tea."

Kanu was so old he could neither see nor hear well, but he still accepted each responsibility with enthusiasm.

The tea was ready, as were the sweets, the whole conical pile of them—the base layer of pistachio mounds, the center almond bars that Nikhil had rolled by hand himself, and on the top three lychees from the garden, so precariously balanced, a single misstep would have upset their delectable geometry.

When he returned to the balcony, he saw Sharma walking up the cobbled lane, his oiled hair shining in the late-afternoon light. The typists greeted him with a verse from a Bollywood number—Sharma's boxer's jaw and darling eyes reminded the typists of an emerging movie star—and Sharma shook his head and laughed.

Kanu limped downstairs to let Sharma in, and Nikhil waited in the living room while the two of them made their way up.

"And what is the special occasion?" Sharma said, eyeing the pile of confections with a boyish grin.

Nikhil refused to say. He allowed Sharma to have his fill, watching with satisfaction as his fingers became honey-glazed from the offering.

Afterward, when they lay on the great divan—hand-carved and older than his mother's ghost—Nikhil breathed deeply to calm his heart. He feared the words would be eaten in his chest, but he'd been planning to tell Sharma for days, and there was no going back now. As evening settled, the air between them became heavy with the sweetness of secrecy, but secrecy had a short wick.

"My dearest, fairest boy," he said. "I want our love to increase."

Sharma raised his eyebrows, those lines thickly drawn, nearly fused. Who better than Sharma to know Nikhil's heart? Who but Sharma to take it all in stride?

"I desire to have a child with you," Nikhil said.

Nikhil had trouble reading Sharma's expression in the waning light, so he repeated himself. His fingers were shaking, but he took Sharma's hand anyway, gave it a squeeze.

"I heard you the first time," Sharma said.

A rare cool wind had prompted Nikhil to turn off the ceiling fan, and now he could hear the rum sellers on the street enunciating prices in singsong Urdu.

He touched Sharma's face, traced the line of his jaw, unsure still of how his lover had received his news. Likely, Sharma was still mulling—he formed his opinions, Nikhil believed, at the pace the street cows strolled.

Nikhil waited out the silence as long as he could. "Listen," he finally said. "The country is changing."

"A child diapered by two men," said Sharma. "Your country is changing faster than my country is changing. What about the boys from Kerala?"

They had learned about a schoolteacher and a postal clerk who'd secretly made a life together. Unfashionably attired and chubby cheeked, they seemed too dull for the news. A few months ago, locals threw acid on their faces. Even in the black-and-white of the photographs, their scars, along the jaw, the nose, the better half of a cheek. Ten years since man had landed on the moon, and still.

"We are not boys from Kerala. We are protected."

No ruse better than a woman in the home, Nikhil had argued over a year ago, and eventually Sharma had agreed to a marriage of convenience. Kanu, who had loved Nikhil through his childhood and even through his years of chasing prostitutes, had arranged for a village woman who knew about the two men's relationship but would never tell.

Nikhil rummaged through his *almirah* and returned with a gift in his hands. "You close your eyes now."

"Oh, Nikhil." But Sharma closed his eyes, accustomed now perhaps to receiving precious things.

Around Sharma's neck, Nikhil tied his dead mother's necklace. It had been dipped in twenty-four karats of gold by master artisans of Agra. Miniature busts of Queen Victoria decorated its circumference. A piece for the museums, a jeweler had once explained, but Nikhil wanted Sharma to have it. That morning, when he'd visited the family vault to retrieve it, he'd startled himself with the enormity of what he was giving away, but what better time than now, as they were about to begin a family?

"Promise you'll dream about a child with me."

"It is beautiful, and I will wear it every day, even though people will wonder what is that under my shirt."

"Let them wonder."

"You are entirely mad. Mad is what you are."

Nikhil was pulled back to the divan. Sharma, lifting Nikhil's shirt, placed a molasses square on his belly, teasing a trail of sweetness with his tongue.

Nikhil closed his eyes and allowed himself to be enjoyed. Down below, the rum sellers negotiated, the prices of bottles fluctuating wildly.

Afterward, they retired to the roof. Their chadors cut off the cold, but Nikhil still shivered. When Sharma asked what the matter was, Nikhil kissed the spot where his eyebrows met. There was another old roof across the street, where grandmothers were known to gossip and eavesdrop, but he did not care. Let them hear, he thought, let them feel this wind of enormous change.

The next morning, while Sharma washed, Nikhil said, "I want you to toss the idea to your wife. Get Tripti used to the matter."

Sharma dried himself so quickly he left behind footprints on the bathroom's marble floor. "Toss the idea to my wife. Get her used to the matter," Sharma said, before he changed into his working clothes, leaving Nikhil to brood alone.

Tripti would have few issues with the arrangement of a child, Nikhil believed. After all, at the time of her marriage to Sharma, her family was mired in bankruptcy, her father had left them nothing but a reputation for drink and dishonesty, and she herself—insofar as he recalled from his sole meeting with her, at the wedding—was a dour, spiritless creature who deserved little of the bounty that had been provided her. What little else he knew was from Kanu's reports. Extremely pliable, Kanu had first said. Then, closer to the wedding: a little stubborn about the choice of sweets. She wants village kind. On that note, Nikhil had wilted—let her have her desserts, he'd said, the wedding paid for, and the matter removed from mind.

The next few days, when Sharma was away at the village and at the foundry, Nikhil paced around the house, overcome by the idea of a child. He'd always dreamed of becoming a father but had never believed it would be his due until this year's monsoon, when, in the middle of a deluge, his forty-two-year-old sister had given birth to a girl. The rain had been so fierce no ambulance could ferry them to the hospital, so the elderly women of the family assumed the duties of midwifery and delivered the child themselves. The first moment he saw his niece he nearly believed in God and, strangely, in his own ability—his *right*—to produce so perfect a thing.

He couldn't bring Sharma to his sister's house to meet his new niece, so the next week he'd spent their Thursday together sharing photos; if Sharma experienced the same lightness of being, he didn't let it show. All Sharma said was, "Quite a healthy baby she is."

It was true. She'd been born nine pounds two ounces. The family had purchased a cow so that fresh milk would always be available.

Nikhil convinced himself that Sharma had opened his heart to the idea of fathering, but the exuberance of this conclusion led to certain practical questions. Sharma's wife would be the carrier of the child, but where would the child live? In Sharma's house in the village, or in Nikhil's house here in the city? If she lived in the village, which Nikhil admitted was the safer option, how would Nikhil father her, how would she receive a proper education?

These questions consumed the hours. When he went to check on his tenants, he was distracted and unable to focus on their concerns. A leaky toilet, a broken window, the group of vagrants who'd squatted outside one of his properties—all these matters seemed trivial compared to his imagined child's needs.

The next week, the afternoon before he would see Sharma again, he stepped into a clothing store on Rashbehari Avenue to calm his mind. It was a shop he'd frequented to purchase silk kurtas for Sharma or paisley shirts for himself. He told the attendants he needed an exceptional outfit for his niece. They combed the shelves and found a white dress with a lacy pink bow. He imagined his daughter wearing it. From his dreaming he was certain a girl would come out of their love—Shristi was what he'd named her—Shristi enunciating like a princess, Shristi riding her bicycle up and down Kakulia Lane.

Early on, they'd agreed Nikhil would avoid the foundry, but he was feeling so full of promise for Shristi that he did not deter himself from continuing down Rashbehari Avenue toward Tollygunge Phari, nor did he prevent himself from walking to the entrance of Mahesh Steel and asking for his *friend*.

Sharma emerged from the uneven music of metalworking with a cigarette between his lips. His Apollonian features were smeared with grease. His hands were constricted by thick welding gloves, which excluded the possibility of even an accidental touch. When he saw Nikhil, Sharma scowled. "Sir," he said, "you'll have the parts tomorrow."

Though he knew Sharma was treating him as a customer for good reason, the tone still stung. Nikhil whispered, "See what I have brought." He produced the perfect baby girl dress.

"You have lost your soup," Sharma whispered back. Then, so everyone could hear, "Babu, you'll have the parts tomorrow. Latest, tomorrow."

Nikhil tried again, "Do you see the collar, the sweet lace?"

"You should go to your home now," Sharma said. "Tomorrow, I'll see you."

But that Thursday Sharma failed to visit. Nikhil and Kanu waited until half past nine and then ate their meal together by lamplight.

Thursdays because it was on a Thursday that they had met three years ago, that time of year when the city is at its most bearable, when the smell of wild hyacinth cannot be outdone by the stench of the gutters, because it is after the city's short winter, which manages, despite its brevity, to birth more funerals than any other time of year. In the city's spring, two men walking the long road from Santiniketan back to Kolkata—because the bus has broken and no one is interested in its repair—are not entirely oblivious to the smells abounding in the wildflower fields, not oblivious at all to their own smells.

He supposed he had fetishized Sharma's smell from the beginning, that scent of a day's honest work. The smell of steel, of the cheapest soap. The smell of a shirt that had been laundered beyond its time. The smell of his night-bound stubble. He allowed his hand to linger on Sharma's wrist, pretending he was trying to see the hour. An hour before sunset. An hour after. He did not remember exactly when they parted. What did it matter?

What mattered were the coincidences of love. The day he saw Sharma for the second time he counted among the small miracles of his life.

Sharma was drinking tea at the tea stall on Kakulia Lane. He was leaning the weight of his body on the rotting wood of the counter, listening to the chai wallah recount stories. Later, he would learn that Sharma had landed a job at a nearby foundry and that this tea stall was simply the closest one, but in that moment he did not think of foundries or work or any other encumbrance, he thought instead of the way Sharma cradled his earthen teacup, as if it were the Koh-i-Noor.

Oh, he had said, did you and I . . . that broken bus . . . What an evening, yes?

A question that led to Thursdays. Two years of Thursdays haunted by fear of discovery, which led to a wedding, because a married man who arrived regularly at Kakulia Lane could not be doing anything but playing backgammon with his happenstance friend. What followed was a year of bliss. He considered this time their honeymoon. They were as seriously committed as any partners who'd ever shared a covenant, and shouldn't that show?

Sharma did visit the following Thursday, though the matter

of his absence the week before was not raised. Instead of their usual feast at home, they ate chili noodles doused with sugary tomato sauce at Jimmy's Chinese Kitchen, along with stale pastries for dessert. Sharma was wearing Nikhil's family necklace under his shirt, with just an edge of the queen's image peeking out from the collar. Seeing his gift on his lover's body released Nikhil from his brood, and for the first time that night, he met Sharma's gaze.

"You're cross with me," Sharma offered.

It wasn't an apology, but Nikhil was warming to the idea of a reconciliation.

"Anyway, Tripti and I have been discussing the issue of the baby."

Tripti and I. He so rarely heard the name Tripti from Sharma's lips, but that she could be in league with him, discussing an *issue*? Unjust was what it was.

"It's in part the physical act. We eat our meals together. We take walks to the bazaar or to the pond. But that, no, we do not do that."

"Don't worry," Nikhil said. "I shall do the deed. I shall be the child's father." While it was unpleasant to imagine the act of copulation itself, he'd studied the intricacies of the reproductive process and believed his chances were excellent for a single, well-timed session to yield its fruit.

"But you can barely stand the smell of a woman."

What passed over Sharma's face may have been described as amusement, but Nikhil refused to believe his lover wasn't taking him seriously—not now that he'd opened his heart like a salvaged piano. "Sharma," Nikhil said. "It shall be a small sacrifice for an enormous happiness."

"Oh, Nikhil, do you not see that we are already happy? Anything more might upset what we have. We should not tempt the gods."

Nikhil ground away at the pastry in his mouth until the

memory of sweetness dispersed. The things Sharma said. As if there were a cap on happiness in this world. It was Sharma's village religion talking again, but there was something more. He sensed in the way Sharma held his hands in his lap, the way he kept to the far side of the bed when they retired for the night, that Tripti had wormed something rotten into him. He was vulnerable that way, Sharma was.

When Nikhil awoke the next morning, Sharma had already departed, but in the bathroom, which he'd lovingly reconstructed from Parisian prints, with a claw-foot tub and a nearly functioning bidet, he found Sharma's stubble littering the marble sink. Sharma had always been fastidious in the house, taking care to wipe away evidence of his coming and going, and the patches of facial hair offended Nikhil. He studied their formations, searching for patterns. When nothing could be discerned, he called for Kanu to clean the mess.

Only one train went to Bilaspur, a commuter local. For two hours, Nikhil was stuck next to the village yeoman, who'd gone to the city to peddle his chickens and was clutching the feet of the aging pair he'd been unable to sell, and the bleary-eyed dairyman, who smelled of curd and urine. The only distraction was the girl with the henna-tinged hair who'd boarded between stops to plead for money, whose face looked entirely too much like the child he envisioned fathering.

When he reached the Bilaspur terminus, he was relieved to see the rows of wildflowers on either side of the tracks, to smell the bloom of begonias planted by the stationmaster's post.

It wasn't difficult finding Sharma's home. With money from the foundry and regular gifts of cash from Nikhil, Sharma had purchased several hectares of hilltop land and built a concrete slab of a house, garrisoned with a garden of squash, cucumber, and eggplant, and with large windows marking the combined living and dining area. Nikhil found the structure too modern, but that was Sharma's way—he had never swooned over the old colonials of Kakulia Lane.

From inside the house, Nikhil could hear the BBC broadcast, which was strange given Tripti didn't understand English. Nikhil tiptoed toward the open living-room window, and from there he spied. Sharma's wife was holding a book on her lap, mouthing back the words of the BBC announcer.

"BER-LIN WALL," she said. "DOWNING STREET."

She had a proud bookish nose—adequately sized for the resting of eyeglasses—a forehead that jutted too far forward, reminding Nikhil of a depiction of Neanderthal gatherers, and the slightest of chins, which gave to her appearance a quality of perpetual meekness. Her sari was stained with years of cooking. Her only adornments were the bright red bindi on her forehead and the brass bangles that made music whenever she turned a page.

There were certain topics Nikhil and Sharma had left to the wind, foremost the matter of Sharma's marriage. In the beginning, Nikhil experienced a shooting pain in his abdomen whenever he thought about Sharma and Tripti coexisting in domestic harmony, though over the past few months that pain had numbed; the less he'd thought of Tripti, the less she existed, but here she was now—the would-be mother of his child. He rapped on the grill of her window.

"Just leave it there," Tripti said without looking up from her book.

It was the first time she'd ever spoken to him. Her voice, which was composed of rich baritones, seemed rather forceful, and her demeanor, that of the lady of a proper house, left him feeling uncertain about his next move. At last, he said in a Bengali so refined it could have passed for the old tongue of Sanskrit, "Perhaps you've mistaken me for the bringer of milk. I am not he. Madam, you know me but you do not know me."

The words had sounded elegant in his head, but when spoken aloud he flushed at their foolishness.

She looked up to study his face, then his outfit, even his shoes now rimmed with the village's mud. "I know who you are," she finally said. "Why don't you come inside?"

He had not planned beyond this moment. He had allowed his feet to step onto the train at Howrah, imagined a brief meeting, a quick exchange at the doorstep, ending with a mutually desirable pact.

"I can't stay long," he said. Sharma would be home in another hour, and Nikhil had no wish to see Sharma in the same vicinity as his wife.

While he settled into the living room, Tripti puttered around the kitchen. The house was decorated with wood carvings and paintings of gods and goddesses. Parvati, the wife of Shiva, smiled beatifically from a gilded frame, and her son the remover of obstacles was frozen inside a copper statuette. From the plans Sharma had gloated over, he knew a hallway connected the three bedrooms of the house—one for Tripti, one for Sharma, and the last a prayer room—and he wondered now who slept where, how their mornings were arranged, what politics were discussed, what arguments were had, where the laundry was piled.

Tripti brought two cups of tea and a plate of sweets. "Homemade," she said. He'd been raised to fear milk sweets from unfamiliar places, but out of politeness, he took the first bite—a little lumpy, only mildly flavorful.

"Sharma is always praising your cooking," he said, but it was a lie. They never bothered to discuss Tripti's cooking; in fact, Nikhil had teased that they were lovers because of his talents in the kitchen. Still, it felt appropriate to compliment this woman, and he continued in this fashion, standing to admire the Parvati painting, which he described as "terribly and modernly artful."

"Nikhil Babu," she interrupted. "Are you here to discuss the matter of the child?"

He sighed with relief. Until that moment, he'd been unsure about how to broach the subject.

"You know," she said, "we discuss our days. We may not be lovers, but we are fair friends."

He experienced what felt like an arthritic pain in his shoulder, but it was only the collar of his jealousy. At least they were not *best* friends.

She pointed to the book on her coffee table, an English-language primer. "Unfortunately, it's just not on our horizon. You see, I'm going to university. I shall be a teacher."

"University," he said. "But you did not even finish eighth grade."

"That is true, but at Bilaspur College, the principal is willing to accept students who display enormous curiosities."

He found it improbable that she would be able to absorb the principles of higher learning, but he had no particular wish to impede her efforts. Education was a challenge he understood. "You want to improve yourself? Wonderful. If you are with child, I will have tutors come to you. Not professors from Bilaspur College. Real academics from the city."

But it was as if she had not heard him at all. She submerged a biscuit in her tea and stared out into the garden.

"Whose happiness are you after, Nikhil Babu?" she said. "Yours and yours only?"

He found himself grinding his teeth. The great bane of modernity. Though the country had opened itself to the pleasures of the other world—cream-filled pastries, the films of Godard, a penchant for pristine white-sand beaches—he did not care for the consequences, the dissolution of ordering traditions, with whose loss came poor speech, thoughtless conduct. A village woman addressing him without the slightest deference.

"Perhaps you should enroll in a school for proper manners," he said.

Tripti eased her teacup down. He followed the geometry of her sloping wrist, but there was no break of anger in her face.

"Listen," he said. But how could he explain that his want for a child had become rooted in his body, in the bones of his hands and the ridge of his knee, where just that afternoon the girl on the train who'd emerged from the rice fields to beg in the vestibules, whose outstretched palm he would normally loathe—there was no way to lift the country by satisfying beggars—had touched him. Had he not smiled back and touched her hair?

"If you're planning to catch the last train back," she said, "it's best you go now."

He chewed another of Tripti's lumpy sweets. When properly masticated, it would have the consistency to be spat and to land right between Tripti's eyes. But Tripti had turned away from him and resumed her studies. Soon he was all chewed out; he had to show himself out of the house.

By the time he reached the train station, the six o'clock was arriving at the platform. He squatted behind the begonias by the stationmaster's post and waited to see if Sharma was aboard. With the afternoon's disappointment, he felt he deserved to see Sharma's face, even if only covertly. See but remain unseen. In that moment, he could not have explained why he did not peek his head out of the tangle of flowers, though a glimmer of an idea came, something to do with the freedom of others—how, in this village of Sharma's birth, unknown and burdened, Nikhil could never be himself. Sweat pooled where his hairline had receded. How old the skin of his forehead felt to the touch.

As passengers began to disembark, those who were headed for the city clambered aboard. He looked at the faces passing by but did not see Sharma. The first warning bell sounded, then the second, and the stationmaster announced that the train was nearly city-bound.

He saw Sharma as the crowd was thinning out. He was walking with someone dressed in the atrocious nylon pants that were the fashion, and perhaps they were telling jokes, because Sharma was doubled over laughing. In all their evenings together, he couldn't recall seeing Sharma laugh with so little inhibition as now, so little concern about who would hear that joyous voice—who would think, What are those two doing? He watched Sharma walk along the dirt road toward his house, but it was an entirely different progress; he was stopping to inspect the rows of wildflowers on the path, to chat up the farmer who'd bellowed his name.

He kept watching Sharma's retreating form until he could see nothing but the faint shape of a man crossing the road. It was then he realized that the city-bound train, the last of the day, had left without him; he sprinted into the stationmaster's booth and phoned his house. It took several rings for Kanu to answer. "Yello?"

"Oh, Kanu," he said. "You must send a car. You must get me. I am at Bilaspur."

The connection was poor, but he could hear Kanu saying, "Babu? What is happening? What is wrong?"

There was no way to express how wounded the afternoon had left him, and he knew the odds of securing a car at this hour, so he yelled back into the phone, "Don't wait for me, Kanu. Make dinner, go to bed!"

He asked the stationmaster if there were any hotels in the village. A room just till the morning, he said. The stationmaster shrugged and pointed vaguely in the direction of the dirt road.

There were no hotels, he soon discovered. Either he would sleep underneath the stars or he would announce himself at Sharma's house to spend the night. He was certain he couldn't do the latter—what a loss of face that would be—but the former with its cold and its unknown night animals seemed nearly as terrifying.

He paced the town's only road until he grew hungry. Then he headed in the direction of Sharma's house, following a field where fireflies alighted on piles of ash. He had no wish to be discovered, but in the waning daylight that would soon turn into uninterrupted darkness, he felt as anonymous as any of the mosquitoes making dinner of his feet.

When he reached the entrance to Sharma's house, he could smell the evening's meal: lentil soup, rice softened with clarified butter. He could see the two of them together in the kitchen. Sharma was slicing cucumbers and Tripti was stirring a pot. The way Sharma's knife passed over the counter seemed like an act of magic. Such grace and precision. Soon, he knew the lentils and rice would be combined, a pair of onions diced, ginger infused into the stew, the table set, the meal consumed. He watched, waiting for the first word to be spoken, but they were silent partners, unified by the rhythm of their hands.

They moved into the dining room with their meal, and he crawled to the open kitchen window. Sharma had left his mother's necklace on the kitchen counter, next to the cheap china atop the stains of all meals past. What he was seeing couldn't be dismissed: Sharma had treated his greatest gift as if it were nothing more than a kitchen ornament. Nikhil's hand snaked through the window to recover the heirloom, and he knocked over a steel pan in the process.

Sharma rushed to the kitchen and began to yell, "Thief, stop," as if it were a mantra. Nikhil scurried down the hill, the necklace secure in his grip, and when he paused at the mouth of the town's only road and turned back, he thought he saw Sharma's hands in the window, making signs that reminded him of their first meeting, when in the darkness those dark fingers had beckoned. Nikhil almost called back, but too much distance lay between them. Whatever he said now wouldn't be heard.

Kate Cayley

The Bride and the Street Party

MARTHA REGARDED HERSELF SKEPTICALLY, and imagined skepticism from the other mothers at the table. She had too many children (four), and not for a discernable reason (religion, twins), she was too young (twenty-eight), she was disordered and apologetic. She made stuffed baby toys out of felt and organic wool, her breasts strained through old tank tops. Her blondness was suspect. It was not an alarming, seductive blondness. She was freckled and angular and snub-nosed. A child, pinkish, peddling a bike home from a violin lesson, earnest and a little sad. She did not convince.

Her breasts were leaking. Denton was probably carrying their crying youngest through their house, cursing lavishly.

"I know this is going to be a difficult one, but we need to talk to the family," Bronwyn was saying, raking one hand through her hair, "and ask them if they can route the car somewhere else or just have her walk to the car, that might be even better, if the car was on a different street. We've got the chalk drawing on their street. And the lemonade and bake sale. And one of the bands. And the craft table. They'll have to understand this is a community event. It's for the whole community. I'm sure they'll understand."

"But it's her *wedding*," Martha said plaintively, louder than she meant to. "It's a shame, isn't it? It's her wedding."

Bronwyn, Marley, and Alison looked at her expectantly, and she looked back at them over the table in Bronwyn's kitchen, and then down at her hands laid in front of her, limp and white among the mugs of tea, the lists and phones and plate of cookies. She should have used her evening better. She didn't even want to be on this committee. Outside, she could hear her son Noah and Bronwyn's son Max playing.

Martha had the watchful aggrieved boredom of mothers, but she smiled often as cover for her sleeplessness, and so was praised for cheerfulness. The women surrounding her, on or beside benches, in yards and community centers, at school pickups, on her street, calling greetings from the open windows of their cars, their open screen doors, appeared competent and discerning. They complained freely, and their complaints seemed more forceful and justified than her own. She had not put a hard-won career or artistic practice on hold in order to raise children. Her memory before the birth of Noah went as far as the first half of a degree in history. After: diapers, splatters of yogurt, little jars of fruit mush, tears, mysterious stains. The other women seemed to have had more time to consider the question of what they wanted, and they had refined and elaborated on that question, as a moral problem to be excavated and solved.

Her own problem was Noah, eight, loner, lonely, prone to abrupt rage. At first they said he was like his father, but Denton had a friendliness and self-assurance that made her shrug off the swearing, the jumpiness, and occasional door slamming. He was a big, jovial man, already losing his hair, and his whole back and his arms were blue-black with ink (Bronwyn had a few tasteful tattoos along her back and shoulders, delicate as leaf veins), and he roared his approval and disapproval. He was liked. She liked him. He liked himself.

Noah was different. A thin boy, taut as a tuned string, his blue eyes frantic, his hair sticking up in light brown tufts. He reminded Martha of a fledgling—something quivering and naked, perilously close to an edge. At six months old, he'd screamed if she tried to put him down, and yet being touched seemed to hurt him too. She'd dreaded changing him so much that she'd let sores fester along his bum and legs.

He was sly now. He said mean things, cried if another child stared too hard in the playground, hit children running past. There were meetings, conversations that altered course when Martha approached. She did not want to seem defensive; she could not defend. She lay in bed picturing the confusion of his wide-open eyes, often red-rimmed (he was a strong swimmer, and loved the nearby public pool, his clothes carrying a whiff of chlorine). He was not invited to the houses of classmates after school, or to birthday parties. Max was his one friend, a vigorous and noble busybody, like his mother. Like his mother, he wanted dependents. Martha watched as Noah bore patronage, came home in furtive sorrow that she, from experience, pretended not to see. She trembled for him, she loved him, but sometimes, as he passed by her with his head down, or looked away when she spoke, she imagined him kicking someone in the face, throwing a match into the rainbow slick of a gasoline spill, in front of a stranger's quiet, sleeping house.

Outside, the boys played.

"But it's her wedding," Martha said again, more loosely.

Before she had to say anything else, Max ran in with a nosebleed and Noah behind him, eager and fearful from the look of blood, and in the scuffle and tears and exclamations that took over the kitchen, the question of shame was left. The nosebleed had nothing to do with Noah, Max had fallen off his skateboard with Noah nowhere near him, and in her relief Martha forgot to bring the wedding up again. The meeting finished with Max sitting on Bronwyn's lap with ice on his neck, and Noah standing behind Martha's chair, gripping the back of it with both hands.

"I'll talk to the family," Bronwyn said to Martha in the hall. "I'm sure they'll understand." She waved as they all walked down the stairs.

"I feel like we live in a village," Bronwyn called to Martha, "don't you?"

Martha had never lived in a village, but she nodded, and envied Bronwyn her emphatic goodwill.

On the way home, Noah let her hold his hand, and the small victory buoyed her up enough that even walking in the door to Denton calling out, "Where the fuck have you been? All she wants is boob!" only made her laugh and kiss him hard so that he grinned at her, delighted as a child offered a present. Ella stopped crying, smothered into Martha's breast. And Noah was already climbing the stairs; she heard the water running as he brushed his teeth. It will be all right, she thought, and kissed Denton again. Maybe it will be all right.

It is all well meant, goodness knows. None of it is intended as hostility to the people who have lived in this part of Toronto since the seventies, who seem older than they are, who attend church, who wish to launch their granddaughter from the house in which she grew up, who have rented the shining white limousine to which she will descend, on the morning of her wedding, swaddled in synthetic lace, the groom only a willing accessory to her brash, temporary magnificence. The street festival has been carefully planned, and every effort has been made to include everyone, and these efforts have been made in good faith by the families who have organized it, families who have begun to buy the houses that the older people have sold, or that their children have sold after their deaths. They have moved into these small houses and they have made them beautiful according to their ideas of beauty, they have painted the walls in the friendly deep colors of Van Gogh paintings, they have exposed the red brick that was hidden under brown or yellow vinyl siding, they have laid new floors and built back decks. They have worked hard, and have a right to stake a claim, and the street festival, the chalk drawings and sidewalk sale and music and cookies and bubble machine, are part of that claim. They are good people, and few of them are rich, though they have the pliancy of some money, and may safely accumulate modest debt. Even though Martha and Denton bought their house through an estate sale, a leaking and rotting shell of a place, and Denton worked over every inch of it himself while they lived with his mother and Martha helplessly nursed Sam, the second of her babies, and felt sidelined and useless, the down payment came from her grandmother. She knows that, however uneasy it makes her, she falls on the side of the radiant houses, the vigorous, educated people, who don't clip coupons even though they are daunted by the price of groceries, and that these worlds, the world of those burnished floors and new kitchens, and the world of bleached sidewalks and tiles with pictures of the Holy Family, will not be entirely reconciled.

She looked out the skylight that Denton installed in their attic room, and listened to Denton's heavy breathing and Ella's soft whoosh, and thought of the wedding, and, on the floor below her, her three other children—Noah sleeping lightly or also awake, looking out the window, his heart beating like an old-fashioned watch.

"Mama! I want you!" (Sally, three, scooped up from the table with one arm while Martha reached for Sam with the other, his glass of milk teetering.)

"Mama! I spilled!" (The glass rolling on the floor, though not shattered.)

Denton left the house early, trying to finish a job installing cabinets, working for a friend who paid him in cash, then going to his other job, putting in windows and doors on the four tiny new houses down the street, squeezed onto one wide lot.

Martha counted to ten in her head, like Bronwyn recommended, watching the gray-white flow. When that wasn't enough, she turned away in time to see Noah lift Ella down from the changing table, swinging her around fast, her naked legs hunched against him.

"NOAH! STOP!"

"She's a superhero!"

"Sam, get a towel."

She resolved to be kind. Putting Sally down, she approached Noah.

"Give her to me, sweetie."

"She loves it!"

"She's not a toy."

"She's flying!"

"She'll pee on you!" Sam yelled from the kitchen doorway.

Noah dropped Ella. There was a moment of hush that Martha found riveting, as if everyone might, in that moment, agree to let whatever had happened pass unmarked, though no one ever did. Ella wailed, Martha screamed at Noah, Noah flung himself away from her, Sam gawked, Sally squealed.

She sat on the couch, nursing Ella, half-noticing that Sally and Sam had carefully spread three large clean towels over the spilled milk and left them there, seeping.

After collecting the late slips from the school office, after cursory pats and good-byes ("I love you!" she called anxiously after Noah, and he smiled his flinching smile, waved one raw pink hand), Martha walked along Dundas Street, a list of groceries in her head, Ella purring in her sleep, curved in the sling, her smooth forehead warm against Martha's chest.

Worming through the grocery list, the necessity of an evening meal, the towels she had left on the kitchen floor, was the sense she should say something to Bronwyn. She rehearsed speeches about the street party and the car that would take the bride to church. In her imaginary speeches she withdrew her offer of the craft table, she provoked a disagreement that resulted in the scuttling of Max and Noah's friendship, which she needed more than Bronwyn did, she took a principled position and became subtly worthier, she exiled herself from a society she already stood on the fringes of, and was left with no one to talk to, and all this happened in her head before she crossed the second light to the supermarket.

She'd stepped into the road when she saw the man on the bike. The bike was too small for him, and his addict-thin body was bent over it, his spine curled like a scythe. He wore a red bandana, track pants, a black windbreaker buttoned up to his scrawny throat. His eyes were red-veined blue, and the knuckles on both hands were bruised. He clutched the handlebars as he wove in and out of traffic at full speed toward her, his head held low, his face rigid with anger, ignoring, or maybe enjoying, the honks and panicked shouts as he swung into the path of the cars. She ran to the other side just in time, and turned back to see him hurtle out into the oncoming rush of the intersection. Cars swerved or stopped, he got through to the other side, shouting, and disappeared down a side street. By the time she kept walking, nothing had happened, except the rush of blood inside her at having seen his eyes.

Denton managed to come home early; Martha took Noah to the pool, leaving Denton in the playground with Ella sleeping in the stroller, Sally and Sam digging in the sand. She hoped Denton wouldn't smoke, another thing he did that made their family unwholesome, though she felt this reflected only on her, while

Denton, blowing expert rings over the back of the bench, reading a novel, carried off a rakishness that was forgivable.

She tried to swim beside Noah but he wanted to dive and splash, affronting a stately old man who plowed, puffing, through the deep end, so she lapped away, leaving Noah to his territory. The water flickered under the halogen lights, sound bounced off the walls as each person found an orbit, avoiding touch or speech. She loved the strange order of the swimmers, the way each person found a flare path, rarely colliding even while striking out apparently at random. It had the civility of eighteenth-century dances.

She floated on her back, thinking of the man on the bike. She'd looked at him and he'd looked back at her and sped up on his bike, toward her, toward her baby, his expression unchanging. He was willing to make her a casualty of his anger, making him inhuman or more than human ("Nietzsche!" Denton had yelled at her, years and years ago, waving *Beyond Good and Evil* in her face as she laughed, naked in his bed). She spun around in the water, watching Noah dive and hover at the bottom of the pool, fighting the buoyancy of his body, his fists clenched.

A row of Styrofoam heads were lined along the wall of the pool deck, used by the lifeguards in first-aid training. Faces perfectly smooth, pert flapper noses, cursory swirls of ear, and mouths forming sterile open circles, reminding her of the porcelain lip of a sink. One of the heads slumped sideways, its mouth caught over the ear of the one beside it, faintly obscene.

She pulled herself out of the water, shaking her head.

She should have sent a text first, but she didn't know what to say, so she walked over to Bronwyn's house in the dusk of the summer evening, pretending to herself that she was putting Ella to sleep, gripping the stroller as she eased it onto the curb, hoping she would find Bronwyn on her porch. The porch was empty. Steeling herself, she lifted Ella out and reached for the bell. Before she touched it, her phone rang.

"Come home right now."

They'd fought, they always fought, she thought, putting ice on the blue bulge on Noah's forehead. Denton had no malice in him, but his son baffled him. Denton was solid, Noah liquid. She should never leave them alone.

"I'm sorry."

"I know."

"I didn't think he'd—"

"I know."

A fight about homework: Denton had yelled, Noah had cried, Denton had yelled louder, and Noah had run up the stairs, with Denton in pursuit, Noah had run all the way to the top floor and, turning back first to see if Denton was watching him from the bottom of the stairs, he'd bashed his head into the brick of their exposed chimney.

"And he just came back downstairs like that, *bleeding*, and he *looked* at me—"

"You weren't listening!" Noah shrieked. "You never listen!"

"And I know I shouldn't yell—"

"Mama, it hurts—"

"I don't know what to do anymore—"

"We don't need to talk about this now," said Martha, in the voice she hated. A loving, brittle calm, the chime of maternal reassurance. She kissed Noah to the left of his bump. He received the kiss passively. The bump would be deep purple by morning.

It was eleven thirty, she wanted to go to sleep, and Denton was crying. He was failing, a failure of love or patience, a failure, he said, of sympathy, he was not the right father for this easily broken child; he cried. No one would have believed her, if she'd told anyone how Denton cried, and how easily afterward he let it go, how grateful he was for her permission, which allowed him to finally shrug, and laugh, and fall asleep before she did, one arm slung casually across her waist. Her own eyes were dry as sand. She turned away from him to Ella, who clawed lightly at the sheet, looking for milk.

"You came to my house?" Bronwyn asked the next day as they walked away from the school doors.

"You saw me?"

"Max said he saw you come up the steps."

"I got a call. Noah—you know."

Bronwyn touched her shoulder, nodding.

"Can we sit?" Martha asked.

They sat on a bench.

"Are you okay?" Bronwyn asked, her brow creased. "I mean, you seem—are you really okay?"

"I'm fine."

"Noah?"

"Noah's fine." She sounded angry, and then she felt angry. "I think we need to move all the stuff off that street," Martha said.

"What street?"

"The street where Zalia's wedding is."

"Zalia?"

"The bride."

"Oh—you mean—oh. No, Zalia's the grandmother. The bride is Ashley."

A short pause. If I were Bronwyn, Martha thought, I would make a joke, I would turn this into a joke and make us both laugh.

"I'm sorry. I've thought about this a lot. I think it isn't fair to make her walk to the car."

"Fair?"

"I know it's supposed to be for everyone, and it is, I know it is, I can see that, I agree with you, I agree, but it isn't really, I don't think it is, and I can't sleep, I think we need to move everything over, or I'm not going to do it, the craft table I mean, I can't, I just can't."

"I'm sorry you feel that way."

"I do. I do."

"It would be a loss."

Martha wanted to speak but couldn't. She wasn't going to cry, she wished she could, even if crying was the way women threw punches.

"But I talked to them," Bronwyn was saying. "I've already talked to them."

"When?"

"Yesterday. To Zalia."

"She doesn't speak English, I thought."

"I speak Portuguese. My mother was from Lisbon. Did I never say?"

Martha shook her head, mortification complete.

"I thought I did," Bronwyn said, tiny flicker of a smile. "Of course, the dialect is slightly different. They don't mind. Really, they don't. Anyway, no one's making her walk to the car. How did you get that idea? She'll just be picked up a little earlier, that's all. A scenic route to church."

Ella mercifully woke up, was lifted out, cooed over.

"I miss that age. You're lucky. All those babies."

"Yes."

"You shouldn't worry so much. You have so much to worry about. And it's all been settled. But if you'd rather not run the craft table—"

"No, no, of course—"

"Maybe that would be better anyway. You have so much on your plate."

"It's fine."

"I do wonder if it would be better. For the whole thing. If we didn't have it. I've been thinking. Maybe better to skip it? It's such a generous offer, but those things can be so messy."

"I don't mind."

"I think it might be a better choice not to have a craft table. Maybe next year. When you're less overstretched."

This was final, Martha could see. She got up. Bronwyn remained on the bench.

"We should really get the boys together. Maybe on the weekend?"

"That would be great."

"Saturday? No, wait, Max has a birthday party. Sunday morning?"

"Sunday morning."

She made herself walk home along a different route, past the controversial house. She thought of the bride, whose name was not Zalia. She could barely picture her. Whereas Bronwyn knew her grandmother, probably knew some of the details of her life. Am I like Noah, Martha thought, miscalculating the world? Seeing malevolence where there is none?

The stroller caught in a crack in the sidewalk, she stumbled and cursed as loudly as Denton would, and as she recovered herself she imagined, behind the curtains of the bungalow, a flicker of interest, a pair of peering eyes.

She put the ready squares of cotton for the craft table away, stuffed the finished animals into a bag in the back room, which was full of boxes and empty bottles and jars, mismatched things, postponed things. Her for-later room, when there was time.

And she'd still be young, when she found time to finish all her projects, to sort and divest. Bronwyn had been forty when Max was born, but Martha could get Ella launched on the school system and still be still-young. It was smug to feel that (she gave an oddly proportioned rabbit a punch, loosely knotted the bag), but smugness might need to be the thing that got her through.

She'd embroidered the animals with red and blue thread, and they had black beads for eyes. She'd kept them simple: these were models, to show the children how to do it. Another time. And she could always give them as Christmas presents, or new baby presents. They were sturdy and artless. Only, the beads were too black. It made them look watchful, the way real animals and birds were watchful. Cunning. She would snip them off and embroider complicated and beautiful eyes, friendly brown eyes, with fine lines of thread for lashes.

Bronwyn was right anyway, Martha thought, on the day of the festival. She could never have managed it. Sally had the flu and was home with Denton, watching a movie. It was too hot to fiddle with stuffing, guide small sweaty fingers. She had very little sympathy to spare when it was this hot. She would have spoken sharply to other people's children, been impatient at their disappointment, when the thing they'd imagined in their head and the thing they had made didn't match.

The streets were crowded and it was hard to push the stroller. She kept losing sight of Noah and Sam, briefly allowing herself to panic, then spotting a flash of familiar T-shirt, the back of a head. Swathes of the neighborhood were cordoned off; she saw Emily, Alison's younger daughter, gleefully leaping from the curb to the road and back. Martha was afraid of cars, and had made her children afraid (she was also afraid of strangers, highways, crosswalks, airplanes, and other, less tangible things), but the zest of Emily's jump, her manic eyes, felt sad to her. As if she, Alison, all of them, were raising a generation so obedient, so correct, that the smallest, most sanctioned deviation took on more weight than it could bear. There was a mythical kingdom, somewhere in her head, in which her children and the children she saw every day ran loose in open fields, built structures out of discarded wood and rusted nails, like the clips she sometimes watched on YouTube of rural communes in the seventies, in which grubby, jubilant children ripped up handfuls of dried grass beside their hoeing parents, or helped out in a makeshift dairy. She knew that those places had been full of infighting, that the food had run low, that many of those children had grown up eager to move to cities and assert their private and precious identity as best they could, insulating themselves with their houses and possessions. But there was something about the records of that time, before her own birth, that was luminous and tender, making her feel that she had cocooned and short-changed her own children through a failure of nerve. Maybe that would have saved Noah, she thought, catching sight of him standing alone, and then wondered why she thought he was already lost.

They ate fish and chips on the sidewalk before pushing their way on into the park. Bronwyn had made a dance for the end of the evening, working with volunteers, some professional dancers like herself, some not, and a choir made up of older people who liked to sing. It was growing dark when the audience gathered, sitting on the steep side of the hill looking down into the soccer field, and beyond that a parking lot.

The soccer field was edged with huge white paper lanterns. It was a still evening; they did not move in the wind. Noah sat on one side of Martha, Sam on the other, Ella slept. The waiting people grew quiet, the park grew darker. As the light emptied out, the lanterns seemed bigger, solemn. Music began: something instrumental, vaguely familiar, a blurred soft-industrial sound that pulsed and looped, and a row of white lights came on at the far side of the field, Christmas lights probably, or smaller versions of the paper lanterns.

When the lights came on Martha saw a row of people sitting on the pavement where the parking lot met the grass. It looked like forty or fifty people, sitting there, close to each other but not touching, men and women and children, all wearing pale shirts and gray pants or skirts and brown ties. They looked across the field at the audience, and they smiled, and seemed to be listening to the music. Then they stood and began walking slowly over the half-lit grass. The formation broke—some people came forward, some held back, some walked to one side while others continued straight ahead, a few people sat abruptly down on the ground. Martha snorted internally. But as she watched, the sheer size of the group overwhelmed her, and their deliberate movements, their hesitations and digressions, began to be beautiful. Closer, they lost the look of clones of one another, even though she didn't know who all of them were. Max was there, solid and formal, moving slightly out of step. Marley, holding her daughter's hand. Martha noticed the glint of gray in Marley's hair. She recognized more people, surprising people: the man who owned the convenience store, an older woman who lived alone on Martha's street and who was so hostile to the children that they called her a witch, but here she looked frail and sincere, walking in time to the music, looking out over the heads of the watchers.

The music stopped. The dancers kept moving over the grass. Then Martha saw the choir standing to one side by a big tree. They were dressed in the same uniform, but they were all old, standing a little stooped, deep lines in their faces like creases in dough. And they began to sing.

Do you realize that you have the most beautiful face?

Martha cried. Not much, no falling tears, just a few small pricks around her eyelids.

Do you realize that everyone you know someday will die?

She saw Bronwyn afterward, standing in a little knot of people. Her broad white face, her hair foaming over her bony shoulders. She was hugging one of the dancers, closing her eyes as she held the woman, and Martha saw she was crying benevolently, like it was nothing. Whatever it was in Bronwyn that she wanted to thank was not present in Bronwyn's face. She wanted to thank the dance itself, for being simple and ardent and making her feel loved and known, but that wasn't true of Bronwyn herself. Except it was. It must be.

She got up from the grass, she found her sons, she took them home.

When she saw Bronwyn next it was Monday, and both were worn down by the weekend, the long stretch of Sunday after the party. A spattering of confetti still clung to the church steps like dirty snow, but Martha had seen the grandmother going into her house with her groceries, bent with the weight of an ordinary weekday morning, in her flat, brown shoes. She wondered if Ashley had gone on a honeymoon, and tried to picture her, but could only imagine scratchy white lace, the swooping train of a cheap wedding dress.

Bronwyn hugged her.

"Come have a coffee."

Martha hesitated, and agreed.

They walked companionably toward the café, and Bronwyn did not mention the wedding, or the craft table, or the dance, and Martha was grateful. Noah had had one of his dreams again, in which something was chasing him. She and Denton called it The Crooked Man, and when he had this dream he screamed in his sleep and for a long time afterward, held between them like a bundle of sticks. She wondered if it dated from the nursery rhyme, read to him casually, years ago, before she realized how careful she had to be.

> *There was a crooked man*
> *And he walked a crooked mile*
> *He found a crooked sixpence*
> *Upon a crooked stile*
> *He bought a crooked cat*
> *Which caught a crooked mouse . . .*

This man staggered through Noah's mind and sometimes broke to the surface, grinning, reaching out thin arms.

"I really loved the dance."

"Thanks, thanks so much, that means a lot to me."

She is going to say something, Martha thought. When they reached the café, when they sat curling their hands around the mugs. Bronwyn would cut her out in some way. Cut Noah out.

Crossing the street, they both saw him. The young man on the bike, furiously threading his way through the cars. He was shouting something but so many horns were sounding that Martha couldn't hear what it was. She grabbed Bronwyn's arm to pull her back onto the pavement but before he reached them he darted into the oncoming lane and was hit by a white van. The man flew over the low handlebars, with his arms flung wide, describing an arc in the air, and as he flew Martha sensed the same hush she felt before she screamed at one of her children, a lull in which it might still be possible for his unhappy body not to meet the road.

Bronwyn ran forward and held his head as another driver got

out and dialed 911, and the man in the van stumbled onto the pavement, shaking.

"He came at me. He just came at me."

Martha found herself taking the man's arm, supporting him.

"Is he—is he dead?"

"No."

"He's dead."

"No. No, he's not."

"I killed him."

"No."

Blood ran over Bronwyn's lap.

"I fucking killed him."

"No. No."

Sirens, getting nearer, the intersection swarmed with paramedics. Martha couldn't see Bronwyn through the huddle of uniforms, and then Bronwyn was led away, someone was wiping her hands, covering her shoulders with a blanket.

Martha stayed beside the driver. He was gray under his stubble, his hands working together, his whole body trembling. It wasn't his fault, but he would think it was, if he were a decent man, even if it wasn't true. She'd rather be guilty and decent than convinced of her own innocence. The young man was lifted onto a stretcher and into an ambulance, which sped away. Maybe they would be able to save him, Martha thought. I can't. I can't.

Amit Majmudar

Secret Lives of the Detainees

1. Ansar al-Banna

ANSAR AL-BANNA WAS THE first prisoner to start scream-ing in his own cell, before anyone had touched him. His interviewers, for all their ingenuity, found themselves emptying flare guns into the pulsing sun of his pain. Ansar observed their efforts with mild irritation, barely interrupting the scream he'd brought with him. The Doberman gazed into the two-way mir-ror with its jaws puzzled shut, like an actor working with an uncooperative animal.

The base physician was summoned. A CT scan showed six kidney stones in each kidney, with one of them about an inch down Ansar's right ureter, tearing its slow way from his kidney to his bladder. Ansar had passed kidney stones before, jagged bits of quartz crystal that tinkled in the bowl, so the diagno-sis struck him as no miracle of Western medical science. Ansar knew this pain well, not that familiarity made the pain any friendlier. Every year or so, he peed blood and did something that felt like birthing a baby through his dick. Turmeric water didn't help, and neither did spinach: so much for his grandmother's remedies, picked up from a Hindu quack who used to live in Peshawar before the Partition. This was the old stone pain, all right, and even the USMC bullet he'd taken in his right thigh was no match for it. If stone pain hadn't desensitized him to bullet twinges, he wouldn't have kept firing back for as long as he had. When the time came to run, the leg had buckled.

Now there was a rod through that femur, placed in him at an American field hospital, an unwanted gift. It blazed white and gave off spiky rays on the CT scan, like a star embedded in his thigh. Ansar hated the American Army doctors. They worried about his welfare too much; unlike the uniformed officers, they shook hands with their translators; they numbed cuts before stitching them. Ansar had never been treated so kindly by other men in his life. White men, the old ones with silver, the young ones with light-brown hair. Their kindness interfered with his hating of them. He had to remind himself: they are saving you to pass you on. They are fixing you so there is something to break.

Ansar's interviewers were faced with a dilemma. They simply could not compete with the spike of calcium tearing through him. Their repertoire could trouble only the surface of his body. After some discussion, they did something counterintuitive: they treated his pain. A pump with a button delivered a short-acting opiate. They tamped his pain down to nothing, showed him the button that had done it, and waited while the opiate wore off and his pain returned.

You were part of Mansur Ikhwan's guard, they said. Tell us how he found out about the strike.

Seconds passed, and his pain resumed its insurgency. The pump and hovering thumb were waved before his face.

How did Ikhwan find out six minutes before the strike? Who called him with word?

No answer. His interviewers could not understand that Ansar had passed a half-centimeter basalt boulder last March. His penis had oozed blood for hours afterward, as if someone had stuck a pipe cleaner up there and scrubbed. Back then, he had bitten a sponge to keep from waking his mother and grandmother, who thought he worked at a factory "in the city" and had no idea he was shooting at Americans in Afghanistan. It was good to come home to them every eight months or so, and he didn't want them to remember his howling. Today he had hatred and residual Fentanyl to keep him quiet. Hatred brought beauty to his lips, and he started reciting under his breath. A small blood spot started dilating on his crotch.

His interviewer, shaking his head at the two-way mirror, snatched out the IV and fetched him a bucket. The tug of a drawstring dropped his pants. The bucket wasn't wired for electricity, but when his urine made its noisy spritz-dribble-spritz, he felt like he was peeing on an electric fence. The questions kept coming as his body began to shake uncontrollably, drops of urine and blood everywhere—the floor, even the walls. There were two interviewers in the room at this point, and Ansar strafed them without intending to. Their arms went up and they scrambled out of the room, overturning a tool kit and emerging cussing into the control room, their pants and boots and bare cheeks minutely dotted pink. The door was left open, and Ansar glimpsed a bank of screens and the two outraged interviewers slapping their pants and wiping their faces on their sleeves.

For the first time in two years, Ansar heard laughter. At least a dozen other interviewers were guffawing at their two bespattered colleagues. Ansar felt a cactus sprout out of his penis, and the culprit fleck landed in the bucket.

2. Marwan Malik

All of Marwan Malik could bear captivity, just not his hands. His hands fluttered at the ends of his arms like birds tied to stakes. The authorities thought they were being merciful by refraining from forced labor, but Marwan's hands would have treasured some calluses. Didn't the grounds have any rocks that needed breaking? Were there no salt mines on the whole island? Who was scrubbing their bathrooms? Marwan's hands would have reconciled themselves to crocheting American flags on a pattern. Anything that put them to use.

Back in his Lahore days, his hands had been industrious little spiders. They made Marwan the only john in the history of Lahore brothels who took the time, after he had finished, to bring the whore to climax. He never did this with his tongue—they were whores, after all—but his hands, one on top, the other inside, went into a deft, rhythmic routine that finished even the most jaded Saimas and Razias of the Shahi Mohalla. The whores were confused at first and could not figure out if he expected them to refund a portion of the fee. But Marwan's hands reciprocated of their own free will: they would not let the rest of him drop off to sleep until they, too, had finished something.

Because they loved tasks. Tasks were their food. How they had taken to shoelaces when, at age twenty-three, he bought his first pair of real shoes, and the shoe-store clerk had shown him how! Expensive shoes: hard to remember when such things had mattered. His hands did and undid and redid those shoelaces for an hour, marveling at this bow-tying that turned his feet into wrapped presents. His hands were perfectionists. When they had no tasks, they fiddled. Cigarettes: his hands demanded them, not his lungs. His hands took apart radios and fingered the components, learning weights and shapes until his hands could have reassembled the machine without looking.

What to do, what to do? His hands could not go twelve hours without waking up and throttling his sometimes less than eager penis. His hands started fixing wristwatches for friends, small appliances for strangers in apartments. Malik was good at this. A repair shop downtown tried to hire him and then, when he refused, started bad-mouthing his work—don't trust that fellow Malik, he isn't certified, works out of a shack, we're always fixing things he's stabbed and scratched with his Phillips screwdriver. It didn't matter. His hands were soon well known. They pursued everything with the ease of instinct and the conscience-blank curiosity of science. Can we do this? It was all one form of fidgeting or another. Toasters with wires that wouldn't glow anymore. Smartphones that needed jailbreaking. Bombs that needed timers. Whatever it was, the hands handled it.

In his solitary cell at the base, Marwan's hands slowly began to go mad. They crawled down to his penis every few hours, but his penis played dead until they left. They would then trek back north to pick his already picked-clean nose with a frenzy that left him bleeding. The blood would make his hands lay off for a while. When the little inside-the-nostril tears he gave himself scabbed over, he picked the scabs. His hands sought out the springs under his cot, tight parallel loops, just to feel something designed and machined. They read the rust pocks in the raw-metal frame like braille. At last, his hands attacked each other, one hand's fingers biting down on the back of the other. The camera saw Marwan wring his hands in what looked like despair. This was what the interviewers were waiting for, this moment when Marwan's hands turned on each other. The interviewers, in their control room, glanced at one another; one pressed a button and rose from his swivel chair. When the cell door hissed open and the light slapped him across the face, his hands rose by reflex, one palm in front of either eye, like prayer.

3. Nadeem Nadeem

Most of the men were there for good reason, though none of them were charged with anything in particular. There were

Yemeni schizophrenics who heard voices telling them to go to Afghanistan and kill the Americans. There was a Berlin cab-driver who attended a watched mosque and had no idea his every text message blinked up on a screen in Colorado. These men were there with cause, though not exactly "legally."

Not so Nadeem Nadeem. Nadeem Nadeem was an actor with Liverpool's Straw Man Burning Theatrical Company. Straw Man Burning put on plenty of Pinter, which could have been suspicious, but they stuck to the apolitical earlier stuff, not because they were cowards but because they had taste. They also put on Rod Furman's *Apachistan*, where Marines-versus-Afghans alternated with cowboys-versus-Apaches, scene by scene. There were monologues in that one about Power and Extermination. Nadeem Nadeem played Sharif Mohammed (in turban) and Running Foot (in feathered headdress). That production was politically charged.

The play they were putting on then, though, with an Arts Council England grant, was classical repertoire, was beyond reproach, was *Lear*. They reset it during the Thatcher era and cut eighty minutes off the text, but still, *Lear*. Their version wasn't just a hit; they got invited to present it at the Playwright's Theater in Chicago. There was NEA money involved, an international theater initiative of some sort, which meant free tickets for the troupe.

Nadeem Nadeem took his art seriously, so if he was playing Keith Lear, who had made his fortune in aeronautics, and was now, in his bearded old age, dividing his holdings among his three daughters, well, Keith Lear was going to have a Lear beard. Nadeem grew out his beard as soon as he won his campaign for the part against Peter Wilkins, who was, he argued, too skinny. By the time the troupe left for America, Nadeem Nadeem had a full beard that tickled his breastbone.

He was supposed to have left with them, on the same flight. The next two weeks of his life would have been very different had his mates been there to raise hell in his defense. But Nadeem Nadeem was in love with a needy, ethereally pale, easily hurt Finnish youth named Jussi, and Jussi wanted to spend the weekend together before his trip. So Nadeem drove down to Dudley, where Jussi shelved avocadoes at a co-op, and together they watched *Spider-Man 2* in the theater and slept in and ate eggs. So he left on Sunday instead of Friday. Allah punished him for those four orgasms—even though they were so mild that Nadeem, watching himself in the mirror, the bearded goatman tupping the golden androgyne, wondered whether he was, in fact, going to cheat on Jussi in Chicago. There would be opportunities. He would see.

At Heathrow, Nadeem Nadeem the actor discovered he shared a name with Nadeem Nadeem the international terrorist. Fortunately, he looked nothing like the photograph on file for Nadeem Nadeem. Under his beard, that is. Because *that* Nadeem Nadeem took Islam as seriously as *this* Nadeem Nadeem took method acting.

An understandable mix-up, gentlemen, said Nadeem Nadeem with thespian flair. Simply fetch me a razor, and I shall save us all a great deal of time. I prefer the Schick Quattro with the ProGlide strip, but anything you've seized from the security queue will do.

This attempt to procure a sharp object did not go undocumented. Nor did Nadeem Nadeem's name, which was a 100 percent match with that of Nadeem Nadeem. The more English he spoke, the more it seemed the devil quoted scripture to his purpose. They put him to sleep and flew him thousands of miles in the wrong direction. He awoke in a cell and walked his hands across the walls, the actor reduced to mime.

During his interviews, though, Nadeem Nadeem performed. He performed like one of those frill-necked lizards that discourage predators by opening their mouths wide and splaying a very

Elizabethan ruff. Mamet and Pinter, one terse, one surly silent, would not serve, only the bedlam Bard at his most superflux-shaking. Mad scenes poured out of Nadeem, his own lines and Poor Tom's as well, and at his wildest he turned to the two-way mirror and shouted *Rive your concealing continents, and cry These dreadful summoners grace*, wept *I am a man More sinn'd against than sinning*. Far away, in another time zone, Peter Wilkins, knock-kneed in a stage beard, delivered the same lines with just as much passion, only feigned for art's sake, not to save his life. Yet the applause that met his performance was greater. Nadeem got no reaction but silence from his interviewer. So he divided his kingdom once again; once again he reproached Goneril, bantered with the Fool, and ended up back on the heath. This time—*Blow, winds, and crack your cheeks!*—Nadeem ripped the beard off his face, fistfuls of straggly black hair, the skin pig pink and the pores oozing, five full fistfuls until his face was his own.

The system, as it turned out, was not completely broken. Nadeem got an apology and a knockout pill, and soon the lost man found himself in London, his face smelling of Old Spice and his passport in his pocket. The troupe was still in Chicago, but he had stopped caring about theater or even Jussi. Nadeem Nadeem began calling lawyers and a journalist from *The Guardian* who wrote about this kind of thing. America, it turned out, was very hard to sue. But he did get a five-hundred-word story about his mistaken-identity "ordeal" and a photograph. That led to a radio segment, seven whole minutes during which he talked about how he had been illegally detained for two weeks in an American prison he still didn't know the location of. A student organization at Leeds University called him to give a talk, even gave him bus money and a free dinner. Nadeem wondered whether he might write a book about his experience. If only he had been tortured—he was always having to answer with the pregnant phrase *Not physically* when asked that. Perhaps he should make it a novel? Someone left a death threat on his voice mail; he was elated. How dangerous-endangered he had become, how very Rushdie!

All of a sudden, though, the media lost interest, and so did the Muslim haters. Nadeem found himself selling cold product. Richer stories—stories with actual torture scenes—trumped a story of what was essentially a mix-up. Meanwhile, in his social circle, his two weeks in American custody became his identity. Backstage, at art showings, at book-launch parties, getting coffee with new people, it was how he was introduced and what he was expected to talk about. The liberal-arts majors in thick-rimmed spectacles, the messy-haired poet-activists, the friends of friends all wanted to know if he had been tortured.

Not physically, he said; and then, more quietly, for effect: Not . . . *physically.*

4. Tawhid Khan

Tawhid Khan readied his couplets overnight and held them in his mouth like smoke. He had no way to etch them anymore. An Action Team had seized his stash of Styrofoam-cup shreds and pared his fingernails past the cuticle. Interviews, he knew, were recorded, transcribed, reproduced, studied, interpreted. So when the hose was removed from his mouth, he would scream

The mare's broken. Let her gnaw the bit.
It's only to work the leather soft.

And then he would go quiet. The question would be put to him again, and he would present another couplet from a different poem. So, two or three couplets later, when he screamed

Why do you smile, Qaidi, while you sleep?
This lump on my head's a pillow, feather-soft,

no one recognized the distinctive bone structure of the ghazal. The transcript was lineated as prose, the rhyme-refrains lay scattered, and the analysts—usually poli-sci majors who had learned the language to increase their marketability (much as they used to learn Russian and now were learning Chinese)—had little feel for the conventions of Urdu poetry.

Qaidi, "prisoner," had been Tawhid's pen name even before his imprisonment. But it led to speculation about who Qaidi was and whether Qaidi was still active. The analysts flagged the name after a few sessions and directed the questioning. Who's Qaidi, the interviewers demanded. Tell us who Qaidi is, When were you put in contact with Qaidi, Where did you last see Qaidi, What is Qaidi's full name, Is Qaidi in contact with al-Jabbari, Is Qaidi a code name, How did you communicate with Qaidi? Tawhid, on his next interview, gave a clear answer.

You put me in prison. Why ask me *Who's Qaidi?*
I'm both the true Oneness and the one true Qaidi.

This was no riddle. *Tawhid* meant Oneness—of God, but also of poet and pen name. Tawhid's father had been a famous preacher, something that had worked against his case from the beginning. So the next time they interviewed him, he gave them couplet after couplet with the refrain of *Qaidi* because they struck him across the jaw whenever he offered any verses, however well-turned, that did not end that way. And when he shouted his final couplet, they still weren't satisfied, so, realizing they would keep at him unless he delivered Qaidi, he extemporized couplets on the same rhyme and refrain. Twenty, twenty-three, twenty-five couplets: his questioners felt they were close to Qaidi, on the verge of some revelation about Qaidi that might lead to a cascade of arrests, if only they could get Taw-hid to talk about Qaidi instead of mynahs, mirrors, grandfather clocks, doors opening onto gardens, Layla's eyes, train whistles, blue kites with yellow streamers, envelopes sealed but never addressed, cigarettes, cats, streets, waterfalls, and the armies of Sikander. Tawhid would have kept going. Urdu ran out of rhymes. Besides, he could not bring himself to mar his form. This ghazal's marathon twenty-six couplets, he knew, would be his crowning work, preserved and parsed; Qaidi would live on, even if only in the imagination of his enemies. Hadn't it been his aim, since his boyhood, to be outlived by his verses?

So he went silent under the questions and blows. The Dober-man was brought in and led away, and the man with the monkey wrench, and the man with the pork. Tawhid Khan had been set free of fear. When his wrists were untied, his body spilled itself off the chair and pooled at his interviewer's feet. The interviewer knelt, saying *Shit* and *Don't you dare* as he loosened the draw-string of the hood and revealed a swollen face, its eyes rolled all the way back, the poet secure in his immortality.

Lesley Nneka Arimah
Glory

WHEN GLORY'S PARENTS CHRISTENED her Glorybe-togod Ngozi Akunyili, they did not foresee Facebook's "real name" policy, nor the weeks she would spend populating forms and submitting copies of her bills and driver's license and the certificate that documented her birth on September 9, 1986, a rainy Tuesday, at 6:45 P.M., after six hours of labor and six years of barrenness. Pinning on her every hope they had yet to realize, her parents imagined the type of life that well-situated Igbos imagined for their children. She would be a smart girl with the best schooling. She would attend church regularly and never stray from the Word (amen!). She would learn to cook like her grandmother, her father added, to which her mother countered, "Why not like her mother?" and Glorybetogod's father hemmed and hawed till his wife said maybe he should go and eat at his mother's house. But back to Glorybetogod, whom everyone called Glory except her grandfather, who called her "that girl" the first time he saw her.

"That girl has something rotten in her, her chi is not well."

Husband pulled wife out of the room to prevent a brawl ("I don't care how old that drunk is, I will fix his mouth today") and begged his father to accept his firstborn grandchild. He didn't see, as the grandfather did, the caul of misfortune covering Glory's face, which would affect every decision she made, causing her to err on the side of wrong, time and time again. When Glory was five, she decided after much consideration to stick her finger into the maw of a sleeping dog. At seven, shortly after her family relocated to the United States, Glory thought it a good idea to walk home when her mother was five minutes late picking her up from school, a decision that saw her lost and sobbing in a Piggly Wiggly parking lot before night fell. She did a lot of things out of spite, the source of which she couldn't identify—as if she'd been born resenting the world.

That's how, much to her parents' embarrassment, their Glory was nearing thirty, chronically single, and working at a call center in downtown Minneapolis. She fielded calls from disgruntled home owners on the brink of foreclosure, reading from a script that was intricate and logical and written by people who had never before spoken on the phone to a human being. In all their calculations about her future, Glory's parents had never imagined that on April 16, 2013, at 5:17 P.M., Glory would receive another email refusing to restore her Facebook page. Nor could they have conceived that Glory would be the sort of person for whom this misfortune would set rolling an avalanche of misery, which led her to contemplate taking her life.

She called her mother, hoping to be talked out of it, but got her voice mail and then a text saying, "What is it now?" (Glory knew better than to respond.) A call to her father would yield a cooler response, and so she spent her evening on the edge of her bed, neck itching like crazy, contemplating how a bottle of Moscato and thirty gel-filled sleeping pills would go together. The note she wrote read:

I was born under an unlucky star and my destiny has caught up with me. I'm sorry Mummy and Daddy that I didn't com-

*plete law school and become the person you'd hoped. But it was
also your fault for putting so much pressure on me. Good-bye.*

All of this was true, and not. She was unlucky, yes, but it
was less Fate and more her terrible decision making and lazi-
ness that saw her flunk out of college, along with her propensity
for arguing with professors and storming out, never to return.
She eventually graduated with a shameful G.P.A. Then came
law school, to which she gained entrance through a favor of a
friend of a friend of her father's, thinking that her argumentative tendencies could be put to good use. But she managed to
screw that up too, choosing naps instead of class, happy hours
instead of studying. She was unable to do right, no matter how
small the choice. These foolish little decisions incremented into
probation, then a polite request to leave, followed by an impolite
request to leave after she staged a protest in the dean's office.

It was also true that her parents put pressure on her. Yet theirs
was the sort of hopeful pressure that would have encouraged a
better person.

Glory fell asleep after a glass and a half of wine and woke to
find the pills a melted, bitter mass in her fist. In the morning
light, her melodramatic note mortified her, and she tore it up
and flushed it down the toilet. At work, avoiding the glare of her
supervisor and the finger he pointed at the clock, she switched
on her headphones to receive the first call: Mrs. Dumfries. Her
husband had died and she had no clue where any paperwork
was. Could Glory help her keep her house? Glory read from her
script, avoiding the "no" she was never allowed to utter. Then
there was Glen, who was actually Greg, who was also Peter, who
called every day at least four or five times and tried to trick the
customer service reps into promises they couldn't keep. Little
did he know that even if Glory promised him his childhood

home, complete with all the antiques that had gone missing after the foreclosure, she would only be fired and he would be stuck in the same two-bedroom apartment with his kids. All day the calls came in, and Glory had to say no without saying "no," and the linguistic acrobatics required to evade this simple answer wore away her nerves.

At lunch, she ate one of the burritos that came three for a dollar at the discount grocery store and a nice-looking sandwich that belonged to one of her coworkers, and checked her email again. Even though her Facebook account hadn't yet been restored, she walked by the lobby of the advertising agency that dominated the top two floors of the building. Before she reached the glass doors, she paused by the wall to the right, on which the agency had mounted the logos of the companies it represented. She took a photo of herself in front of the logo of the jewelry megachain. When her Facebook page was restored, she would post the picture, with the caption: "Worked on my favorite account today. The best part is the free samples!"

Then her cousin in Port Harcourt would like her post, and another friend would confess her envy, and others still would say how (OMG!) she was *sooo* lucky. And for a moment, she would live the sort of life her parents imagined for her those many, many years ago.

After her lunch break, she sank back into her seat and was about to switch her headset on when he walked in. Glory knew he was Nigerian right away by his gait. And when he spoke, a friendly greeting as he shook her supervisor's hand, her guess was confirmed. He wore a suit, slightly ill-fitting, but his shoulders made up for it. He joined a group of trainees across the room.

He had an air of competence that she found irritating, reading from the script as though he had memorized it and managing to make it sound compassionate and genuine. At one point, he noticed her staring, and every time she looked at him after that, he was looking at her, too.

She culled bits and pieces of him over the rest of the day, eavesdropped on impressed supervisors who sang his praises. He was getting an M.B.A. at the U. He had grown up in Nigeria but visited his uncle in Atlanta every summer. After his M.B.A., he was going to attend law school. His parents were both doctors.

Glory knew what he was doing, because she did it as well: sharing too many details of her life with these strangers, signaling why she didn't belong here, earning $13.50 an hour. She was something better than a "customer service representative"—everyone should know that this title was only temporary. Except in his case, it was all true.

He smiled at her when she was leaving, a smile so sure of reciprocation that Glory wanted to flip him off. But the home training that lingered caused her to avert her eyes instead and hurry to catch the bus.

Her phone dinged. "Why did you call me, do you need money again?" A text from her mother. *No*, she wanted to respond, *I'm doing fine*, but she didn't. After a week, her mother might send $500 and say this was the last time and she'd better not tell her father. Glory would use the money to complete her rent or buy new shoes, or squirrel it away to be nibbled bit by bit—candy here, takeout there—till it disappeared.

Then, when her mother couldn't restrain herself anymore, Glory would receive a stern, long-winded lecture via email about how she wouldn't have to worry about such things if she were married, and why didn't she let her father introduce her to some of the young men at his work? And Glory would delete it, and cry, and retrace all the missteps that had led her to this particular place. She knew her birth story, and what her grandfather had said, but it never made a difference when the time came to make the right choice. She was always drawn to the wrong one, like a dog curious to taste its own vomit.

· · ·

The next day, Glory arrived at work to see the man sitting in the empty spot next to hers.

"Good morning."

"Hi."

"My name is Thomas. They told me you are also from Nigeria? You don't sound it."

"I've been here since I was six. I hope you don't think I should have kept my accent that long."

He flinched at her rudeness, but pressed on.

"I don't know many Nigerians here. Maybe you can introduce me?"

Glory considered the handful of women she knew who would *love* to be introduced to this guy, still green and fresh. But they saw little of her real life, thought Glory an ad exec with a fabulous living, and any introductions would jeopardize that.

"Sorry, I don't really know anyone, either. You should try talking to someone with real friends."

He laughed, thinking she was joking, and his misunderstanding loosened her tongue. It was nice to talk to someone new who had no expectations of her.

"So, why are you slumming it here with the rest of us? Shouldn't you be interning somewhere fabulous?"

"This is my internship. I actually work in corporate, but thought I should get a better understanding of what happens in the trenches."

"Wait, you're here voluntarily? Are you crazy?"

He laughed again.

"No, it's just . . . You wouldn't understand."

"I'm not stupid," Glory said, thinking he thought that of her. "So fuck you."

She ignored his "Whoa, where did that come from?" and switched on her headset, turning her dial to the busiest queue. The calls came in one after the other, leaving Thomas little chance to apologize if he wanted to.

An hour later, he pressed a note into Glory's palm. *I'm sorry,* it read. *Can I treat you to lunch?*

Her pride said no, but her stomach, last filled with the sandwich she had stolen yesterday afternoon, begged a yes.

She snatched up his pen. *I guess.*

"Mom, I'm seeing someone." Glory typed and deleted that sentence over and over, never sending it. Her mother would call for sure, and then she'd dissect every description of Thomas till he was flayed to her satisfaction. Her father would ask to hear the "young man's intentions" and the cloying quality of their attention would ruin it.

Thomas would delight them. He went to church every Sunday—though he'd learned to stop inviting her—and he had the bright sort of future that was every parent's dream. He prayed over his meals, before he went to bed, when he woke up. He prayed for her.

Glory despised him. She hated the sheen of accomplishment he wore, so dulled on her. She hated his frugal management of money. She hated that when she pressed him for sex, he demurred, saying that they should wait till they were more serious.

Glory couldn't get enough of him. She loved that he watched Cartoon Network with the glee of a teenager; loved that he could move through a crowd of strangers and emerge on the other side with friends. He didn't seem to mind her coarseness, how her bad luck had deepened her bitterness so that she wished even the best of people ill. He didn't seem to mind how joy had become a finite meal she begrudged seeing anyone but herself consume.

She wanted to ask him what he saw in her, but was afraid the answer would be qualities she knew to be an illusion.

They talked of Nigeria often, or at least he did, telling her about growing up in Onitsha and how he wanted to move back someday. He said "we" and "us" like it was understood that she would go back with him, and she began to savor a future she had never imagined for herself.

She'd been to Nigeria many times, but it was the one thing she kept from him, enjoying, then loathing, then enjoying how excited he was to explain the country to her. He didn't know that what little money she scraped together was spent on a plane ticket to Nigeria every thirteen months, or that over the past few years, she had arrived the day after her grandmother's death, then the day after her great-aunt's death, and then her uncle's, so that her grandfather asked her to let him know when she booked her ticket, so that he could prepare to die. Thomas still didn't know she was unlucky.

She kept it secret to dissuade any probing, not yet aware that people like Thomas were never suspicious, as trusting of the world's goodness as children born to wealth. When she visited her grandfather, with whom she had negotiated a relative peace, they sat together in his room watching TV, Glory getting up only to fetch food or drink for them. Nobody knew why she made the trips as often as she did, or why she eschewed the bustle of Lagos for his sleepy village. She couldn't explain that her grandfather knew her, saw her for what she was—a black hole that compressed and eliminated fortune and joy and happiness—and still opened his home to her, gave her a room and a bed, the mattress so old the underside bore stains from when her mother's water broke.

Near the end of her last stay, their conversation had migrated to her fate.

"There is only disaster in your future if you do not please the gods."

The older she got, the more she felt the truth of it: the deep inhalation her life had been so far, to prepare her for the explosive exhalation that would eventually flatten her.

"Papa, you know I don't have it in me to win anyone's favor, let alone the gods'."

They were both dressed in shorts and singlets, the voltage of the generator being too low to carry anything that cooled. Glory sat on the floor, moving every half hour to relish the chill of the tiles. Her grandfather lounged on the bed.

When he began one of his fables, she closed her eyes.

"A porcupine and a tortoise came to a crossroads, where a spirit appeared before them. 'Carry me to the heart of the river and let me drink,' the spirit said. Neither wanted to be saddled with the spirit, but they could not deny it with no good reason.

"'I am slow,' said the tortoise, 'it will take us many years to reach it.'

"'I am prickly,' said the porcupine, 'the journey will be too painful.'

"The spirit raged.

"'If you don't get me to the heart of the river by nightfall and give me a cup to drink, I will extinguish every creature of your kind.'

"The tortoise and the porcupine conferred. 'What if you carry me,' said the tortoise, 'while I carry the spirit? We will surely make it by nightfall.'

"'I have a better idea,' said the porcupine. 'These are no ordinary quills on my back. They are magic quills capable of granting any wish. The only condition is that you must close your eyes and open them only after your wish is granted.'

"The tortoise and the spirit each plucked a quill, eager for desires out of reach. They closed their eyes. That's when the porcupine snatched the quill from the tortoise and jammed it into the flesh of his throat. He filled the spirit's hands with blood, which it drank, thinking the gurgling it heard to be that of the river. But spirits know the taste of blood, and this one lashed out at the porcupine, only to find that it could move no faster than a tortoise. The porcupine continued on his way."

Her grandfather's long pause signaled the end.

"Are you hearing me?"

"Yes, but what does it mean?"

"If you can't please the gods, trick them."

The time with her grandfather had eased the pressure building in her, but then she came back stateside to another stream of catastrophes. Keys left on the plane. An accident in which her foot slipped on the pedal made smooth by the car insurance check she had forgotten to mail. A job lost for lack of transportation, which is how she ended up disappointing former home owners in the petri dish of a large call center.

Thomas, on the other hand, was a lucky man. He always seemed to find money lying around in the street, although never so large an amount as to induce alarm or guilt. He got what he wanted, always, and attributed it to ingenuity and perseverance, unaware of the halo of fortune resting on his head. When she had him write the request to restore her Facebook page, it was back up in a day. He would have been appalled to know that she sometimes followed him when they parted ways after work, watching with fascination as he drew amity from everyone who came close.

Some of that luck rubbed off on her, and she found herself receiving invitations to long-standing events she hadn't even known existed. Igbo Women's Fellowship of the Midwest. Daughters of Biafra, Minnesota Chapter. Party, Party, a monthly event rotated among different homes. Sometimes, as she watched Thomas charm a crowd with little effort, she wondered how it was that one person could be so blessed and another not. They had been born in the same state to parents of similar means and faith. Even taking into account the rewards of his maleness, it seemed to Glory that they should have been in the same place. She began to think of his luck as something that had been taken from her, and viewed this relationship as a way to even her odds.

At last they were serious enough for Thomas, and the sex was, not mediocre exactly, but just good—not the mind-blowing experience she had expected it to be. Thomas was moved, and thanked her for trusting him, and she said "You're welcome" in that cutesy, girlish way she knew he would like, even though what she really wanted was for him to not be such a gentleman and fuck her silly.

But the more he said "us" and "we," the less quickly she deleted that "Mom, I'm seeing someone" text. One day, instead of sending it, she posted a picture of her and Thomas on her Facebook wall, setting off a sequence that involved her Port Harcourt cousin calling another cousin who called another and so on and so forth, until the news got to her mother, who called her right away. It took thirty-seven minutes.

Glory waited till just before the call went to voice mail to pick up.

"Hello?"

"Who is he? Praise God! What is his name?"

"Thomas Okongwu."

Her mother started praising God again. Glory couldn't help but laugh. It had been years since any news she delivered over the phone had given her mother cause for joy, and she felt a blush of gratitude. She told her mother about Thomas and his ambitions, getting more animated as her mother got more excited. She ignored the occasional hint of disbelief on the other end of the line, as if her mother couldn't quite believe her daughter had gotten something right.

After that, it was like *everything* she did was right. Her job, long pilloried, was now a good thing. No career, her father said, meant that she could fully concentrate on her children when they came along. That she was terrible at managing money became a nonissue. You see, she had picked the perfect man to make up for her weaknesses. Kind where she was not, frugal where she was not. Successful.

Glory stared at her father's email, meant to comfort but instead bringing to mind the wine and pills and what they could do to a body. She moved it to a folder she had long ago titled EVIDENCE, meant to make the case if she chose to never speak to her father again.

When Thomas asked if she'd like to meet his mother, who was free to travel as his father was not, Glory knew the right answer and gave it. But she panicked at having to impress this woman. Her parents had been easy. Thomas was impressive. She was not.

"Why do you want me to meet her?" The question was a bit coy, but Glory wanted some reassurance to hold on to.

Thomas shrugged.

"She asked to meet you."

"So, you didn't ask her if she wanted to meet me?"

After a patient rolling of eyes, Thomas gripped her shoulders and shook her with gentle exasperation.

"You're always doing this. Of course I want you to meet her and of course she wants to meet you. You're all she ever talks about now, look."

Thomas dialed his cell phone, and after a pause, he said, "Hey, Mum, she's right here. I'll let you talk, but don't go scaring her off."

Glory heard the woman laugh on the line and say something that made her son laugh too. Then the warm phone was pressed to her ear, and a voice just shy of being too deep for a woman greeted her.

Glory tried to say all the right things about herself and her family, which meant not saying much about herself. She wanted this woman to like her, and, even beyond that, to admire her, something she wasn't sure she could accomplish without lies. She had already pretended to quit her advertising job on her Facebook wall—a "sad day indeed," an old college friend had said, worded so that Glory suspected he knew the truth. (She unfriended him right away.) But Thomas's mother could not be so easily dismissed. Glory trotted out her parents' accomplishments—engineer mother, medical-supply-business-owner father—to shore up her pedigree. Then she mentioned more recent social interests of hers, like the Igbo women's group, leaving out Thomas's hand in that. All the while, her inner voice wondered what the hell she was doing. *Tricking the gods*, she replied.

The day Thomas's mother flew in, Glory cooked for hours at his apartment, soliciting recipes from her own mother, who took much joy in walking her through every step over the phone. By the time he left for the airport, his apartment was as fragrant as a *buka*, with as large a variety of dishes awaiting eager bellies.

His mother was tall and Glory felt like a child next to her. His mother was also warm, and she folded Glory into a perfumed, bosomy hug.

"Welcome, Ma," Glory said, then wanted to kick herself for sounding so deferential.

"My dear, no need to be so formal, I feel like I've known you for years, the way my son goes on and on. It's me who should be welcoming you into the family."

His mother complimented each dish, tasting a bit of one after the other and nodding before filling her plate. It was a test, and Glory passed and felt gratified.

Thomas squeezed her leg under the table, a reassuring pressure that said, *See? Nothing to worry about.* But what did a person like him know about worry? When his mother questioned her about her work, it was clear she assumed Glory worked in corporate with Thomas, and neither of them dissuaded her. Yet it rankled Glory, who couldn't decide whether Thomas had stretched the truth into a more presentable fit or had simply overlooked the possibility that his mother would make such an assumption.

It didn't seem to matter to Thomas's mother, who expressed her delight that Glory would soon leave and come to stay with her in Nigeria, something Glory and Thomas had never discussed. He squeezed her leg again, the pressure less reassuring: *Please don't argue with my mother.*

Glory felt it then, that peculiar itch at the back of her neck that flared up when she came to a crossroads. She ignored the sensation and returned Thomas's squeeze, and he relaxed, changing the subject to his mother's schedule for the next day, which he and Glory would have off.

Thomas excused himself, leaving the two women to talk alone. He promised to be back in an hour and left to run an errand. Every minute that passed without Thomas by her side, Glory felt as though a veil was slipping off her, revealing more and more of her true nature. She didn't say or do anything different, but she felt his mother close off a bit, leaning back as though to consider what manner of girl she was.

After thirty minutes, his mother's pleasantness cooled to politeness and Glory excused herself to the bathroom before it chilled further. *You have to come back now,* she texted Thomas. *Now!*

And he did, interrupting a lie his mother could have uncovered with very little research. Perfect timing as always. Always perfect.

Not long after, the ease between the two women returned, but the more they talked, the more his mother touched on the expectation that Glory would drop everything and go back to Nigeria and live there with her hypothetical children, in her mother-in-law's house. If the idea had been hers, Glory might not have minded it—but this was being discussed as a given, not a choice. Thomas was most comfortable in Nigeria and would move back when he was done with schooling to join his wife, who would already be settled. And Thomas was a man who got what he wanted. All the "we" and "us" now felt less like a collaboration and more like a general compelling his troops. It surprised Glory to realize that she was not the only one scheming.

After they took his mother to her hotel, Thomas and Glory idled in the parking lot, each waiting for the other to break the silence. Then, offering neither apology nor explanation, Thomas placed a box in Glory's lap. She opened it, the hinge levering to reveal a ring that, just a year ago, she would never have imagined receiving anytime soon, or ever. The itch returned to her neck.

A part of Glory had always thought to win her parents' good graces by her own merit. She believed that one day, she would eventually stumble into accomplishments that she could hold up as her own, that the seeming chaos of her life would coalesce into an intricate puzzle whose shape one could see only when it was complete. That this ring was to be her salvation—she couldn't bear it. And yet, salvation it was. Acceptance into many proper folds. Lies she would never again have to tell. She could lose herself in the whirlwind of Thomas, golden child turned golden man.

But then Glory thought of the first time she had turned her luck with something truly reckless, the thing with the dog. She had felt itchy all over and there was her uncle's dog, napping. A thought wormed into her head that the itch would go away if she touched the dog's tongue, and it was suddenly the right and only thing to do. She rubbed the scar on her thumb, thinking of all the times she had picked stupid over sensible, knowing, just knowing, she'd gotten it right. She could not afford to get it wrong this time.

She looked at the ring, and resentment and elation warred till one overcame the other and Glory made another decision.

Martha Cooley

Mercedes Benz

I

THEY PASSED IT ON the way back from Cremona, on a mild evening in July.

In the low foothills of the Apennines on the Parma side of the Cisa Pass, the light was harshly golden; by the time they approached Borgotaro, the sun's rays were no longer in their eyes but came at them aslant. Huge clouds bloomed and drifted above them. Twisting below, the wide rocky riverbed of the Taro was intermittently visible, little streams emptying into it: Erbetello, dei Cani, Pizzarotta. Descending, the streams cut stony runnels that zigzagged erratically downward, as though someone had scored the earth with a huge sharp stick.

She marveled at the autostrada, its construction such a feat of engineering—all those high viaducts over valleys and rivers, the long well-lit tunnels, the curves on the Parma side of the pass, the varying elevations of the parallel roadways. The entire autostrada system had taken over a decade to build, and its maintenance, Eligio'd said, was a ceaseless job. The A15 stretch between Emilia-Romagna and the Ligurian Sea had been among the toughest to complete, because of the mountains. Quite tricky to design, actually. Lots of foreign engineers came to see it and learn how such roads were built.

There was little traffic on their side; only cars, since trucks were forbidden on Saturdays and Sundays. They proceeded at a good clip, seldom having to pass anyone, staying mostly in the right-hand lane. Shortly after the tunnel called Il Partigiano, she noticed there weren't any vehicles on the other side, heading toward Parma. Not a single one.

Weird, said Eligio when she remarked on this absence. You're right, I hadn't noticed. . . . Nothing's coming at us.

Emergency lights flashed several hundred yards ahead of them on the opposite roadway. Eligio pumped the brakes lightly.

Tell me what you see, he said as they slowed down. I need to keep my eyes on the road.

The accident had happened between Borgotaro and Berceto, on a sharp curve.

At the point where it occurred, the two lanes heading toward Parma were separated from theirs by a thin median strip and a pair of sturdy guardrails. The opposing lanes were elevated slightly, perhaps ten feet; just beyond them a hill ascended steeply, walled in concrete for a few yards till low shrubs and thick grass took over. The roadway had very narrow shoulders on either side—as was the case, she'd noticed, for most of the curves on the A15. Apparently there hadn't been room to make wider shoulders; the curves hugged a series of thin ridges.

Several emergency vehicles were parked in the middle of the roadway on the other side. A pair of men in neon-orange jumpsuits moved about quickly, yelling; one man gestured at an ambulance, urging it forward. From nearby a police siren blared. A car, a gray sedan (later, in her memory, it was neither large nor small, old nor new, just an ordinary automobile), lay tipped over and pressed against the guardrail; she noted, fleetingly, a black tarp on the ground. A barricade had been erected a hundred yards before the overturned car; flashing its lights, the ambulance skirted the barricade and drew up next to the sedan. Then the lights were behind them, the scene receding as they proceeded.

What a mess, said Eligio.

The vehicles ahead of them had slowed to a crawl as they passed the scene, so he'd been able to take a quick look himself. *Rubbernecking*, she told him it was called. A kind of instinct, an impulse that manifested in circumstances like this. The traffic on their side picked up speed, but on the opposite roadway the halted cars snaked as far as they could see. Drivers were standing around talking; whole families gathered alongside their cars. She watched a mother pushing a stroller slowly along the highway's thin shoulder. Did all these people have bottles of water? Were they sharing provisions up and down the line, like soldiers at the front? Hard to say how long they'd be stuck there, knowing nothing of what'd actually happened. Waiting for someone to tell them the story.

II

Earlier that summer, she'd developed a strong and, to her, startling attraction to certain kinds of cars. Luxury European brands such as Mercedes, Audi, Lamborghini, BMW, Porsche—prohibitively expensive, latest-model cars. Nothing she'd ever had the slightest interest in driving, which made the attraction all the more peculiar.

At first, sitting in the passenger seat, she found herself noticing the elegance of expensive cars' taillights as they zipped by. Ordinary cars had rear lights shaped like ugly lozenges, or set in silly overlapping circles, or wrapped awkwardly around the side of the car like bad sunglasses. Or, worst of all, designed as a series of loudly blinking dots, like a Times Square news flash. But the taillights of luxury sedans were sized in perfect proportion to the cars' rear windows and bumpers and weren't in the least ostentatious.

Overall, too, the designs of costly cars were more refined than those of normal ones. Of course the refinements didn't change a basic fact: all cars, fancy ones included, were aggressive, in appearance as well as function. So much metal and chrome, the side mirrors and antennae and dashboard icons, all of it a form of weaponry. . . . Not worth thinking about, really—the basic craziness of sitting in a metal box hurtling along with a bunch of other metal boxes, all of them weaving from one lane to another. And a good percentage of the drivers were sleepy or texting or drunk or drugged.

Luxury sedans, though, could announce their efficiency and power without overdoing it. They offered their owners an illusion of safety, neatly packaged as exclusivity. You're different, their murmuring engines seemed to say to their drivers. Exempt from the usual dangers.

She wondered about her obsession with high-end cars. They were just like the rest, simply a means of getting from A to B, so why care? The purported sexiness of expensive models, their rapid acceleration, their leather interiors and high-tech gadgetry: all that stuff had never before meant a thing to her.

To Eligio her newfound interest in expensive cars was amusing, something he could tease her about. *You actually want one of those?* he asked at one point, gesturing with his chin as he drove. A Mercedes or a Porsche? I can't imagine it.

No, of course not. They had a Volkswagen, a Golf, compact and fuel efficient. It'd belonged to Eligio's former father-in-law;

too old to drive any longer, he'd given the car to them a few years earlier. The Golf had a hundred thousand kilometers under its belt. Though a bit nicked and scratched, its upholstery torn on the driver's side, the car suited their needs just fine.

Maybe you're having a midlife crisis, Eligio said as she gazed at a black Jaguar whipping past them. Usually it's boring heterosexual guys who get excited about expensive cars, you know, when they're having a midlife crisis. . . .

It is pretty strange, she responded.

He smiled. Well, everyone has a midlife crisis if they get to live that long. It's just a matter of what shape it takes.

Whenever she said or did something out of character, Eligio liked to tease her about it. It didn't happen daily—her being or acting out of character—but when it did, he made sure to draw it to her attention. Not roughly; lightly.

Why're you startled? he'd ask when she surprised herself with some unexpected reaction. Past a certain point, you can't fool yourself. . . . I mean, you can go ahead and insist *I'm just X*, but you know you're Y, too, and Z. . . . It's one of the reasons I'm attracted to you. You're a mongrel, is that the word for it? My favorite mongrel.

Sometimes his teasing troubled her. Mostly, though, she liked it, since it was linked with his desire. And he was right: she was a mess of contradictions. She admired other women her age, pushing sixty, who seemed to cohere as they aged. Perhaps their coherence was mainly at the level of their social selves, a function of habit or necessity. Within themselves, privately, maybe those women felt as mercurial and blurry as she often did. Well, not blurry, exactly: incompletely inventoried. Like a house with unexplored rooms.

Let me count the ways, she'd sometimes say in response to Eligio's teasing.

That phrase was a code between them. Not long after they'd married, she'd read aloud to him the sonnet from which it came, Elizabeth Browning's "How Do I Love Thee?" Eligio hadn't heard of the poem, though he did know Browning had lived in Florence with her poet husband. Casa Guidi, their apartment was called; it sat nearly across the street from the Palazzo Pitti. A house museum, these days. She liked imagining the Brownings in Florence, writing and taking walks and talking politics. They'd let their son play with other kids along the banks of the Arno, almost like a pair of expat poets might do now, she told Eligio. They'd lived like real Florentines.

Only without the parking hassles, he said. And renting an apartment near the Palazzo Pitti would cost you a fortune today. Lucky poets!

Listening to the poem, Eligio had pronounced it old-fashioned. Which of course it was. But also beautiful, especially *when feeling out of sight / For the ends of being* . . .

Those lines were clunky in translation. How best to say or explain them in another language? Groping—that's what Browning had meant. Her love for her husband had groped blindly for the borders of self, so as to reach and cross them. A vast, hungry love, Elizabeth's, yet simple and fluid, too. Rising like water *to the level of every day's / Most quiet need.*

What a strange verse, Eligio'd said after she read the poem aloud again, at his request. It starts off as a list, then it goes haywire. . . . All those rational reasons for love—but by the end, the poet says she'll love her man more after death than beforehand. Wow!

Eligio liked the expression *going haywire.* There was nothing like it in Italian.

Groping, he said. In English, doesn't that word have a sexual connotation?

It does sometimes. It can be vulgar, like a guy grabbing a girl's ass on the subway. Or it can be what teenagers do with each other in sleeping bags at sleepovers. Which isn't vulgar, just sort of confused.

Ah, said Eligio, smiling. Well, searching for the borders of self—is that how you put it?—ought to be more like that. Confused. Without any reasons or lists.

III

At the start of that summer, when her attraction to luxury cars arose—after twelve months had gone by, a year spent in the small stone house they'd rented for her sabbatical leave—they bought the old *canonica* up by the church. It stood at the end of a cobbled lane, just below the castle gates.

Almost no one lived full-time on the lane, which served as the spine of the medieval *borgo*. In summer, a few of the lane's houses filled as owners and their extended families returned for vacations; during the rest of the year, though, the lane was deserted. The *borgo* wasn't the easiest place to reach. Most cars were too wide to fit through the arch at the upper entrance, where the main lane T'ed out. Residents with small-enough cars didn't like bringing them up; side scrapes happened easily. Even the oldest inhabitants usually parked at the base of the village and walked up the hill to the arch.

The *canonica*, they'd learned, was once the local priest's house; before that, it'd belonged to peasants who'd worked the church's land.

Across from the front door of the house was the ramp to the castle; to its left sat the church. The castle's upper garden was visible from the front door, its tomato vines bordering a high stone wall. At the back of the *canonica* were pomegranate and fig trees, along with an old cistern no longer in use. A low wall ran the length of the church's piazza; beyond it, the terrain dropped precipitously into dense copses of trees.

It's like you could fall right off this hill, said Eligio one day as they stared downward. Unless you cling to the church, of course, he added, poker-faced. Then he smiled. I sure never thought I'd be bargaining with the church for a piece of its property!

Me neither, she said. I guess you'd call it an accident of fate.

Yes. *Una felice circostanza.*

The view from the house was what'd attracted them initially: the other side of the Magra Valley, lushly green, where the hills of Groppoli rose up from the river.

The house itself, they agreed, would be terrific when redone, but best of all was the quiet and light all around them. Throughout the valley the light was limpid and serene; breezes played across fields bordering the river. During the day, birdsong was the only noise save for the slight, low hum of a car or truck wending between Monti and Villafranca.

Evenings were peaceful, too, though on summer weekends, a disco's annoying thump could be heard some nights. Trouble in paradise, said Eligio one night shortly before they closed on the purchase of the house. It was a Saturday, close to midnight; they were standing by the *canonica*, gazing up at the inky, star-filled sky.

That music, you mean?

Yeah. Not the end of the world, though. We're lucky. When the house is done, we'll get to stand here quietly and see all this—the stars, the darkness—whenever we want.

Not just see it but live it, she said.

Yeah. I didn't think you could say it like that in English.

Well, he added, smiling, there's no going backward now—we've already begun living it. . . .

They hadn't planned on buying the house, hadn't even known it was for sale till a neighbor mentioned the church wanted to get rid of it. The proceeds, they were told, would go into the village bell tower, which was badly in need of repair. The price was low.

Eligio raised his arms over his head, fingers outstretched toward the glittery sky. Then he dropped his arms abruptly to his sides: his way of releasing tension.

You know, renovating a run-down house in a near-empty *borgo* isn't exactly a normal thing to do, he said. I bet our American friends will think we're nuts for buying this place. A lot of Italians would say the same thing . . .

Eligio liked the word *nuts*. Like *haywire*, it had no Italian equal.

Oh, they won't say that, she said. It's a good deal.

Fixing it up will end up costing most of what I've got. That means you'll have to pick up more of our expenses when we get home.

I know. And I'm not saying I'm not scared.

Before buying the house, they'd found a local architect who declared it solid and safe. All the rooms were bright and dry, though the house had been locked up unaired for several years. There was mildew on some walls, but no serious water damage. The main things needed, the architect said, were a new roof and a set of metal struts for protection against earthquakes.

Eligio had pressed for a rationale; the struts weren't cheap. Antiseismic regulations were enforced in the region, the architect explained. There'd never been a really bad quake in their locality, but small ones did happen from time to time. They'd have to spend the money.

He wasn't wrong about the region. A few weeks before, a mild earthquake had occurred in the middle of the afternoon. She'd been sitting with Eligio in the rental house, sipping coffee, and felt the ground do something it wasn't supposed to do. As soon as the tremors ended, they'd gone up to the *canonica* to see if it'd been damaged; several days later, a structural engineer confirmed that the house was fine. They'd been fortunate: only an hour away, lots of homes had sustained damage.

Seems we've bought a strong house, Eligio said to the engineer at the end of his inspection.

Yes, but the antiseismic struts were important, the engineer responded. Just to be *al sicuro*.

On the safe side, said Eligio by way of explanation when the engineer left. We ought to stay on the safe side.

An odd expression. In English, anyway. As though in any setting or situation there were always two sides, safe and unsafe, and you'd necessarily have to cross from one to the other; and you might not know which side was which, hence might find yourself suddenly no longer on the safe but the unsafe side— unable to recross, to go back to wherever you started from.

Right after the earthquake, Eligio had taken her hand as they walked up to the *canonica*. To reassure her—and himself, too: the money they'd just plunked down wasn't going to be wasted. The house would survive earthquakes and anything else: the so-called acts of God. There'd be no flooding; of that she was sure. They were too high above the river. The bell tower was the tallest structure in the village, so it'd take the brunt of any lightning—had already done so, a few years back; there was a blotch on its side where the burn had happened. What about tornadoes? No, not in this part of the country. But there'd be heavy rainstorms, hard winds. Snow and ice, too.

The climate-related stuff wasn't so worrisome, though. It was scarier to think about the future of the village itself, already near-deserted except for those weeks in July and August when people came back to air out their mattresses and trim their little plots. A dozen or so families would gather each evening at the base of the village; the elders would trade nostalgic stories about growing up in the *borgo*. But none of these returnees were deeply invested in the village's future. Their lives happened elsewhere, in towns and cities up north: Como, Brescia, Milan. How much longer would the village attract fresh visitors, especially if no one took care of the decrepit houses flanking the main lane? What if the vines and trees already encroaching upon the *borgo* were victorious? That tangled undergrowth was already a fire hazard. . . .

And then there was the castle. Its octogenarian owner had died that autumn, leaving insufficient funds for its upkeep. If the castle went into decline, the village would eventually empty out; there'd be little reason for anyone new to come visit or live there. Nobody would be adventuresome or crazy enough to show up out of the blue, purchase a falling-down house, and restore it. She and Eligio would be left with a renovated *canonica* worth next to nothing, and virtually no human neighbors— merely an expanding community of feral cats, plus martens and the occasional fox. Might the wild boar near the cemetery down the road grow bold enough to come up and root around, too?

It'll be okay, Eligio'd said quietly after the engineer's departure, sensing her thoughts. No teasing in his voice.

The *canonica*'s been through a lot and survived, he added. But we do need to be ready.

For what?

Worse beatings.

Like what?

You know, health problems, other unexpected things . . . But we'll deal. Isn't that how you say it in English?

She'd thought again, hearing him say that, of Elizabeth Browning's poem. Of how the poet had redirected her passion from the old griefs, as she'd called them—all her prior losses and sufferings—to her newly beloved, her husband. To Robert's unexpected arrival in her life.

And how it'd been like that for herself and Eligio, too: emotion redirected from anguish to ardor. *With my childhood's faith*, Browning wrote. *With a love I seemed to lose / With my lost saints*—seemed to lose, yet managed to find again. And somehow to reconceive. How surprised by that Elizabeth must've been! Perhaps Robert had teased her about being surprised.

Even worse beatings. Eligio was right: anguish would come again, how not? Some sort of illness. One of them would have to go first, and the other would be left. The earthquake to come . . . But putting it like that was too dramatic. He'd tease her if she said it aloud.

IV

All during that summer, as the contractor began gutting the house and the struts were put in place, they did a fair bit of driving in their Golf—the little silver chariot, as Eligio called it.

They went to Parma several times to see Eligio's daughter and her family; to Lerici for swims in the sea; to Sarzana to meet with the architect. Each time they returned home, the Golf climbed uncomplainingly up and down the twisty road to the village. She pictured the car with a mind, a will, telling the car's body to conserve its energies, stay in shape, last awhile longer.

They went to Cremona a handful of times as well, to visit Eligio's former father-in-law, Bertrando, the Golf's original owner. Bertrando was a senile ninety-five-year-old with a full head of hair. He always recalled their names yet was stunned to hear they were living just a couple of hours away. They kept reminding him of this fact, but the information wouldn't stick. *Davvero*, he'd say incredulously, really, I had no idea, I thought you got married and were living in New York . . . Yes, they told him over and over, we did get married, and we do live there, usually. But we're here now, living in Lunigiana for a year.

Bertrando had no idea. For him, the information about her sabbatical and their move to Italy had come and gone, evanescing like a scent he'd sniffed for an instant. It didn't matter how many times they'd passed the vial beneath his nose. Watching him express bewilderment, seeing him confused over and over, she'd found herself wishing there were a switch in a person's mind that might be turned on and off, so particular feelings and understandings could be put out of reach. So sources of worry or distress might be tamped down, at least for a while. A false peace, of course, but compelling. Pain not banished but distanced.

Bertrando had done that with his daughter's death: put it out of reach. Not on purpose, not consciously, yet the fact had been erased from his daily thinking. He never alluded to it.

A pragmatist, Bertrando was. An emotional pragmatist. Unlike Eligio, whose eyes would well up if a strong emotion caught him unprepared. He'd weep outright if he needed to, without embarrassment. For as long as she'd known him— during the final couple of years before his wife Serena died, when it was clear she was ill yet unclear she'd really not make it; during the days when, after the metastasis was diagnosed, what lay ahead for her was something neither Serena nor their two adult children could confront head-on; and during the final hours of her life, when, unbeknownst to Eligio, Serena was having the heart attack that killed her before cancer could finish the job—during all of that, Eligio had let distress wash over him again and again, let it swamp him and take him under. And then he'd let himself bob to the surface again—gagging and heaving and sputtering, but alive. In his own way Eligio, too, was an emotional pragmatist. He grasped what Bertrando knew: you felt things, joyful or awful, it didn't matter, and you moved with the current they carried you on, knowing the current would change. You didn't flail. You just moved.

V

They'd been en route home from a visit to Cremona when they came across the accident.

During the hour or so they'd spent with him in his apartment, Bertrando had spoken, as he always did, solely of the past. Though he possessed vivid memories of his youth, he could recount almost nothing of the present, or even of his wartime experiences. He did know that the younger of his two daughters, the dead one's sister, would be out with her husband that evening. And that one of his pair of granddaughters would be making him dinner.

What a strange life he's had, Eligio said as they wound their way through Cremona, aiming for the Po River and the autostrada beyond. I mean, think of it. . . . First Bertrando served in Mussolini's army, and then after the switch in 1943, he reported to the Americans. Imagine that! From one day to the next, your enemies turn into friends and your friends into enemies. . . . But for Bertrando it was all more or less the same.

Why?

Because his country was at war. So he had to serve somebody—had to do what he was told. Then after the war he got married and had two girls, so the war was something he didn't have to think about anymore. Then he lost his wife and moved in with his younger daughter—and meanwhile Serena and I got married and had kids and made a life of our own. And then Serena died. Bertrando was left without his wife and his older child. But he's got two more girls now—his granddaughters.

Eligio paused. They were at the entrance to the autostrada; he pulled a ticket from the tollbooth, and they merged into the traffic heading for the Cisa Pass.

What is it, she asked. You're thinking something.

Yeah . . . You know, I've always admired Bertrando. He's simple, straight. But the thing is, he's never been able to love anyone but himself. Not that he's nasty; he's just totally . . . I guess I'd say self-possessed. Is that the right word for it? You've spent a little time with him, what do you think?

I'm not sure, she said. To me *self-possessed* implies self-confident, but in this case, it's like . . . I feel that Bertrando owns himself, belongs to himself. And other people have nothing to do with that. So he doesn't have to worry about feeling confident.

Yeah, said Eligio, that's right, that's it. He just lives his life his way, and is basically uninterested in how other people do it. He's his own little fortress. All locked up nice and tight. Never hostile or aggressive; just *chiuso*, closed.

VI

The drive over the pass was dramatic no matter the weather.

There were the flat plains of wheat and corn outside Parma, then the gently ascending slopes, and a little later the deep ravines and treeless summits of the mountains. Here and there was a tucked-away cluster of farmhouses, mostly abandoned; occasionally, a barn commanded a small clearing. An august landscape, this one. No wonder the partisans hid out in these hills during the war: if a person wanted to vanish, he could do it easily here.

They drove the first forty-five minutes without talking much. Listened to a CD of Janis Joplin singing "Summertime," that no-no-no of hers at the end part praying, part keening. "Me and Bobby McGee" next, the ballad soft at first, then careering into wails. Then "Mercedes Benz" with its comic plea: *Oh Lord, won't you buy me a night on the town. . . .* They sang along to that one, Eligio's fingertips tapping the steering wheel.

Later she recalled there'd been an older-model station wagon (were cars still called by that name?)—a Mercedes—ahead of them, not long before the traffic on the other side stopped. An elegant navy-blue station wagon. On a sharp curve before Borgotaro, the Mercedes passed a sluggish truck, performing the pass in midcurve. The speed and smoothness of the maneuver made it seem as though there were no centrifugal leftward pull, no destabilizing strain on the vehicle. As though the Mercedes's chassis couldn't possibly leave the ground. The station wagon swept past the truck, then returned to the right-hand lane.

Whew, she whistled softly.

Not a good idea, Eligio said. You should never pass a truck on a curve. You should always just hang behind.

People do it, I've seen it happen before.

I know, but it's just not worth it. Sometimes the truck will move slightly to the left as it's going around the curve, without realizing it—because it's being pulled there by its own weight. So you could get squeezed between the truck and the guardrail. Or just thrown off balance, into a spin.

. . .

Ahead of them, the Mercedes passed another car and zoomed ahead.

Ciao, she said, waving at its receding rear lights.

You know, Eligio continued, this stretch of the autostrada is famous for being difficult to drive. If you go too fast it's really a problem, especially on curves. There aren't any shoulders, just the guardrails between lanes, and if the road's not—oh, I know the word . . . yeah, banked. If it's not banked just right . . .

I'd say that Mercedes wasn't having any trouble taking that curve.

Those kind of cars handle the road really well, Eligio said. If we tried that in this car—

Don't worry, I won't ever try! But what a car, that Mercedes, such a clean design. . . . Did you see its rear lights? So much nicer than those of that Fiat over there. Or that Lancia. No comparison.

Honestly, I never realized you noticed such things! What one learns about one's mate while driving. . . .

I usually don't notice. But that model of Mercedes was really handsome. Or should I say pretty? Not sure which is the right adjective. . . . Anyway, I quite fancy that car.

Eligio frowned in confusion.

Fancy? he asked.

That's how Elizabeth Browning might've said it. With a British accent. It means, "I'm really infatuated."

Ah, *infatuato*, said Eligio, smiling.

Yeah. Elizabeth Browning might also have said she was mad about the car—crazy about it. Like when I tell you, *sono pazza di te*.

He smiled. Ah . . . so you'll have to decide on the right word. Well, it's your love affair, you should call your object of desire whatever you want!

She wrapped her fingers around his right forearm, its muscles firm as he held the wheel.

I'll think up a list of words, she said, and show it to you.

VII

That, she recalled later—the moment when she alluded to making a list, and Eligio turned to her and murmured (so quietly she almost didn't hear) *and I'll count the ways*—was just before the traffic on the other side vanished. As if all the cars had run into the hills, like the partisans.

Within a minute they were driving past the site of the accident. An hour later, they were home. And the next afternoon, Eligio reported on what had happened on the A15.

A man was driving; his wife was in the passenger seat. They were headed to Bologna, to the airport, to pick up their son. The man lost control of the car on the curve, and the wife was killed. She was fifty-seven. No other car was struck. There weren't any witnesses, or at least no one who could give a clear account.

What about the man, the driver? she asked.

He was seriously injured.

Does he know . . . ?

I have no idea. The article didn't say.

What kind of car was it?

A four-door sedan—that was the only description given. He was going too fast, for sure. I don't know if he was trying to pass someone.

The tarp, she thought, must have been covering the wife's body; the ambulance had been there for the man. At that point the husband hadn't known what'd just happened to him, to the car, to the wife. His body in shock if not in pain. His mind shut down.

And when he awoke in the hospital (if he hadn't already) and asked where is she, my wife, how is she? And when the son would have to tell him, *Papà*, you never made it to the Bologna airport to pick me up, you crashed into the guardrail and flipped over, it happened on one of the viaducts, I waited for you, I tried phoning but no answer, then the police called and told me, but no one can explain, no one understands why . . . ?

VIII

That summer ended, and her sabbatical leave ended as well. They had to go home—back to what they'd taken to calling their other life, though the one they'd lived for a year in the village was their other life, too. Even more other, in fact, than the urban, American one. Other and centrifugal, pulling them up and away from what they'd grown accustomed to, the *borgo* and its quiet.

We've become in-betweeners, said Eligio. Or I have, anyway. Neither Italian nor American.

Unmoored, she thought sometimes—they'd been unmoored. Which wasn't itself a bad thing, just unnerving, because you had to accept whatever waters moved you.

Back in the city, she recalled Bertrando's face, its placid expression.

He'd had two daughters, and one of them died when she wasn't supposed to. Leaving a husband and grown kids, a sister, a grandchild who'd never know her. Serena would've wanted—wouldn't she?—not just her father but her husband and kids to let themselves get knocked over and pulled down, and then somehow get up. She'd been scared to talk about dying: to admit out loud it'd happen. Her family'd had to go along with her silence. But Eligio'd understood.

Perhaps the man who'd been driving the crashed sedan, recovering now in a hospital near Parma, no longer had an intact mind or heart. Eligio'd had more time than that driver to prepare for what would happen; not a lot, but enough. He'd let himself get knocked over. And he'd had, afterward, a friend in America to turn to and talk with, grow closer to, trust. He'd be the first to say that was just pure luck.

In the fall, a month or so after their return to the States, their architect sent them an email with a report on the work under way. The roof of the *canonica* had been redone, he stated. *Tutto al sicuro*, without mishap.

The contractor sent photos. She gazed at pictures of the roof with its terra-cotta tiles; of the valley, its swaths of green changing color now. In the photos the rest of the village looked utterly empty. Of course the undergrowth was still encroaching, the martens and foxes still paying nocturnal visits. But if an earthquake were to happen, the house would be fine.

Back in the city, they spoke of how the other life was waiting over there, or simply passing. They worked, read, took walks, made love—the same things they'd done in the village, only without the quiet.

The light in the city's nice, too, Eligio said one evening. Different, yet nice. But the quiet of the *borgo* . . . that's what I miss. The city will never give it to us. Well, who knows, once we get back there—it'll be different, too. All over again. Don't think it won't change.

She'd taken his hand, run her forefinger across the ridged knuckles. Like mountains, valleys; as if permanent, immutable. Sensing, he'd leaned in and kissed her.

It'll change, it all changes, he said. And we'll deal.

IX

She'd stopped being interested in cars. In the city they didn't drive; they took subways and buses.

Now and then, with winter approaching, she wondered about the man who'd been driving the car that had crashed. Did he survive his injuries? And his son, what sort of life was he having now?

She pictured the son getting into his own car and heading toward the autostrada. He and his parents had lived somewhere in Liguria; his home was probably still there. He'd enter at Sarzana and make the turn for the A15, a few kilometers north. It'd be the first time for him on that stretch of road since the accident. He'd pass Aulla and go through the long tunnel after Pontremoli, then another before Berceto. He'd note the names of various streams; he'd see stone farmhouses dotting the hills. He'd take the curves and wonder where exactly it'd happened, what it'd sounded like, if his mother had died instantly. What his father had understood in that instant when he lost control.

And then the son would think about exiting at Fornovo. He'd do it. He'd exit and pull to the side and contemplate taking a narrow road up into the mountains, going higher and higher till he couldn't see or hear the autostrada any longer, then ditching his car and walking into the dense woods. He'd picture pine needles and cones underfoot, their dark sponginess, layers burying layers. But he'd fear getting lost; it was late in the day, he ought to head home.

So he'd make a left and return to the autostrada entrance in the opposite direction. Approaching the Cisa Pass, he'd slip a CD into the player—some music, relief, distraction. The low rays of sun slanting across his face would make him want to shut his eyes. Perhaps he'd sing along with the music, mindlessly at first, then really hearing the words: *Oh Lord, won't you buy me a Mercedes Benz. . . .*

He'd want to stop then. Lie down on dark pinecones, or asphalt. Not get up. May he be lucky, she thought. May he surprise himself somehow, and keep going.

Manuel Muñoz

The Reason Is Because

NEVER MIND THAT EXCEPT for Shawna, the daughter of one of the elementary school librarians, no other girl in Nela's junior class had ever gotten pregnant. The way her mother made it sound, girls her age were pushing strollers around United Market, standing in line with their WIC coupons instead of being in school. But Nela knew this wasn't true. The looks she got at the grocery store proved it. Shawna, a skinny white girl who had worn long sweaters to her knees to fool everyone, had been sent off to relatives in San Diego before she had her baby. Nela had nowhere but here, and she was the only one.

The only what? The only pregnant girl in school? The only young mother? "The only girl your age . . . ," as her mother would say when she started in on her. From the moment Nela had to admit to her mother what had happened because of Lando Quintanilla, she had felt the word *only*, understood why Shawna had gone away to San Diego, where she could be only without anybody knowing her.

Nela had dropped out of classes before she had begun to show and didn't miss school at first. Not the gossip and the whispering, which her friend Luz reported to her. But it was

September again, and the baby was waking at dawn, the worst of the summer heat giving way to cooler mornings. Nela took to sitting at the top of the stairway leading up to their second-floor apartment. She held the baby and longed for the boring days at the high school. At least there, her daydreaming didn't seem so pointless. She looked down at the parking lot of the Las Palmas complex and watched it empty out by eight thirty in the morning. Nela's mother scoffed with resentment, muttering about their neighbors making too much money to be on Section 8. This wasn't true, Nela knew, judging by the cars coming back coated with the fine dust of the fields. People were finding jobs that might pay under the table to keep an apartment like theirs from scrutiny. It was a savvy that Nela understood now, with the baby in her arms, and it made her sad for knowing it, for having grown into wishing for different things.

From what Luz had told her, Lando Quintanilla was still in school, walking around the hallways like he had gotten away with something, like everyone didn't know that he was the father of Nela's baby. Lando, who used to leave school at the end of every day without even a pencil in his hand, was in it for real now, according to Luz. Come next June, he of all people would have a diploma.

What he would do with it was another matter, but as Nela's mother kept insisting, he recognized now that it was important to stay in school. "His elevator don't go all the way to the top," her mother said, "but at least he'll go places." Whatever places those were, Nela's mother hadn't been, and neither had her father, wherever he was. By the emptiest part of the morning, the parking lot was nearly deserted. Nela could hear the faint but constant filter of TV game shows through the open windows. By noon came the stuttering rush—"*¡Córrele, córrele!*"—that sent Doña Hortencia, who played bingo on Radio Bilingüe, running to the pay phone in the laundry room, too late to call in her prize.

Always too late, Nela thought, every time she saw her, but it was hard not to think of herself at school, pushing away the books that had been placed in front of her. She knew now that a boy was nothing to wish for and that even a dumb wish like Doña Hortencia's bingo playing was better than what she had ended up with. The look of dejected pride that Doña Hortencia wore on the way back from the laundry room saddened Nela. "*Bien safada*," Nela's mother said of her, but Nela always smiled back at Doña Hortencia. The other women at Las Palmas left the door to the common laundry open, even when the manager complained. They maintained a small stack of dimes on top of the phone, just in case Doña Hortencia got there in time but had no coins. Nela envied her a little. At least she was dreaming.

A little help was all Doña Hortencia needed, a voice always calling from the dark doorway of her apartment, encouraging her to run, run, run. Nela could only wish for as much, passing the days mostly on the steps, sometimes with the baby, sometimes not. Her mother turned on the television in the morning and kept it on all day. Whenever the baby woke for a feeding, Nela ate too, a single piece of bread folded over with something in the middle. By three in the afternoon, when the Donahue show came on with its male strippers on Fridays, Luz would stop by to report on school.

"He's still there," Luz always told her, as if nothing was going to change. Nela secretly wanted Lando to drop out, if only for her mother to move on to someone else's failure. Today, Luz said it even before she made her way up the stairs to join her. She put down her math book with a cover made from a United Market paper bag, her otherwise pristine Pee-Chee folders with nothing in them. She spent the days with her chin in her hand, writing the name of the boy she swooned over in tiny letters. ALONSO ALONSO ALONSO, as if she could will him into her life.

Luz was no fool. She went to school in the long denim skirts that her parents ordered her to wear, her hair plain and straight all the way down the back. But she saw Alonso on the sly when-ever she could. Still, it surprised Nela when she said, almost casually, "The Raisin Day Festival is this weekend." She thought Luz had forgotten all about their town's annual parade.

"Are you going?" Nela asked.

"Just to the carnival. It starts tonight. You want to come?"

"My mother won't want to babysit."

"So bring the baby with you."

"She would never let me take the baby out in the middle of all those people."

"Whose baby is it?" Luz asked. "Hers or yours?"

It was tough talk from Luz, arrogant and full of her not knowing the long drag of Nela's mornings, the hours spent as she second-guessed herself. It made Nela think of the days after the baby was born, agreeing to name the baby after Lando. The last name, right down to the Junior and everything. "It's not that easy, Luz," Nela said.

"Sure it is." Luz pointed down the stairs, and Nela followed her finger out to the horizon beyond the parking lot. "One step at a time." Luz marched down a few of them as if to show her but turned back quickly when she saw that Nela was unmoved. "Seriously, though. Or get Lando to take care of it. He doesn't even give you alimony."

"Child support, *mensa*. We never got married."

The baby stirred a bit but Luz, still looking like she might have an answer to that, stayed quiet for a moment.

"You know what I mean," she said, her voice a little lower once she was sure that the baby had gone back to sleeping. "He doesn't help you. Does he even come over?"

"Sometimes," Nela answered. The real answer was almost never. His visits came unannounced, a friend of his waiting down in the parking lot with the car still running while Lando ran up the stairs to knock on their door. Sooner or later, their neighbors would look out to see who the car belonged to, Lando's friend tossing a half-lit cigarette to the cement when the staring got to be too much. A quick honk told Lando to hurry up. "At least the baby sees him," Nela's mother would tell her. "It's important for a baby to see his father."

Nela's mother said stupid things like that, blind to Lando's real reasons. He was checking on Nela, making sure that no other guy was around, the way he stood in the doorway, barely holding the baby and crooking his neck to see past Nela into the apartment. It angered Nela that he would want no one in her life, even when he didn't want to be with her. She knew better now, just as she knew better that it had been a mistake to name the baby as she had, just as she knew better why her mother hadn't kicked her out of the apartment when she announced her pregnancy. "You're her dependent," Luz had explained, one of the few times she used a big word right. "They'd move her downstairs to the efficiency apartments, and no one wants one of those."

"Maybe I'll go to the parade tomorrow morning," Nela said.

"The parade's boring," said Luz. "If I want to see a bunch of kids on the back of a truck, I'll go to my *tío*'s house. Come to the carnival."

"The baby—"

"Leave the baby here," said Luz. "Or take him with you." She sighed heavily and tilted her head at Nela, impatient. "See—you just don't know how to make people do what you want."

"What do you mean?"

"All you have to do is listen to what your mom wants you to do and then do the other thing," said Luz. Before Nela could protest that Luz was wearing the long denim skirt and pressed white blouse that her parents demanded, she saw how Luz had only given up on the clothes to gain their trust. If she followed orders, she could go places. She could go to the carnival. She could see Alonso on the sly.

"Your problem is you ask," Luz continued. "You don't have to ask anybody if you don't want to. No matter what you do, it's always the right thing. Because you want to do it. See what I mean?"

If Nela had been in a mood for argument, she would've told Luz that she was the one who had encouraged her to keep staring back at Lando Quintanilla. But the baby wasn't Luz's fault or Lando's or hers, Nela told herself. That was her mother's way of thinking. The baby was just a baby, and she could put it to bed while she went to the carnival, just for a little bit.

Nela stood up without announcing anything to Luz, the baby still quiet in her arms, and walked to the door of the apartment. She opened it gently to pass through, her mother looking up to see if the baby was sleeping or not. Nela left the door slightly ajar to signal Luz to wait for her, that she wouldn't be long. Before her mother could whisper, "What's Luz still doing here?" Nela had put the baby down in its crib.

"I'm going to the carnival real quick," she said, and rushed to the door before her mother could protest. "Where do you think you're going?" her mother hissed after her from the landing, but Nela, halfway down the steps, didn't answer, Luz following in surprise right behind.

"That's how you do it," Luz said, her voice catching with nerves, since she wasn't the one doing the brave thing. But that's how it was, Nela decided. Everyone knew better than she did, everyone knew what had to be done. She took no comfort in Luz's encouragement as they headed for the park in the center of town. It was as hard to keep walking as it was to not turn back.

Later on, when she returned to the apartment, she would endure her mother. But right now, the walk in the fading afternoon light reminded Nela that it was Friday, and she could see the weekend anticipation on the faces passing by as cars drove over to the carnival. She was aware of their ages now, the young married couples, the ones without children, none of them tired from being up at six in the morning because of a baby. Girls their age were heading to the park on foot, little brothers and sisters in tow. This was the crowd they would get—the baby-sitters, the ones who took the children out to leave the homes with a temporary peace. This was the order of things in their town, and Nela thought of her mother back at the apartment, the things she must be saying under her breath.

The carnival was still a day away from being full tilt, but the kiddie rides were running and so were more than a few food and game booths. Enough people milled around to make it hard to find a seat, but they caught an empty spot at one of the wooden picnic tables. Nela had left the apartment too quickly to even bring money along. Luz, looking around for any sign of Alonso, made no motion to buy her even a soda for the trouble.

"There he is," Luz said, but Nela had spotted him long before that, Alonso tall and shallow-chested, still wearing the pressed dress shirt that his churchgoing parents bought for school. He wore them even on Fridays, when all the school athletes, not just the football players, were asked to wear their letterman jackets. Alonso was on the track team, slightly hunched, his strides long and gangly. Nela had never found him attractive, but now that she was away from classes, away from Lando Quintanilla, away from all the boys at the high school, she had had a long time to consider what was desirable and good. Like Luz, Alonso was practicing a careful rebellion. Like Luz, he was biding his time until he was out of his parents' grasp. She respected this patience now, all the makings of their secret plans.

"He brought a friend," Nela said.

"That's his cousin," Luz said quickly. Nela thought her answer was too forced, too nonchalant. She kept her eye on the cousin as the boys approached, and the closer they got, the more assured Alonso appeared by comparison. His cousin stood beside him, smaller and rounder.

"This is my cousin Javi," Alonso said.

"Hi, Nela," Javi said, and as soon as he said her name, Nela knew that Alonso and Luz would be leaving them alone.

Alonso's loose and awkward arms took solid hold of Luz and started to pull her into the crowd. "You want something to eat?" Luz asked her, as if they were coming back soon. "I'll bring you something, promise," she said, calling over her shoulder.

"I can get you a soda," Javi offered. "I'm kind of thirsty anyway." He dug into his pockets and pulled out a couple of dollar bills.

"That's nice of you," Nela agreed, afraid to disappoint him. Javi ducked over to one of the concession carts to stand in line, and she watched him, squat and dumpy, how ridiculous to send him along at all, a guard by Alonso's family against whatever trouble they thought their goody-goody son could get into. It was too early out, the park too full of little kids, for anyone to carry on like that. Nela felt a little sorry for Javi, his fat head waiting patiently for the concession line to move forward, oblivious to what other teenagers did when they had a chance to be alone. His concentration was on the food order, his pudgy fingers counting two of each thing to the man in the paper hat. It was impossible to think of him as the same age as Alonso, as Luz, as her. He looked like one of the freshman boys trapped in an adolescence that wouldn't hurry along, couldn't turn him fast enough into a guy like Lando Quintanilla, who filled out a plain white T-shirt, his dark biceps taut just from resting his arms on the desk, a senior who did things in his *tío's* Buick Riviera that a boy like Javi could only imagine.

He came back to the table with his arms so loaded with food and an eagerness to eat that Nela was hesitant to ask if any of it might be for her. Javi pushed a small plate of nachos and a soda her way.

"I don't have any money on me," she said.

"That's okay," he said, with a mouthful of taco.

"You go to school here?"

"I'm from Reedley," he said. "Not here."

"What year are you?"

"Same age as Alonso. I'm a senior."

"I wouldn't have guessed that."

"Believe it," said Javi. They ate for a little while before Javi said, "We met before. Only, I think you don't remember. We met here at the carnival. Three years ago or something."

Javi was right. Nela didn't remember. She remembered meeting a cousin of Alonso's, but if Javi was short and pudgy now, she couldn't imagine the weak impression he would have given her back then. She had been full of easy distraction, the playfulness of being with friends her age at the park for the first time without their parents, the older boys showering them with attention. She and Luz had gotten whistles all night. By the time Nela had figured out that the boys had no use for Luz and her long denim skirt, she had gone giddy with the flattery, laughing in the dark at even the stupidest of jokes, the boys trying hard to impress her. Even if she had met Javi then, her eyes would have been on the senior boys—the boys who promised to win her stuffed animals at the ball toss, the waistbands of their boxers peeking from the tops of their beige Dickies as they lifted wallets from their back pockets.

"It's okay," Javi said and then, without hesitation and much to her surprise, "you weren't my kind of girl anyway."

"You got a lot of nerve," Nela said, pushing away her food.

"It's true," he said. "What's wrong with saying the truth?"

"Why wasn't I your kind of girl?"

"Does it matter?" Javi asked. He ate, looking around vaguely, and Nela followed his eyes. He looked at none of the girls passing by, not even the junior high girls, the ones the senior boys never failed to drool over.

"You gay or something?"

"No," Javi said. "See what I mean, though? You have to find a way to put somebody down if you don't like what they say. Just like your boyfriend."

"I don't have a boyfriend."

"Lando isn't your boyfriend?"

"Lando *wasn't* my boyfriend," she corrected him, only to quickly see that she wasn't correcting him of very much.

"Call him whatever you want," Javi said, "but I think he's an asshole."

She turned to look around for Luz, to look for Alonso's slender and towering height, but it was harder now, the sun gone down to dusk and more and more people around. "I don't even know why I came."

"Hey," said Javi, "I'm sorry. I shouldn't be saying things. It's just the way you looked at me like that."

"Like what?"

"Like I wasn't good enough for you."

"You trying to be good enough for me?"

To that, Javi had no answer, but as Nela kept turning this way and that, she caught a glimpse of Lando Quintanilla. Just his shaved head turned to the side, but enough to know that it was him, enough to know that Javi was right, however Javi knew who he was. She wished she had been nicer to Javi then, when it sunk into her that Lando Quintanilla had brought someone with him to the carnival. Somewhere in the thickness of the crowd, he was holding someone else's hand, but there were too many people now, too many bodies, for Nela to get a good view.

"Thanks for the food," Nela said, a little sheepishly. She had been staring into the crowd too long, and when Javi didn't answer, she worried that he had spotted what had distracted her.

"The Reedley carnival has better tacos," he said, wiping his fingers. He gathered their paper plates and used napkins and rose from his seat. "You done?"

"Yeah, thanks," she said and watched Javi as he took her trash to a nearby bin.

Lando Quintanilla surprised her, maneuvering out of the crowd and to the head of the wooden table. "Who's the fat fuck?"

Nela didn't answer him. She didn't raise her head to him either, not even to look past him, to see what girl was standing over there waiting for him.

Javi made his way over and, without saying anything to Lando Quintanilla, sat back down.

"You know she has a kid, right?"

"Lando . . . ," she tried.

"I'm not talking to you," he said, keeping his eyes on Javi.

"Yeah, I know," said Javi. "And?"

Before Nela could say his name again, that other girl said it, an impatient plea, a hurry-up tone. She hated him for it, the way he had turned into the kind of guy whose name always had to be said out loud like that, to get him to stop, to get him to hurry up, to get him. The girl's voice called out one more time.

"This is bullshit, Nela," Lando said, but she refused to raise her head to look at him go. It took Javi speaking to know that he was long gone.

"See," said Javi. "I told you he was an asshole."

"I never said he wasn't."

"He's still looking in this direction."

"So why are you looking over there?" Nela asked. "I don't want any trouble with him."

"You're prettier than the girl he's with," Javi said. After a beat, he added, "She's from Reedley," and Nela stayed in that pause, a taunt to her curiosity. Her eyes took to the amber lightbulbs of the game booths, the large plush animals floating silly in the dusky sky above them. She could hear a girl shrieking in glee, the tumble of milk bottles, and she didn't have to look over to see it was a young couple who hadn't made any of her mistakes.

"Excuse me," said Javi, but she ignored him. "Excuse me," he said again, and then again. He said it enough for Nela to realize that he wasn't even speaking to her. "Do you have a pen I can borrow?" he asked an older woman passing by, who fished in her purse and pulled one out. He grabbed a stray napkin on their table. "Give me your number," he said to Nela.

"Javi, you're sweet and everything—"

"Trust me on this," said Javi. "He's still looking over here."

"Why do you want trouble?"

"It's not trouble," he said, and then he started scribbling. "It's just for show anyway."

When it occurred to Nela what he was doing—what he was willing to do to give Lando Quintanilla the same gut-punch feeling she had when she had spotted that other girl—she caught a flash of Luz's beaming face breaking through the crowd, coming back with ALONSO ALONSO ALONSO. It was time to go back home.

"It's for the phone in the laundry room. We don't have one at our place."

Javi looked at her so sweetly that the embarrassment of having to admit that went away almost as it came. He noted it in a rush.

"See, I wasn't long," Luz said, her eyes on Javi as he slipped the napkin into his pocket. She let go of Alonso's arm, and Alonso, staring dumbly at her, made no protest when she grabbed Nela's hand.

"You giving them a ride home?" Javi asked.

"We're walking," Luz begged off, even though it was near-dark already, and she pulled Nela from the bench. For all her big talk, Nela knew that Luz feared being seen in Alonso's car, but she admired the quick risk Luz took in kissing Alonso's cheek.

"Bye, Javi," Nela said. They walked briskly home, moving through the dark but familiar streets of their neighborhood. She and Luz were doing as they pleased, but here she was, thinking of the old stories her mother told of what happened to girls in the dark. Luz shared in her hard breathing, silent. It was only when they turned the last corner and the light of the Las Palmas complex came into view that Luz spoke.

"Thanks for coming with me."

"If you wanted me to come just so you could see Alonso, you should've just said so."

"That wasn't why. You had a good time, right?"

"With Javi? Give me a break."

"He's kind of sweet, if you ask me."

As they approached Las Palmas, they could hear the soft rumble of an idling engine. They had been too far up the block to make out the parking lights. Nela knew instantly who it was.

"You should cross the street before he sees you," Nela said.

"Lando?" Luz asked. "He was there?"

It was too late to even tell her about it. "I'm just going straight up the stairs and closing the door behind me," Nela told her. "So unless you want to hear him yelling, I'd just go home if I were you."

"I'll walk you to the door," Luz said.

"Go on," Nela urged, and gave her a little shove to cross the road and hurry home. Almost as soon as Luz was swallowed by the dark end of the street, his voice called out, patient but demanding. "Nela . . . Nela . . ." She picked up her pace, her eyes fixed on the landing of the apartment where, to her surprise, the silhouette of her mother sat waiting.

"Nela . . . ," his voice said.

Her mother rose to her feet as soon as she saw her, the bundle in her arms. She glared down at Nela as she made her way up the stairs. "He came here looking for you, and what do you want me to say, huh? Huh?" Her mother spoke loudly, and Nela sensed the neighbors looking out of their windows. They had been looking even before she had gotten there, drawn by a man yelling, an infant crying.

"Stop moving the baby like that," she told her mother.

"Now you got two babies to take care of," her mother said. "Or maybe I've got three."

"Nela . . ."

Her mother handed her the baby. "I'm not taking care of your problems for you no more. I'm just telling you." She turned to go back inside the apartment as Lando came up the stairs.

"So you just hanging out at the park now, or what?"

"Lando, go home. Like you weren't doing the same thing."

"If you let me see the baby more often . . ."

"Knock it off."

The baby started to cry.

"Who's the guy?"

"None of your business, Lando. Why do you care anyway?"

"Because it's not right."

"I don't want to argue right now. And besides, you're making the baby cry."

"Hand him over, then," Lando said. "You're the mom and you're not even holding him right. Here," he said, reaching out.

He reached out with one arm. Only one arm, and that was why Nela pulled the baby closer.

"I'll show you," Lando Quintanilla said, and he took the baby from her with both hands with an ease that froze her. She was stuck in place when he calmly held the baby over the landing, its feet kicking loose over the open air.

"Nela!" She could hear Luz's voice way off in the dark.

"*Ay, dios mio . . . ,*" said someone down below.

"I swear to God, Nela, if I see you out like that with another guy, I'll hurt somebody. You hear me? You understand me?"

Her mother's door had shut against the fearful whispering down below that now grew into admonition. "*¡Desgraciado!*" someone finally said. Someone spoke up and Nela wished it had been her voice. But she couldn't join them as they called out. "*¡Eso no es de hombres!*" When the voices yelled out for the *policía*, Lando Quintanilla shoved their baby back into her arms and bounded down the stairs, almost knocking over Luz at the bottom. Nela clung to the baby's fingers helplessly, her own hands useless, and tried to still its crying.

"Nela . . ." Luz said her name as if she had some explaining to do. She came up the stairs, and Nela closed in on the baby, her shoulders huddled down around him. She could shield her tears from Luz, but she could not tamp down her cries, the only thing her voice could do. "Why did he do that, Nela?" Luz asked, the wrong question to the wrong person. Down below, the parking lot stayed silent, but Nela knew without looking that the neighbors were as watchful as ever, trying to figure out what had happened, why it had happened. She hated that they would see the reasons. She hated that they would talk about that girl who lived with her mother, that boy who came around to bang on their door.

From the laundry room came the ring of the telephone, endless, because no one did laundry at that hour. The phone stayed silent for a moment and then it rang again. Luz seemed not to hear it, but Nela counted each of the rings, knew the waiting behind it. Below, finally, came the shuffle of the house slippers and Doña Hortencia, rushing to the laundry room, saying "*¡Córrele, córrele!*" to herself. It was not the call she was expecting. It was not the right time of day. It was not the Radio Bilingüe announcer at the other end.

The phone began ringing once more and Nela finally raised her head, her tears dried. She saw Doña Hortencia standing in the parking lot, looking at the open door to the laundry room. She went in to answer the phone one more time. "*¿Bueno?*" Nela could hear her say. "*¿Bueno?*" and then her house slippers shuffled back across the concrete.

Out of the shadows, a woman came to gather her. Nela knew instantly that it was Doña Hortencia's mother, though she had never—not once—seen her before. The woman was old but patient. She put her arms around Doña Hortencia to lead her back home and looked up at Nela and Luz. "She confuse," the woman said, raspy and apologetic, but strong and loving. "She just confuse."

Gerard Woodward
The Family Whistle

IT HAD BEEN A good day for Florian. She'd had some success in the shops, being among the first in the queue when she heard there was real coffee for sale in Faber's, and had managed to buy half a kilo of arabica. Then she had found a pair of white silk stockings in Schmidt's and didn't even have to queue for them. On her way back, she had dropped briefly into her husband's bar on the Promenadeplatz and had shown him—in a furtive moment, while she sat chatting with his weather-worn manageress, Myra—the stockings, and he had given her a quick, appreciative kiss, promising to bring home something good when he closed that afternoon. But then he always did, if only a single sweet pastry left over from the day, or one slice of black ham. By means of such little luxuries they felt richer than they had ever been before the war, though, by any accepted standards, they were far poorer.

By the time Florian returned to their third-floor apartment on Max Joseph Strasse, closing the reassuringly solid oak door behind her, it would be just half an hour or so before Wilhelm joined her. She may as well have waited in the café so they could come home together, but Wilhelm never liked her doing this, since she always got involved in the clearing up. Florian enjoyed helping, but Wilhelm insisted that his own wife should never be an employee, no matter how casual.

Florian went into the dining room and placed her gleanings of the day on the table, laying them out like a little trove. She spent a while arranging them, as though she were an artist preparing a still life. The tin of coffee formed the centerpiece. The silk stockings, still folded, shimmered beside it. A packet of eggs. A handful of black cherries. A block of butter. Everything so perfect, beautiful, promising.

There was a knock at the door. A quiet, rather tentative knock, like that of a nervous child expecting to be told off. Was Wilhelm back so early—had he forgotten his key? It had happened once or twice before, so Florian went straight to the door and opened it.

A man stood outside. Tall but desperately thin, with vague, hollow eyes and sucked-in cheeks. He wore a nearly new, unbuttoned greatcoat over filthy, tattered clothing. A few years ago, one frequently saw this sort of man wandering hopelessly in the city, led sometimes by a stern-looking woman, sometimes by children. The returning soldiers, starved and stunned, often from years in captivity, struggling to recognize the country for which they had fought. They were turning up even now, mostly from Soviet labor camps. After the war, the Russians had hung on to their prisoners with a grim, sulky determination. She presumed this man was one such, and had forgotten where he lived. She wondered if she should give him something—perhaps a piece of cake—before sending him on his way.

"Florian," came the surprisingly deep though trembling voice. It was not a voice she recognized, any more than the face from which it came; and the shock of hearing her own name spoken, and of seeing the smile forming on that same mouth to reveal gray, broken teeth, made her cling to the door ever tighter. The smile hung on the face like a pinned memo, expecting the same in return. When she didn't oblige, the expression changed to one of hardened disappointment. The head cocked itself, the chin turned up, bathing the face in light from the apartment's hallway, which allowed Florian to examine the man's eyes closely for the first time. Little, distant pearls. "What's wrong, Florian? Don't you know your own husband?"

It was a foolish response, but without thinking, Florian slammed the heavy door shut with such force that the dinner gong, which had sat unused on the hall table for fifteen years, found its own voice and chimed smugly. The man on the landing had been slow to react, but now he was knocking sharply.

"Don't be idiotic, woman. It's me, Wilhelm. Let me in."

Florian leaned her back against the door. Her breath was short, her heart unsteady. She could see, down the long tiled hallway, her still life on the dining-room table, and suddenly felt protective of it.

"What is it, Florian? Have you got another man? I'm reasonable—we can talk it through." He had found the crack in the door, the little hairline fracture that ran vertically a few inches from the hinge. At some points it was just wide enough to act as a peephole. No one would notice it at a glance, but this man had brought his lips to it, talking so closely that Florian could see a patch of moisture forming on the plasterwork.

"A little misunderstanding. It's been a long time, after all, Florian—no one would blame you. I've been through hell. When did you last hear from me, eh? I was in Libya. You know what happened? I rowed across the Mediterranean in a little dinghy, no bigger than those on the boating lake in the park. I was the last German out of North Africa. Saw every one of my comrades killed. Made it all the way to Sicily. Greeted like a hero in Syracuse—they said they would recommend me for the Iron Cross, first class. Then the next thing those bastards did? Sent me straight to the Russian front without even a day's leave. Out of one cauldron, straight into another, though you wouldn't call the Russian front a cauldron—more an icebox. A deadly, deathly icebox. Can you hear me, Florian? Why won't you let me in?"

Slowly, through the door, the voice was doing its work: monotonous, quiet, and—though still tremulous—under extreme control. The tremor was masking something more resonant beneath, a profound undertone that Florian was beginning to recognize. The man gave a loud cough; spittle shot through the crack. She caught a tang of his breath, an empty-larder smell.

"Florian, if you saw what I had to go through on those snowy plains. Little boys, my fellow soldiers, not much older than our sons. Boys of eighteen years, and some younger, having lied about their ages to get into the army—such patriots, you would have been proud of them, Florian. And the Russians were merciless, when we got bogged down. I thought I was lucky to be taken prisoner. They took very few, instead slaughtering our boys like vermin; I saw whole schools of young men wiped out by a single flamethrower. That's how it seemed to me, Florian. Those boys, so young. And we prisoners soon learned we weren't so lucky, after all, but were to face an ordeal far worse than death—far, far worse. Marched across icy wastes, half-naked, starved. Some ate insects and spiders. It was a shame on mankind, what they did to us. And all the while taunting, *You're nothing but a filthy Nazi.* And I would call back, always, *And you're nothing but a filthy Communist.* They would laugh at me, Florian. They would laugh at me, then beat me across the face. . . ." The voice paused. In the ensuing silence, only their breaths spoke. "I know you are still there, Florian. I can see your shadow under the door. And I can smell you, I can smell all the smells of our home. Nothing has changed. I long to greet our children. Why won't you let me in?"

Florian came away from the door and turned round to face

it. She cleared her throat, unsure, quite, of what tone to use. She decided to try to sound as neutral and as matter-of-fact as possible.

"I am sorry, sir, but I must ask you to go away. If you are claiming to be my husband, then you are very mistaken."

Outside, a shuffling sound, as though the man were repositioning himself, devising a new strategy.

"Florian, you are being stupid. You are shocked, I know. We have all changed. It has been too long. Locked up all those years, we didn't know if the war was still going on, if we had lost; all we heard was rumor, no real news. They let me out a month ago—and only then did I learn that the war has been over for four years. Those devils! And now I come back to find my country in ruins. People wretchedly thin, undernourished, but not the Jews—they look well fed. I passed through the city center today and wondered who these healthy people were, with their signs saying, *Open the gates of Palestine, set us free.* They were Jews, Florian, Jews staging a demonstration, making demands, and no one spoke a word against them."

"No—you mustn't think like that."

"Oh, I know. Don't worry—I've been told what to think. We're all hanging our heads now, aren't we, saying, *It was nothing to do with me?* I've seen them already on the trains, wringing their hands, making me sick to my stomach, Florian. So I've got to accept that I fought on three fronts, lost all my friends, and spent seven years in a labor camp for nothing? And now my own wife refuses to acknowledge me. For God's sake, Florian"—he thumped the door; she imagined he'd hit it with his head—"open up and let me in."

"I can't."

"Why in heaven's name not?"

"You don't understand, whoever you are"—she had raised her voice, was almost shouting—"my husband was returned to me more than three years ago, in 1946, and we have been living happily together since. Wilhelm saw me through the darkest days of those terrible winters. Now he works, he is supporting us. You, whoever you are, you are not my husband."

Another long silence.

"What are you talking about, Florian? I am your husband, standing here now, locked out of my own home."

"No. I am sorry, but you have made a mistake."

"Florian, I think I know what has happened. The man you believe to be your husband is nothing but an impostor, a former friend from one of the camps. Of course, we talked a great deal about our lives. We made pacts, like all the men did, that if anything should happen to one of us, the other—if he survived— would inform the dead's loved ones. In the course of all those years, I told him so much about you, about our life, that he could pass himself off as me. He knows all our secrets. We did look similar—same height and build, we could be taken for brothers—and then you must have been easily led, having not set eyes on me in all that time, wondering how much I could have changed. You were ready to make allowances for me being not quite the same, for being different in some indefinable way. Isn't that what you felt when you first met this man?"

Florian was thinking back to the day that Wilhelm appeared. It had been under similar circumstances, a knock at the door, a cautious conversation, but in that moment she'd had no reason to doubt him. By then the war had been over for a year, and the city seemed empty of men. It was rumored that millions of soldiers were still held in camps, hundreds of thousands in Europe—by the Americans, the French, the British—many more in Russia. Why was this barbarism allowed? Germany was no longer a threat; it no longer even existed. Her neighbors said that the prisoners' status had been changed, reclassified as Disarmed Enemy Forces, and so they were no longer protected by the Geneva Convention. How depraved, to get around a law or a treaty simply by changing the names of things. The men gradually returned, but in tatters, skeletal, ashen, some dying within days. Married women lived in dread of what figures might appear on their doorsteps.

Florian and the children had been fortunate. Not a single bomb or shell had landed on their street, nor within a hundred yards of their building. And when the occupying armies arrived, for some reason they hardly bothered with the upper levels, rarely climbing beyond the second floor. Her family was troubled only once, when someone tried to batter down their door, but it had stood firmly. The sole danger was in leaving the apartment to find food and water.

So they had survived, and when Wilhelm called, things were just beginning to resume something like normality. She'd been down to her last drop of perfume; by chance she had applied it that very morning, in a kind of ritualized, reverential act of self-anointing, knowing it could be a long time before she saw any more. And upon their first embrace, Wilhelm had said, "Ah, to breathe that scent again, after all these years . . . ," which did strike her as odd. She had been using this brand only since 1943, when a friend had given her the half bottle. It should have been a strange smell to her husband.

The man outside the door suddenly burst upon it, in a brief cry of frustration.

"This is nonsense, Florian; you cannot have been so foolish as to have been taken in by that fellow. You know what he is? A nasty little con man. He told me that, before the war, he was well known in Berlin. He owned a nightclub in Friedrichshain, until it was closed down by the Nazis. Only it wasn't a nightclub like you or I would think of going to. It was nothing more than a knocking shop. A brothel. You wouldn't believe the stories of his life then. They amused me while we were in the camp, but only in the way that men together will be amused by such stories—in the real world they would have disgusted me. And I dread to think how many times he must have got the clap. Florian, if you have been intimate with this man, you are at great risk—I'll be frank with you—at great risk of catching something horrible."

"Stop it," Florian abruptly called back through the door. "I won't listen to such talk. How could I believe you are my husband when you stoop so low as to tell such tales about a former friend?"

She was distressed, because she had indeed suffered since taking the new Wilhelm into her bed. An awful urinary infection that lasted for weeks. The doctor explained that he'd seen it all before in the wives of recently returned soldiers. "I am afraid that even the warriors of the Wehrmacht were guilty of taking things further than is necessary from a military point of view," he'd said. She wished he'd spoken in less vague terms, until realizing afterward that Wilhelm had probably ravished some poor Russian woman on his way to Stalingrad, just as the Russians had done on their advance in the opposite direction. "It will all come out in the wash," the doctor had concluded, giving her an encouraging pat on the rump as she left his surgery, his customary parting gesture.

"A former friend who does this to me—what do you expect? That I should just let him move in on my family and not care about it? What would you think of me then, Florian? I'm amazed at you, that you could be so easily deceived. You cannot believe for a moment that I am not your Wilhelm. My memories are your memories. Our wedding day in the Church of St. Ludwig, and that excellent reception provided by your father—'the old goat,' I used to call him—and you told me off, remember? That strange party where we met, held by that official of the union—I can't recall his name, but you were somewhat over-dressed. How could I ever forget the vision of you on that night, in that white dress sewn all over with mother-of-pearl, with that high neck, almost like a ruff? And I was surprised, the first time

I saw your skin, that it shone in just the same way. I could stand here for hours recounting the moments of our courtship in every detail, yet surely you won't make me do so before you let me in."

Florian sobbed as this man described her beauty through the door, because the other Wilhelm had said almost exactly the same things, about the wedding, about the dress.

"You say you told your friend all the details of our past. How do I know you aren't that friend, now trying to pass yourself off as my husband?"

The man laughed. "Think about it logically, Florian. If I were the friend, and had been released three years after the true husband, why would I come here pretending to be him, when I would know that he was already home, that he would have settled himself back into his old family, made love to his wife in such a way that she remembered every touch, every scented breath? It would be a waste of my time. If you have two men claiming to be your husband, it is clear that the first to appear would be the impostor."

Yes, Florian could not help but appreciate the cogency of this argument. And Wilhelm was such a logical, methodical person, always cutting through her wayward, woolly ideas with the sharp instrument of his reasoning.

"And where is this other Wilhelm? I would very much like to meet him. Is he cowering now in the back bedroom, or has he already hopped out of the window and down the fire escape?"

"No, he is at work."

"Work. Well, I expect there is a lot of work for a joiner now, with all these houses being rebuilt. He must be doing very well."

Florian was silent. She knew that Wilhelm's failure to take up his old trade would count against him from this man's perspective. Her husband had said that he couldn't carry on with it because of eye problems; instead he'd managed to find employment in one of the few bars that was still open in those days. He'd worked very hard indeed, partnering recently with a Berliner—admittedly, a rough man—to open their own café on the Promenadeplatz. A respectable bar serving the clerks and office personnel of the business district, not some shady, seedy gin palace or knocking shop, like this other man had suggested.

"Is he a good joiner, this Wilhelm of yours?"

The moisture on the plasterwork had gathered into drops, now running in parallel down the face of it.

"If you don't go away," Florian said, "I will have to call the police." It was her last attempt at resolve. How she loved the Wilhelm who had returned to her. She had never known anyone so kind, so loving, far more loving than he'd been in the days before the war, when, almost instantly after their marriage, his romantic streak had seemed to evaporate. The new Wilhelm loved and treasured his children, and they, though older and with few memories of their father, responded in kind. Initially anxious about having this stranger come to live with them, they soon adored him, and—unexpectedly—started to talk about their childhoods for the first time, as though realizing that their lives were beginning to make a story.

The man outside spat on the floor—Florian couldn't be sure, but that's what it sounded like: a click on the stone slabs of the landing. A dirty habit that her true husband would never practice.

"So when will he be home, this husband?"

"Soon."

She regretted saying it. A man so determined to stake his claim would lie in wait for her Wilhelm, challenge him when he came up the stairs. Perhaps it would get violent.

She heard the man's voice, farther away now. He was talking to someone else—one of her neighbors—probably auditioning his claimed identity on this person; but there were few left who would know her Wilhelm, so many having fled the city in 1945, so many dead. She could make out just a few words, asserted in an agitated, bullying tone: "You must remember me. Look at my face, look at it . . ." Of the interrogated one's replies, she discerned only a faint, apologetic murmur, to which the man rejoined dismissively, "To hell with you, then." His footsteps returned to the door, and a soft thump resonated against the wood, a diffuse, distributed noise that was demanding not entry but something else. Then a sliding, shifting, rubbing sound, as if he were nervously polishing her door. He must have been leaning his back against it. She could picture him, one leg raised and the knee bent so the sole of his boot rested on the lower panels. A cough, a shuffling, a little moan and sigh of pleasure, as though—denied access to her—he were making use of the surface in closest proximity to what he desired, as though the old woodwork were the extreme outer layer of her self, a sort of skin.

There was a tapping and clicking of metal—a busy, industrious clamor, things being unwrapped and unscrewed. Was he going to have lunch out there? Then a horribly close scraping that seemed, for a moment, to rip the door open, as if it were made of cardboard—a match being struck against it. He'd been rolling a cigarette, and the smell of tobacco seeped into the apartment. It was not a brand she recognized, certainly not the Ecksteins Wilhelm used to smoke, but some awful, coarse Russian kind from the Crimea or somewhere.

Where would this end? She tiptoed up the passage to the dining room to glance at the clock on the mantelpiece. Twenty past two. The café would have closed for the afternoon. Wilhelm might be home in minutes. She gazed again at the goods on the table. The cherries, the coffee, the stockings.

"Hey, are you still there?" he suddenly called out, seeming to sense her remove.

"You must go now," Florian said, realizing her furtiveness had no purpose, and walking noisily back to the door. "This is a pointless exercise. I know you are not my husband, you know it, that person on the landing you just spoke to knew it. Leave this minute, or I will call the police."

"You have a telephone that works?"

She opened her mouth to answer, but nothing came out.

"No matter. I have just thought of a way of proving my identity to you once and for all. Do you remember the family whistle?" He spoke directly through the crack again, a puff of rank smoke preceding his voice. "We never used it much, but in that time it was important we had a way of identifying each other, the children included. You remember? It went back to my father's days in the trenches, the signal he gave. You could whistle it to me now, couldn't you? And you know that your husband would never, ever, ever teach anyone else the family whistle, no matter how close a friend, no matter how trusted a comrade in arms. It would be a key to unlock everything. I'll tell you what, that first Wilhelm of yours, that fake joiner who comes home to you every night, his hand punctured like a sieve with his bad nailing and sawing, I bet you a thousand American dollars he has never whistled our family whistle. He couldn't do it."

"And you can?"

Florian understood the end was near. She had never asked the first Wilhelm for the whistle—she'd never even thought of it—because the first Wilhelm hadn't needed to prove anything. She heard this new man wet his lips, she heard his inrush of breath, and then the whistle: moist, raspy, beautiful. She recalled it from the days of their courtship, when he would offer it through the door of her uncle's vacant basement flat, where their early liaisons occurred. Later, he'd taught it to the children, so they would know whom to let in. How could she ever forget it, this haunting tune, which began with two repeated notes (*like the call of a cuckoo*, she thought), then a trill, a quick flourish, and it was gone? Where had it come from—perhaps a Mozart symphony, or a long-lost music-hall lament? No words were spoken by either husband or wife as Florian delicately turned the lock, lowered the handle, and slowly pulled the door toward her.

Then suddenly it was in her face, knocking her back against

the wall, sweeping aside all the quietness and gentleness that had silted their conversation. Wilhelm grabbed hold of a shrinking Florian, took her by the shoulders, examined her face in a frenzy, then stuck his mouth right on hers and kissed it, forcing his tongue inside in a hunger for taste rather than an affection or passion, as if confirming her identity. For her part, she caught the strong flavor of that bitter tobacco, and nothing but emptiness beneath it.

He grasped her head, his rough, dry fingers probing about her scalp and chin, working her mouth open once more, moving the jaw as though a broken piece of gadgetry. Then he did the most extraordinary thing—he blew into her. She felt the gust of cold, acrid air, followed by a spasm of pain. He'd bit her tongue; tears streamed from her eyes. Wilhelm stepped back, wiping his lips, and pulled her up by her hair so they were face-to-face.

"You rotten, little whore," he said. "I would be within my rights to thrash you to death for this. So just say a prayer of thanks to the almighty that I'm not a man given to jealousy."

As he pushed her roughly along the hall, toward the dining room, she begged for a moment in the bathroom to flush the blood gathering in her mouth.

Once alone, she tried to compose herself. Wilhelm, her first Wilhelm, was due back any minute. She could lock herself in here and wait for him to return, but then how could she warn him?

By the time she came out of the bathroom, he had taken off his greatcoat, and she was shocked at the emaciation of the body beneath, as though he could drift away in a breeze. His strength was all in his anger.

"You will give me something to eat first, then I will wash, then we will see to other business."

At the sound of a key in a lock, both heads turned to the front door. But the new Wilhelm had put the bolt on.

He seized Florian again, whispered urgently into her ear. "If you're still uncertain, just ask that man for the family whistle. I will give the two of you that final chance. Ask him for the family whistle, and see what he does."

The key ceased its shifting in the lock.

"Florian, are you in there?" That voice, so mellifluous and musical—how could she ever think it belonged to her husband? "I can't get in. Florian."

She approached the door quietly.

"Florian—can you come to the door? It's stuck."

"Wilhelm," Florian called.

A pause.

"What's wrong, Florian? Is there something wrong?"

"Wilhelm. Listen to me . . ." She looked to the man now beside her, who nodded insistently. "I want you to give me the family whistle."

"What?"

"Through the door, give me the family whistle."

There was silence. Such a long silence. Florian stood two feet from her husband, hoping, believing, just for an instant, that she might hear that same melancholy tune far more sweetly sung. But what she heard instead were footsteps departing, moving slowly at first (backward, she imagined), then pausing at the top of the stairs, before descending, quickly, lightly, down the first flight, and the second. Then they were gone.

She turned. Wilhelm was already in the dining room. She could see him through the doorway. He examined the things on the table—opening the tin of coffee, pressing his nose in and sniffing, closing his eyes with pleasure—then gestured with a big, sweeping arm for her to join him.

Fiona McFarlane

Buttony

THE CHILDREN WANTED TO play Buttony.

"All right," Miss Lewis said, and she clapped her hands five times, in the rhythm that meant they must be quiet and copy her. They were quiet and copied her.

"All right," she said, with that smile she reserved for the sleepy, silly midafternoon. "We'll play. Joseph, get the button." The children approved the justice of this appointment; that was apparent in the small, satisfied sigh they made together. They watched Joseph walk to Miss Lewis's desk. Joseph was a compact, deliberate boy, and his straight black hair fell to his shoulders. He wore his uniform in a way that seemed gentlemanly but at the same time casual. He was both kind and beautiful, and they loved him.

The button lay in a special tin in the right-hand corner of Miss Lewis's top drawer. The children listened for the sound this drawer made as Joseph opened it. They knew that the shifting sound of the drawer opening meant largesse—gold stars or stamps or, in exceptional cases, gummy frogs—and that Miss Lewis's bounty was capable of falling on them all, but fell perhaps more often on Joseph. Alternatively, the sound of the drawer opening meant Buttony.

All the children handled the button with reverence, but none more so than Joseph. He was gifted in solemnity. He had a processional walk and moved his head slowly when his name was called—and it was regularly called. His attention was made more valuable by its purposeful quality. He never leaned in confidentially to hear a secret; the other children came to his ear and whispered there. Miss Lewis liked to call on him in class just to see his measured face rise up out of that extraordinary hair. His beauty had startled her, until she'd met both parents—Vietnamese mother, Polish father—and then he'd seemed like the solution to something. When he held the yellow button out before him in the dish of his hands, Miss Lewis could forget the mustard-colored cardigan it had fallen off one winter day. The button was no longer limited by its cheap yellow plastic; it seemed to pulse with life. The children looked at it, and at Joseph, without appearing to breathe. Miss Lewis wanted her children to live in a heightened way, and she encouraged this sort of ceremony.

"Close the drawer, Joseph," she said, because she found she liked nothing better, after admiring him, after giving him the opportunity to be admired, than to gently suggest a mundane task. Miss Lewis could close that drawer with her hip. Joseph used a shoulder. The sound of the drawer closing released the children. Now they hurried to line up at the door.

They always played Buttony outside.

"Quietly, quietly!" Miss Lewis scolded, brushing the tops of their heads as they filed past her into the corridor, led by Joseph and the button. She followed them out. In the next-door classroom, 3A recited times tables under the priestly monotone of Mr. Graham. The other side of the corridor shone with 5B's scaled depiction of the solar system. The children claimed to like blue Saturn best, with its luminous rings, but Miss Lewis was fond of Neptune. She always put out a finger to touch its smooth crayon surface as she passed.

They gathered under the jacaranda tree. The day was sweet and green. Miss Lewis leaned against the tree and crossed one ankle over the other. Her ankles were still slim; she wasn't so very old. The children formed a circle around Joseph, and there was something very natural about this, about Joseph being in the middle of a circle. Grave Joseph. He stood with the button as if at some kind of memorial service. Then he raised it to his lips and kissed it. No one had ever kissed the button before, and some of the other children raised their fingers to their lips. Miss Lewis pursed her mouth. One boy—she didn't see who—let out a brief scoff, but was ignored.

"Put out your hands," Miss Lewis said, and the children lifted their cupped hands.

"Close your eyes," Miss Lewis said, closing her own eyes. She was often so tired, in the midafternoon, that this handful of seconds in which to close her eyes seemed the true blessing of Buttony. To stand under the jacaranda tree in the bright day and make darkness fall, and then to hear Joseph's voice. His eyes were open, of course. He made his way around the circle, and as he touched each set of hands he said, "Buttony."

"Buttony, Buttony," twenty-one times. Miss Lewis counted them out, and when he was finished—all twenty-one pairs of hands, because none of her children were absent that day, no one was sick or pretending to be—she opened her eyes. The children stood motionless in the circle, and now their hands were closed, each set clasped together, possibly holding the button. Joseph returned to the middle of the circle. He looked up at Miss Lewis and she looked at him, and it was as if, from inside that hair, he were acknowledging sorrow and solitude and fatigue, and also routine and expectation and quietness. And, because he was only a boy, trust. Miss Lewis nodded, and Joseph nodded back.

"Open your eyes," Miss Lewis said. She loved to see all her children open their eyes at once. They always smiled, as if relieved to see the light on the other side of their eyelids. They giggled and pressed their hands together, and looked at one another's hands, and looked at Joseph, and wondered who now had the button. Oh, that beautiful button: mustard-colored, Joseph-kissed. Round as a planet on one side, sharp as a kiss on the other. Joseph stood with his hands behind his back. His hair hung over his eyes. It was hard to puzzle Joseph out in Buttony. The children delayed for a fond moment, as if wanting to leave him alone with his secret a little longer. Miss Lewis surveyed the circle to see who was blushing, whose head was raised higher than usual, who was smiling at having been favored with the button. She also looked for the disconsolate signs of a child who was clearly buttonless.

"You start, Miranda," Miss Lewis said.

Miranda rubbed her right ear against her right shoulder. She swayed on one leg.

"Xin," she said. Xin produced a goofy smile. Then she opened her hands: there was no button there.

"Blake," Xin said. Blake grinned and threw his empty hands over his head.

Blake said Miranda. Miranda said Josie. Josie said Osea. Osea said Ramon. Miss Lewis closed her eyes. She opened them again and thought, Jyoti. It took eleven more children to guess Jyoti. She was one of those girls you didn't suspect. Her socks slipped. She had a mole on her left cheek. It was like Joseph to have picked Jyoti. It was like Jyoti to stand burning invisibly in the circle, hardly able to believe her luck. Her hands unfolded, and there was the button. The other children craned to look. For a moment, they loved her. For a moment, she held Joseph's kiss in her hands. She stepped into the middle of the circle, and Joseph took her place. She raised the button to her lips, but didn't kiss it.

"Hands out, eyes closed," Miss Lewis said, and darkness fell. "Don't forget, Jyoti. No giving the button to the person who was just it. Don't give the button to Joseph."

It was necessary to remind the children of this rule at the beginning of every game; otherwise, they were capable of handing the button over to Joseph at any opportunity. As it was, Jyoti picked Archie, and Archie picked Joseph. Joseph picked Mimi, who picked Miranda, who picked Joseph.

The afternoon grew brighter. Planes flew overhead in all directions. The jacaranda dropped its spring flowers. Every now and then, Miss Lewis saw faces at the windows of classrooms, as other children looked out to see them playing Buttony. How long had they been playing now? These children could spend the whole afternoon hoping to be chosen by Joseph. They would never tire of it. Joseph picked Ruby picked Ramon picked Joseph picked Liam S. picked Liam M. picked Joseph. Joseph said, "Buttony, Buttony, Buttony" twenty-one times. Miss Lewis closed her eyes and kept them closed when she said, "Open your eyes." The children, in turn, said, "Buttony, Buttony, Buttony." She uncrossed her ankles and crossed them again and thought, Every day could pass like this, quite easily. Every day could be sweet and green with the jacaranda and the children and the sun and the planes. And then, at the end of them all, the sweet days and the children, would you open your eyes? Would your hands fall open?

Would they be empty?

Miss Lewis looked. Joseph stood in the circle.

"Hands out, close your eyes," she said, and the children obeyed. They bent their heads as if praying. She was moved by the tenderness she saw come over each of them. They were like children in a fairy tale, under a spell.

She looked at Joseph, and he was watching her, so she nodded at him. His face was impassive. He made her think of a Swiss Guard at the Vatican. He received her nod by beginning to walk around the circle, and each hand he touched trembled, and the children lowered their heads still further as he passed them. Their hands closed like sea anemones. Joseph hadn't yet given away the button. Fifteen, nineteen, twenty-one times he said, "Buttony." Then he raised his neutral face and looked at Miss Lewis and opened his mouth and placed the button inside it. The button made no indentation in his cheek. Miss Lewis crossed her arms. You will solve this, she thought, and suffer for it. Joseph blinked inside his hair.

"Open your eyes," Miss Lewis said. The children lifted their heads into the burden of their love for Joseph. They smiled and squirmed and began to guess: Phoebe, Ruby, Usha, Archie, Blake. Joseph turned toward every name as it was called, as if waiting to see who might produce the button. Liam S., Bella, Jackson, Xin. Twenty names, and twenty hands falling open. Only Jyoti remained. She stood with her rigid hands, with her desperate smile, with her socks slipping. No one wanted to say her name. They wanted her to give herself up. Miss Lewis, too, wanted Jyoti to give herself up. Eventually, Ramon said, "Jyoti." Jyoti opened her empty hands.

The circle laughed. Miss Lewis had found that children, as a rule, didn't like practical jokes. There was a certain kind of laughter that, in children, was a howl. Ramon took Jyoti's wrists and inspected her hands. No one looked at Joseph, but they all saw Jyoti: the mole on her cheek, the dusty mark where she'd rubbed her shin with the heel of her shoe, the crookedness of her teeth. Jyoti might have been crying. Ramon threw her wrists down as if discarding them. Then all the children save Joseph and Jyoti began to cry out, just as they'd done when they wanted to play Buttony. They stamped their feet and kicked at the grass. They shook their uniforms and looked up into the branches of the jacaranda tree, as if they might find the button there. The circle broke open as they shook and kicked and shouted, and faces appeared again in classroom windows.

Miss Lewis watched Joseph stand there with his mouth closed and his hands behind his back. Although the circle had broken, he seemed still to be in the middle of it. He was only a boy, and he was alone and proud and terrible. Miss Lewis stepped away from the tree. She would order him to open his mouth and spit out the button. She would make him say what he had done, how he had stood and watched the children guess; she would shame him, and the faces in the windows would see it. But first she must settle the children. She clapped her hands five times in the rhythm that meant they must be quiet and copy her. They were quiet, but they didn't copy her. She saw the way they looked at her; she saw their fury.

Ramon came first, to pull at her pockets. Then Josie, who had lost a tooth that morning; her mouth was open as she searched the grass at Miss Lewis's feet. Osea and Mimi scratched at the scabbed bark of the tree. Miss Lewis swatted and slapped, but the children still came. They opened her hands and dug in her elbows. Liam S. squatted to peer up her skirt, and when she crouched to stop him it was Jyoti who pulled the pins from her hair, as if the button might be hidden in its roots. Now Miss Lewis cried out. She lifted her head and saw 3A's Mr. Graham running toward her. And Joseph was behind him, not quite running, not altogether, but like a shadow, long and blank and beautiful.

Reading *The O. Henry Prize Stories 2017*

The Jurors on Their Favorites

Our jurors read the twenty O. Henry Prize stories in a blind manuscript. Each story appears in the same type and format with no attribution of the magazine that published it or the author's name. The jurors don't consult the series editor or one another. Although the jurors write their essays without knowledge of the authors' names, the names are inserted into the essay later for the sake of clarity. —LF

David Bradley on "Too Good to Be True" by Michelle Huneven

I do not claim that I can write a short story as it ought to be written. I do not even claim to know how a short story ought to be written, although for many years I was almost daily in the company of writers making the attempt.

In those years, I taught fiction writing. As such, my essential duty was to critique short-story manuscripts by applying accepted principles laid down by masters of the art—Philip Sidney, John Dryden, Edgar Allan Poe, Mark Twain, George Orwell . . . and Strunk & White. Occasionally I envied a student's story. I never envied the struggle to make it short. Or perhaps I felt a twisted envy; that was a struggle I, as a writer, had never won.

Truth told, as both a writer and a reader, while I had always loved story, I had loved the long, not the short, of it. My struggle as a teacher was to conceal this prejudice from my students. I taught that, according to Edgar Allan Poe, "there should be no word written . . . not to the one pre-established design," that dramatic unity was most fully achieved by a narrative that could be read at one sitting, and that while "undue brevity is . . . exceptionable . . . undue length is yet more to be avoided." I accepted the affinity some of them felt for the styles of Ernest Hemingway, Raymond Carver, and Amy Hempel (or maybe Gordon Lish) and tried to respect their aesthetics, even as I critiqued their sentence structure, especially as I understood that brevity was valued by editors in the markets where they dreamed of placing their work.

Personally, while I agreed with Poe on intentionality, I found undue length less exceptionable than undue brevity; I'd never thought a tale more elegant just because I could read it between (or during) bathroom breaks. And it seemed to me the narrative defined the length of a "sitting"; a tale with words set in delightful proportion, I believed, could hold children from their play and old men in the chimney corner.

Not that I did not appreciate clever conceits of compression or disliked any writing that conformed to minimalist principles. But on a dark and stormy night, while sitting by a roaring fire with a glass of bourbon and a book, what I wanted was an old-fashioned story, à la Chaucer, Rabelais, or Balzac, with a beginning, middle, and ending, with characters whose lives were not "complicated" but complex, who inhabited not a "narrative space" but in a certain place and time and, moreover, in a moral universe that arced, not always toward justice, but toward resolution—and a writer who was not afraid to clearly draw the curve.

I admit all this because I know my aesthetics are unfashionable—all right, antiquated—and because I admire most of these stories . . . certainly more than one. I greatly admire "Secret Lives of the Detainees," which makes a moral statement with precisely drawn vignettes that both delight and instruct. I greatly admire "The Buddhist," which realizes the metaphysical, dramatizing a character's hunger and thirst for enlightenment . . . and the price he pays for it.

But my choice is "Too Good to Be True." Here there be characters whose lives became real to me, though very different from my own. Here was the dilemma that summoned my sympathy, though by the grace of God I do not go there. Here was the story that twisted my emotions, raising and dashing my hopes. Here was the Point of View that made me look at what I did not want to see. Here was an ending that turned ambiguity into finality . . . and back.

This was the story that kept me sitting longer than I wanted and haunted me even after my glass was empty and the fire was out.

David Bradley is the author of two novels, *South Street* and *The Chaneysville Incident*, which was awarded the 1982 PEN/Faulkner Award. He has received fellowships from the Guggenheim Foundation and the National Endowment for the Arts. His essay "A Eulogy for Nigger" was awarded the 2015 Notting Hill Editions Essay Prize. Bradley has taught at Temple University, the Michener Center at the University of Texas at Austin, and the University of Oregon. Born and raised in western Pennsylvania, he now lives in Southern California.

Elizabeth McCracken on "Secret Lives of the Detainees" by Amit Majmudar

In the end, for me, it comes down to jokes. I loved so many of the stories in this year's *O. Henry*, as I always do. Since reading this year's collection I have thought particularly of "Mercedes Benz," whose characters are shockingly endearing and real, and whose shape winds like a road; and of "Night Garden," with its unforgettable dog and snake at the center, its sneaky revelations.

But these days I am particularly drawn to the absolute realism of absurdity, and so my favorite story here is "Secret Lives of the Detainees," a story that is both charming and about terrorism, minutely moving and very funny, sad, funny, strange. Possibly I'd be a sucker for any story that opens with kidney stones and ends with poetry, but the story is something quite extraordinary, both incredibly intimate and, at the same time, about Our Historical Moment, since it is about four men who are being detained on suspicion of terrorism. Each story—it is, in a way, a tiny collection of interconnected stories—is about a different detainee: the man whom torture cannot touch because he is being tormented by his own urological system; the man whose hands cannot stop, no matter the work at hand; the poet whose pen name means "prisoner"; and my personal favorite, the actor Nadeem Nadeem, whose name is a "100 percent match" for Nadeem Nadeem, a terrorist. It's a story of opposites: funny but brutal, or funny and brutal: absurd, real, brilliant.

Elizabeth McCracken was born in Boston, Massachusetts. She is the author of the story collections *Here's Your Hat What's Your Hurry* and *Thunderstruck & Other Stories*, for which she won the Story Prize; the novels *The Giant's House*, a finalist for the National Book Award, and *Niagara Falls All Over Again*; and the memoir *An Exact Replica of a Figment of My Imagination*. She's received fellowships from the Guggenheim Foundation, the National Endowment for the Arts, the Liguria Study Center, and the Radcliffe Institute for Advanced Study. She holds the James A. Michener Chair in Fiction at the University of Texas, Austin.

Brad Watson on "Buttony" by Fiona McFarlane

"They were like children in a fairy tale, under a spell," the narrator of this strangely beautiful, brief story says at one point. And so was I, reading about these children and their weary, mysteriously distracted teacher, Miss Lewis. The story beguiles you into something that feels almost dreamlike, a state in which the most pervasive feeling is a tingling, soporific sense of the strangeness of *being*. Of being a child. Of being a lonely schoolteacher, disappointed in life, who both loves to indulge and to exert control over her charges. Of being beneath the blue contrail–scarred sky under the beautiful blue flowers of a jacaranda tree, a magical tree. The strangeness of playing a game that is magically invested with the thrill of something much greater: the thrill of being chosen as someone special among many. The strange thrill of being anointed by a beautiful boy-child to be for a moment the one whom everyone else envies, even if in every other moment you are the plainest of the bunch. Yet there is something subtly sinister in the air of this story, even in its first paragraph, a thing you sense at the edge of your mind but which edges closer to the center in every one of its quiet, stealthy, measured moments. Here is Miss Lewis, who seems a bit intoxicated by fatigue and the "sleepy, silly midafternoon" and our sense that she takes an almost sensual pleasure in manipulating the children's emotional sensations. That she dallies with some kind of inscrutable danger. The grave, solemn, yet slightly impish nature of the preternaturally perceptive boy Joseph, a silent but mesmerizing child-presence whom Miss Lewis both adores and attempts to use in an oddly proprietary fashion. The collective "small, satisfied sigh" the other children make when Miss Lewis asks Joseph to collect "the button," the very ordinary-turned-magical medium used in their favorite game, a game invented by Miss Lewis herself—the whole business has the air of something both innocent and cultish. And in this way Fiona McFarlane captures something quite essential about the experience of childhood, as well as the illusion of the ostensible power adults hold over children.

This illusion soon dissolves in the midafternoon air beneath the jacaranda tree in the yard outside the schoolhouse where other children, not privileged to be schooled by an inscrutably loving and needy and manipulative teacher who does not play by the rules, sit behind their desks toiling away at multiplication tables and geography maps, occasionally peering out the windows at the apparently lucky children in Miss Lewis's indulgent care.

Until it all falls apart, and the story becomes a tale of all-too-realistic horror, and who is the one to have engineered it all? Joseph? Miss Lewis, herself? Or is it something about the very nature of being alive in our surreal, real world, conjured for us here so vividly in a mere twenty-two hundred words?

Brad Watson was born in Meridian, Mississippi. His stories have been published in *Ecotone*, *The New Yorker*, *Granta*, *The Idaho Review*, *Oxford American*, *Narrative*, *The Greensboro Review*, and *Yalobusha Review*, as well as various anthologies including *The Best American Mystery Stories* and *The Story and Its Writer*. He is the author of the story collections *Last Days of the Dog-Men* and *Aliens in the Prime of Their Lives*. His novels *The Heaven of Mercury* and, most recently, *Miss Jane* were finalists for the National Book Award. Watson teaches in the MFA program at the University of Wyoming and lives in Laramie, Wyoming.

Writing *The O. Henry Prize Stories 2017*

The Writers on Their Work

Tahmima Anam, "Garments"
In April 2013, the Rana Plaza building in Dhaka collapsed because of a structural failure, killing over a thousand garment factory workers. It is considered one of the worst industrial disasters in modern history. I had always known about the poor working conditions of factory workers in my hometown, but the image of those men and women being forced to return to Rana the day after cracks had appeared on its walls brought home the cruelty and inhumanity of the industry. I decided to write about these workers, but once I started, I found myself telling a story about the friendship between two women in the factory, about their dreams of finding a home and a life away from their village, their search for security and love. In a sense, the women are exiles—they leave the relative safety of their families and venture into the city alone. I found myself wanting to bring to light not only the difficulties they face but also the possibilities of this new urban context, the chance to create a life untethered to the past. The women protect each other, trade jokes and

sorrows, and sometimes even exploit each other. The factory is a backdrop to all of this—the claustrophobic, oppressive place that makes it all possible.

Tahmima Anam, an anthropologist and a novelist, was born in Dhaka, Bangladesh. Her debut novel, *A Golden Age*, was the winner of the 2008 Commonwealth Writers' Prize for Best First Book. In 2013, she was named one of *Granta*'s Best Young British Novelists. She is a contributing opinion writer for *The New York Times* and was a judge for the 2016 Man Booker Prize. She was educated at Mount Holyoke College and Harvard University, and now lives in Hackney, East London.

Lesley Nneka Arimah, "Glory"

I don't typically write autobiographical work, but I did borrow an old job for this tale, one at a company that was contracted to disburse funds to homeowners affected by the mortgage crisis. The experience was so miserable, I knew I would someday write about it.

I keep a list of story ideas to explore, and when one premise is not enough to support an entire story, I often combine multiple premises to see how they play together. Paired with the misery of the job was the zeitgeist that often follows young women from traditional families who disappoint their parents. There are many ways a young woman can disappoint middle-class Nigerian parents—becoming a writer, for example—but the surest way is to be unpartnered and unsuccessful, as one makes up for the other. Another idea I added was the concept in Igbo cosmology that a person bargains with their chi for what sort of life they'll have on earth, and what might that life look like for a poor negotiator? I played around with these elements until they coalesced into a story.

. . .

Born in London in 1983, Lesley Nneka Arimah grew up in Nigeria before moving to the United States in the mid-1990s. Her work has appeared in *The New Yorker, Granta Online, Catapult*, and other publications. Stories from her recent collection *What It Means When a Man Falls from the Sky* have received awards from the Jerome Foundation, the Elizabeth George Foundation, Commonwealth Writers, Caine Prize, and others. She lives in Minneapolis, Minnesota.

Kevin Barry, "A Cruelty"

In the summer of 2011, I was undergoing some complicated dental work that meant I had to go to Sligo town once a week. I did so by means of a short train ride from the town of Boyle, which is close to where I live in the rural northwest of Ireland. The rhythm of that journey got into my bones, and one day I started to imagine the character Donie, who takes the same train ride for his own, ritualistic reasons and for the comfort of a routine. I knew that the journey was somehow critical to Donie and his sense of himself, but I suspected also that some dark event was waiting for him in Sligo. The story came quickly in this way and wrote itself without difficulty—I was done inside a week. I was working on another story at precisely the same time, a much lighter piece called "Across the Rooftops." I find they often come in pairs like this—one dark, one light, with the latter perhaps giving me the strength for the former.

Kevin Barry was born in Limerick, Ireland, in 1969. He is the author of the story collections *Dark Lies the Island* and *There Are Little Kingdoms* and the novels *Beatlebone* and *City of Bohane*. His awards include the International IMPAC Dublin Literary Award, Sunday Times EFG Short Story Award, Goldsmiths Prize, European Union Prize for Literature, and the Rooney Prize for Irish Literature. His stories have appeared in *The New*

Yorker, Granta, Tin House, and many other journals. He also writes for the stage and screen. He lives in County Sligo, Ireland.

Kate Cayley, "The Bride and the Street Party"

The story began with a paragraph: the opening, exactly as it now reads. Then I got stuck and left it alone for a year, only to return and write the whole thing in a few days. The inspiration had several strands: a program I'd heard on the radio about parents of children who show signs of being disturbed. My children are quite young, and this struck a chord, in a "what would I do?" way. I mulled over this for some time, especially whenever I ran up against my own prejudices. I find parenting is the primal minefield: there is so much judgment involved in it, stemming from the fear that you aren't doing it right, and a deep-seated conviction that any falling short of the ideal is your fault. The main character came to me as a wistful outsider in a rapidly gentrifying neighborhood, separated from her neighbors by her age, the size of her family, and her son's difficulties: an outsider status that is not overt, and that the people around her would deny, but that is there all the same. This then tied in with gentrification itself, which is a pressing reality in Toronto, where I live. What gets displaced, albeit sometimes with regret, as neighborhoods change, and how to at least try to live honorably within that change, recognizing where you stand in relation to it, how you benefit from it. These things become so deeply fraught when they involve our children, because we want to save them, to spare them suffering, in conscious and unconscious ways, and know that sometimes we can't.

Kate Cayley was born in Ottawa in 1978 and grew up in Toronto. She has written two collections of poetry, *When This World*

Comes to an End and *Other Houses*, and a short-story collection, *How You Were Born*, which won the Trillium Book Award and was a finalist for the Governor General's Award. She is a playwright-in-residence with Tarragon Theatre and has written two plays for Tarragon, *After Akhmatova* and *The Bakelite Masterpiece*. She is working on her first novel. She lives in Toronto.

Jai Chakrabarti, "A Small Sacrifice for an Enormous Happiness"

Early drafts of this story began with an image of a man on a balcony in an old neighborhood in Kolkata, India. Dressed in traditional attire, he's stealing glances at the street below. In a neighboring house, a gang of grandmothers watches him with interest. While discovering Nikhil, the story's protagonist, I held on to that ordinary sight. Nikhil is a gay man at a time and in a place where this requires subterfuge, but in the theater of his desires, he's unwilling to let go of the old guard of his mother's ghost. This felt as poignant to me as the love he craves from Sharma. Tripti, Sharma's wife of convenience, came through the process of revision. Her impoverished beginnings hid a fierce grace and ambition. I followed her through the drafts, eager to see who she'd become, and in the way in which revision sometimes leads to the mysterious or the unexpected, I ended up in a field with mosquitoes, the smells of dinner, and a priceless heirloom from the days of the British Raj.

Jai Chakrabarti was born in Kolkata, India, and grew up between India and half a dozen American states. He was a 2015 Emerging Writer's Fellow with *A Public Space* and received his MFA from Brooklyn College. His work has appeared in *Barrow Street*, *Hayden's Ferry Review*, and other publications. He lives in Brooklyn, New York.

Martha Cooley, "Mercedes Benz"

A few years ago, driving on the Italian autostrada halfway between Parma and our home in Lunigiana (the northernmost tip of Tuscany), my husband and I came upon an evidently bad car accident. I know this stretch of highway well; it's curvy, a bit dangerous. The sight of the upturned car rattled me. Thus I began mulling over what might've happened and how it might relate to certain experiences in my own life. This story's more autobiographical than any other I've written. Strictly speaking, its married protagonists aren't my husband and myself; still, their concerns are familiar and close to my heart. Like them, we fixed up a house in a near-deserted medieval village, where we spend part of each year. And we too know there's no "safe side." What I explored in this story was how love confronts this fact—how it handles loss. The story came to me while I was writing essays that I gradually wove into my memoir set in Lunigiana. Without this story, the memoir might not've happened. We all have such moments in our lives—when one narrative pulls others into clearer focus, so we can see our predicaments and possibilities afresh. That's the blessing of stories.

Born in New Jersey, Martha Cooley is the author of two novels: *The Archivist* and *Thirty-Three Swoons*. Her short stories, essays, and translations have appeared in numerous literary magazines. Her most recent book is a memoir, *Guesswork: A Reckoning with Loss*. She teaches at Adelphi University and lives in Queens, New York.

Keith Eisner, "Blue Dot"

This story took twenty-five years to write. I don't mean—heaven forbid—that I worked on it continuously for a quarter century. By the early nineties, the bones of the story—setting, characters, action—were in place. But there was something dreadfully wrong with the tone or spirit of the story. I'd pull it out of a drawer every couple of years, read it, and wince. It was too topical, too infected by a sort of Groovy Sixties nostalgia. Then in 2014, I pulled it out of the drawer again and wrote a new opening sentence beginning with *Once upon a time. . . .* Those four words set me free. The story wasn't, I realized in the final rewriting, about the sixties or drugs or hippies, but about fable and storytelling—possibly the most transformative thing we humans do.

Keith Eisner teaches writing at his local senior center. He earned an MFA from Goddard College and lives in Olympia, Washington.

Michelle Huneven, "Too Good to Be True"
My mother, who has been dead for almost thirty years, once told me—in a few cursory sentences—about friends with a daughter who kept running away from home. I never met those friends or their daughter, but their situation haunted me, and I always knew I would write about it. One day, with the help of another writer, I jotted down a basic scene-by-scene outline of the story, something I'd never done with a piece of short fiction. Once that framework was in place, specifics began to present themselves: the family, their home, the parents' occupations, and then in a bright burst, the housekeeper, Harriet, who not only observed the household from a privileged vantage point but also enjoyed the confidences of both parents and child. I talked to recovering addicts about pills and street life, and loved the brash, high-humored honesty of their "drug-a-logs." Lucky Gus is my tribute to a darling basset hound I knew who drowned one Christmas Day. A novelist by nature, I had to prune some virulent digressions—one draft recounted at length the story of Harriet and Lois's Al-Anon sponsor and her crack-addled son. It

took around six years from that first outline to a finished draft. I worked on the story in spurts and let it sit for months at a time. One day, I was cleaning my desktop and I found the file, read it, and realized it was a handful of edits shy of finished: somehow, in a resting state, it had, like Jell-O or concrete, "set" and become a story.

Michelle Huneven was born and raised in Altadena, California. She is the author of four novels: *Round Rock, Jamesland, Blame*, and *Off Course. Blame* was a finalist for the National Book Critics Circle Award. She has received a GE Younger Writers Award and a Whiting Award for Fiction. She teaches creative writing to undergraduates at UCLA and lives in Altadena, California.

Mary LaChapelle, "Floating Garden"

I wanted to write about someone very different from me. Boy from Burma was my immediate thought. I imagined that if I was a boy living on a lake surrounded by mountains, I might not think about what country, with its changeable names and boundaries, I belonged to. Especially if I lived on a floating garden. And maybe because my ability to know the country was limited, I imagined him on a journey away from his home—in the confines of a box, in a bundle of bamboo on a ship, in a corrugated metal warehouse—but everywhere doing what he needed to do and eventually making his way to another garden.

Once, a man from the audience came up to me after I finished reading "Floating Garden." "You are writing about Kashmir," he said. "I am from Kashmir." I was glad to hear him say this. Though people reading about the lake and leg rowers and floating gardens, about Nat worship and Buddhism, may recognize the boy's home as Burma, I wanted the story to be about any number of places.

. . .

Mary LaChapelle is the author of *House of Heroes and Other Stories* and stories and essays published by New Rivers Press, Atlantic Monthly Press, *Redbook*, *Columbia Journal*, *Lumina*, *Passages North*, *Newsday*, and *The New York Times*. She is a recipient of the PEN/Nelson Algren Award, a Loft/McKnight grant, and the Whiting Award, as well as fellowships from the New York Foundation for the Arts, Hedgebrook, and the Edward F. Albee and Bush foundations. She teaches at Sarah Lawrence College and lives in Bronxville, New York.

Amit Majmudar, "Secret Lives of the Detainees"
"Secret Lives of the Detainees" came about by serendipity. I had some sketches for characters from an abandoned novel about a CIA "dark site" sitting in a file in a dark recess of my iMac. Over a year later, while clicking around in my archives, I found the sketches and marched them together into the same formal cell, as it were: the form of this short story. I don't know what prompted me to explore that particular file and not the one above or below it; it was labeled simply with a date, and I recall clicking on it at random, just to see what was in it. If I hadn't, these detainees would still be languishing—in indefinite detention—in the sunless Guantánamo of my hard drive.

I didn't consciously set out to portray the spectrum of hardened hater, morally cold technical mind, innocent poet . . . but it seems the pursuit of literary variety introduced a plausibly human variety. I'm also pretty sure I had no grand humanitarian agenda in these vignettes, although the reader is free to read one into them. Terrible though it sounds, I simply wanted to write something interesting. And a guy undergoing torture getting out-tortured by his own kidney stone sounded pretty interesting.

. . .

Amit Majmudar was born in 1979 and is a poet, novelist, essayist, and diagnostic nuclear radiologist. His latest book is a poetry collection, *Dothead*, and he has published two novels, *Partitions* and *The Abundance*. His prose has appeared in *The New York Times*, and his poetry in *The New Yorker*, *The Best of the Best American Poetry*, and elsewhere. He is the first poet laureate of Ohio. He lives in Columbus, Ohio.

Fiona McFarlane, "Buttony"

I encountered the game of "Buttony" in a book called *Paraphernalia: The Curious Lives of Magical Things* by Steven Connor. It struck me as strange and familiar all at once; I was fairly sure I'd never played it, and yet it felt remembered. This uncanny affective pull prompted me to put down *Paraphernalia* and start "Buttony," the only story I've ever written from beginning to end and in one sitting. I was reminded, as I wrote, of the formality of childhood: its rules and rituals, its social pacts and structures. I thought of the long, hot school afternoons of my childhood and the powerful fears and desires I experienced and observed without understanding. "Buttony"—both the game and the story—builds on these fears, these rituals. I hope it evokes a similar strange familiarity in its readers.

Fiona McFarlane was born in Sydney, Australia. She is the author of *The Night Guest* and *The High Places*. Her short stories have been published in *The New Yorker*, *The Best Australian Stories*, and *Zoetrope: All-Story*, among other publications. She lives in Sydney, Australia.

Heather Monley, "Paddle to Canada"
When I was four or five years old, my family was rowing on a lake when we heard thunder. The lightning didn't get too close, our boat was a rowboat, not a paddleboat, and our family did not fall apart afterward like the family in the story. But my memory of that moment—waiting out the rain under trees back onshore—and memories of the story being told and retold became the seed for this story.

The first draft came out in a rush, with all the major parts in place. But it took two or three years of revisions to get the telling quite right. I cut back and expanded, reworded and reshaped. I got to know the characters better, and, as tends to happen when you get to know people better, I saw their bad behavior and also their worth.

This story is about the nature of stories, which is a subject I keep returning to. I like stories that question themselves, that point out the tenuous connection between narrative and truth.

Heather Monley was born in San Jose, California. Her fiction has appeared in *Crazyhorse* and in *The Kenyon Review* as winner of the 2013 Short Fiction Contest. She has an MFA from Columbia University and has received residencies from the Lighthouse Works and PLAYA. She lives in Santa Clara, California.

Manuel Muñoz, "The Reason Is Because"
I've been thinking about Nela and young women like her for a long time. Nela reminds me of girls I grew up with, some of the young women in my extended family. I still don't see people like Nela in most American fiction. I am trying to look past the simple reasons that might be.

The story was a way for me to deal with what has been a long-standing problem in my fiction: how to name the violence that shapes the people I write about—the people I love—without veering into stereotype. Even though I am reluctant to bring the ugliness of Lando's actions to light, I also recognize that it is a necessary way of bearing witness.

Nela, like a lot of people I grew up with, is on the receiving end of a lot of questions, under pressure to answer why or why not. Her situation offers no easy answers, and yet the pressure is on to account. This is why the title became a helpful guide. It's an informal usage, a grammar that is sometimes corrected, even when what comes next is perfectly understood. I imagined Nela beginning a lot of her sentences that way, trying to explain. But I know that world; the answers will never be enough.

Manuel Muñoz was born in Dinuba, California, in 1972. He is the author of a novel, *What You See in the Dark*, as well as two short-story collections, *Zigzagger* and *The Faith Healer of Olive Avenue*, which was shortlisted for the Frank O'Connor International Short Story Award. The recipient of a Whiting Award, he lives and works in Tucson, Arizona.

Joseph O'Neill, "The Trusted Traveler"

The essence of my fiction descends, drizzle-like, from the unconscious's gray, dreary sky, but it's always possible to identify a couple of terrestrial sources. This story resulted from several trips to Nova Scotia, to which I would retreat once or twice a year in the hope of getting some writing done. We rent a hilltop place with a view that's very similar to the one described in the story, and the hours I spent marveling at the ocean and at the nuances of the marine element, and thinking about how I might verbalize that strange visual experience, have found their way into "The Trusted Traveler." The second source is my old English teacher from secondary school, Philip Warnett, a brilliant teacher and thinker who—speaking of influences—was the person most responsible for opening my mind to the possibilities of thinking analytically and imaginatively. I still meet up with Phil from time to time, and he remains the one person in the world who writes me long, entertaining handwritten letters in the old epistolary tradition. In one of these, he described being visited by an old student whom he simply didn't remember teaching, and of course I immediately stole his story—that is, its dramatic gist—and transplanted it to this concocted couple in Nova Scotia who are visited by a former student, also concocted.

Joseph O'Neill was born in Cork, Ireland. He has written four novels, including *Netherland*, which received the 2009 PEN/Faulkner Award for Fiction, and most recently *The Dog*, which was longlisted for the Booker Prize. His short fiction has been published in *The American Scholar*, *The New Yorker*, and several collections of new Irish fiction. He teaches at Bard College and lives in New York City.

Paola Peroni, "Protection"

The story had a long gestation, and it took years and numerous revisions to complete it. The news that somebody I had known intimately all my life had attempted to murder his wife before killing himself had a big impact on me. I wanted to write about this, but I struggled to find the angle from which to approach the narrative.

My own strong reaction of disbelief to this event got me thinking about the impossibility not only of ever knowing others but also of knowing one's self. It was then that I came up with the character of the narrator: a restless woman intrigued and frightened by what she is capable of. I had never before set a story in Rome, and I wanted the setting to be an important character. As the narrative slowly started to unfold, I was propelled by the urge to make sense of the events that inspired the story while being aware of the limits of sense-making. And I was reminded, yet again, of the importance in storytelling of raising questions rather than providing answers.

Paola Peroni was born and raised in Rome. Her short stories have appeared in *The Antioch Review*, *Alaska Quarterly Review*, *Bellevue Literary Review*, *Fence*, *Mississippi Review*, *Post Road*, and other publications. She received a residency from Yaddo. She currently lives in New York, where she works as a psychoanalyst in private practice.

Genevieve Plunkett, "Something for a Young Woman"

I wrote this story in the evenings, after my children were in bed. Putting them to bed required a lot of lying in the dark, waiting for them to go to sleep. Sometimes I would lie there thinking about one sentence that was giving me trouble, rearranging words in a kind of trance. In this way, the story became about the sentence, about making sure that each one could stand this test of darkness.

Genevieve Plunkett was born in Bennington, Vermont. She graduated from Bennington College with a degree in literature. Her stories have appeared in *Crazyhorse*, *The Massachusetts Review*, and *Willow Springs*. She lives in Bennington, Vermont.

Alan Rossi, "The Buddhist"

I wanted to write about Buddhism, meditation practice, and consciousness, though I didn't know how. The original version of this story, which is currently around twenty pages, was about sixty pages long. In these pages, I explored how to write a kind, Buddhist, meditative prose, not meditative in the sense that the prose is lyrical or puts the reader in a trance, but a prose that is based in a specific Buddhist meditation technique (in this case, Vipassana). So, for a lot of pages, I explored what this prose would look like. In Vipassana meditation, the meditator constantly checks her thoughts, feelings, actions, et cetera, and in this way, the meditator is supposed to learn that the self is unreal, that all things are impermanent, and other bits of Buddhist wisdom, so the prose has aspects of this internal "checking," but I also realized that such a practice might also lead the practitioner to a dangerous, overly self-conscious place. Rather than meditation freeing the character from self, there's an overemphasis on the self, which is developed both through the intensely internal, self-conscious prose style and with the laptop. The story became about an individual who is searching for freedom from the self, but he fails to grasp the very important aspect of practice that is letting go, and so the main character sort of spirals inward, further toward his idea of himself (which is my own tendency) rather than out of himself.

Alan Rossi's fiction has won a Pushcart Prize and has appeared in *The Atlantic, New England Review, The Missouri Review, The Florida Review, Fiction,* and other journals. He teaches at the South Carolina Governor's School for the Arts and Humanities and lives in Spartanburg, South Carolina.

Shruti Swamy, "Night Garden"

In real life, I'm a cat lover, but in fiction, I love writing and reading about dogs. They are such tender, goofy, elegant creatures, able to express so much human emotion with their bodies and their eyes. My aunt had a dog I never met who once faced a cobra and won. For many years I had the outline of the story in my mind, and one day at my kitchen table it told itself very simply to me and I wrote it down. There are stories you sweat over, reworking draft after draft, and then, every once in a while, a miracle happens, and a story is started and finished in the space of an evening. This has only truly happened to me once: it is the sweetest feeling I know.

Shruti Swamy was born in California. Her fiction has been published in *AGNI*, *Boston Review*, *The Kenyon Review*, and elsewhere. She received her BA from Vassar College and her MFA from San Francisco State University. She lives in San Francisco, California.

Wil Weitzel, "Lion"

I wrote the first version of this story fast. I wanted it to be about an old man who was an inspiration to me, and I didn't want to think too hard or get tripped up by the words. The way he treated everybody was so special, so generous, that it gave me strength. I tried to have the story reflect that and not go on too long. Also, my wife and I have spent a lot of time on the road together, with me driving trucks or the two of us on foot, or for her fieldwork as a graduate student in political science. The African drylands are one of those stressed ecosystems and climatic regimes that can look empty and make overland travel pretty tough, but the daily challenges to survival there inspire me wherever I go. So I wrote this trying to navigate two worlds.

In revision, I looked for ways to iron out the connections, but those attempts felt flat. When I tried to add logic and clarity, it didn't feel real to me anymore or like it was mine. So I stopped trying to rationalize the story and my life, and focused instead on figuring out what motivated the writing. The story grew out of my looking to the old man for a way forward, for some sort of a clue, because I really didn't know where I was going. I think he showed me the way by being himself.

. . .

Wil Weitzel was born in New York City and has lived in Texas, Washington, D.C., Portugal, and Boston. His stories have appeared in *Conjunctions* and *The Kenyon Review*, among other publications, and he has received an NYC Emerging Writers Fellowship at the Center for Fiction, won the Washington Square Flash Fiction Award, and was a finalist for the David Nathan Meyerson Prize for Fiction from *Southwest Review*. He lives in New York City.

Gerard Woodward, "The Family Whistle"

"The Family Whistle" was inspired by an all-too-brief conversation I had with an elderly German woman I met while I was attending a conference in Berlin a few years ago. She had been a young woman during the fall of Nazi Germany and recounted some real-life examples of what I was later to put into the story—men returning home after the war to find their place has been taken by an impostor. She also told me of the family whistle itself, the musical code that could identify a family member as genuine. The conversation was so brief that I was left with just the scrap of the idea; the rest came through a long process of research into postwar Germany. I've since been surprised by how many people have told me that their family also had a musical code, a family whistle. It was not something I'd heard of before.

Gerard Woodward was born in London in 1961 and grew up there. He has published five novels, five collections of poetry, and two collections of short stories, the most recent of which is *Legoland*. He is a professor of fiction at Bath Spa University and lives near Bath, England.

Publications Submitted

Stories published in American and Canadian magazines are eligible for consideration for inclusion in *The O. Henry Prize Stories*. Stories must be written originally in the English language. No translations are considered. Sections of novels are not considered. Editors are asked not to nominate individual stories. Stories may not be submitted by agents or writers.

Editors are invited to submit online fiction for consideration, but such submissions must be sent to the address on the next page in the form of a legible hard copy. The publication's contact information and the date of the story's publication must accompany the submissions.

Because of production deadlines for the 2019 collection, it is essential that stories reach the series editor by June 1, 2018. If a finished magazine is unavailable before the deadline, magazine editors are welcome to submit scheduled stories in proof or in manuscript. Publications received after June 1, 2018, will automatically be considered for *The O. Henry Prize Stories 2020*.

Please see our website, www.ohenryprizestories.com, for more information about submission to *The O. Henry Prize Stories*. The address for submission is:

Laura Furman, Series Editor, The O. Henry Prize Stories
The University of Texas at Austin
English Department, B5000
1 University Station
Austin, TX 78712

The information listed below was up-to-date when *The O. Henry Prize Stories 2017* went to press. Inclusion in this listing does not constitute endorsement or recommendation by *The O. Henry Prize Stories* or Anchor Books.

Able Muse
Alex Pepple, editor
editor@ablemuse.com
www.ablemuse.com
semiannual

AGNI
Sven Birkerts, editor
agni@bu.edu
www.bu.edu/agni
semiannual

Alaska Quarterly Review
Ronald Spatz, editor
uaa_aqr@uaa.alaska.edu
aqreview.org
semiannual

American Short Fiction
Rebecca Markovits, editor
Adeena Reitberger, editor
editors@americanshortfiction.org
americanshortfiction.org
triannual

The Antioch Review
Robert S. Fogarty, editor
cdunlevy@antiochcollege.edu
review.antiochcollege.org
quarterly

Antipodes
Nicholas Birns, editor
nicbirns@aol.com
www.wsupress.wayne.edu
    /journals/detail/antipodes-0
semiannual

The Apple Valley Review
Leah Browning, editor
editor@leahbrowning.net
www.applevalleyreview.com
semiannual

Arcadia
Chase Dearinger, editor
corey@arcadiapress.org
arcadiapress.org
quarterly

Arkansas Review
Marcus Tribbett, editor
mtribbett@astate.edu
altweb.astate.edu/arkreview
triannual

**The Asian American Literary
    Review**
Lawrence-Minh Bùi Davis, editor
Gerald Maa, editor
editors@aalrmag.org
aalr.binghamton.edu
semiannual

Aster(ix) Journal
Angie Cruz, editor
asterixjournal.com
semiannual

The Baltimore Review
Barbara Westwood Diehl, editor
editor@baltimorereview.org
baltimorereview.org
annual

Bellevue Literary Review
Danielle Ofri, editor
info@BLReview.org
blr.med.nyu.edu
semiannual

Black Warrior Review
Bronwyn Valentine, editor
blackwarriorreview@gmail.com
bwr.ua.edu
semiannual

BOMB
Betsy Sussler, editor
betsy@bombsite.com
bombmagazine.org
quarterly

Booth
Robert Stapleton, editor
booth@butler.edu
booth.butler.edu
semiannual

Boston Review
Deborah Chasman, editor
deb@bostonreview.net
bostonreview.net
bimonthly

Boulevard
Jessica Rogen, editor
editors@boulevardmagazine.org
www.boulevardmagazine.org
triannual

The Briar Cliff Review
Tricia Currans-Sheehan, editor
tricia.currans-sheehan@briarcliff
.edu
www.bcreview.org
annual

Bridge Eight
Jessica Hatch, editor
jared@bridgeeight.com
www.bridgeeight.com
semiannual

CALYX
C. Lill Ahrens, editor
Marjorie Coffey, editor
Beth Russell, editor
Emily Elbom, editor
Rachel Barton, editor
info@calyxpress.org
www.calyxpress.org/journal.html
semiannual

The Carolina Quarterly
Moira Marquis, editor
carolina.quarterly@gmail.com
thecarolinaquarterly.com
triannual

Carve
Matthew Limpede, editor
azumbahlen@carvezine.com
www.carvezine.com
quarterly

Chicago Review
Andrew Peart, editor
editors@chicagoreview.org
chicagoreview.org
triannual

Cimarron Review
Toni Graham, editor
cimarronreview@okstate.edu
cimarronreview.com
quarterly

The Cincinnati Review
Nicola Mason, editor
editors@cincinnatireview.com
www.cincinnatireview.com
semiannual

Colorado Review
Stephanie G'Schwind, editor
creview@colostate.edu
coloradoreview.colostate.edu
   /colorado-review
triannual

The Common
Jennifer Acker, editor
info@thecommononline.org
www.thecommononline.org
semiannual

Confrontation
Jonna G. Semeiks, editor
confrontationmag@gmail.com
confrontationmagazine.org
semiannual

Conjunctions
Bradford Morrow, editor
conjunctions@bard.edu
www.conjunctions.com
semiannual

Copper Nickel
Wayne Miller, editor
wayne.miller@ucdenver.edu
copper-nickel.org
semiannual

Crab Orchard Review
Allison Joseph, editor
jtribble@siu.edu
craborchardreview.siu.edu
semiannual

Cream City Review
Loretta McCormic, editor
info@creamcityreview.org
uwm.edu/creamcityreview
semiannual

CutBank
Kate Barrett, editor
editor.cutbank@gmail.com
www.cutbankonline.org
semiannual

Dappled Things
Meredith McCann, editor
dappledthings.editor@gmail.com
dappledthings.org
quarterly

december
Gianna Jacobson, editor
editor@decembermag.org
decembermag.org
semiannual

Denver Quarterly
Laird Hunt, editor
denverquarterly@gmail.com
www.du.edu/denverquarterly
quarterly

Driftwood Press
James McNulty, editor
Jerrod Schwarz, editor
driftwoodlit@gmail.com
www.driftwoodpress.net
quarterly

Ecotone
David Gessner, editor
info@ecotonejournal.com
ecotonemagazine.org
semiannual

Eleven Eleven
Hugh Behm-Steinberg, editor
elevenelevenjournal@gmail.com
elevenelevenjournal.com
semiannual

Epiphany
Odette Heideman, editor
epiphany.magazine@gmail.com
epiphanyzine.com
semiannual

Epoch
Michael Koch, editor
mk64@cornell.edu
www.epoch.cornell.edu
triannual

Exile
Barry Callaghan, editor
exile2@sympatico.ca
www.theexilewriters.com
quarterly

Faerie Magazine
Carolyn Turgeon, editor
info@faeriemag.com
www.faeriemag.com
quarterly

Fairy Tale Review
Kate Bernheimer, editor
ftreditorial@gmail.com
fairytalereview.com
annual

Fantasy & Science Fiction
Gordon Van Gelder, editor
Charles Coleman Finlay, editor
fsfmag@sfsite.com
www.sfsite.com/fsf
bimonthly

Fence
Rebecca Wolff, editor
Paul Legault, editor
rebeccafence@gmail.com
www.fenceportal.org
semiannual

Fiction River
Kristine Kathryn Rusch, editor
Dean Wesley Smith, editor
wmgpublishingmail@mail.com
www.fictionriver.com
semimonthly

The Fiddlehead
Ross Leckie, editor
tfiddlehd@unb.ca
www.thefiddlehead.ca
quarterly

Fifth Wednesday Journal
Vern Miller, editor
editors@fifthwednesdayjournal
.org
www.fifthwednesdayjournal.com
semiannual

Five Points
David Bottoms, editor
Megan Sexton, editor
fivepoints.gsu.edu
triannual

Flash Fiction International
James Thomas, editor
Robert Shapard, editor
Christopher Merrill, editor
books.wwnorton.com/books
/Flash-Fiction-International
annual

The Florida Review
Lisa Roney, editor
flreview@ucf.edu
floridareview.cah.ucf.edu
semiannual

Fourteen Hills
Bradley Penner, editor
Danielle Truppi, editor
hills@sfsu.edu
www.14hills.net
semiannual

Freeman's
John Freeman, editor
www.freemansbiannual.com
semiannual

Free State Review
Hal Burdett, editor
J. Wesley Clark, editor
Barrett Warner, editor
Robert Timberg, editor
Raphaela Cassandra, editor
www.freestatereview.com
semiannual

Gargoyle
Richard Peabody, editor
Lucinda Ebersole, editor
Rchrdpeabody9@gmail.com
www.gargoylemagazine.com
annual

The Georgia Review
Stephen Corey, editor
garev@uga.edu
thegeorgiareview.com
quarterly

The Gettysburg Review
Mark Drew, editor
mdrew@gettysburg.edu
www.gettysburgreview.com
quarterly

Glimmer Train
Linda Swanson-Davies, editor
Susan Burmeister-Brown, editor
editors@glimmertrain.com
www.glimmertrain.com
triannual

Gold Man Review
Heather Cuthbertson, editor
heather.cuthbertson@
goldmanpublishing.com
www.goldmanreview.org
annual

Grain
Adam Pottle, editor
grainmag@skwriter.com
www.grainmagazine.ca
quarterly

Granta
Sigrid Rausing, editor
editorial@granta.com
granta.com
quarterly

Grey Sparrow Journal
Diane Smith, editor
dsdianefuller@gmail.com
greysparrowpress.sharepoint.com
  /Pages/default.aspx
quarterly

Gulf Coast
Adrienne G. Perry, editor
Luisa Muradyan Tannahill, editor
gulfcoastea@gmail.com
gulfcoastmag.org
semiannual

Harper's Magazine
James Marcus, editor
letters@harpers.org
harpers.org
monthly

Harvard Review
Christina Thompson, editor
info@harvardreview.org
harvardreview.org
semiannual

Hayden's Ferry Review
Dustin Pearson, editor
hfr@asu.edu
haydensferryreview.com
semiannual

The Hudson Review
Paula Deitz, editor
info@hudsonreview.com
hudsonreview.com
quarterly

The Idaho Review
Mitch Wieland, editor
Brady Udall, editor
mwieland@boisestate.edu
idahoreview.org
annual

Image
Gregory Wolfe, editor
image@imagejournal.org
imagejournal.org
quarterly

The Impressment Gang
Pearl Chan, editor
Cassie Guinan, editor
Emily Gaudet, editor
director@theimpressmentgang.ca
www.theimpressmentgang.com
triannual

Indiana Review
Su Cho, editor
inreview@indiana.edu
indianareview.org
semiannual

The Intentional
Kate Jenkins, editor
www.theintentional.com
publication suspended

The Iowa Review
Harilaos Stecopoulos, editor
iowa-review@uiowa.edu
iowareview.org
triannual

Iron Horse Literary Review
Leslie Jill Patterson, editor
ihlr.mail@gmail.com
www.ironhorsereview.com
six issues per year

Isthmus
Ann Przyzyck, editor
Taira Anderson, editor
editor@isthmusreview.com
www.isthmusreview.com
semiannual

Jabberwock Review
Becky Hagenston, editor
bhagenston@english.msstate.edu
www.jabberwock.org.msstate.edu
semiannual

Jelly Bucket
Wendy Gowins, editor
editor@jellybucket.org
creativewriting.eku.edu/jelly
  -bucket
annual

The Journal
Michelle Herman, editor
Kathy Fagan, editor
managingeditor@thejournalmag
  .org
thejournalmag.org
quarterly

Juked
Ryan Ridge, editor
info@juked.com
www.juked.com
annual

The Kenyon Review
David H. Lynn, editor
kenyonreview@kenyon.edu
www.kenyonreview.org
bimonthly

**Lady Churchill's Rosebud
  Wristlet**
Gavin J. Grant, editor
Kelly Link, editor
150 Pleasant St., #306
Easthampton, MA 01027
(no email submissions)
smallbeerpress.com/lcrw
semiannual

The Literary Review
Minna Zallman Proctor, editor
info@theliteraryreview.org
www.theliteraryreview.org
quarterly

Little Brother Magazine
Emily M. Keeler, editor
emily@littlebrothermagazine.com
littlebrothermagazine.com
semiannual

Little Patuxent Review
Steven Leyva, editor
editor@littlepatuxentreview.org
littlepatuxentreview.org
semiannual

London Review of Books
Mary-Kay Wilmers, editor
edit@lrb.co.uk
www.lrb.co.uk
biweekly

The Long Story
R. P. Burnham, editor
rpburnham@mac.com
www.longstorylitmag.com
annual

Los Angeles Review of Books
Boris Dralyuk, editor
boris@lareviewofbooks.org
lareviewofbooks.org
quarterly

The Louisville Review
Sena Jeter Naslund, editor
louisvillereview@spalding.edu
www.louisvillereview.org
semiannual

Make
Sarah Dodson, editor
Joel Craig, editor
info@makemag.com
makemag.com
semiannual

The Malahat Review
John Barton, editor
malahat@uvic.ca
www.malahatreview.ca
quarterly

Mānoa
Frank Stewart, editor
mjournal-l@lists.hawaii.edu
manoajournal.hawaii.edu
semiannual

The Massachusetts Review
Jules Chametzky, editor
Jim Hicks, editor
massrev@external.umass.edu
www.massreview.org
quarterly

Meridian
Helen Chandler, editor
meridianuva@gmail.com
www.readmeridian.org
semiannual

Michigan Quarterly Review
Jonathan Freedman, editor
mqr@umich.edu
www.michiganquarterlyreview
   .com
quarterly

Mid-American Review
Abigail Cloud, editor
mar@bgsu.edu
casit.bgsu.edu/midamericanreview
semiannual

Midwestern Gothic
Jeff Pfaller, editor
Robert James Russell, editor
mgp@midwestgothic.com
midwestgothic.com
quarterly

Mississippi Review
Steve Barthelme, editor
msreview@usm.edu
sites.usm.edu/mississippi-review
semiannual

The Missouri Review
Speer Morgan, editor
question@moreview.com
www.missourireview.com
quarterly

Mount Hope
Edward J. Delaney, editor
Mount.Hope.Magazine@gmail
.com
www.mounthopemagazine.com
semiannual

n+1
Nikil Saval, editor
Dayna Tortorici, editor
submissions@nplusonemag.com
nplusonemag.com
triannual

Narrative
Carol Edgarian, editor
Tom Jenks, editor
info@narrativemagazine.com
www.narrativemagazine.com
triannual

Natural Bridge
Mary Troy, editor
natural@umsl.edu
blogs.umsl.edu/naturalbridge
semiannual

New England Review
Carolyn Kuebler, editor
nereview@middlebury.edu
www.nereview.com
quarterly

New Haven Review
Donald Brown, editor
Nichole Gleisner, editor
Carrie Nolte, editor
Mark Oppenheimer, editor
Brian Francis Slattery, editor
John Stoehr, editor
Sarah Pemberton Strong, editor
editor@newhavenreview.com
www.newhavenreview.com
semiannual

New Letters
Robert Stewart, editor
newletters@umkc.edu
www.newletters.org
quarterly

New Ohio Review
David Wanczyk, editor
noreditors@ohio.edu
www.ohio.edu/nor
semiannual

New Orleans Review
Mark Yakich, editor
noreview@loyno.edu
www.neworleansreview.org
annual

New Pop Lit
Karl Wenclas, editor
newpoplit@gmail.com
newpoplit.com
annual

The New Yorker
David Remnick, editor
themail@newyorker.com
www.newyorker.com
weekly

Nimrod International Journal
Eilis O'Neal, editor
nimrod@utulsa.edu
nimrod.utulsa.edu
semiannual

Noon
Diane Williams, editor
1324 Lexington Ave, PMB 298
New York, NY 10128
(no email submissions)
www.noonannual.com
annual

North Carolina Literary Review
Margaret D. Bauer, editor
BauerM@ecu.edu
www.nclr.ecu.edu
annual

North Dakota Quarterly
Kate Sweney, editor
ndq@und.edu
arts-sciences.und.edu/north
  -dakota-quarterly
quarterly

Notre Dame Review
Kathleen J. Canavan, editor
notredamereview@gmail.com
ndreview.nd.edu
semiannual

One Story
Hannah Tinti, editor
hannah@one-story.com
www.one-story.com
monthly

Orion
H. Emerson Blake, editor
orionmagazine.org
bimonthly

Overtime
David LaBounty, editor
overtime@workerswritejournal
  .com
www.workerswritejournal.com
  /overtime.htm
quarterly

Oyster Boy Review
Damon Sauve, editor
email@oysterboyreview.org
www.oysterboyreview.org
irregular

Pakn Treger
Aaron Lanksy, editor
pt@yiddishbookcenter.org
www.yiddishbookcenter.org
/language-literature-culture
/pakn-treger
semiannual

The Paris Review
Lorin Stein, editor
www.theparisreview.org
quarterly

Pembroke Magazine
Jessica Pitchford, editor
pembrokemagazine@gmail.com
pembrokemagazine.com
annual

Phantom Drift
David Memmott, editor
phantomdrifteditor@yahoo.com
www.phantomdrift.org
annual

The Pinch
Courtney Miller Santo, editor
editor@pinchjournal.com
www.pinchjournal.com
semiannual

Ploughshares
Ladette Randolph, editor
pshares@pshares.org
www.pshares.org
triannual

PMS poemmemoirstory
Kerry Madden, editor
poemmemoirstory@gmail.com
www.uab.edu/cas
/englishpublications/pms
-poemmemoirstory
annual

Post Road
Jaime Clarke, editor
David Ryan, editor
info@postroadmag.com
www.postroadmag.com
semiannual

Prairie Fire
Andris Taskans, editor
prfire@prairiefire.ca
www.prairiefire.ca
quarterly

Prairie Schooner
Kwame Dawes, editor
prairieschooner@unl.edu
prairieschooner.unl.edu
quarterly

Prick of the Spindle
Cynthia Reeser, editor
pseditor@prickofthespindle.com
prickofthespindle.org
semiannual

PRISM international
Selena Boan, editor
Curtis LeBlanc, editor
Christopher Evans, editor
prose@prismmagazine.ca
prismmagazine.ca
quarterly

Profane
Patrick Chambers, editor
profanejournal@gmail.com
www.profanejournal.com
annual

A Public Space
Brigid Hughes, editor
general@apublicspace.org
apublicspace.org
triannual

PULP Literature
Mel Anastasiou, editor
Jennifer Landels, editor
Susan Pieters, editor
pulpliterature.com
quarterly

Raritan
Jackson Lears, editor
rqr@rci.rutgers.edu
raritanquarterly.rutgers.edu
quarterly

Redivider
Paul Haney, editor
editor@redividerjournal.org
www.redividerjournal.org
semiannual

River Styx
Richard Newman
BigRiver@riverstyx.org
www.riverstyx.org
triannual

Room
Chelene Knight, editor
contactus@roommagazine.com
roommagazine.com
quarterly

Salamander
Jennifer Barber, editor
salamandermag.org
semiannual

Salmagundi
Robert Boyers, editor
salmagun@skidmore.edu
www.skidmore.edu/salmagundi
quarterly

Saranac Review
J. L. Torres, editor
saranacreview@plattsburgh.edu
saranacreview.com
annual

The Saturday Evening Post
Steven Slon, editor
editors@saturdayeveningpost.com
www.saturdayeveningpost.com
bimonthly

The Sewanee Review
George Core, editor
gcore@sewanee.edu
thesewaneereview.com
quarterly

Sierra Nevada Review
June Sylvester Saraceno, editor
Laura Wetherington, editor
jsaraceno@sierranevada.edu
www.sierranevada.edu/academics
    /humanities-social-sciences
    /english/the-sierra-nevada
    -review
annual

Slice
Beth Blachman, editor
editors@slicemagazine.org
slicemagazine.org
semiannual

Smith's Monthly
Dean Wesley Smith, editor
dean@deanwesleysmith.com
www.smithsmonthly.com
monthly

The Southampton Review
Lou Ann Walker, editor
editors@thesouthamptonreview
    .com
thesouthamptonreview.com
semiannual

The South Carolina Review
John Morgenstern, editor
screview@clemson.edu
www.clemson.edu/centers
    -institutes/press/journals
    -annuals/south-carolina
    -review/index.html
semiannual

South Dakota Review
Lee Ann Roripaugh, editor
sdreview@usd.edu
southdakotareview.com
quarterly

The Southeast Review
Alex Quinlan, editor
southeastreview@gmail.com
southeastreview.org
semiannual

Southern Humanities Review
Anton DiSclafani, editor
Rose McLarney, editor
shr@auburn.edu
www.southernhumanitiesreview
    .com
quarterly

Southern Indiana Review
Ron Mitchell, editor
sir@usi.edu
www.usi.edu/sir
semiannual

The Southern Review
Jessica Faust, editor
Emily Nemens, editor
southernreview@lsu.edu
thesouthernreview.org
quarterly

Southwest Review
Greg Brownderville, editor
swr@smu.edu
www.smu.edu/southwestreview
quarterly

StoryQuarterly
Paul Lisicky, editor
storyquarterlyeditors@gmail.com
storyquarterly.camden.rutgers.edu
quarterly

St. Petersburg Review
Elizabeth Hodges, editor
editors@stpetersburgreview.com
www.stpetersburgreview.com
annual

subTerrain
Brian Kaufman, editor
subter@portal.ca
www.subterrain.ca
triannual

Subtropics
David Leavitt, editor
subtropics@english.ufl.edu
subtropics.english.ufl.edu
semiannual

The Sun
Sy Safransky, editor
thesunmagazine.org
monthly

Sycamore Review
Anthony Sutton, editor
sycamore@purdue.edu
sycamorereview.com
semiannual

Third Coast
S.Marie LaFata-Clay, editor
editors@thirdcoastmagazine.com
thirdcoastmagazine.com
semiannual

This Land
Michael Mason, editor
mail@thislandpress.com
thislandpress.com
quarterly

The Threepenny Review
Wendy Lesser, editor
wlesser@threepennyreview.com
www.threepennyreview.com
quarterly

Tin House
Rob Spillman, editor
info@tinhouse.com
www.tinhouse.com
quarterly

upstreet
Vivian Dorsel, editor
editor@upstreet-mag.org
upstreet-mag.org
annual

Virginia Quarterly Review
Paul Reyes, editor
editors@vqronline.org
www.vqronline.org
quarterly

Water-Stone Review
Mary François Rockcastle, editor
water-stone@hamline.edu
waterstonereview.com
annual

Weber
Michael Wutz, editor
weberjournal@weber.edu
www.weber.edu/weberjournal
semiannual

Western Humanities Review
Michael Mejia, editor
ManagingEditor.WHR@gmail
    .com
www.westernhumanitiesreview
    .com
triannual

Whitefish Review
Brian Schott, editor
brian@whitefishreview.org
www.whitefishreview.org
semiannual

Willow Springs
Samuel Ligon, editor
willowspringsewu@gmail.com
willowspringsmagazine.org
semiannual

Witness
Dan Hernandez, editor
witness@unlv.edu
witness.blackmountaininstitute
    .org
annual

The Worcester Review
Diane Mulligan, editor
twr.diane@gmail.com
www.theworcesterreview.org
annual

Workers Write!
David LaBounty, editor
info@workerswritejournal.com
www.workerswritejournal.com
bimonthly

Yellow Medicine Review
Tanaya Winder, guest editor
editor@yellowmedicinereview
    .com
www.yellowmedicinereview.com
semiannual

Your Impossible Voice
Keith J. Powell, editor
editor@yourimpossiblevoice.com
www.yourimpossiblevoice.com
quarterly

Zoetrope: All-Story
Michael Ray, editor
info@all-story.com
www.all-story.com
quarterly

ZYZZYVA
Laura Cogan, editor
editor@zyzzyva.org
www.zyzzyva.org
triannual

Permissions

"The Trusted Traveler" by Joseph O'Neill first appeared in *Harper's Magazine*. Copyright © 2016 by Joseph O'Neill. Reprinted by permission of the author.

"Protection" by Paola Peroni first appeared in *The Common*. Copyright © 2015 by Paola Peroni. Reprinted by permission of the author.

"Something for a Young Woman" by Genevieve Plunkett first appeared in *New England Review*. Copyright © 2015 by Genevieve Plunkett. Reprinted by permission of the author.

"The Buddhist" by Alan Rossi first appeared in *Granta*. Copyright © 2015 by Alan Rossi. Reprinted by permission of the author.

"Night Garden" by Shruti Swamy first appeared in *Prairie Schooner*. Copyright © 2016 by the University of Nebraska Press. Reprinted by permission of the University of Nebraska Press.

"Lion" by Wil Weitzel first appeared in *Prairie Schooner*. Copyright © 2015 by the University of Nebraska Press. Reprinted by permission of the University of Nebraska Press.

"The Family Whistle" by Gerard Woodward first appeared in *Zoetrope: All-Story*. Copyright © 2015 by Gerard Woodward. Reprinted by permission of the author, care of Rogers, Coleridge & White Ltd., 20 Powis Mews, London W11 1JN.